Shojo Beat

love★com

Story & Art by
Aya Nakahara

17

love★com

contents ⟨17⟩

The Story So Far...

Risa and Ôtani are their class's lopsided comedy duo, and after an agonizingly complicated journey, they've become a couple! Ôtani has been accepted into a teachers' college, while Risa plans to become a fashion stylist. At the graduation party, Ôtani gets lots of laughs in the class play as Issunbôshi, Kohori-kun finally finds a girlfriend in Abe-san, and things are going well between Risa and Ôtani. And graduation day rolls around!!

When the school representative has a fainting spell, Risa and Ôtani end up on the dais leading the class in a banzai cheer!! There were lots of crazy moments, lots of tears and lots of laughter during their high school years, but it's finally over. And soon, Risa and Ôtani will focus on their future. Now how about a story from the duo's time in middle school?

♥ To really get all the details, check out *Lovely Complex* volumes 1–16, available at bookstores everywhere!!

Shojo Beat

love★com

THIS STORY IS ABOUT THE
TWO BEFORE THEY MET!

Story & Art by
Aya Nakahara

17

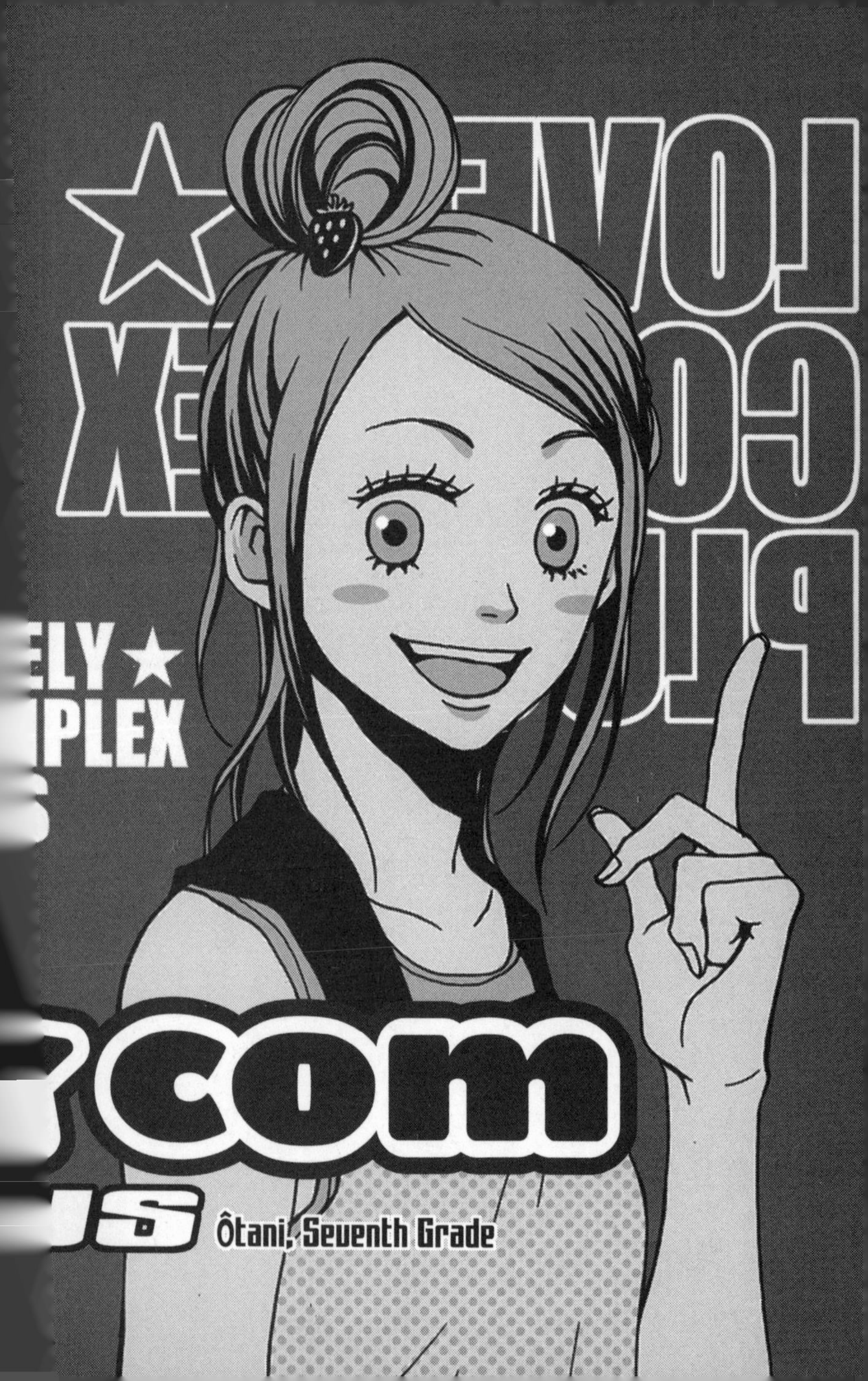
Ôtani, Seventh Grade

LOVELY ☆ COMPLEX PLUS

LO
CO
PL

love ☆

PL

Aya
Nakahara

LOVELY COMPLEX

Love ✿ Com ended in volume 16, so these are bonus stories. See Ôtani in seventh grade, Risa in eighth grade, the two of them in ninth grade... and what everyone is up to after graduation. I hope you enjoy it.

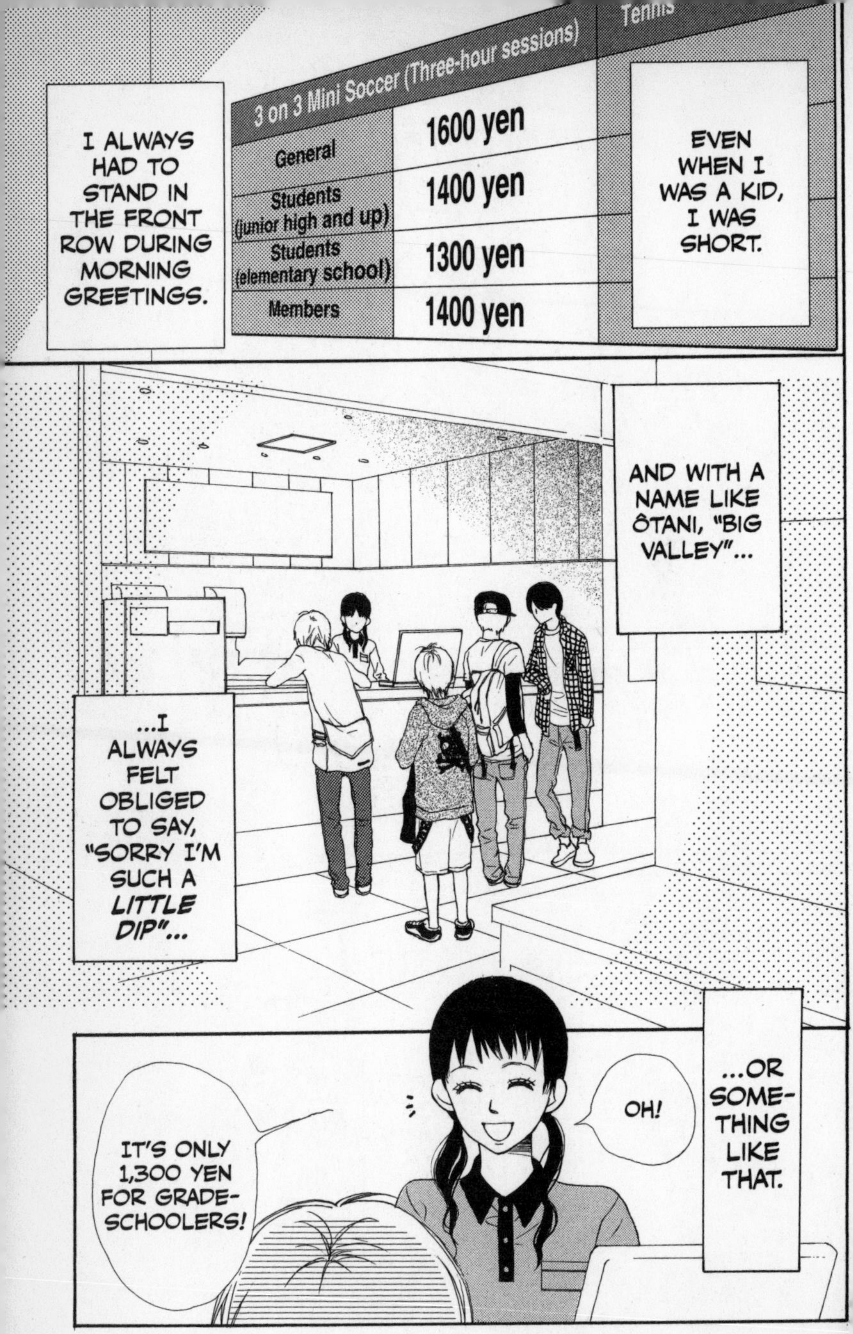
Tennis
EVEN WHEN I WAS A KID, I WAS SHORT.
3 on 3 Mini Soccer (Three-hour sessions)
General 1600 yen
Students (junior high and up) 1400 yen
Students (elementary school) 1300 yen
Members 1400 yen
I ALWAYS HAD TO STAND IN THE FRONT ROW DURING MORNING GREETINGS.
AND WITH A NAME LIKE ŌTANI, "BIG VALLEY"...
...I ALWAYS FELT OBLIGED TO SAY, "SORRY I'M SUCH A *LITTLE DIP*"...
...OR SOMETHING LIKE THAT.
OH!
IT'S ONLY 1,300 YEN FOR GRADE-SCHOOLERS!

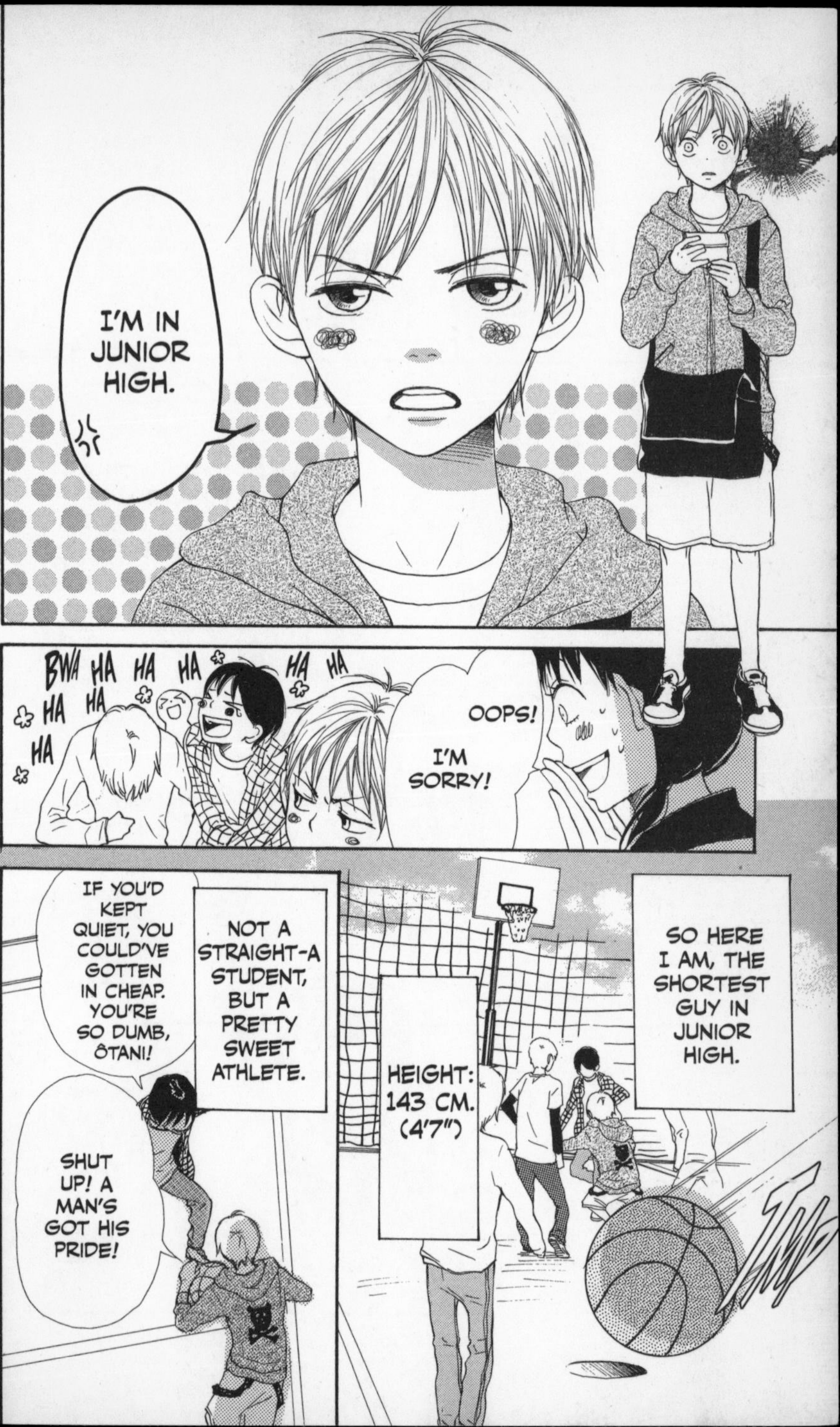
I'M IN JUNIOR HIGH.
OOPS! I'M SORRY!
BWA HA HA HA HA HA HA HA HA
SO HERE I AM, THE SHORTEST GUY IN JUNIOR HIGH.
HEIGHT: 143 CM. (4'7")
NOT A STRAIGHT-A STUDENT, BUT A PRETTY SWEET ATHLETE.
IF YOU'D KEPT QUIET, YOU COULD'VE GOTTEN IN CHEAP. YOU'RE SO DUMB, ŌTANI!
SHUT UP! A MAN'S GOT HIS PRIDE!

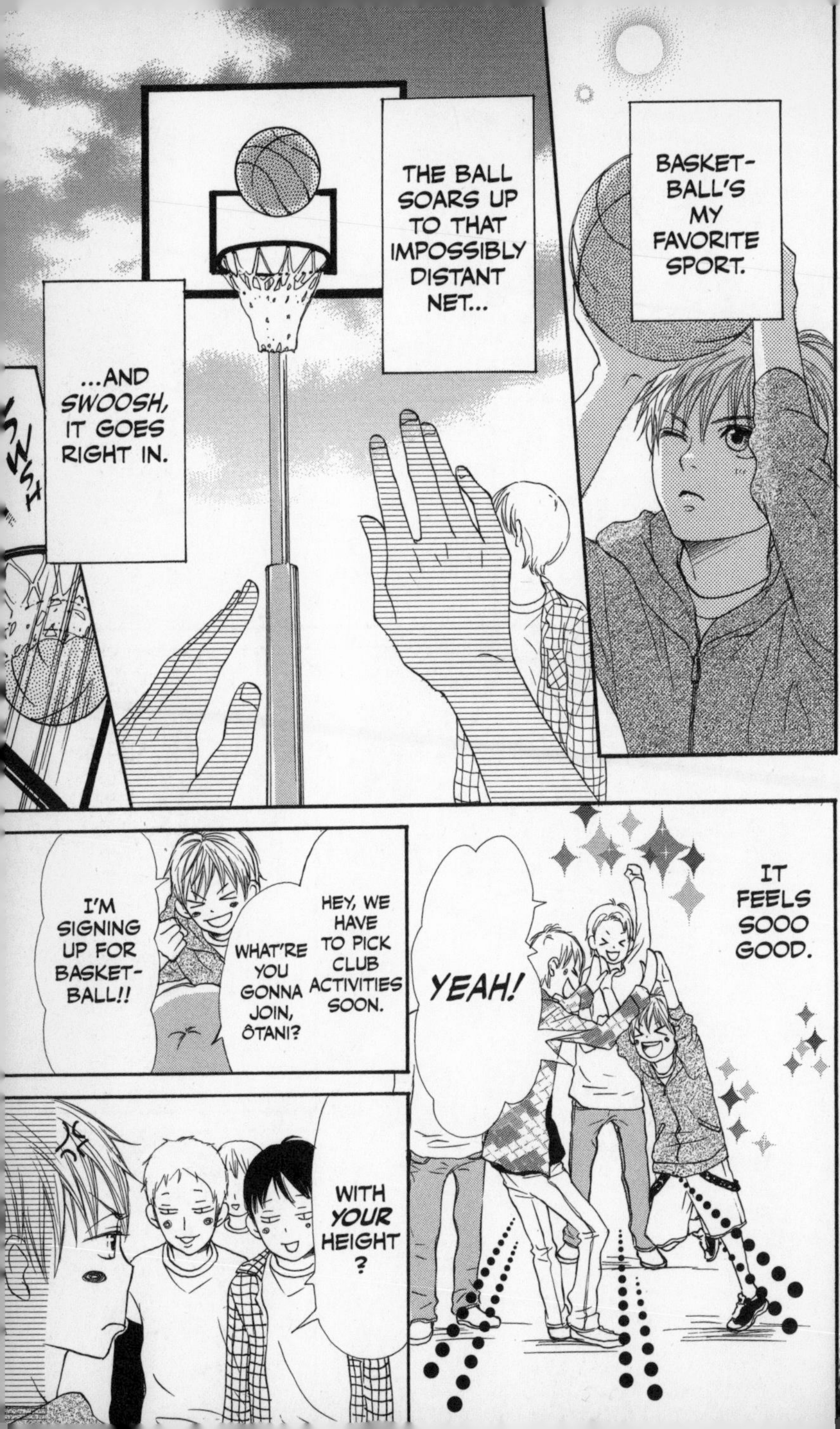
BASKET-BALL'S MY FAVORITE SPORT.
THE BALL SOARS UP TO THAT IMPOSSIBLY DISTANT NET...
...AND *SWOOSH*, IT GOES RIGHT IN.
IT FEELS SOOO GOOD.
YEAH!
HEY, WE HAVE TO PICK CLUB ACTIVITIES SOON.
WHAT'RE YOU GONNA JOIN, ŌTANI?
I'M SIGNING UP FOR BASKET-BALL!!
WITH *YOUR* HEIGHT?

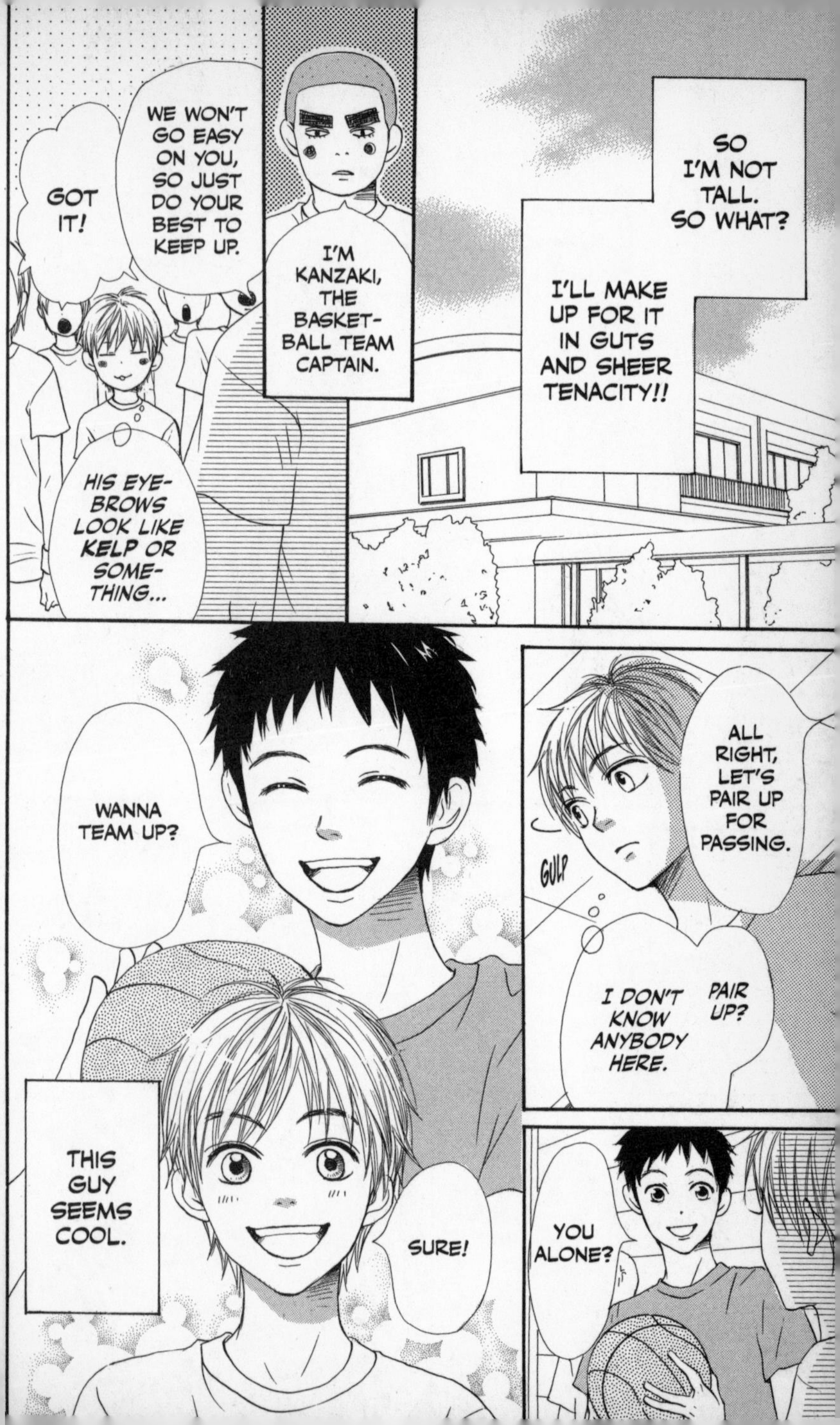
SO I'M NOT TALL. SO WHAT?
I'LL MAKE UP FOR IT IN GUTS AND SHEER TENACITY!!
I'M KANZAKI, THE BASKETBALL TEAM CAPTAIN.
WE WON'T GO EASY ON YOU, SO JUST DO YOUR BEST TO KEEP UP.
GOT IT!
HIS EYEBROWS LOOK LIKE KELP OR SOMETHING...
ALL RIGHT, LET'S PAIR UP FOR PASSING.
GULP
PAIR UP?
I DON'T KNOW ANYBODY HERE.
YOU ALONE?
WANNA TEAM UP?
SURE!
THIS GUY SEEMS COOL.

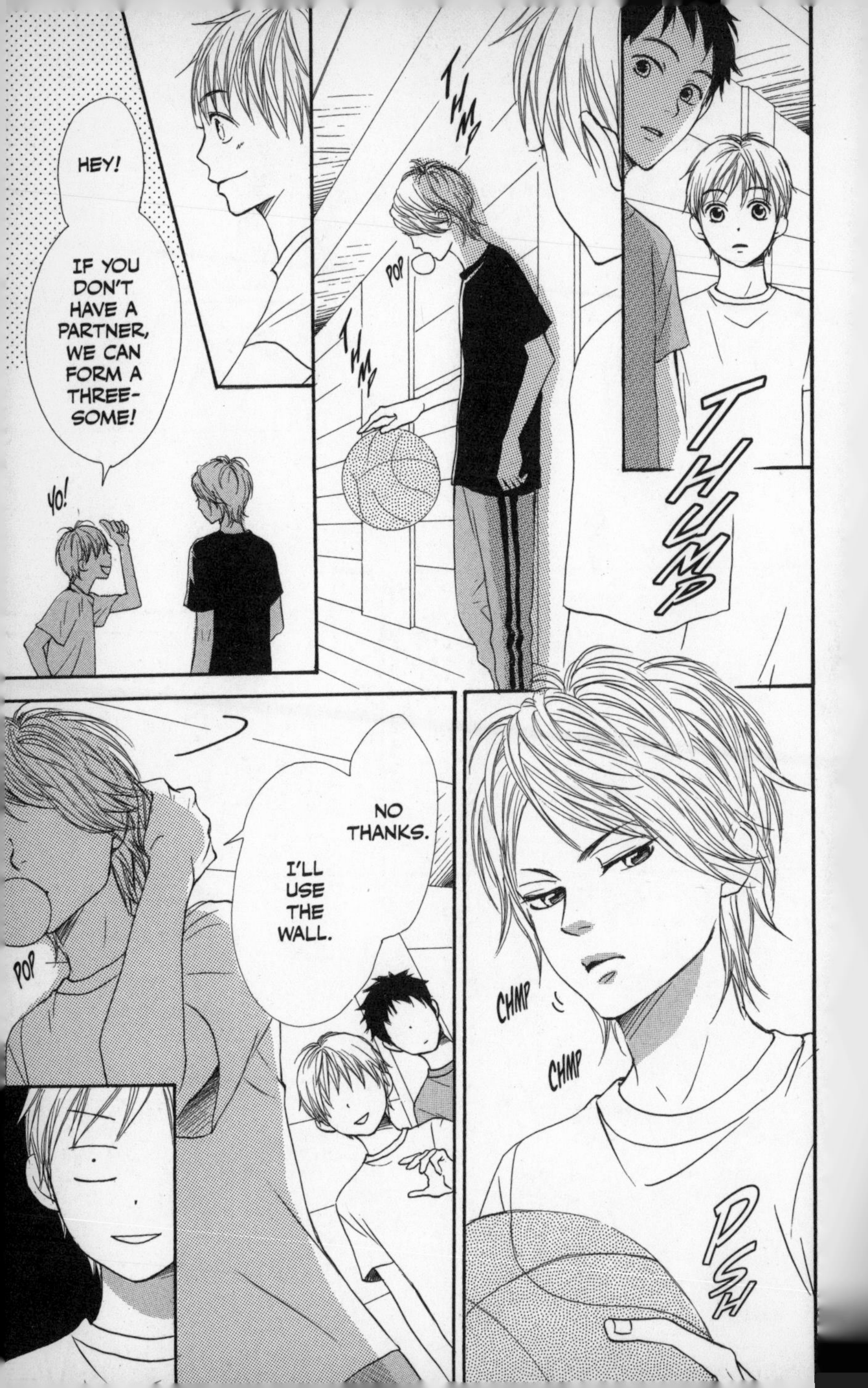
THUMP
THMP
POP
THMP
HEY!
IF YOU DON'T HAVE A PARTNER, WE CAN FORM A THREE-SOME!
YO!
CHMP
CHMP
PSH
NO THANKS.
I'LL USE THE WALL.
POP

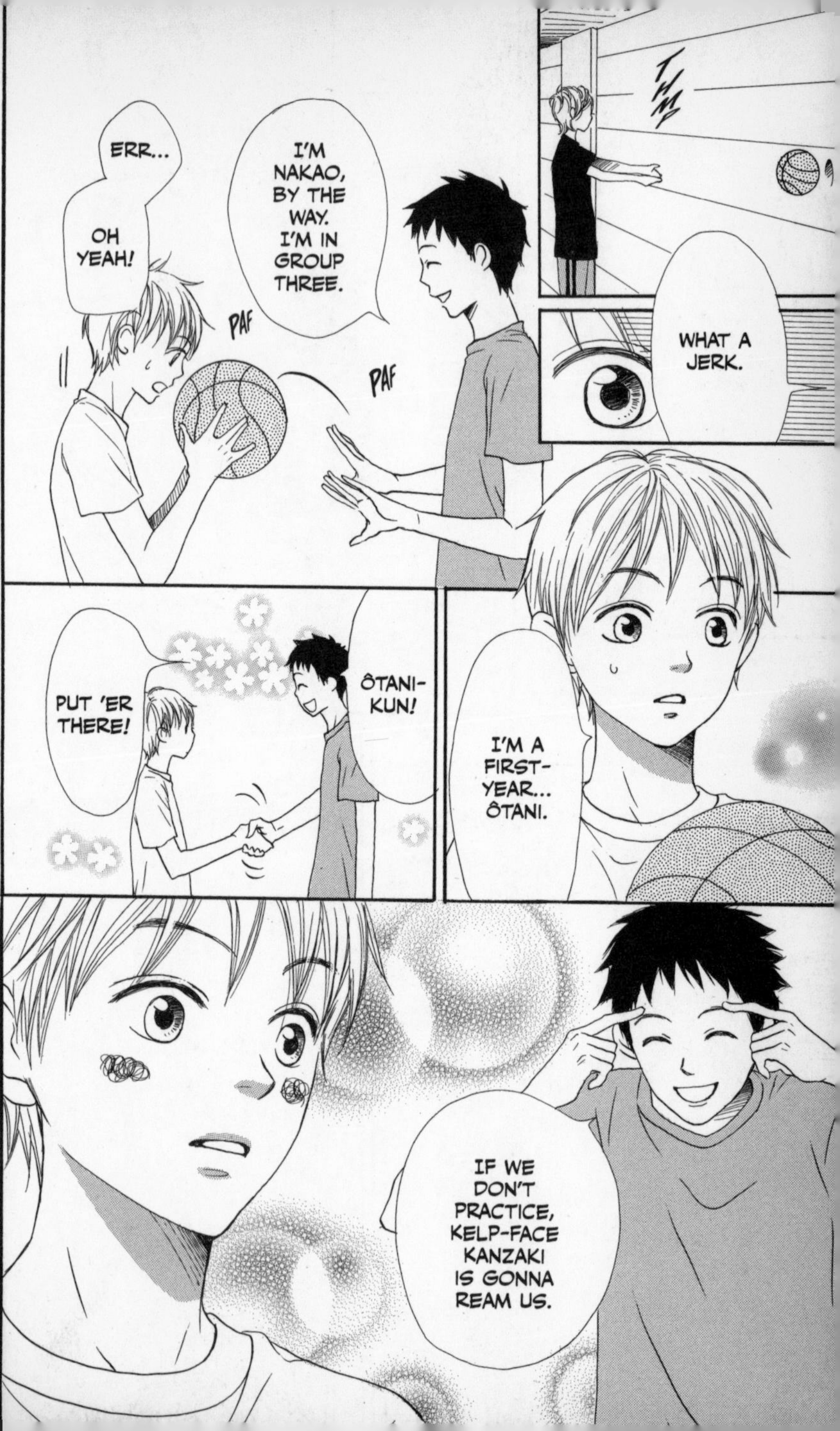
THMP
WHAT A JERK.
I'M NAKAO, BY THE WAY. I'M IN GROUP THREE.
PAF
PAF
ERR...
OH YEAH!
I'M A FIRST-YEAR... ŌTANI.
ŌTANI-KUN!
PUT 'ER THERE!
IF WE DON'T PRACTICE, KELP-FACE KANZAKI IS GONNA REAM US.

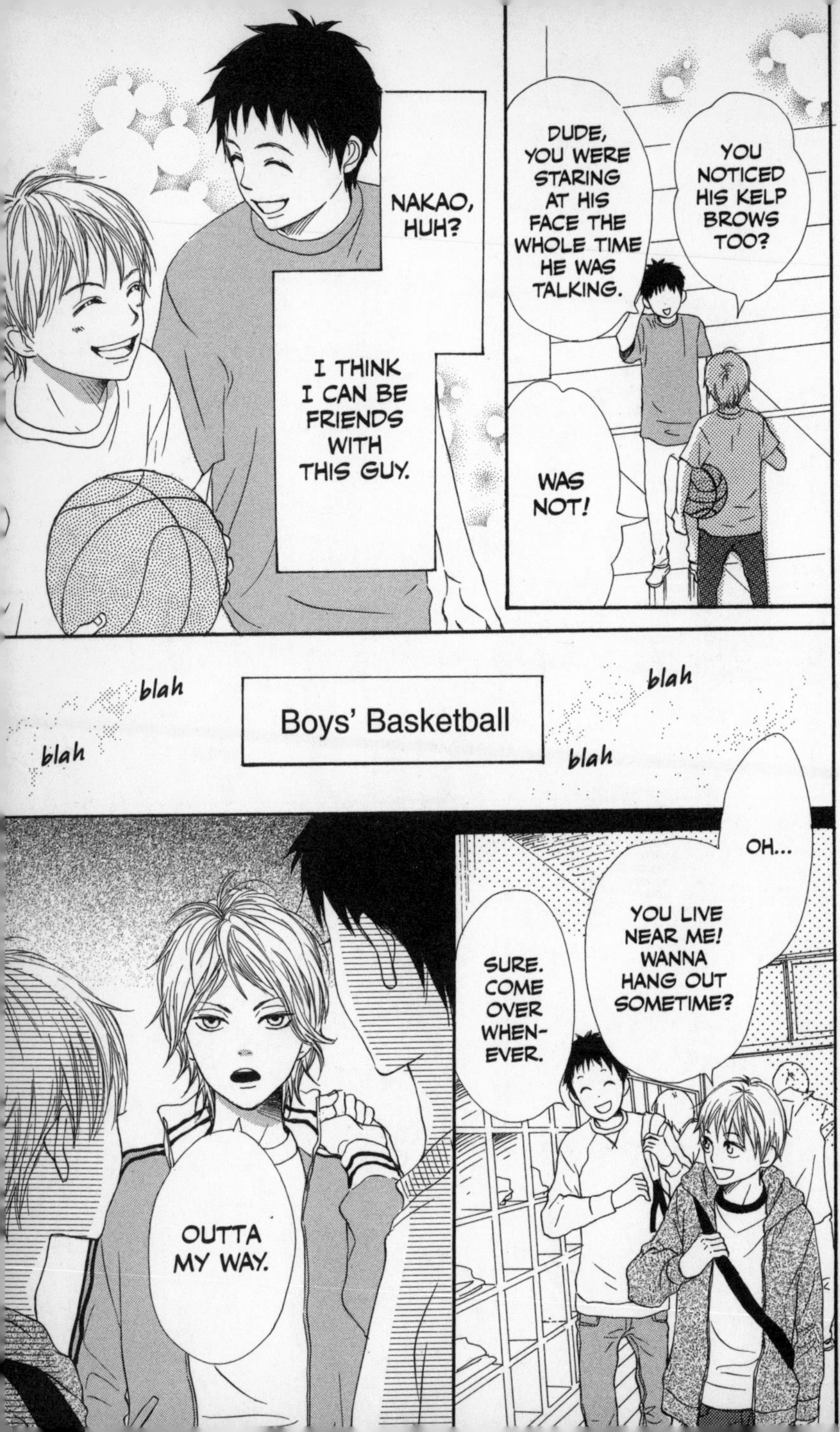
YOU NOTICED HIS KELP BROWS TOO?
DUDE, YOU WERE STARING AT HIS FACE THE WHOLE TIME HE WAS TALKING.
WAS NOT!
NAKAO, HUH?
I THINK I CAN BE FRIENDS WITH THIS GUY.
blah
blah
Boys' Basketball
blah
blah
OH...
YOU LIVE NEAR ME! WANNA HANG OUT SOMETIME?
SURE. COME OVER WHEN-EVER.
OUTTA MY WAY.

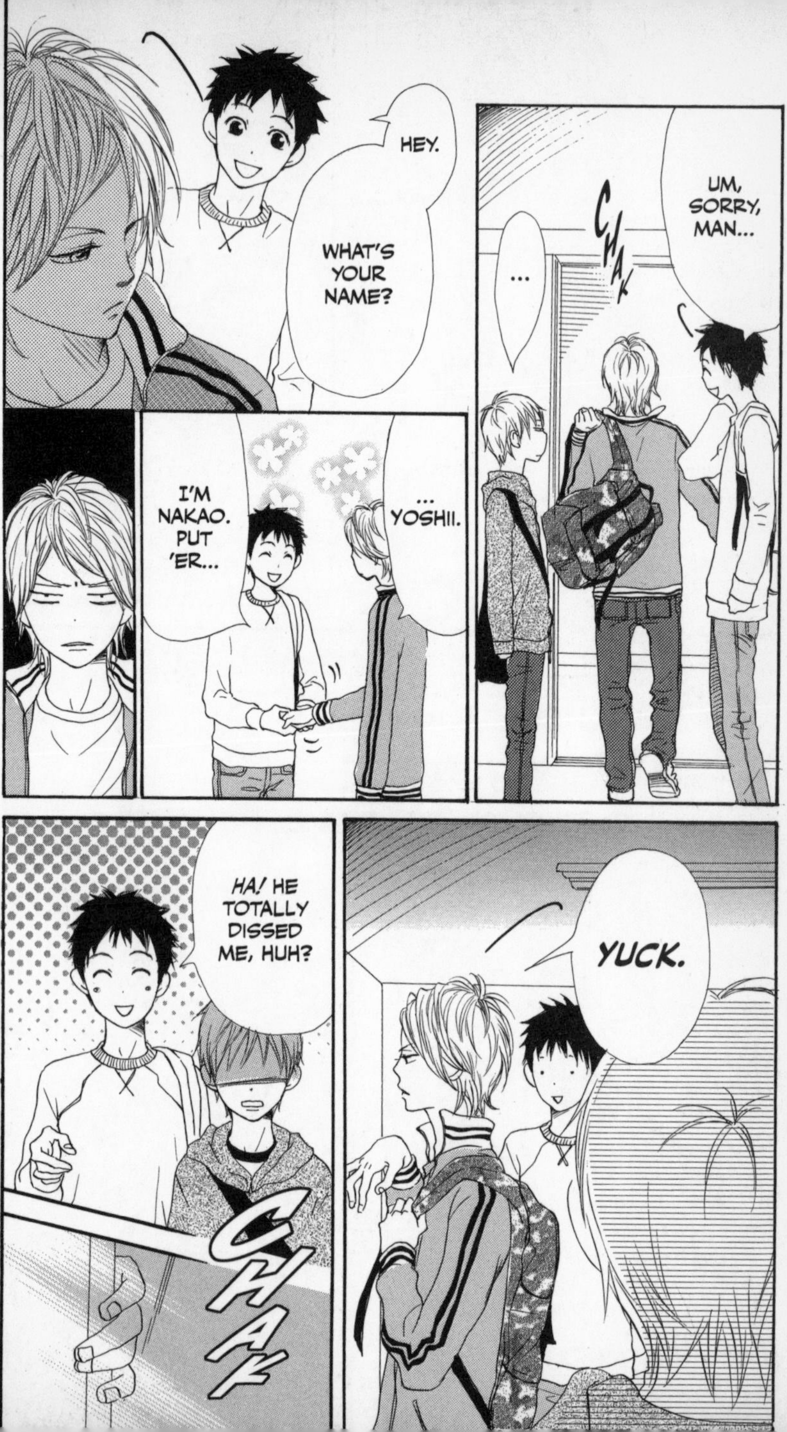
HEY.
WHAT'S YOUR NAME?
I'M NAKAO. PUT 'ER...
... YOSHII.
UM, SORRY, MAN...
CHAK
...
HA! HE TOTALLY DISSED ME, HUH?
CHAK
YUCK.

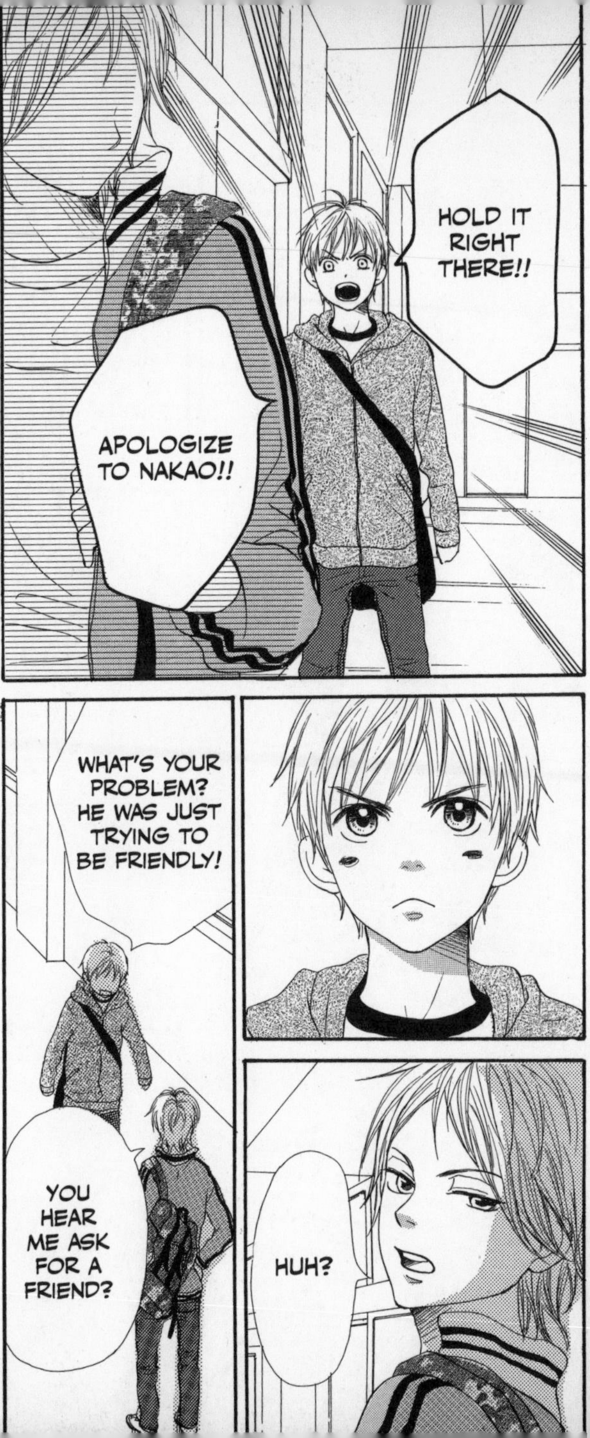
HOLD IT RIGHT THERE!!
APOLOGIZE TO NAKAO!!
HUH?
WHAT'S YOUR PROBLEM? HE WAS JUST TRYING TO BE FRIENDLY!
YOU HEAR ME ASK FOR A FRIEND?

1

Hello! Nakahara here! This collection of bonus stories will be the final volume of *Love★Com*. When I first started the series, little did I imagine it would continue for 17 volumes! I've been so excited through the whole thing...

Okay, okay, I guess I should get serious for the final volume. Or should I write these columns as usual? What a dilemma. It's like a train starting without the passengers... choo-choo...

Either way, guess I've gotta get started!

The *Love★Com* anime started in April of 2007. Nothing could be more exciting for an anime fangirl like me. I've been constantly surprised to see people I've loved and admired for years get involved in the project.

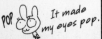

POP It made my eyes pop.

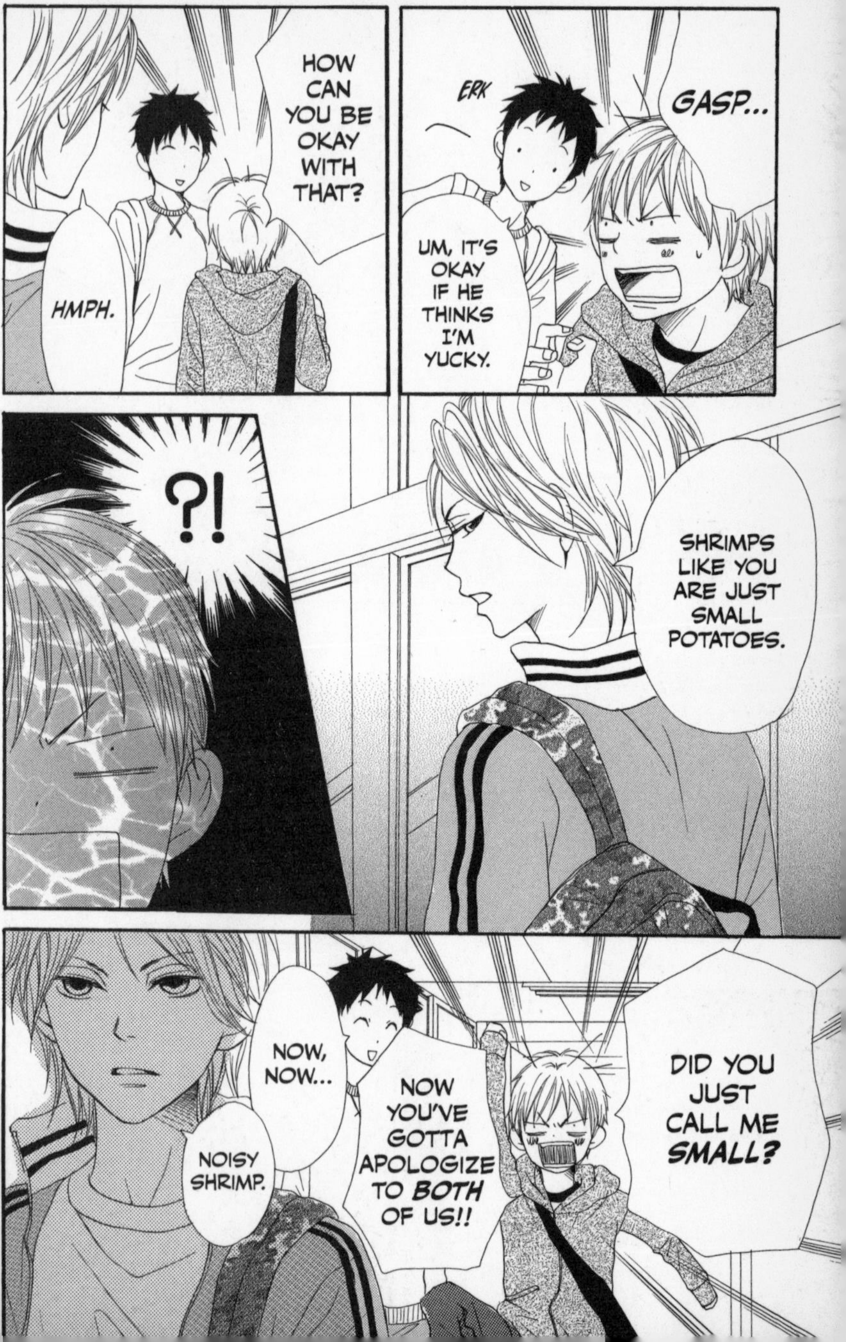
GASP...
ERK
UM, IT'S OKAY IF HE THINKS I'M YUCKY.
HOW CAN YOU BE OKAY WITH THAT?
HMPH.
SHRIMPS LIKE YOU ARE JUST SMALL POTATOES.
?!
DID YOU JUST CALL ME *SMALL?*
NOW YOU'VE GOTTA APOLOGIZE TO *BOTH* OF US!!
NOW, NOW...
NOISY SHRIMP.

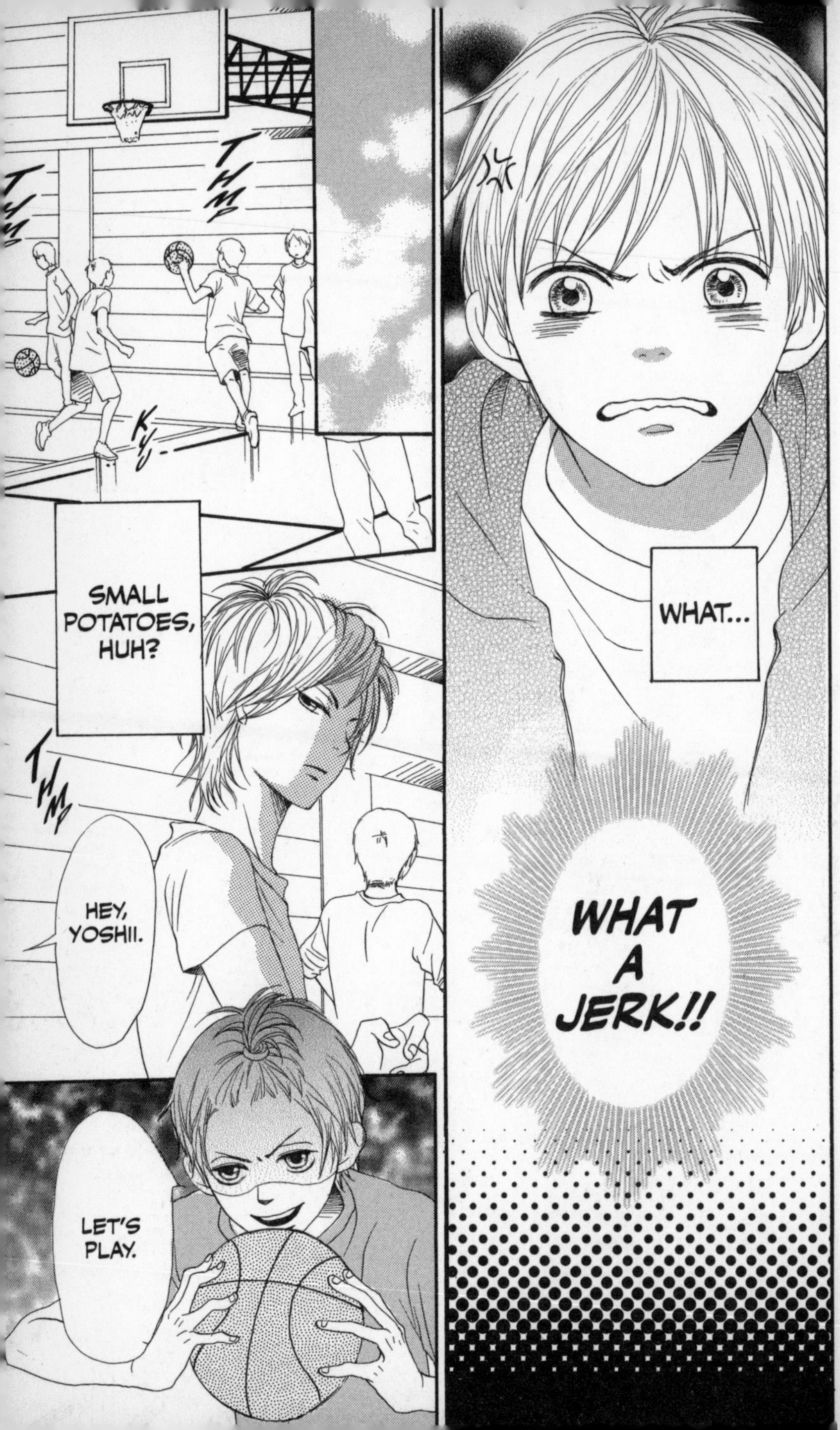
WHAT...
WHAT A JERK!!
THMP
THMP
KYU
SMALL POTATOES, HUH?
THMP
HEY, YOSHII.
LET'S PLAY.

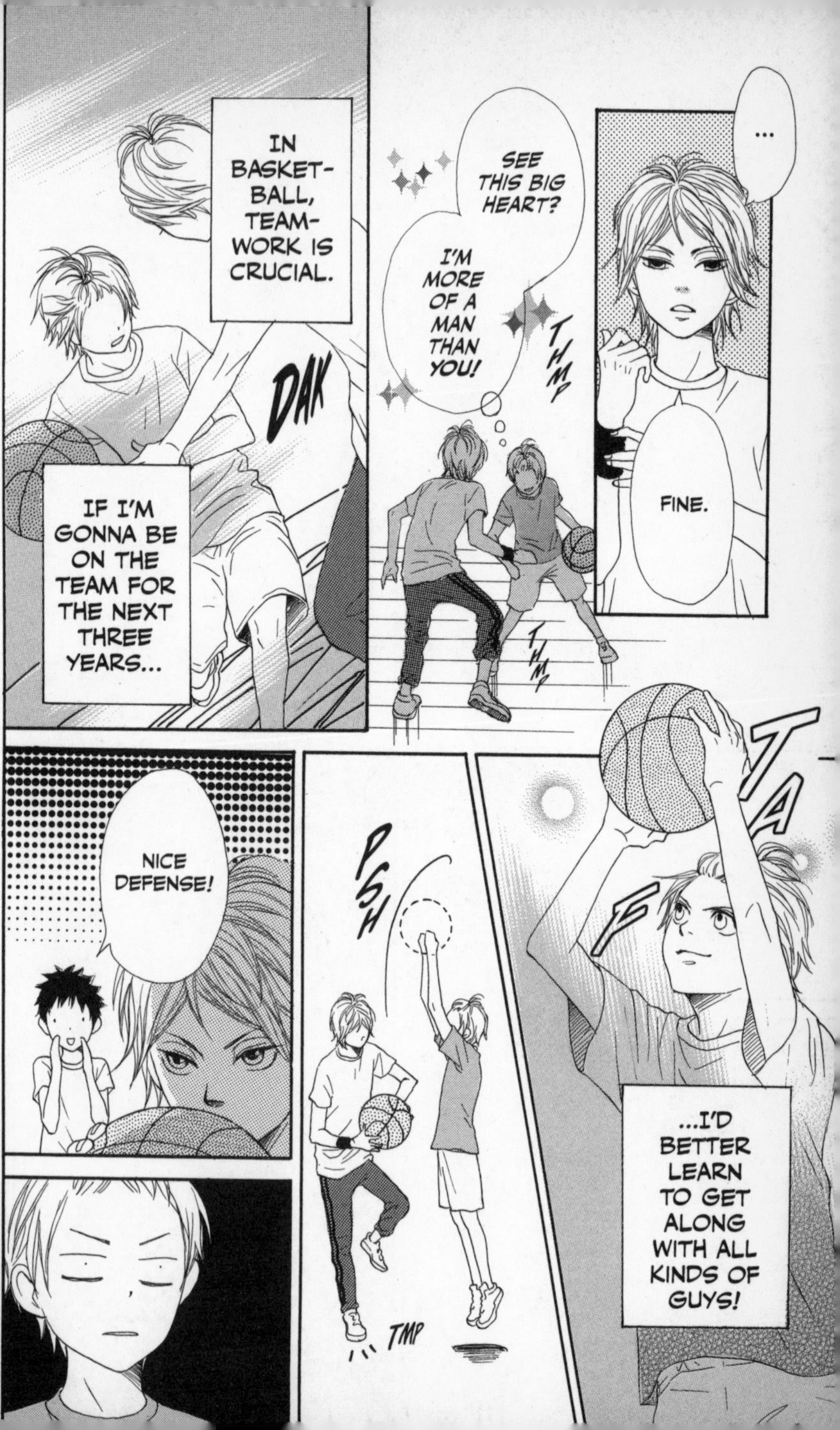
...
FINE.
SEE THIS BIG HEART?
I'M MORE OF A MAN THAN YOU!
THMP
THMP
IN BASKET-BALL, TEAM-WORK IS CRUCIAL.
DAK
IF I'M GONNA BE ON THE TEAM FOR THE NEXT THREE YEARS...
TAF
...I'D BETTER LEARN TO GET ALONG WITH ALL KINDS OF GUYS!
PSH
TMP
NICE DEFENSE!

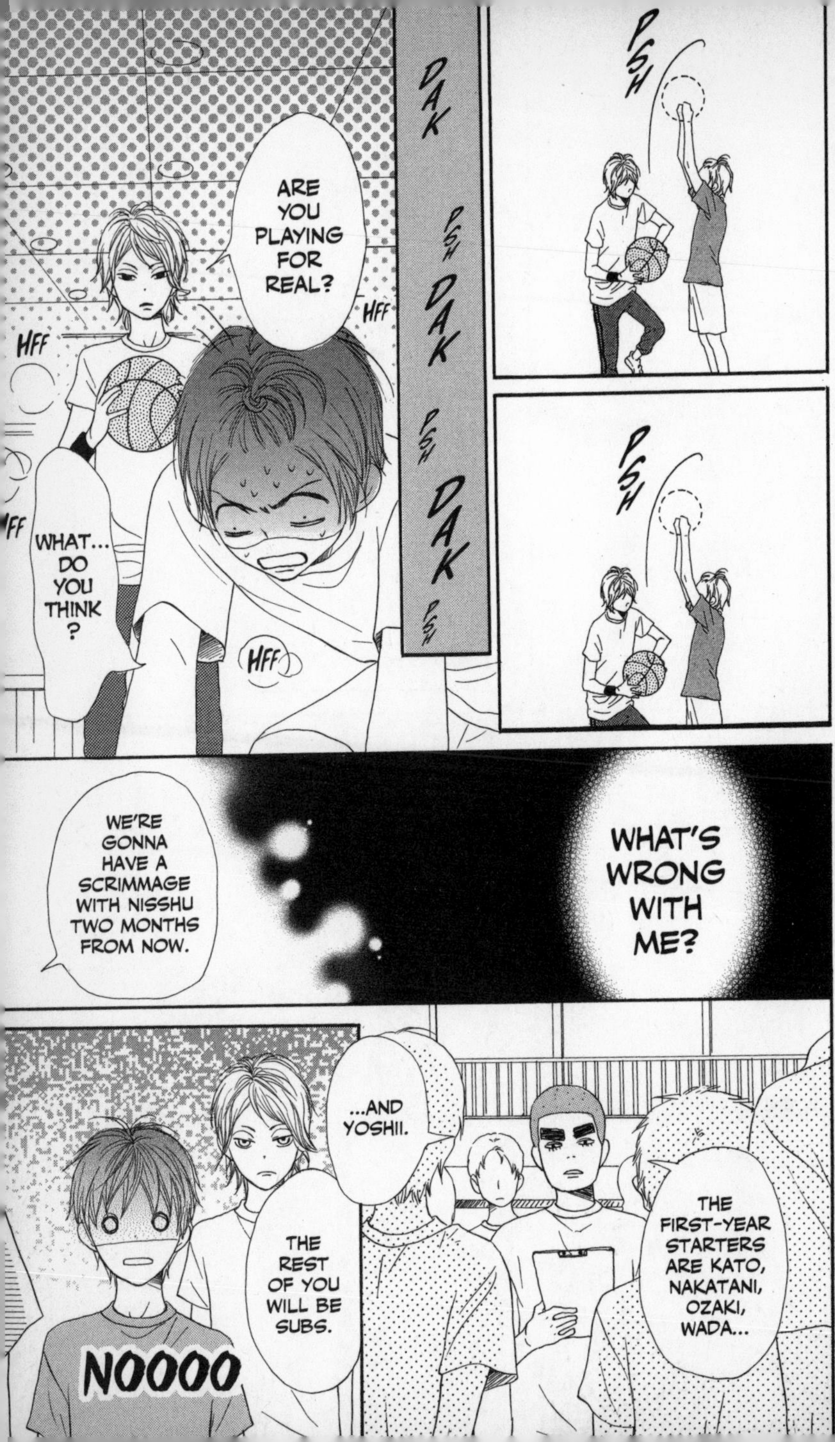
PSH
PSH
DAK
PSH
DAK
PSH
DAK
PSH
ARE YOU PLAYING FOR REAL?
HFF
HFF
WHAT... DO YOU THINK ?
HFF
HFF
WHAT'S WRONG WITH ME?
WE'RE GONNA HAVE A SCRIMMAGE WITH NISSHU TWO MONTHS FROM NOW.
THE FIRST-YEAR STARTERS ARE KATO, NAKATANI, OZAKI, WADA...
...AND YOSHII.
THE REST OF YOU WILL BE SUBS.
NOOOO

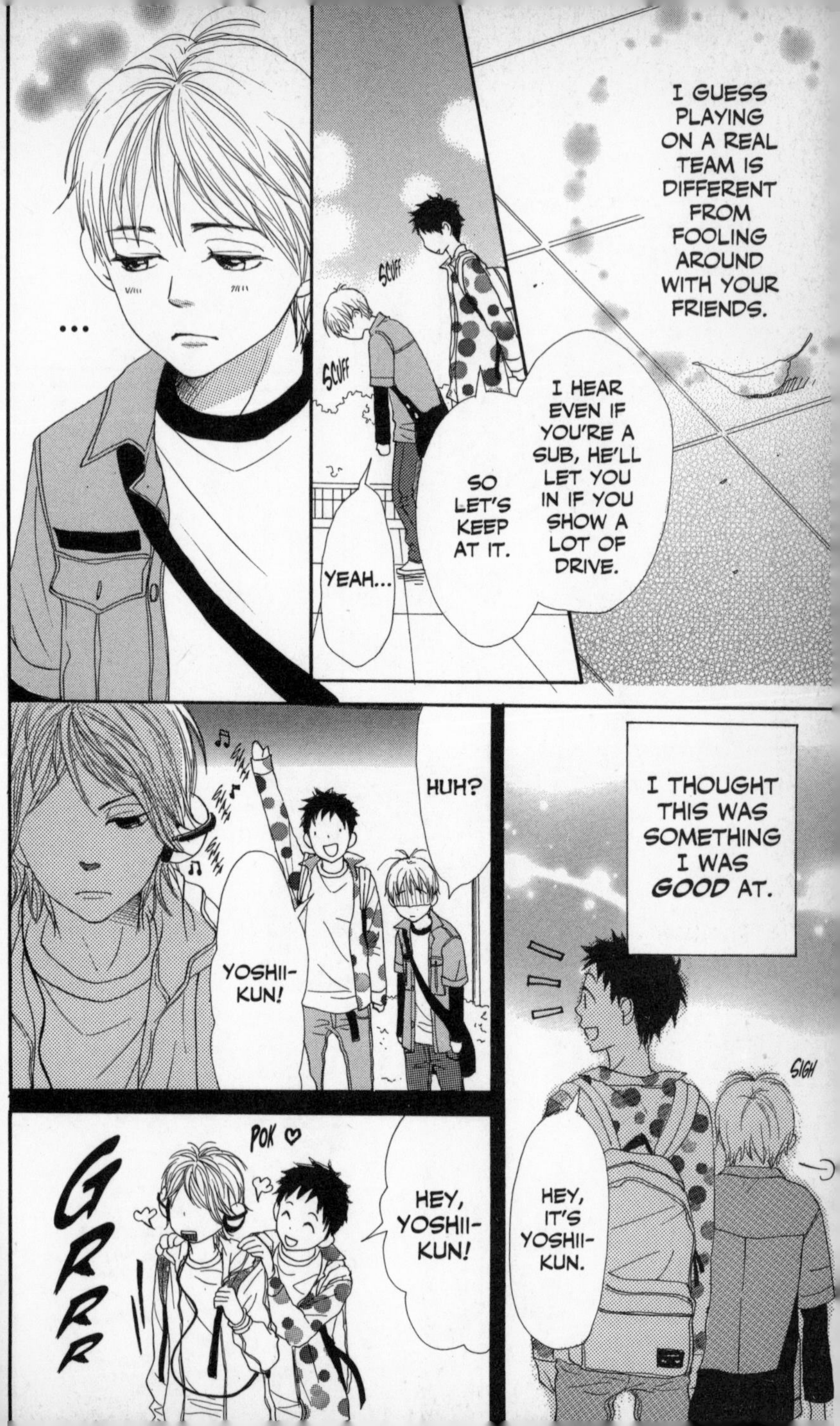
I GUESS PLAYING ON A REAL TEAM IS DIFFERENT FROM FOOLING AROUND WITH YOUR FRIENDS.
SCUFF
SCUFF
I HEAR EVEN IF YOU'RE A SUB, HE'LL LET YOU IN IF YOU SHOW A LOT OF DRIVE.
SO LET'S KEEP AT IT.
YEAH...
...
I THOUGHT THIS WAS SOMETHING I WAS *GOOD* AT.
HEY, IT'S YOSHII-KUN.
SIGH
HUH?
YOSHII-KUN!
HEY, YOSHII-KUN!
POK ♡
GRRR

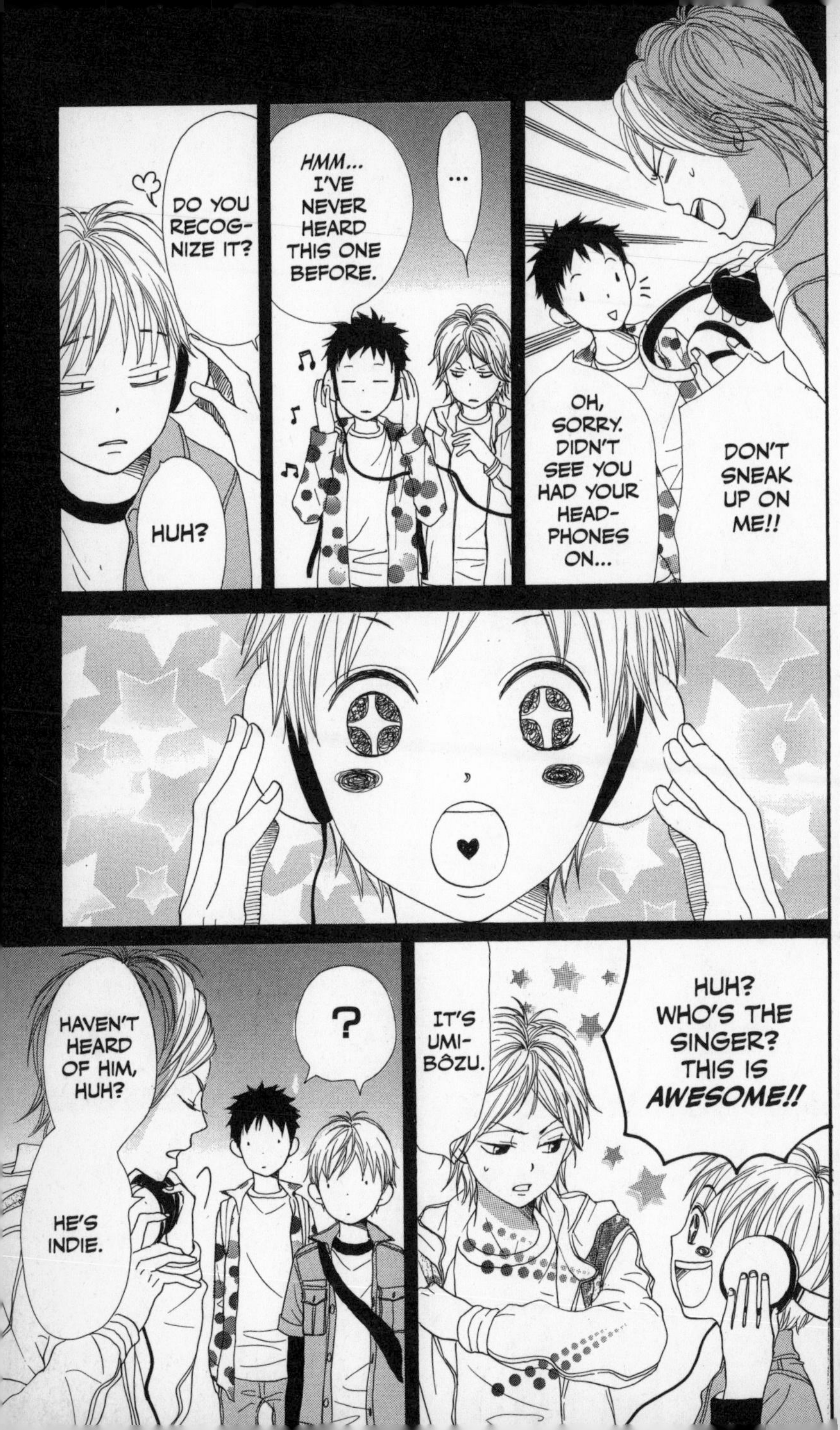
DON'T SNEAK UP ON ME!!
OH, SORRY. DIDN'T SEE YOU HAD YOUR HEAD-PHONES ON...
...
HMM... I'VE NEVER HEARD THIS ONE BEFORE.
DO YOU RECOG-NIZE IT?
HUH?
HUH? WHO'S THE SINGER? THIS IS ***AWESOME!!***
IT'S UMI-BÔZU.
?
HAVEN'T HEARD OF HIM, HUH?
HE'S INDIE.

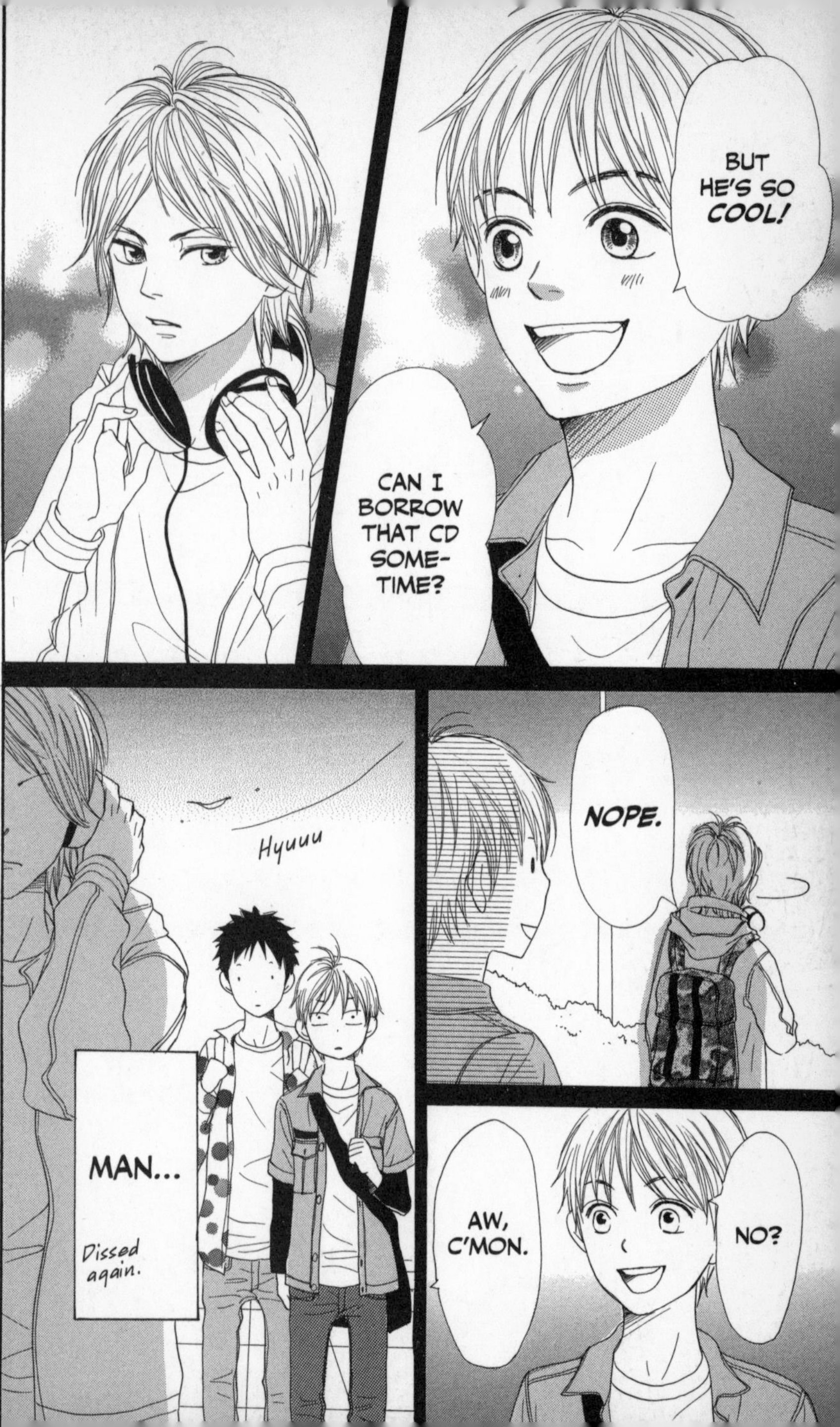
BUT HE'S SO *COOL!*
CAN I BORROW THAT CD SOME-TIME?
NOPE.
NO?
AW, C'MON.
Hyuuu
MAN...
Dissed again.

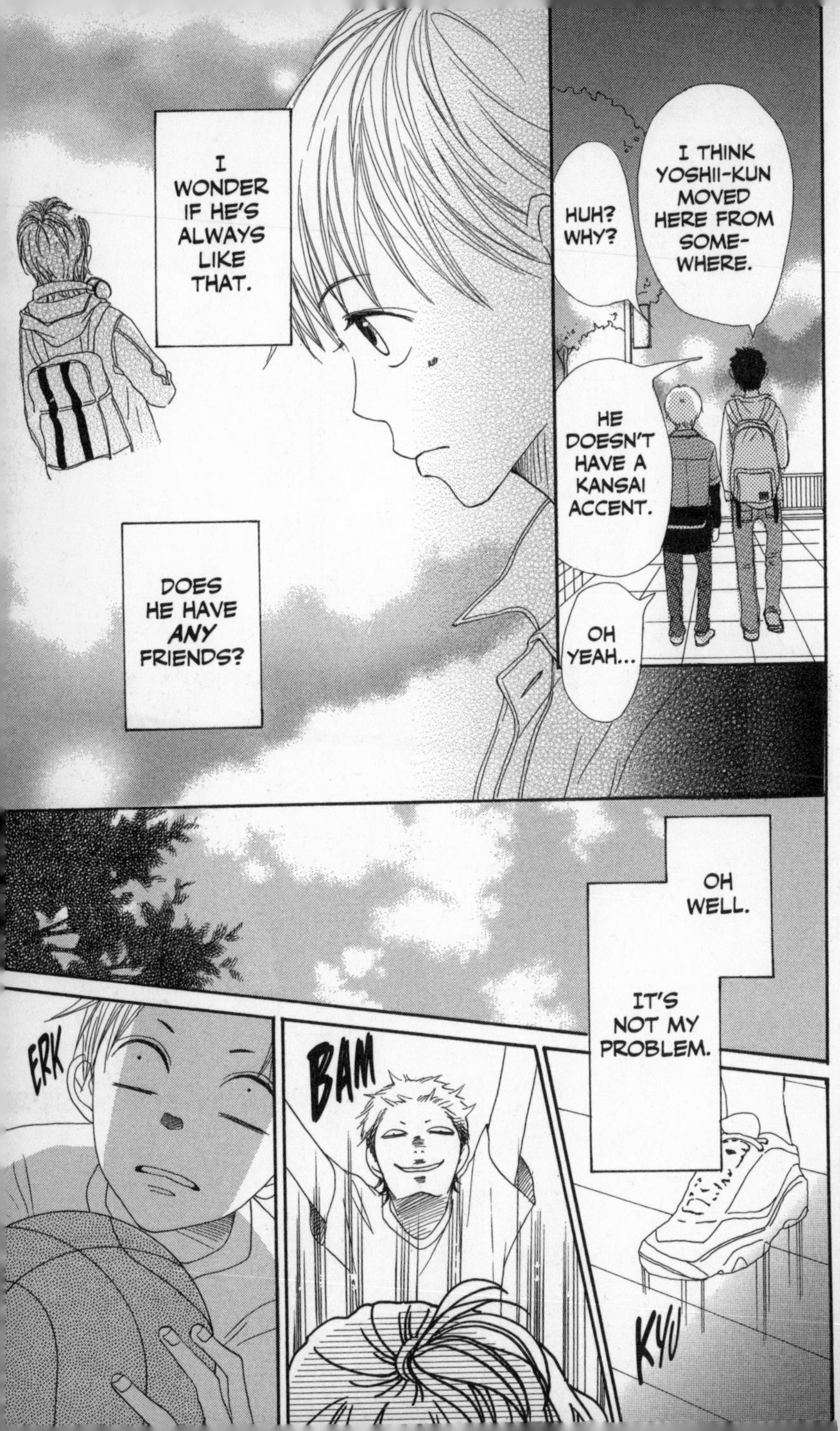

I THINK YOSHII-KUN MOVED HERE FROM SOME-WHERE.
HUH? WHY?
HE DOESN'T HAVE A KANSAI ACCENT.
OH YEAH...
I WONDER IF HE'S ALWAYS LIKE THAT.
DOES HE HAVE *ANY* FRIENDS?
OH WELL.
IT'S NOT MY PROBLEM.
KYU
BAM
ERK

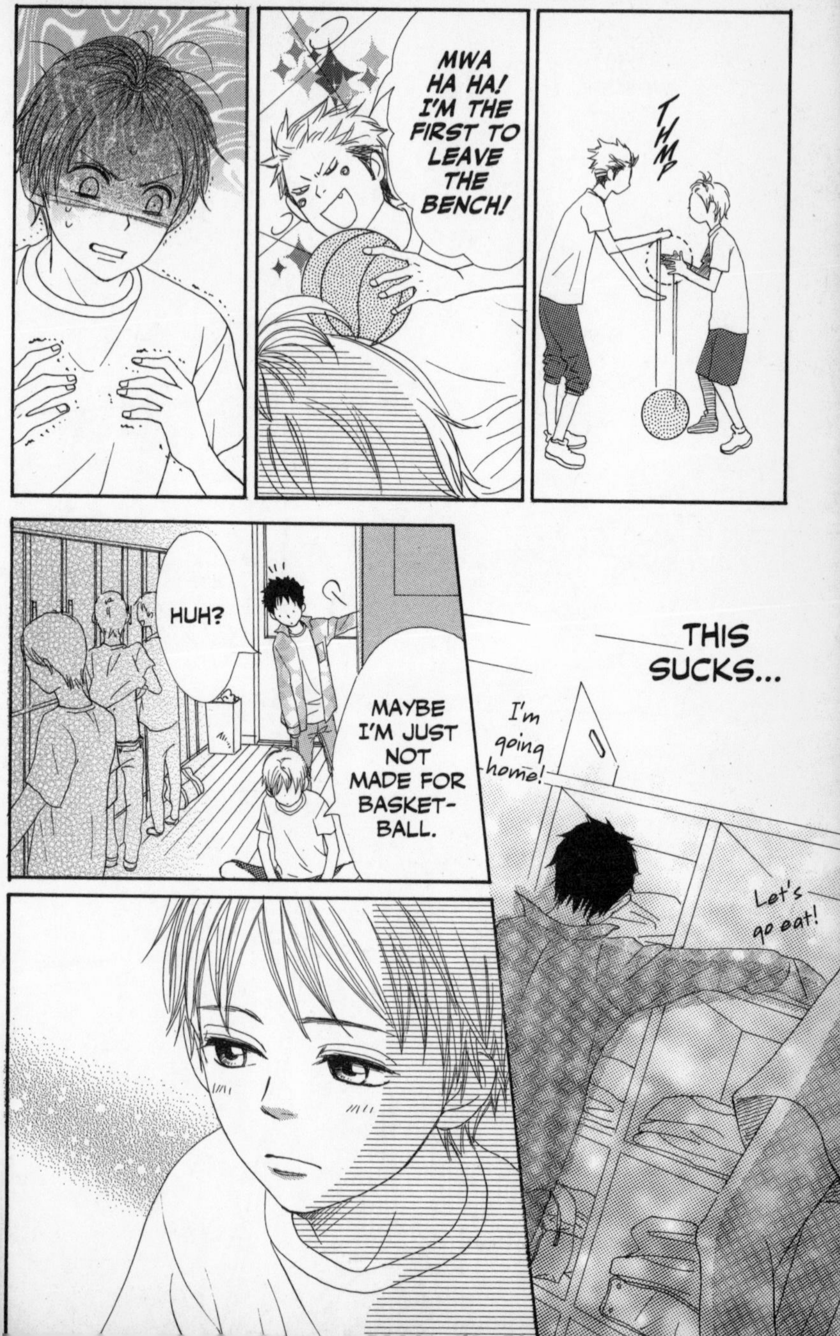
THMP
MWA HA HA! I'M THE FIRST TO LEAVE THE BENCH!
THIS SUCKS...
I'm going home!
Let's go eat!
HUH?
MAYBE I'M JUST NOT MADE FOR BASKETBALL.

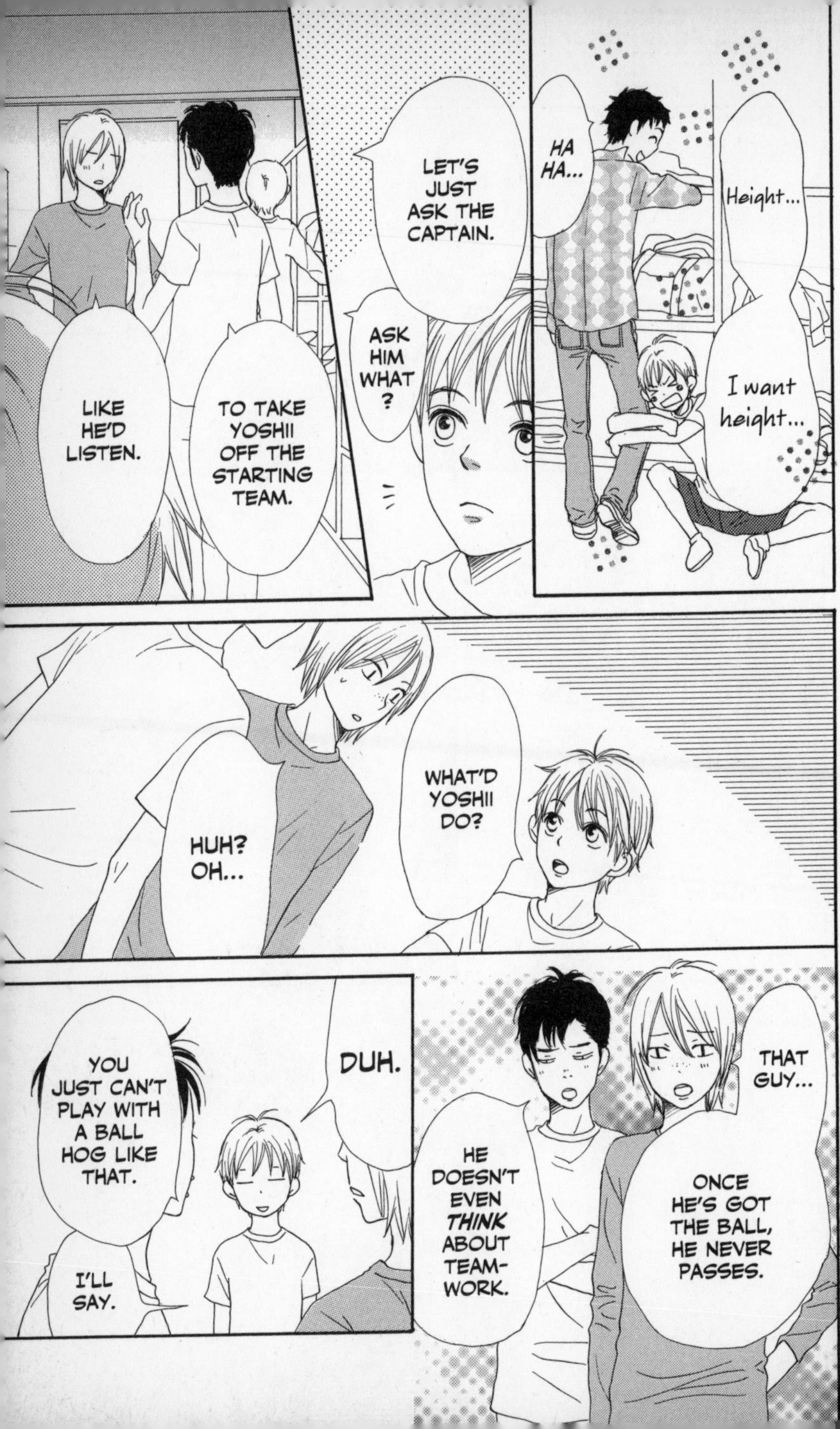
Height...
I want height...
HA HA...
LET'S JUST ASK THE CAPTAIN.
ASK HIM WHAT?
TO TAKE YOSHII OFF THE STARTING TEAM.
LIKE HE'D LISTEN.
WHAT'D YOSHII DO?
HUH? OH...
THAT GUY...
ONCE HE'S GOT THE BALL, HE NEVER PASSES.
HE DOESN'T EVEN *THINK* ABOUT TEAM-WORK.
DUH.
YOU JUST CAN'T PLAY WITH A BALL HOG LIKE THAT.
I'LL SAY.

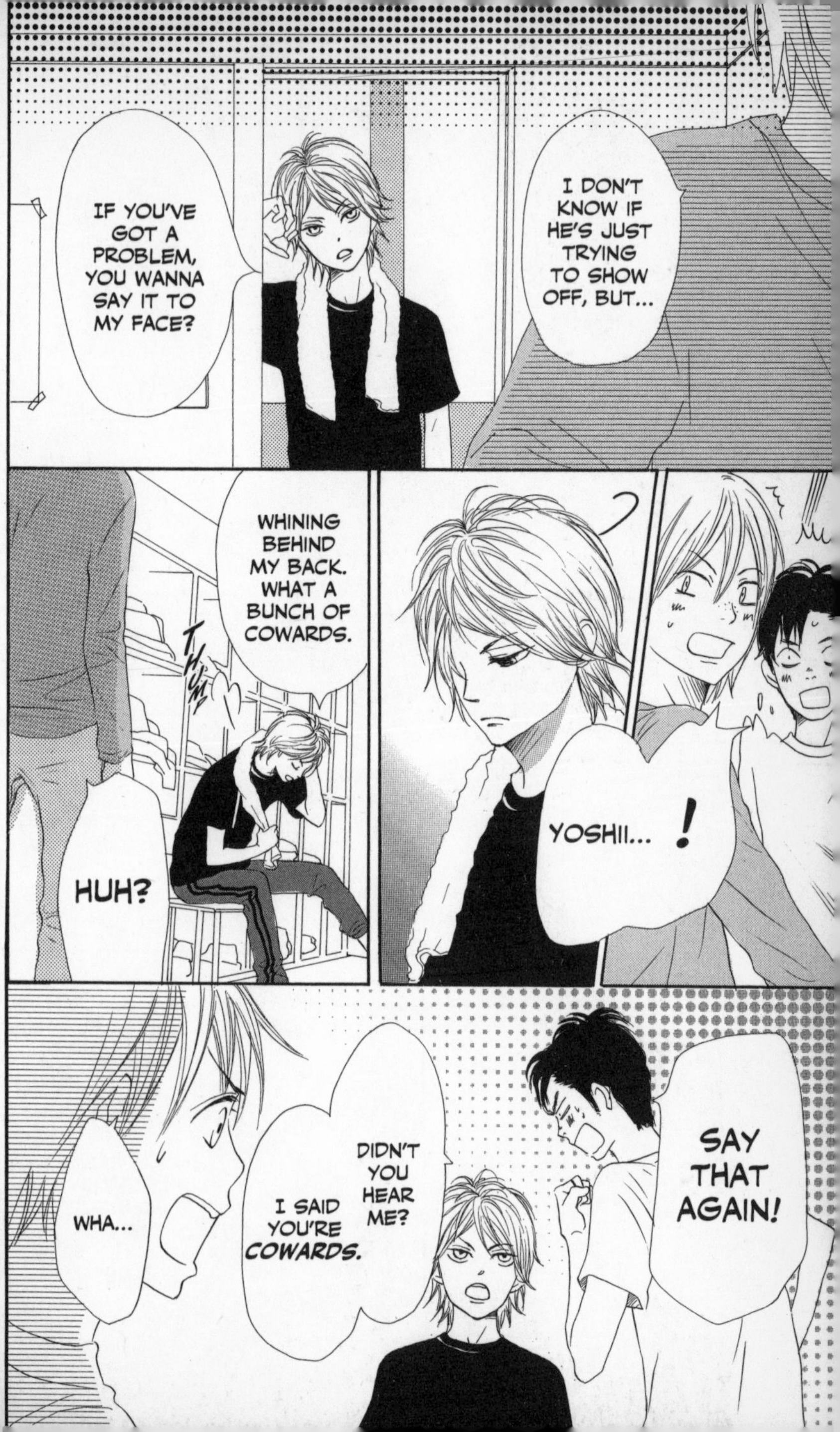
I DON'T KNOW IF HE'S JUST TRYING TO SHOW OFF, BUT...
IF YOU'VE GOT A PROBLEM, YOU WANNA SAY IT TO MY FACE?
YOSHII... !
WHINING BEHIND MY BACK. WHAT A BUNCH OF COWARDS.
THUM
HUH?
SAY THAT AGAIN!
DIDN'T YOU HEAR ME?
I SAID YOU'RE *COWARDS.*
WHA...

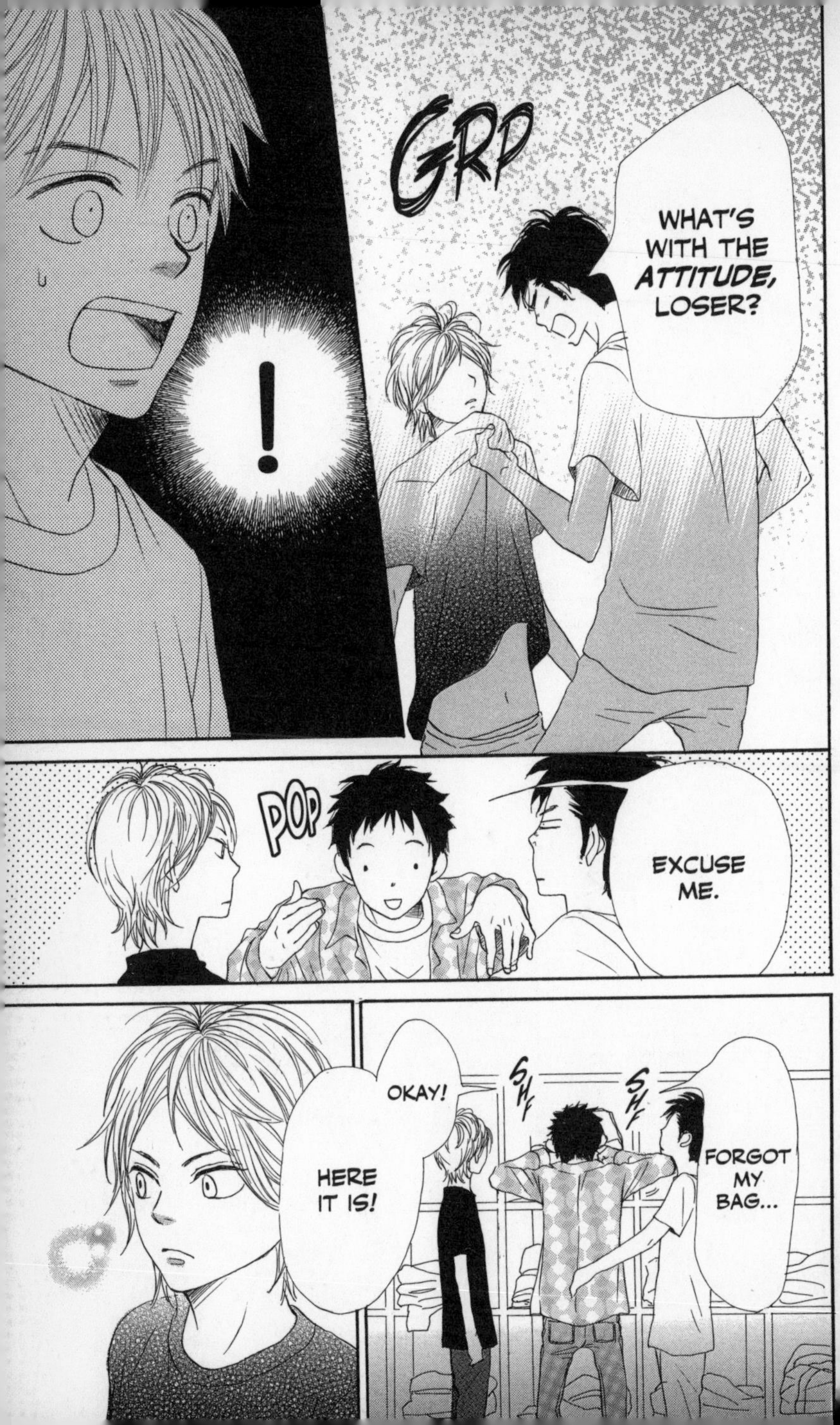
WHAT'S WITH THE ATTITUDE, LOSER?
GRP
!
EXCUSE ME.
POP
FORGOT MY BAG...
SHF
SHF
OKAY!
HERE IT IS!

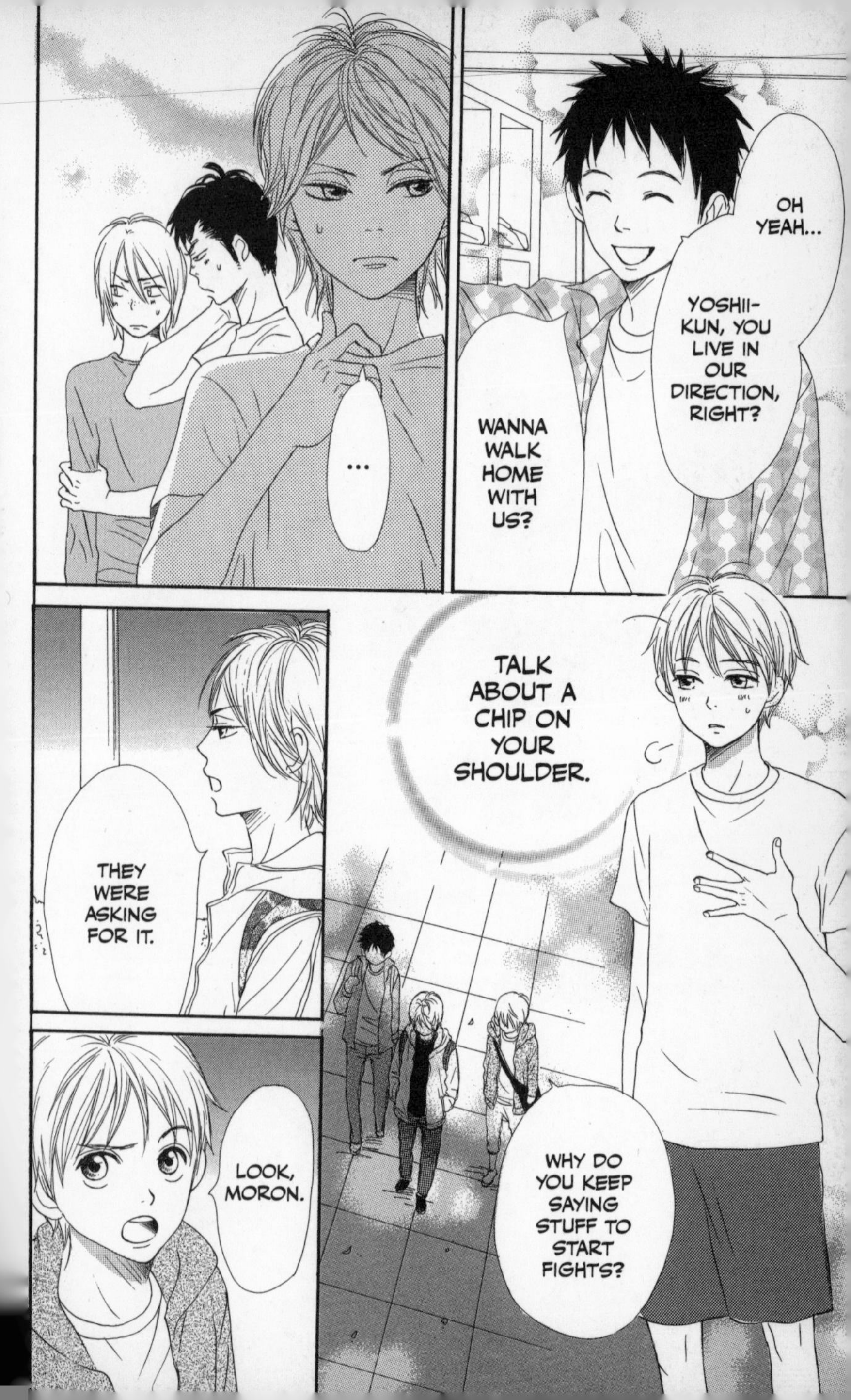
OH YEAH...
YOSHII-KUN, YOU LIVE IN OUR DIRECTION, RIGHT?
WANNA WALK HOME WITH US?
...
TALK ABOUT A CHIP ON YOUR SHOULDER.
WHY DO YOU KEEP SAYING STUFF TO START FIGHTS?
THEY WERE ASKING FOR IT.
LOOK, MORON.

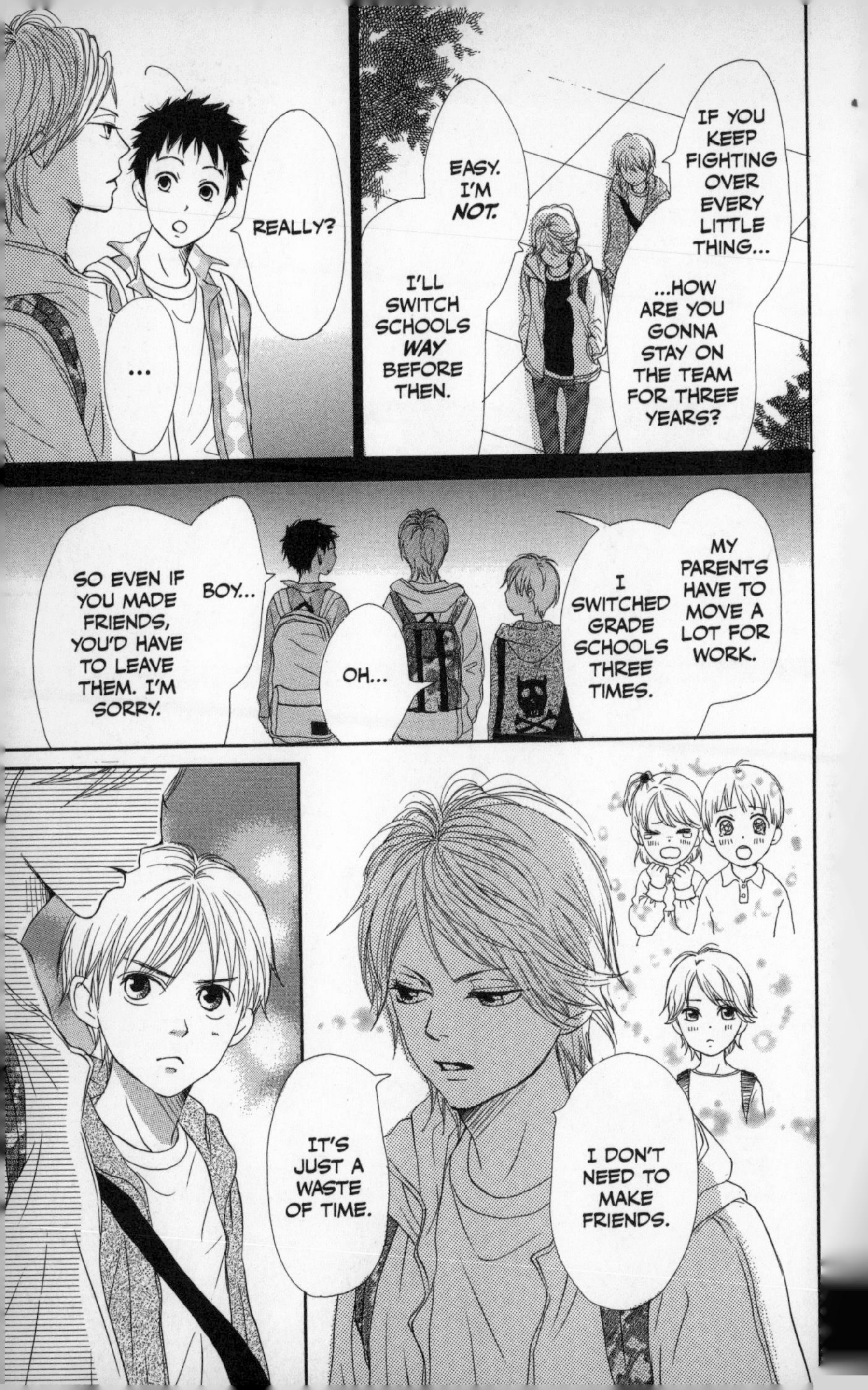
IF YOU KEEP FIGHTING OVER EVERY LITTLE THING...
...HOW ARE YOU GONNA STAY ON THE TEAM FOR THREE YEARS?
EASY. I'M *NOT.*
I'LL SWITCH SCHOOLS *WAY* BEFORE THEN.
REALLY?
...
MY PARENTS HAVE TO MOVE A LOT FOR WORK.
I SWITCHED GRADE SCHOOLS THREE TIMES.
OH...
BOY...
SO EVEN IF YOU MADE FRIENDS, YOU'D HAVE TO LEAVE THEM. I'M SORRY.
I DON'T NEED TO MAKE FRIENDS.
IT'S JUST A WASTE OF TIME.

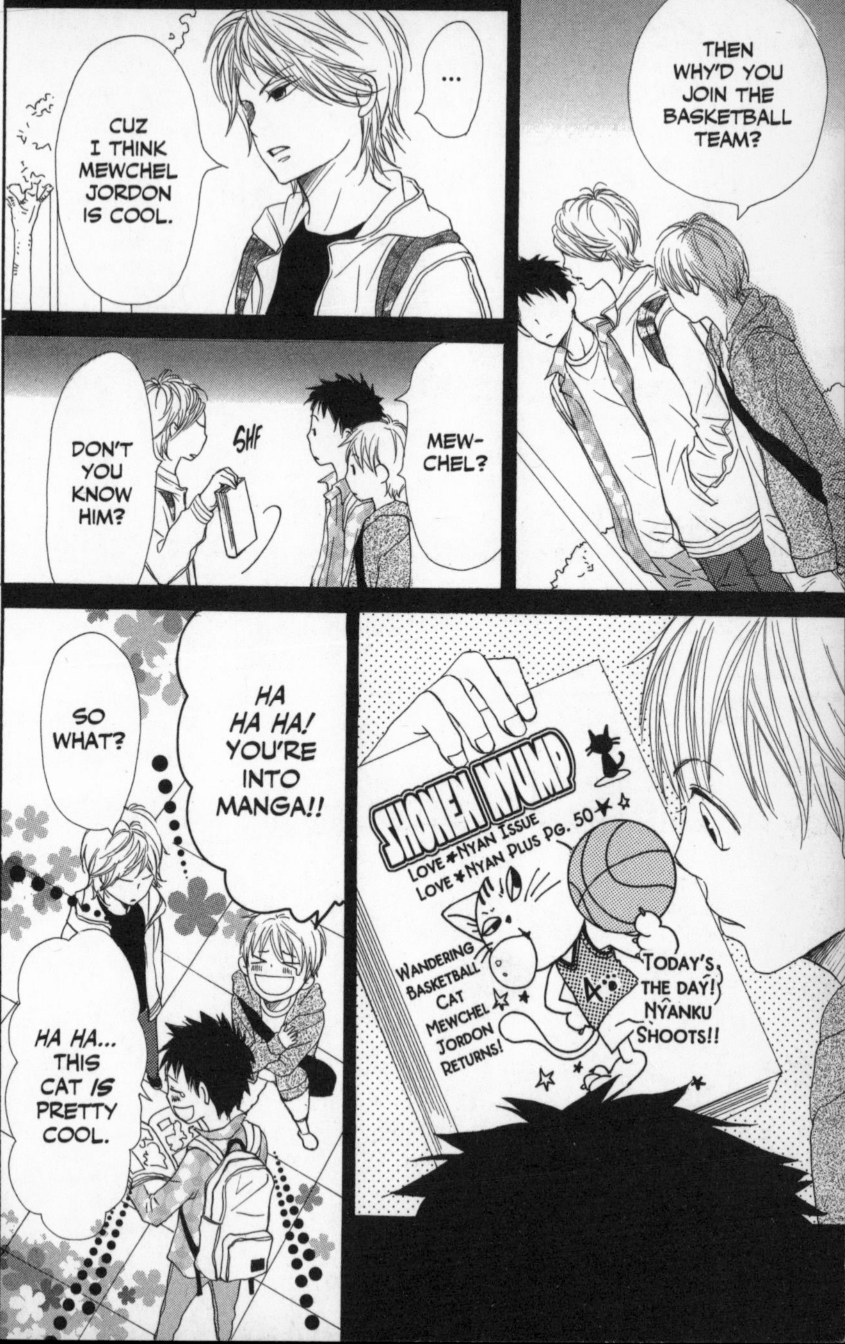
THEN WHY'D YOU JOIN THE BASKETBALL TEAM?
...
CUZ I THINK MEWCHEL JORDON IS COOL.
MEW-CHEL?
SHF
DON'T YOU KNOW HIM?
SHONEN MYUMP
LOVE✶NYAN ISSUE
LOVE✶NYAN PLUS PG. 50
TODAY'S THE DAY! NYANKU SHOOTS!!
WANDERING BASKETBALL CAT MEWCHEL JORDON RETURNS!
HA HA HA! YOU'RE INTO MANGA!!
SO WHAT?
HA HA... THIS CAT *IS* PRETTY COOL.

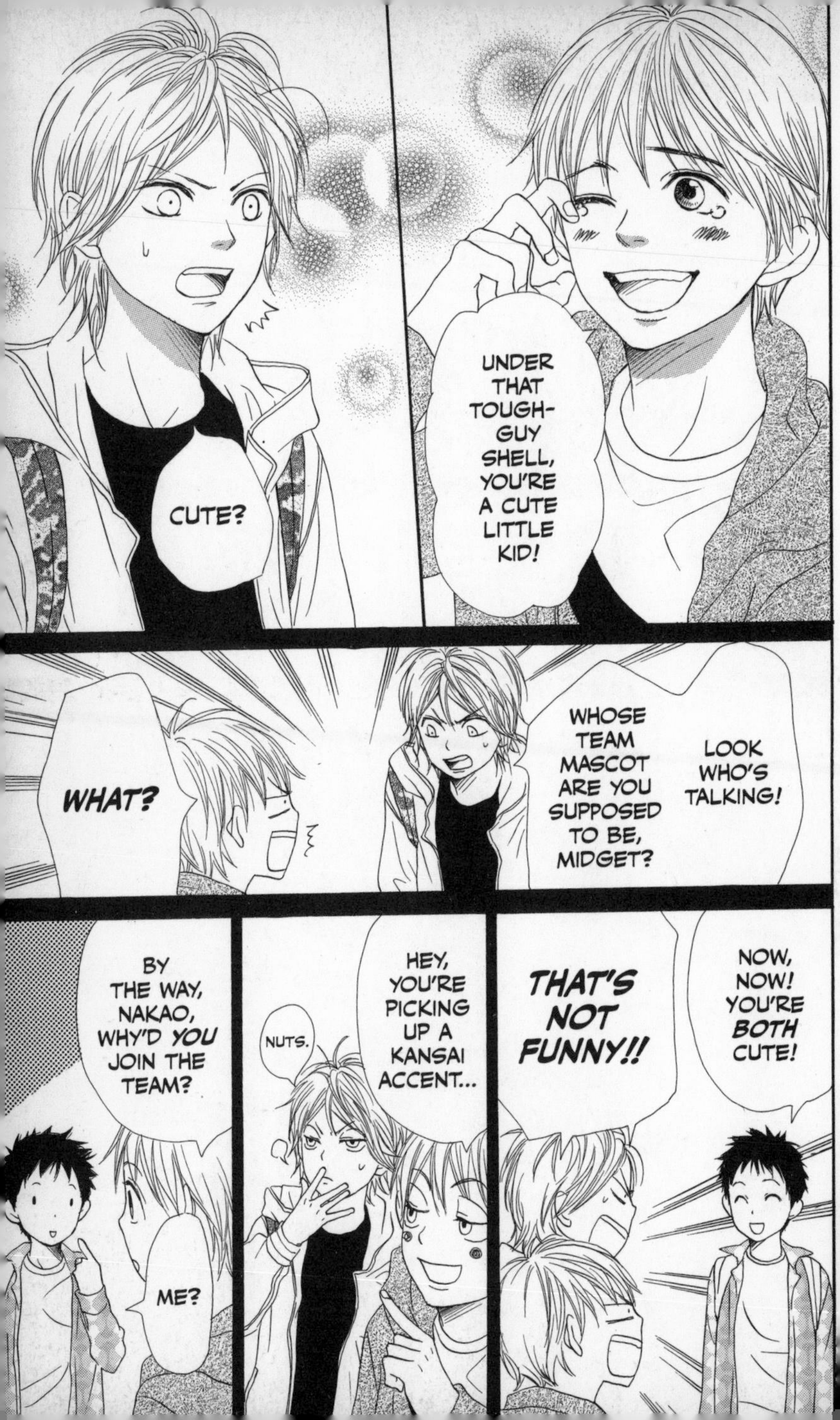
UNDER THAT TOUGH-GUY SHELL, YOU'RE A CUTE LITTLE KID!
CUTE?
LOOK WHO'S TALKING!
WHOSE TEAM MASCOT ARE YOU SUPPOSED TO BE, MIDGET?
WHAT?
NOW, NOW! YOU'RE *BOTH* CUTE!
THAT'S NOT FUNNY!!
HEY, YOU'RE PICKING UP A KANSAI ACCENT...
NUTS.
BY THE WAY, NAKAO, WHY'D *YOU* JOIN THE TEAM?
ME?

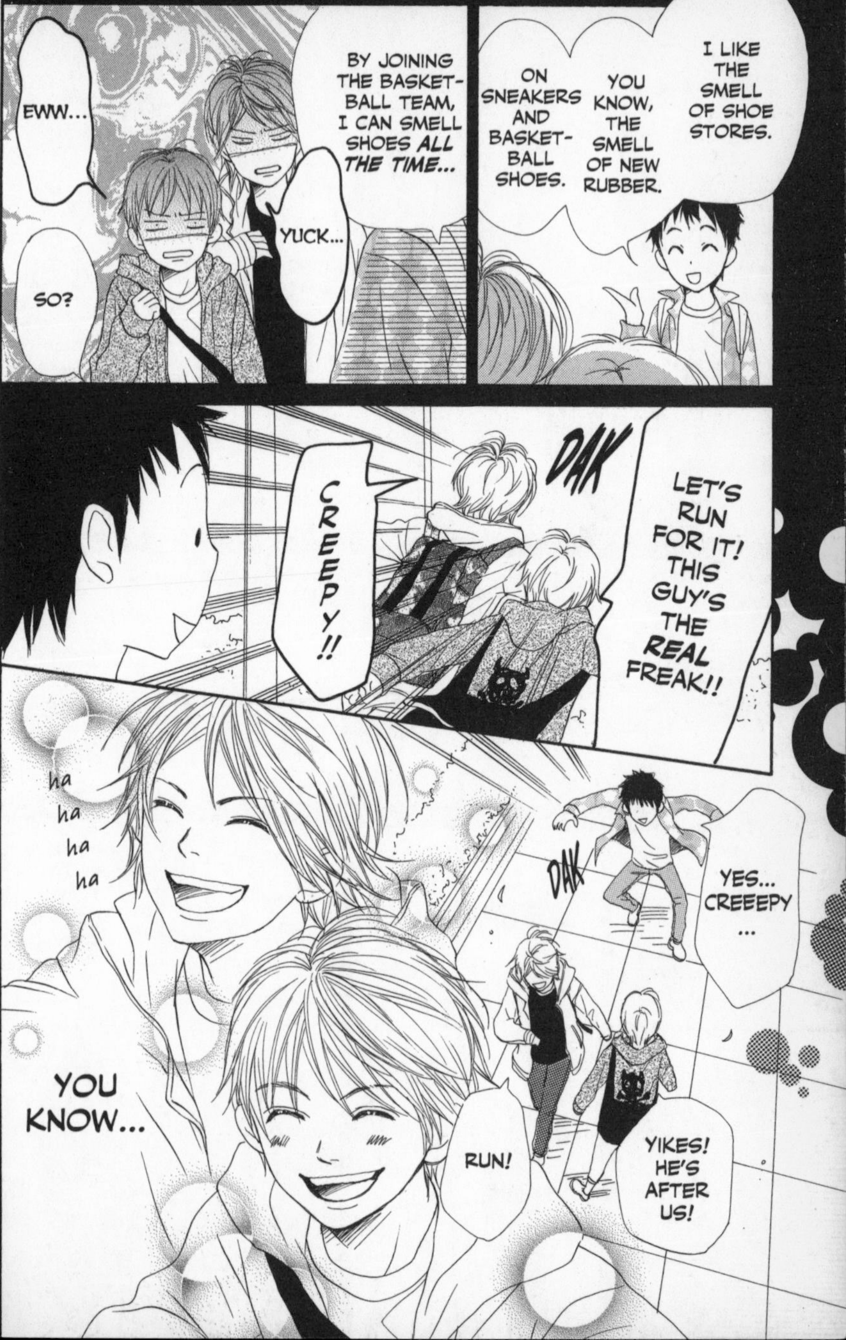
I LIKE THE SMELL OF SHOE STORES.
YOU KNOW, THE SMELL OF NEW RUBBER.
ON SNEAKERS AND BASKET-BALL SHOES.
BY JOINING THE BASKET-BALL TEAM, I CAN SMELL SHOES ALL THE TIME...
YUCK...
EWW...
SO?
LET'S RUN FOR IT! THIS GUY'S THE REAL FREAK!!
DAK
CREEPY!!
YES... CREEEPY ...
DAK
YIKES! HE'S AFTER US!
RUN!
ha ha ha ha
YOU KNOW...

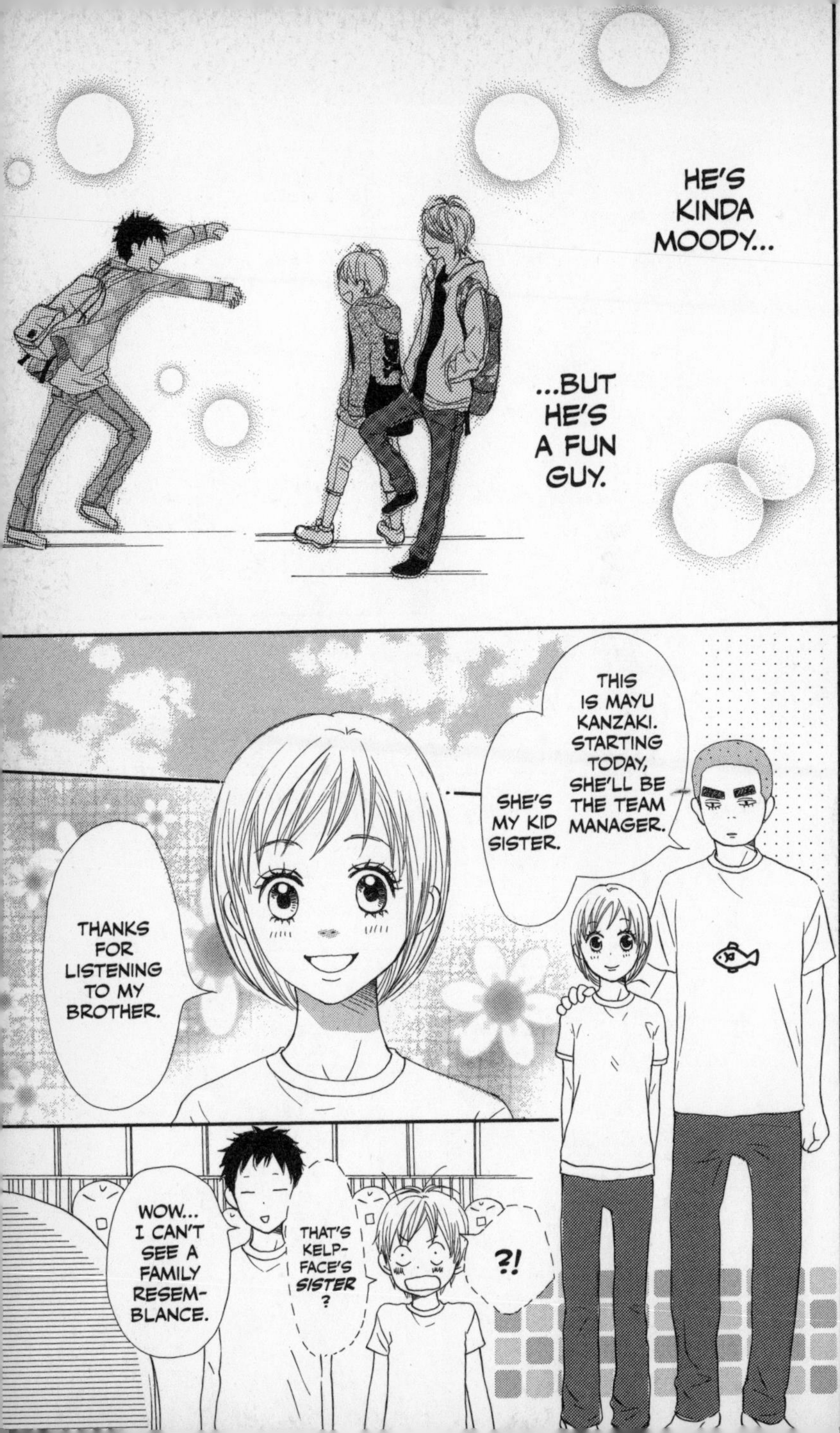
HE'S KINDA MOODY...
...BUT HE'S A FUN GUY.
THIS IS MAYU KANZAKI. STARTING TODAY, SHE'LL BE THE TEAM MANAGER.
SHE'S MY KID SISTER.
THANKS FOR LISTENING TO MY BROTHER.
?!
THAT'S KELP-FACE'S *SISTER*?
WOW... I CAN'T SEE A FAMILY RESEM-BLANCE.

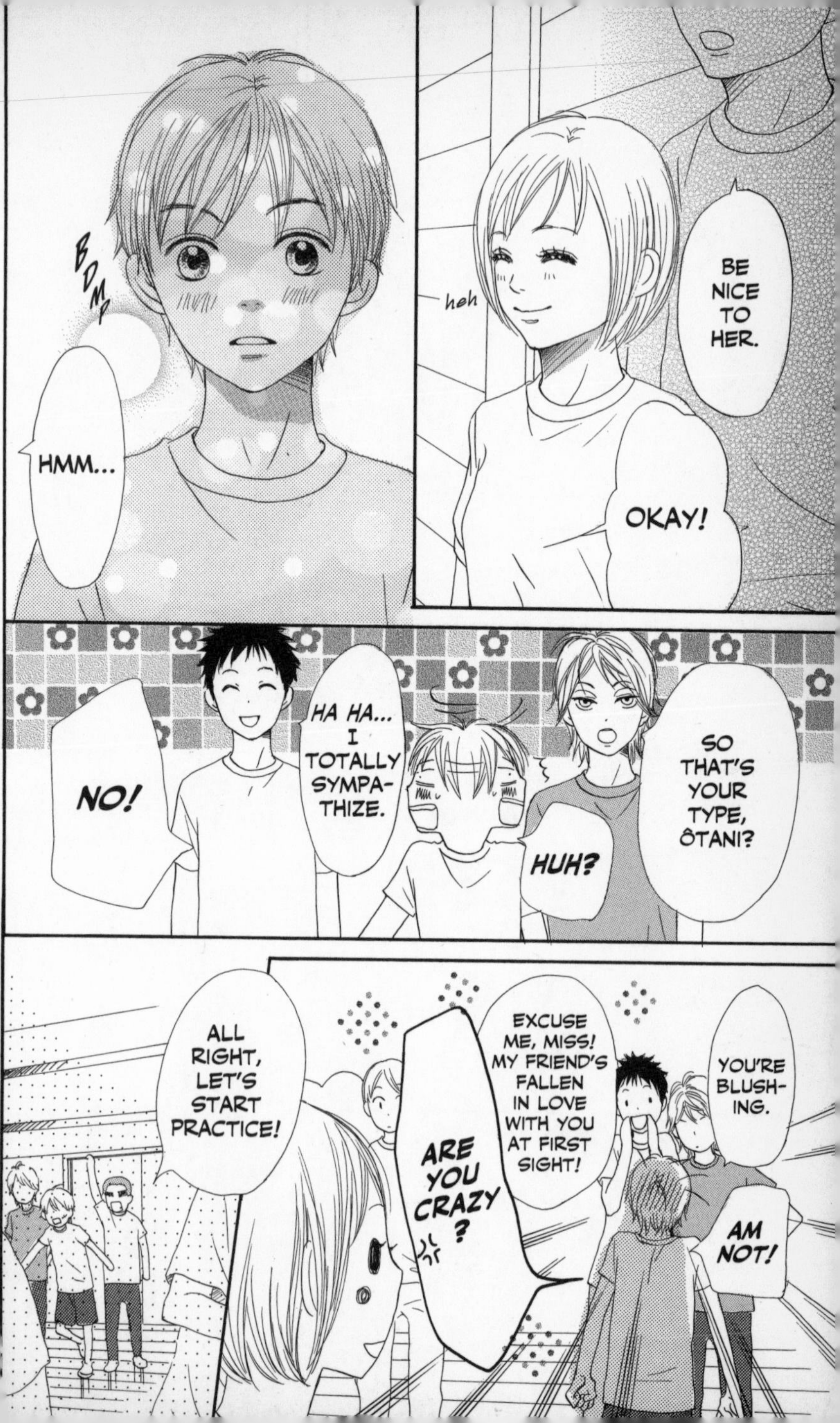
BE NICE TO HER.
heh
OKAY!
BDMP
HMM...
SO THAT'S YOUR TYPE, ÔTANI?
HUH?
HA HA... I TOTALLY SYMPA-THIZE.
NO!
YOU'RE BLUSH-ING.
AM NOT!
EXCUSE ME, MISS! MY FRIEND'S FALLEN IN LOVE WITH YOU AT FIRST SIGHT!
ARE YOU CRAZY?
ALL RIGHT, LET'S START PRACTICE!

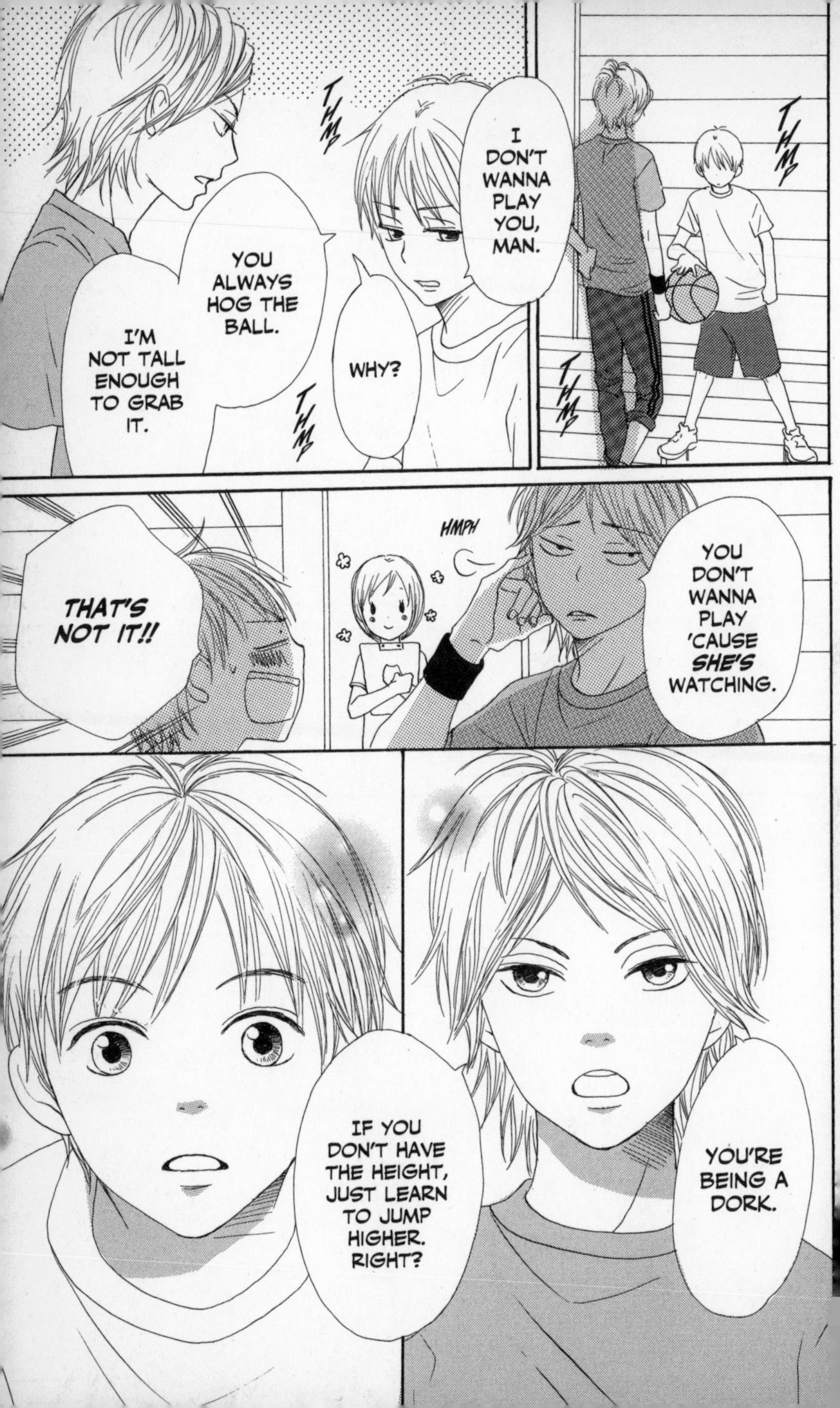

THMP
THMP
I DON'T WANNA PLAY YOU, MAN.
THMP
YOU ALWAYS HOG THE BALL.
WHY?
I'M NOT TALL ENOUGH TO GRAB IT.
THMP
YOU DON'T WANNA PLAY 'CAUSE SHE'S WATCHING.
HMPH
THAT'S NOT IT!!
YOU'RE BEING A DORK.
IF YOU DON'T HAVE THE HEIGHT, JUST LEARN TO JUMP HIGHER. RIGHT?

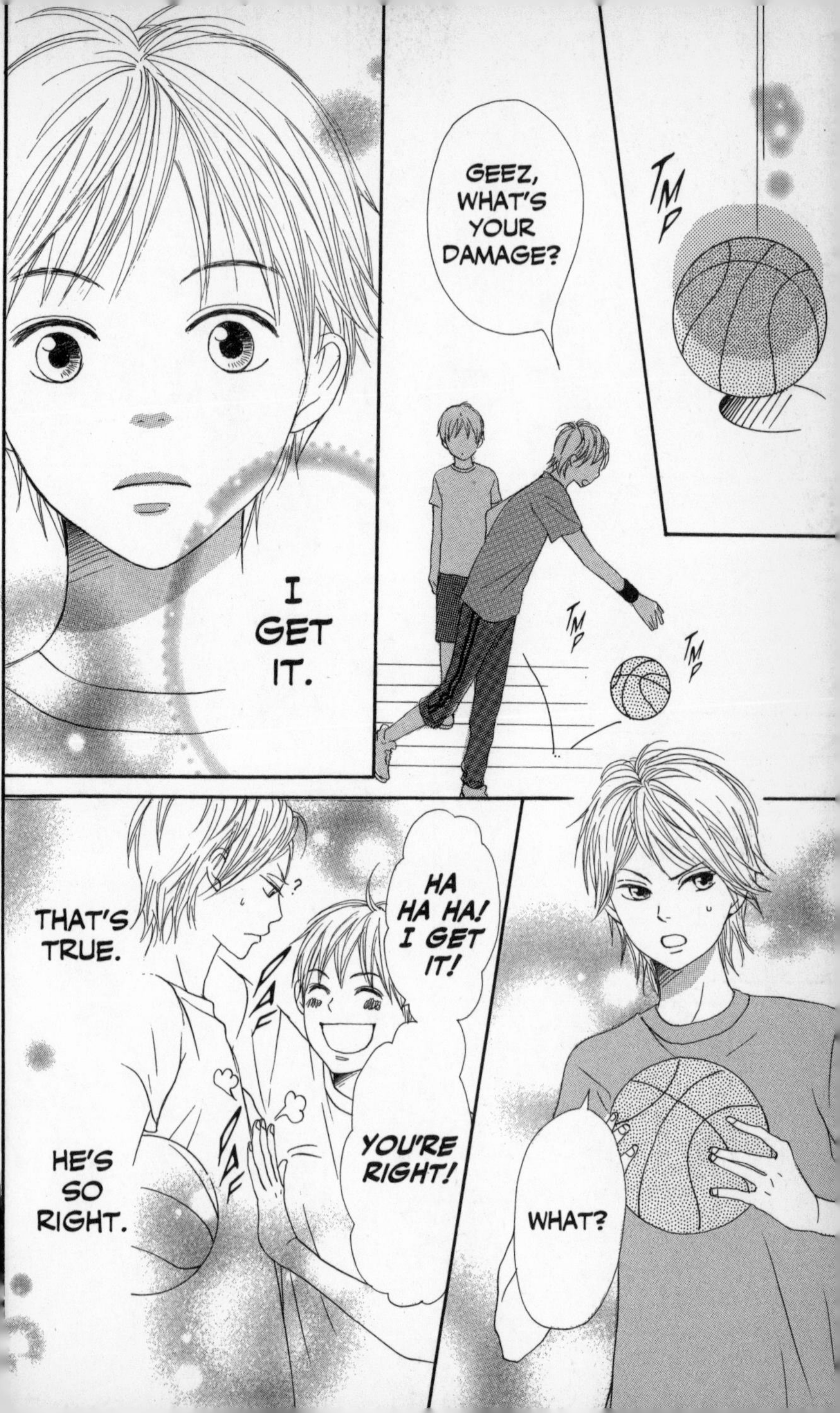
TMP
GEEZ, WHAT'S YOUR DAMAGE?
TMP
TMP
I GET IT.
WHAT?
HA HA HA! I GET IT!
YOU'RE RIGHT!
THAT'S TRUE.
HE'S SO RIGHT.

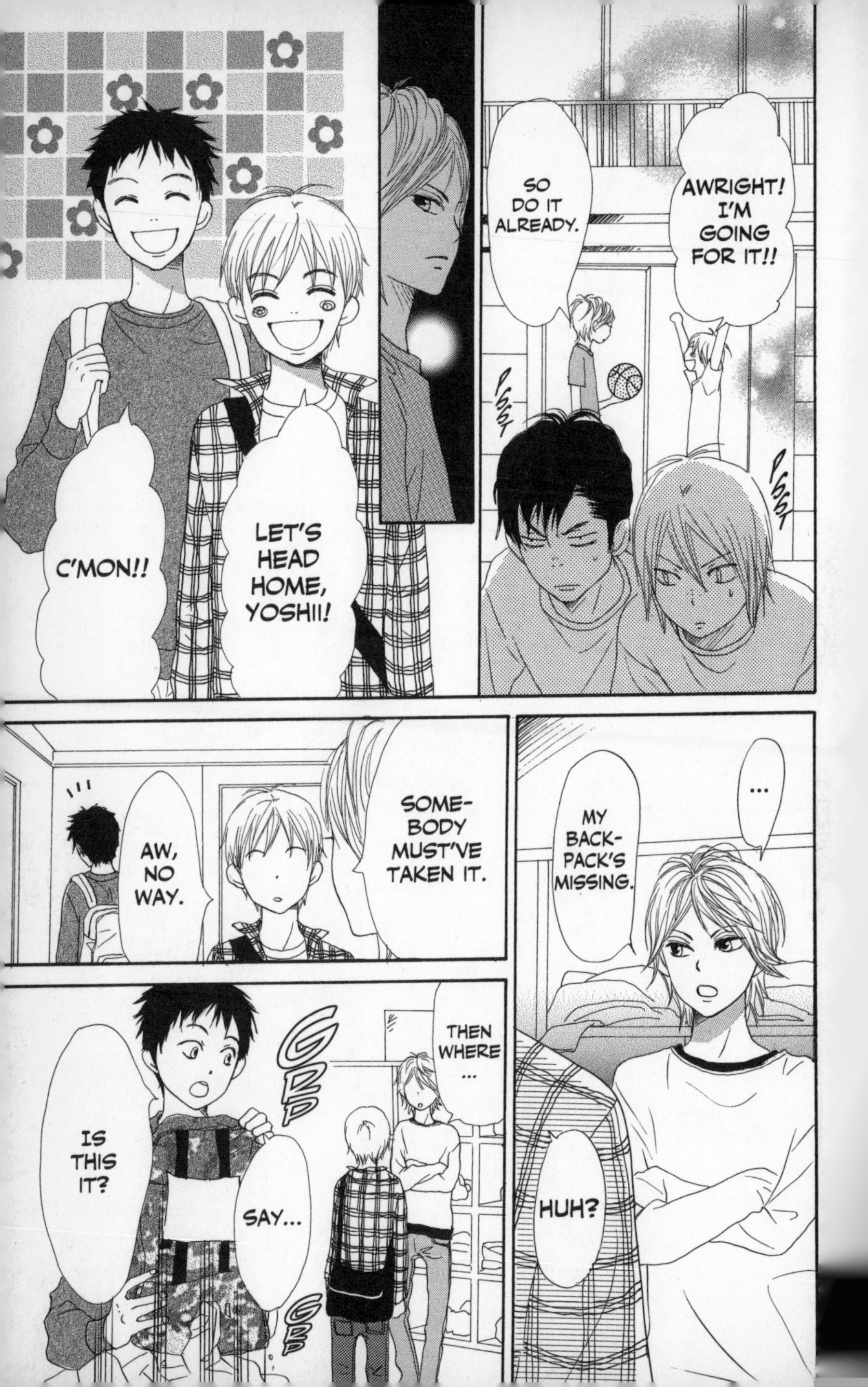
AWRIGHT! I'M GOING FOR IT!!
SO DO IT ALREADY.
LET'S HEAD HOME, YOSHII!
C'MON!!
...
MY BACK-PACK'S MISSING.
HUH?
SOME-BODY MUST'VE TAKEN IT.
AW, NO WAY.
THEN WHERE ...
GRR
SAY...
IS THIS IT?
GRR

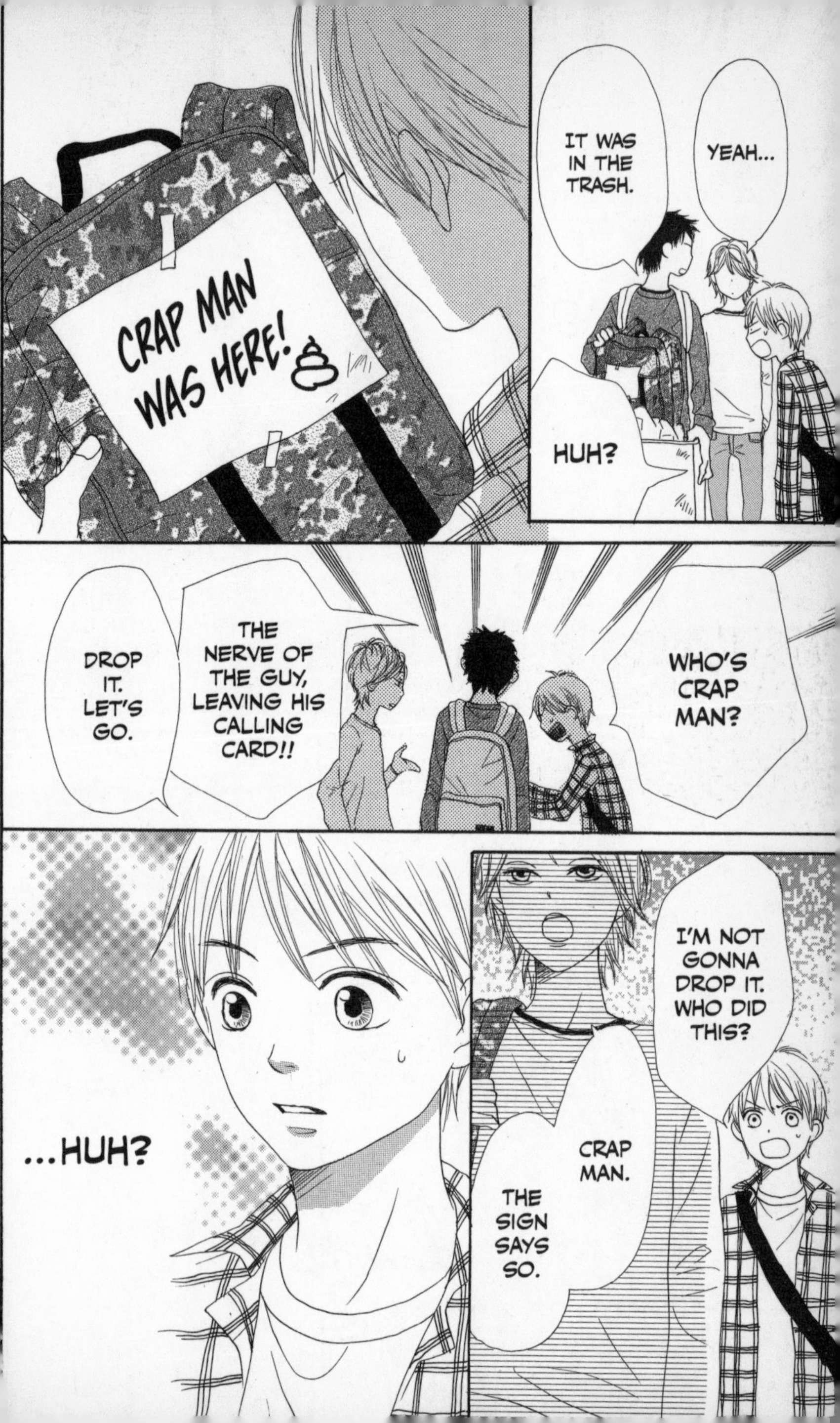
YEAH...
IT WAS IN THE TRASH.
HUH?
CRAP MAN WAS HERE!
WHO'S CRAP MAN?
THE NERVE OF THE GUY, LEAVING HIS CALLING CARD!!
DROP IT. LET'S GO.
I'M NOT GONNA DROP IT. WHO DID THIS?
CRAP MAN. THE SIGN SAYS SO.
...HUH?

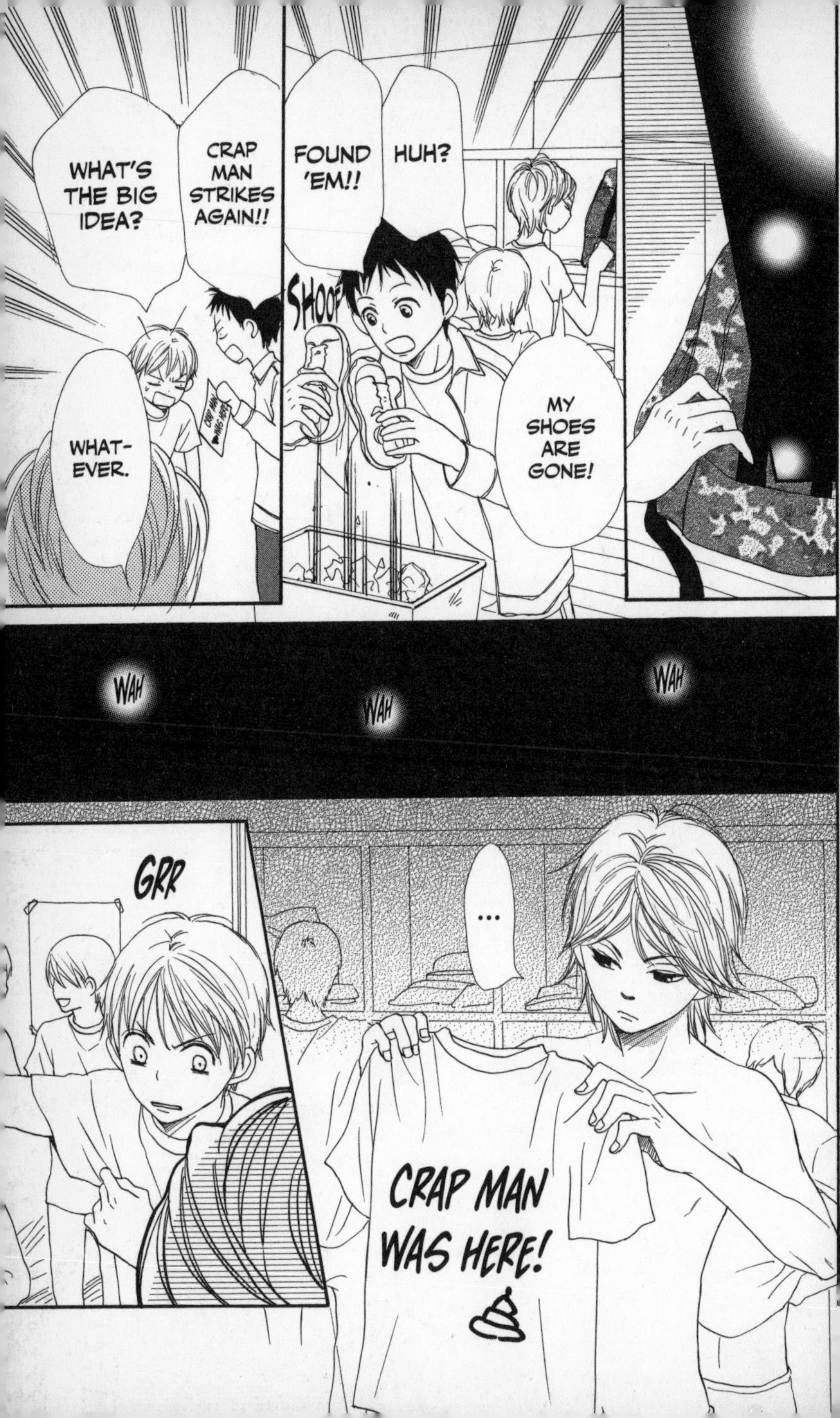
HUH?
FOUND 'EM!!
SHOOF
MY SHOES ARE GONE!
CRAP MAN STRIKES AGAIN!!
WHAT'S THE BIG IDEA?
WHAT-EVER.
WAH
WAH
WAH
...
CRAP MAN WAS HERE!
GRR

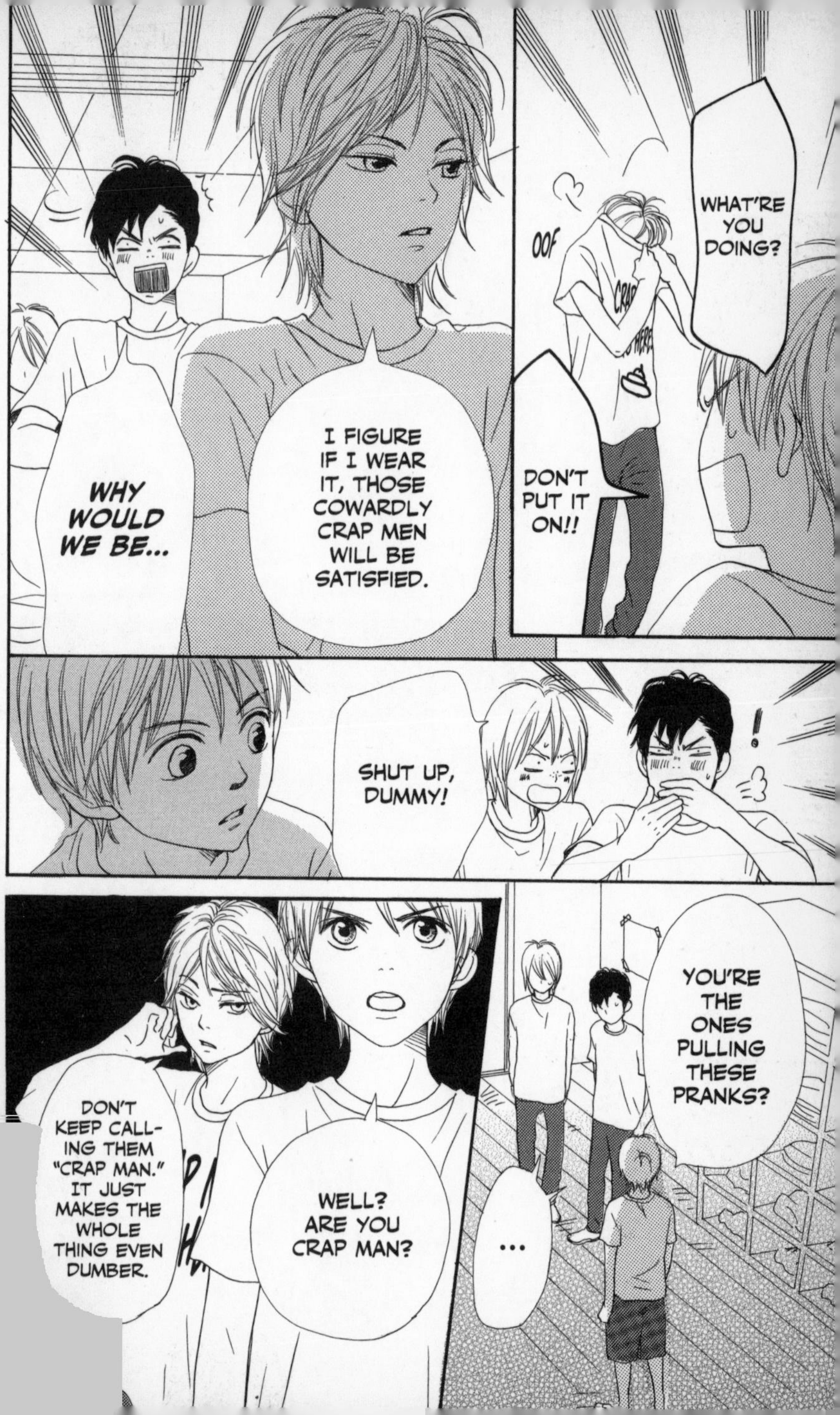
WHAT'RE YOU DOING?
OOF
DON'T PUT IT ON!!
I FIGURE IF I WEAR IT, THOSE COWARDLY CRAP MEN WILL BE SATISFIED.
WHY WOULD WE BE...
!
SHUT UP, DUMMY!
YOU'RE THE ONES PULLING THESE PRANKS?
...
WELL? ARE YOU CRAP MAN?
DON'T KEEP CALLING THEM "CRAP MAN." IT JUST MAKES THE WHOLE THING EVEN DUMBER.

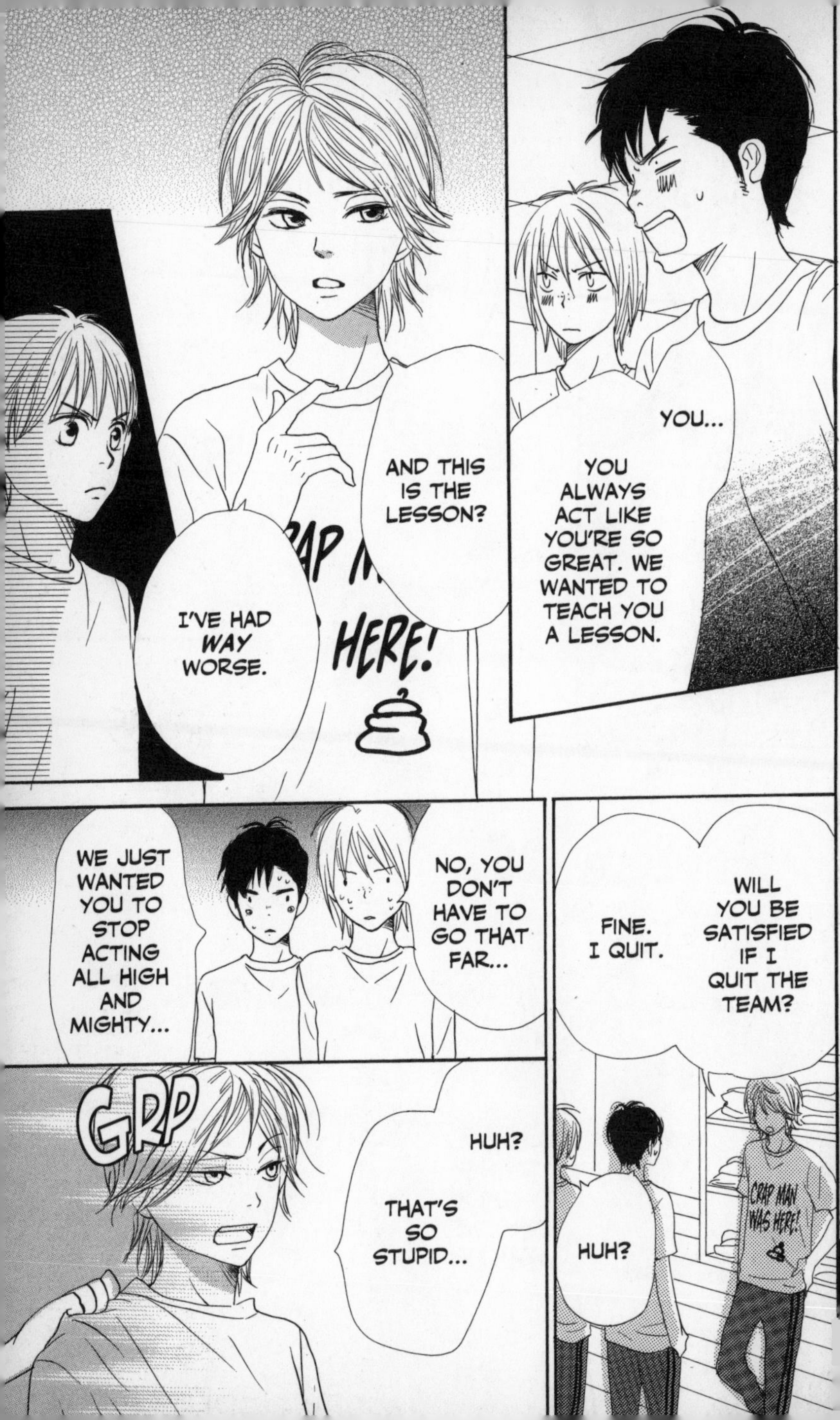
YOU...
YOU ALWAYS ACT LIKE YOU'RE SO GREAT. WE WANTED TO TEACH YOU A LESSON.
AND THIS IS THE LESSON?
I'VE HAD *WAY* WORSE.
WILL YOU BE SATISFIED IF I QUIT THE TEAM?
FINE. I QUIT.
HUH?
CRAP MAN WAS HERE!
NO, YOU DON'T HAVE TO GO THAT FAR...
WE JUST WANTED YOU TO STOP ACTING ALL HIGH AND MIGHTY...
GRP
HUH?
THAT'S SO STUPID...

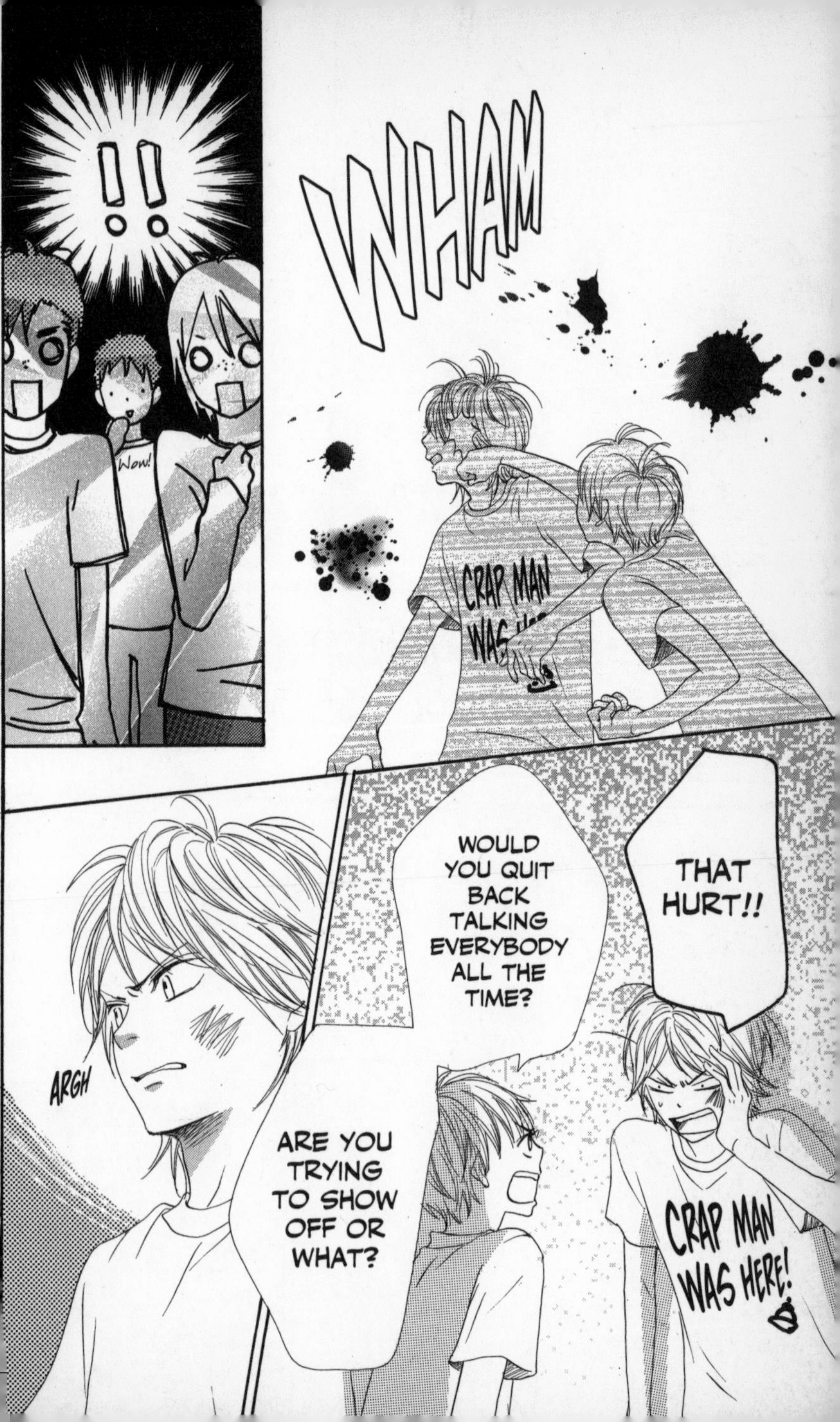
WHAM
CRAP MAN WAS
!!
Wow!
THAT HURT!!
WOULD YOU QUIT BACK TALKING EVERYBODY ALL THE TIME?
CRAP MAN WAS HERE!
ARE YOU TRYING TO SHOW OFF OR WHAT?
ARGH

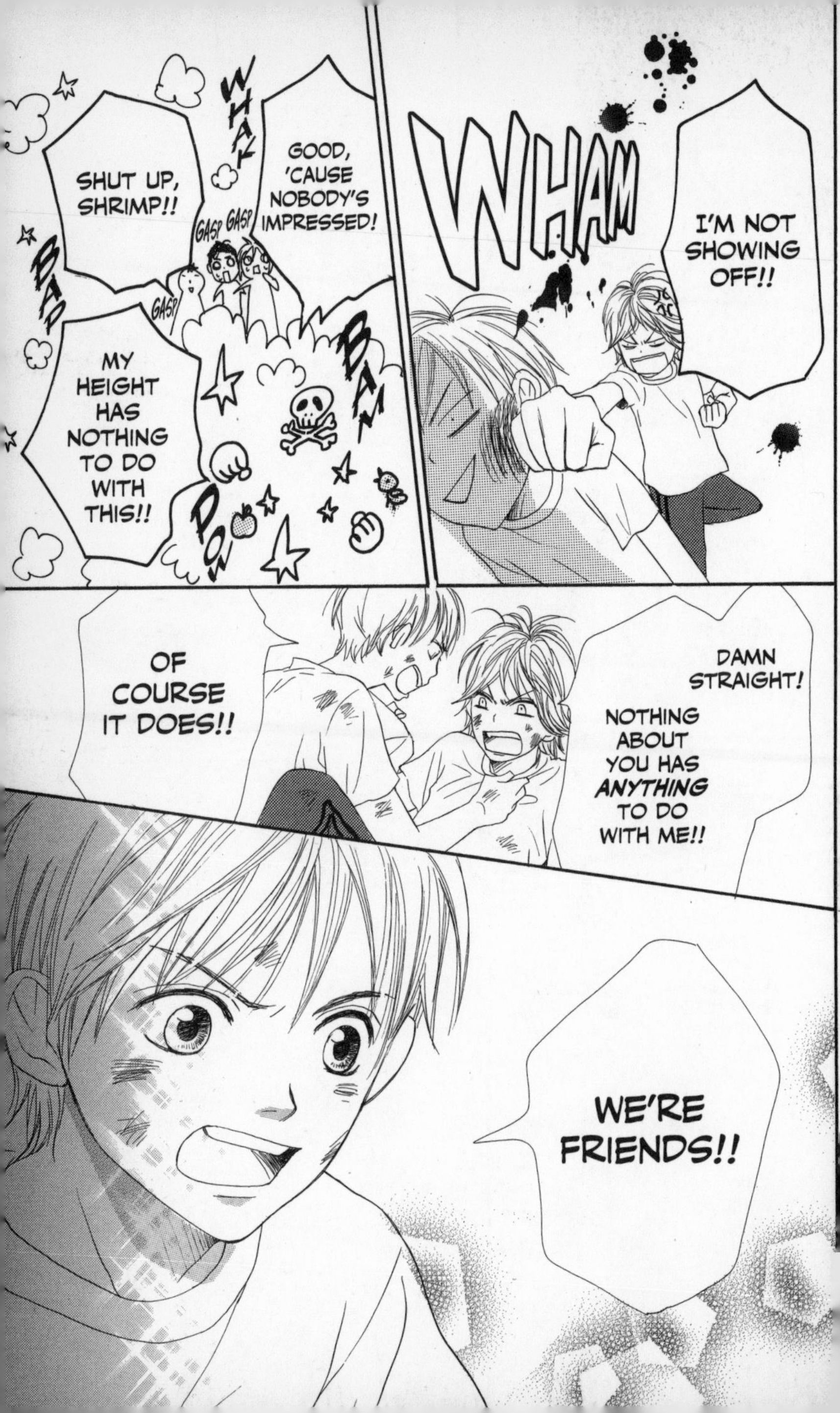
WHAM
I'M NOT SHOWING OFF!!
WHAK
GOOD, 'CAUSE NOBODY'S IMPRESSED!
SHUT UP, SHRIMP!!
GASP GASP
GASP
BAP
BAM
MY HEIGHT HAS NOTHING TO DO WITH THIS!!
POW
DAMN STRAIGHT!
NOTHING ABOUT YOU HAS *ANYTHING* TO DO WITH ME!!
OF COURSE IT DOES!!
WE'RE FRIENDS!!

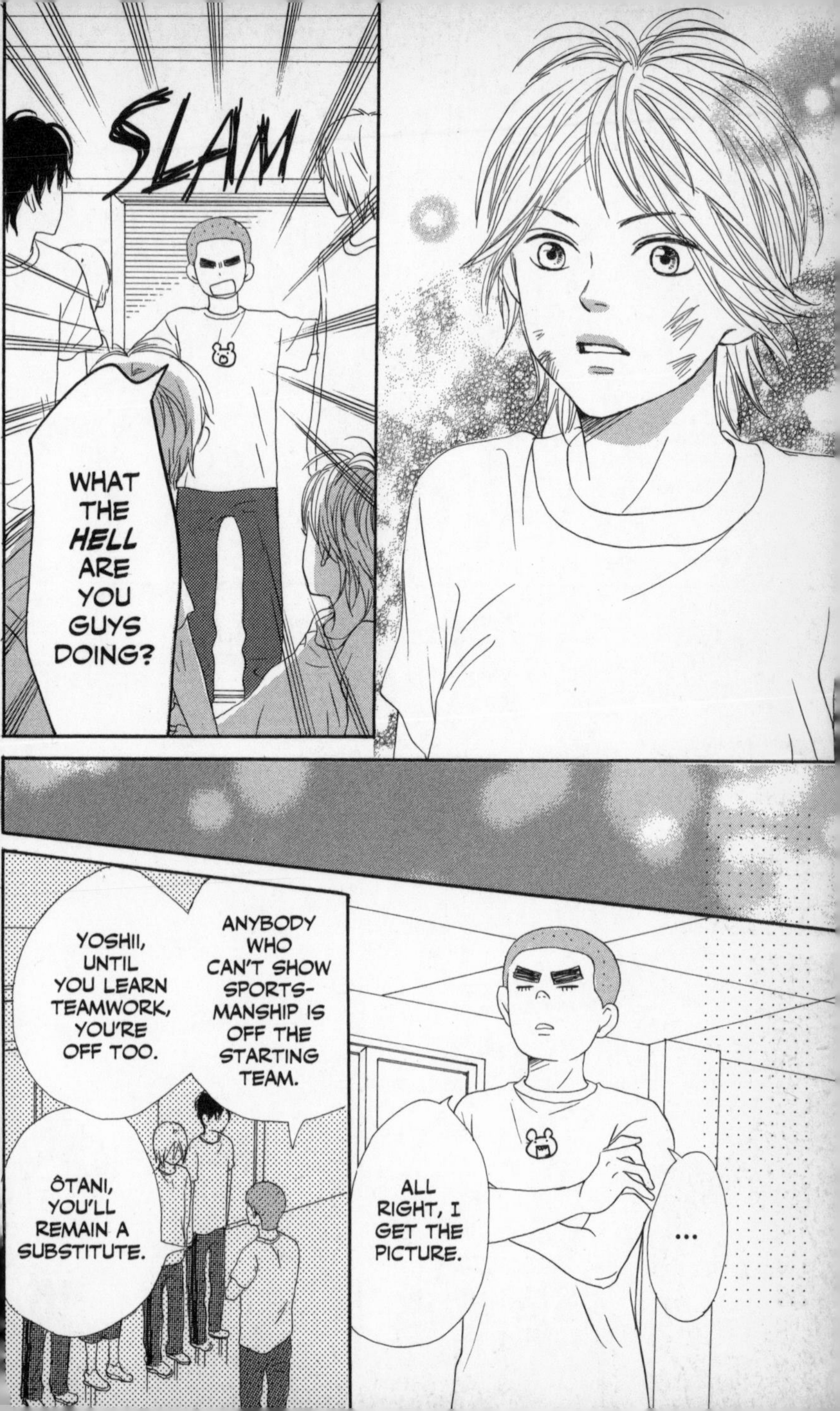
SLAM
WHAT THE HELL ARE YOU GUYS DOING?
...
ALL RIGHT, I GET THE PICTURE.
ANYBODY WHO CAN'T SHOW SPORTSMANSHIP IS OFF THE STARTING TEAM.
YOSHII, UNTIL YOU LEARN TEAMWORK, YOU'RE OFF TOO.
ŌTANI, YOU'LL REMAIN A SUBSTITUTE.

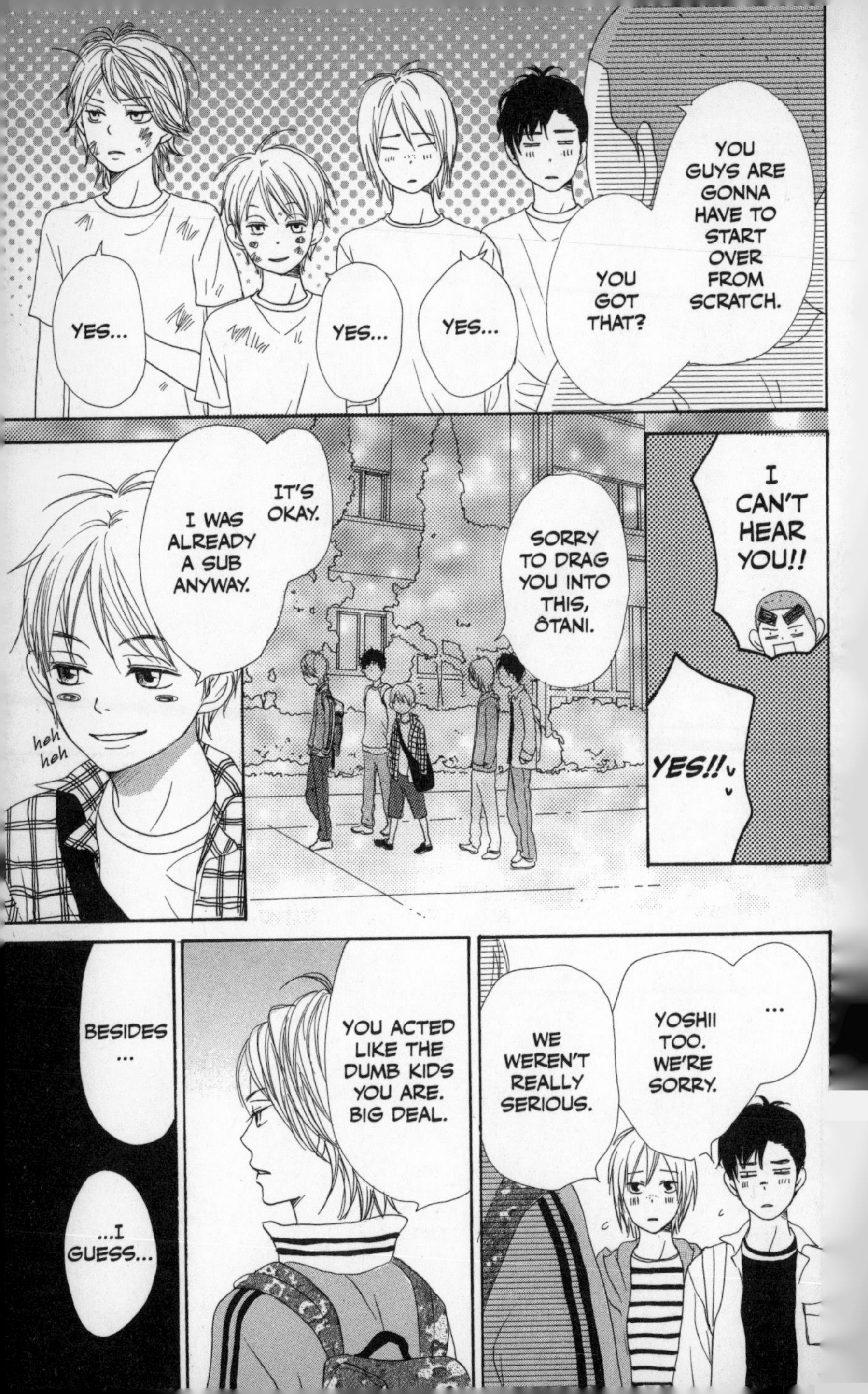
YOU GUYS ARE GONNA HAVE TO START OVER FROM SCRATCH.
YOU GOT THAT?
YES...
YES...
YES...
I CAN'T HEAR YOU!!
YES!!
SORRY TO DRAG YOU INTO THIS, ÔTANI.
IT'S OKAY.
I WAS ALREADY A SUB ANYWAY.
heh heh
...
YOSHII TOO. WE'RE SORRY.
WE WEREN'T REALLY SERIOUS.
YOU ACTED LIKE THE DUMB KIDS YOU ARE. BIG DEAL.
BESIDES ...
...I GUESS...

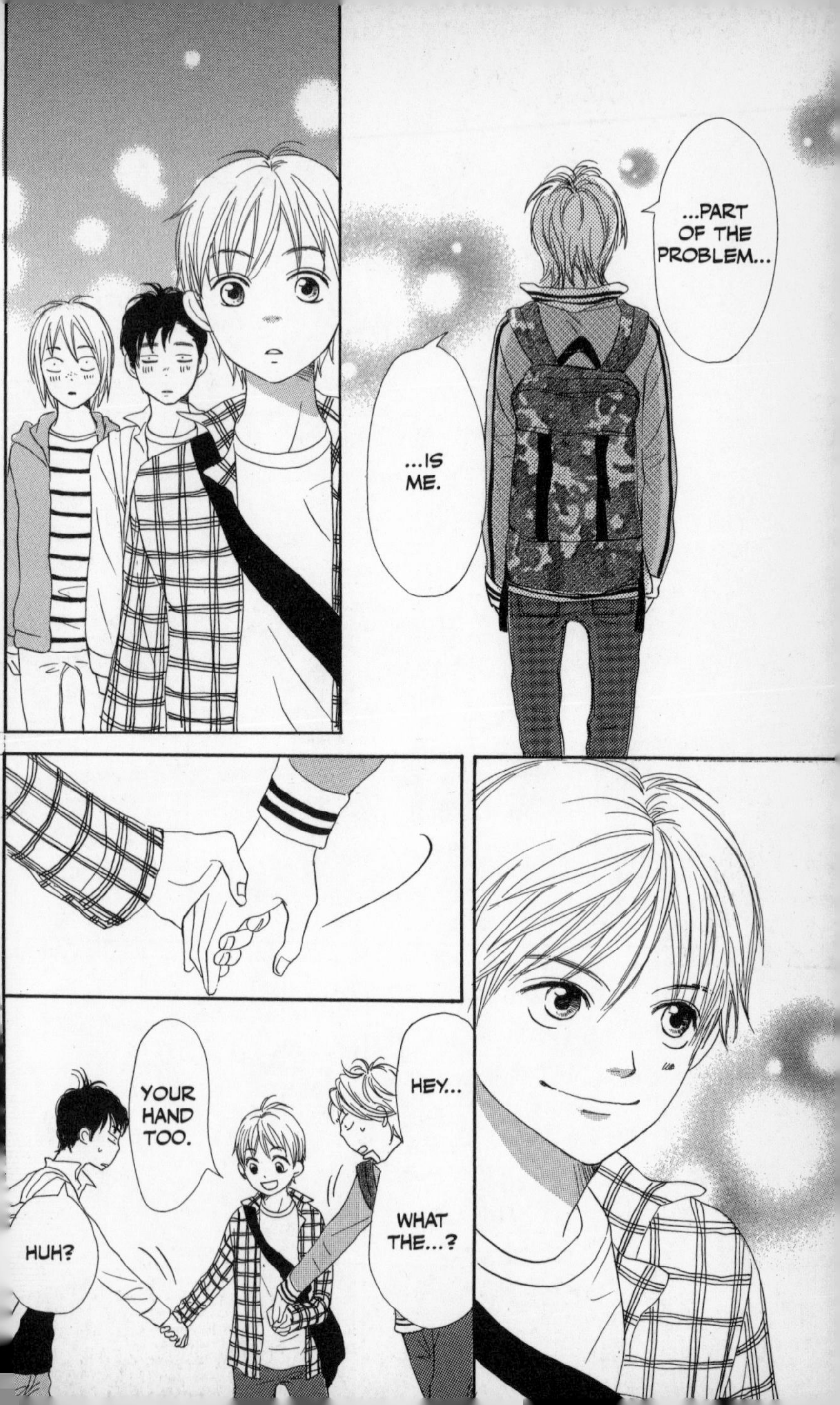
...PART OF THE PROBLEM...
...IS ME.
HEY...
WHAT THE...?
YOUR HAND TOO.
HUH?

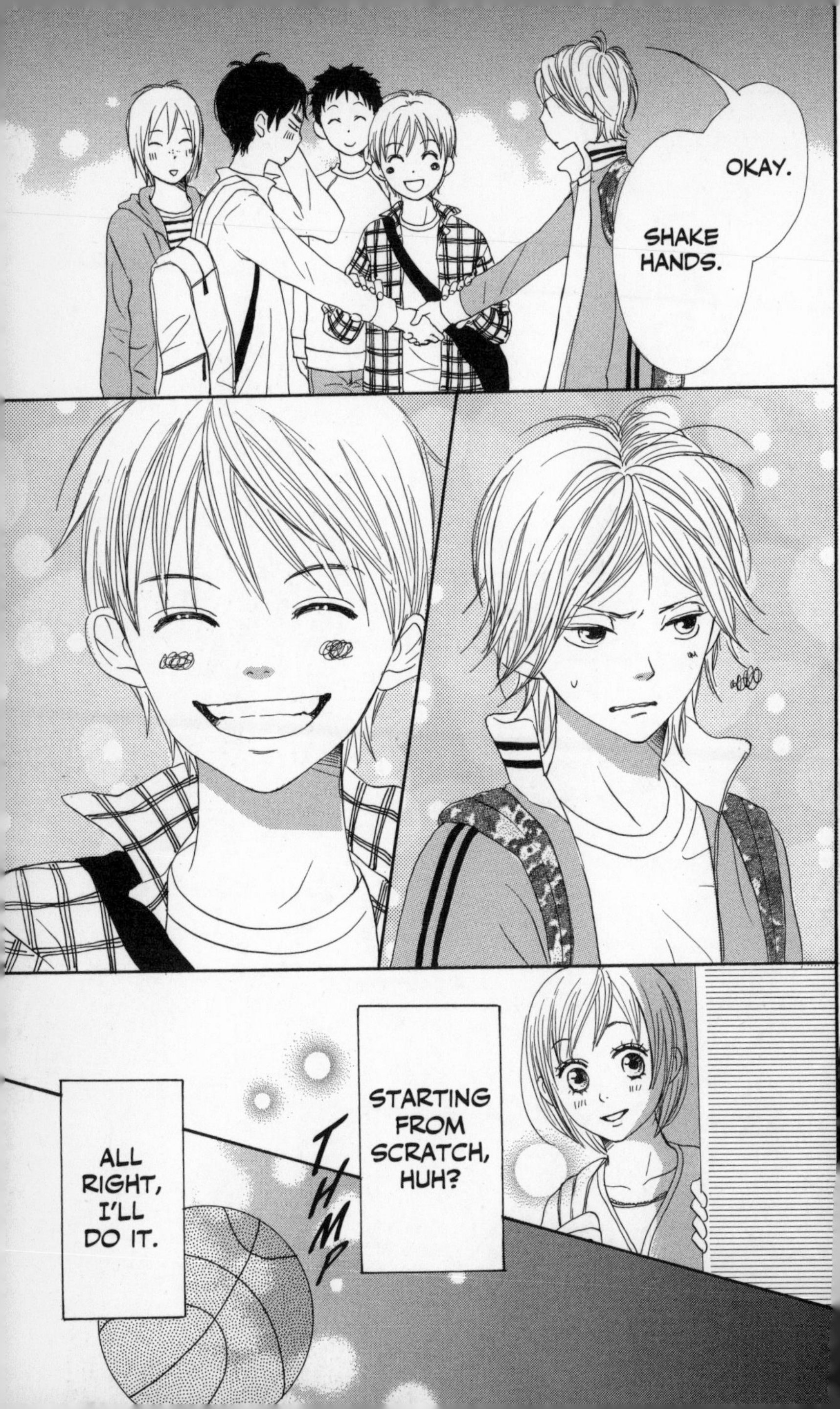
OKAY.
SHAKE HANDS.
STARTING FROM SCRATCH, HUH?
THMP
ALL RIGHT, I'LL DO IT.

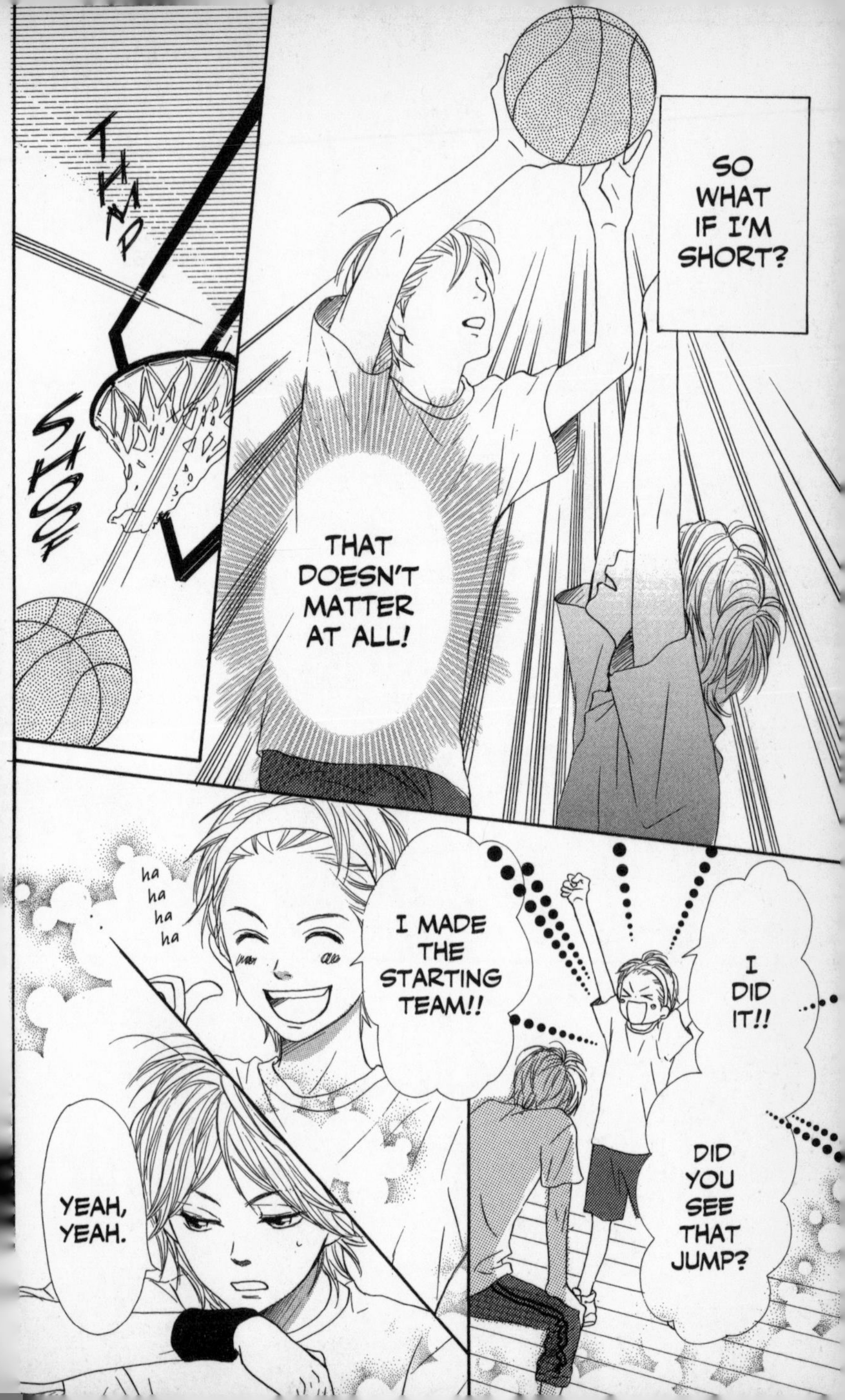
SO WHAT IF I'M SHORT?
THAT DOESN'T MATTER AT ALL!
THUMP
SHOOF
I DID IT!!
DID YOU SEE THAT JUMP?
I MADE THE STARTING TEAM!!
ha ha ha ha
YEAH, YEAH.

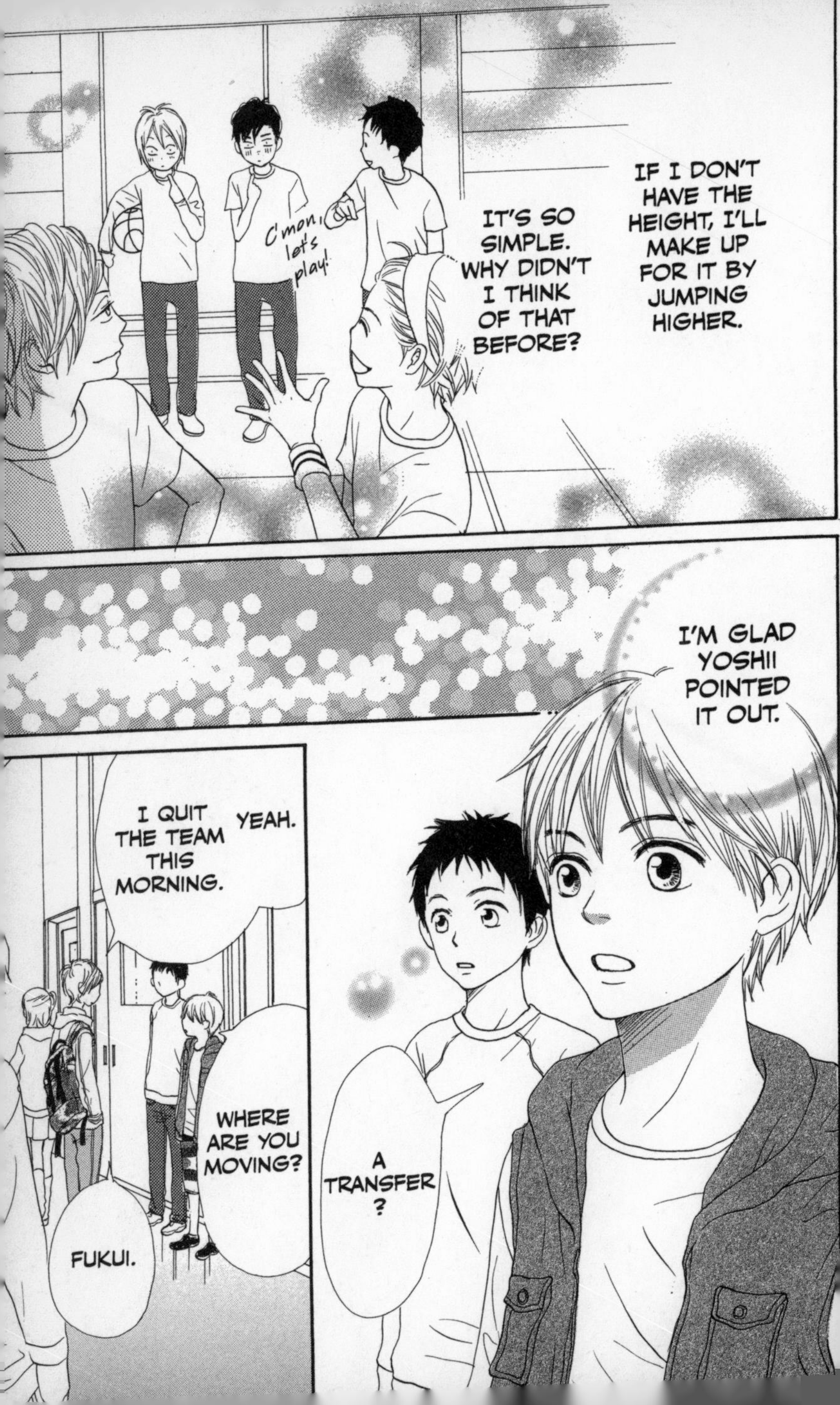
IF I DON'T HAVE THE HEIGHT, I'LL MAKE UP FOR IT BY JUMPING HIGHER.
IT'S SO SIMPLE. WHY DIDN'T I THINK OF THAT BEFORE?
C'mon, let's play!
I'M GLAD YOSHII POINTED IT OUT.
A TRANSFER?
YEAH.
I QUIT THE TEAM THIS MORNING.
WHERE ARE YOU MOVING?
FUKUI.

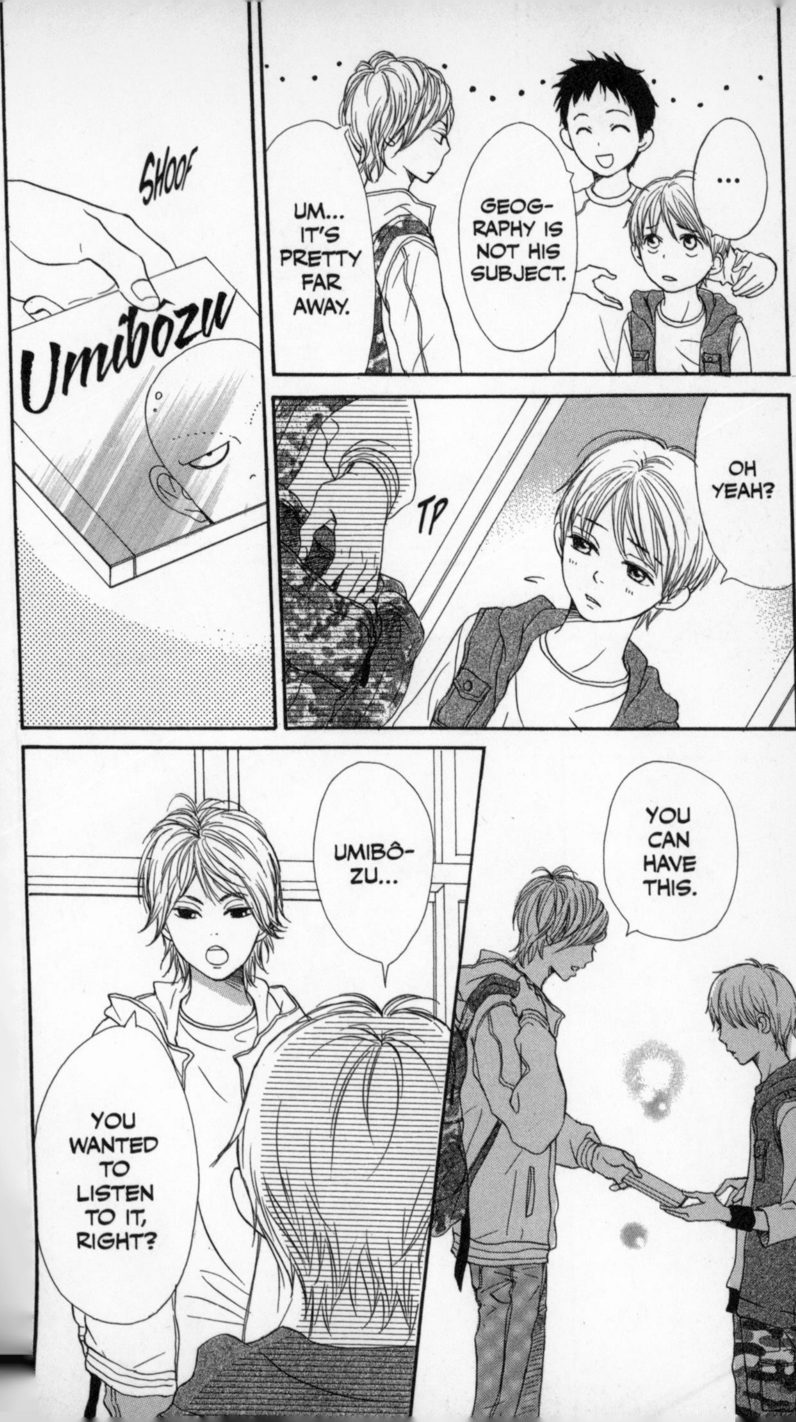
...
GEOG-RAPHY IS NOT HIS SUBJECT.
UM... IT'S PRETTY FAR AWAY.
OH YEAH?
TP
SHOOF
Umibôzu
YOU CAN HAVE THIS.
UMIBÔ-ZU...
YOU WANTED TO LISTEN TO IT, RIGHT?

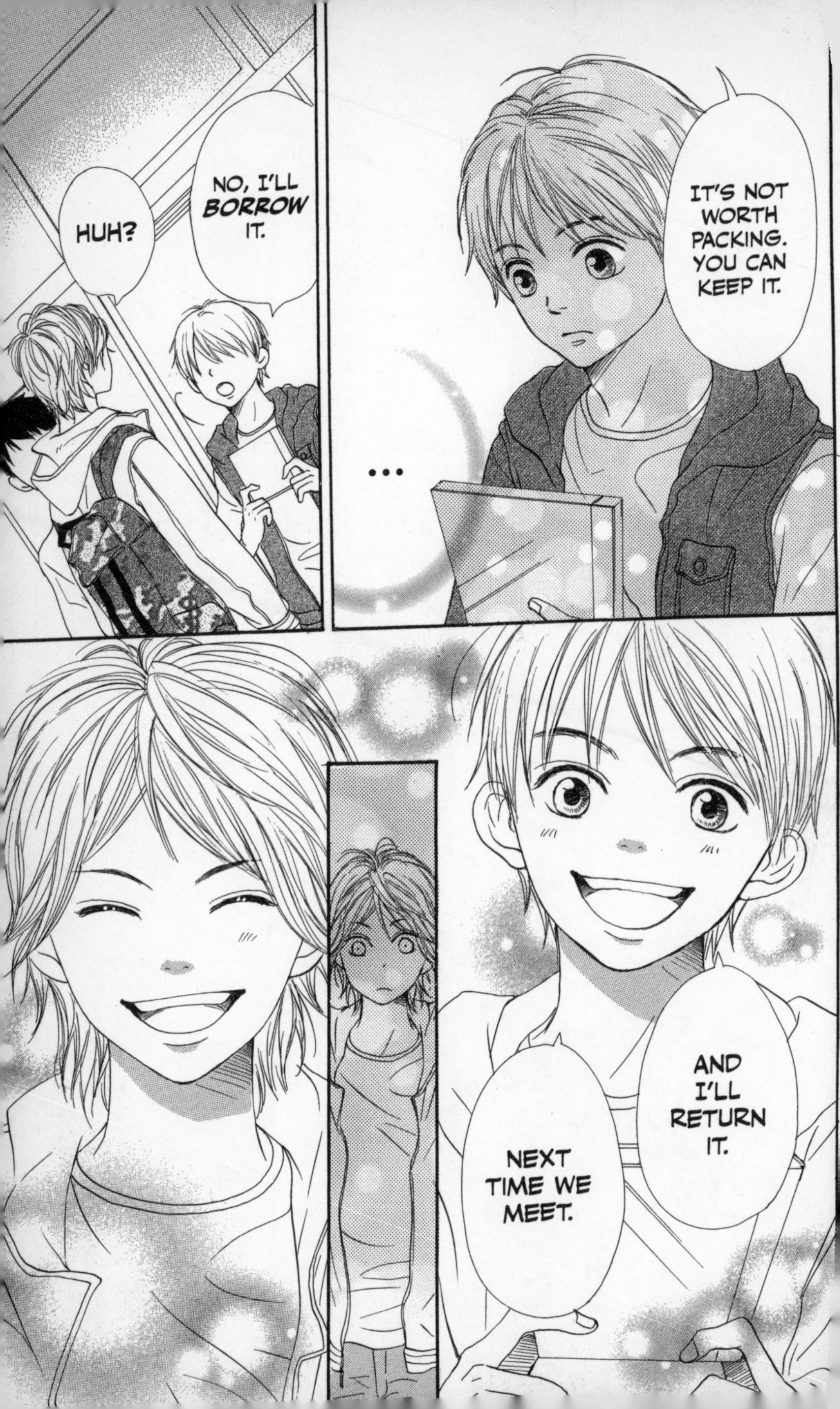
IT'S NOT WORTH PACKING. YOU CAN KEEP IT.
...
NO, I'LL *BORROW* IT.
HUH?
AND I'LL RETURN IT.
NEXT TIME WE MEET.

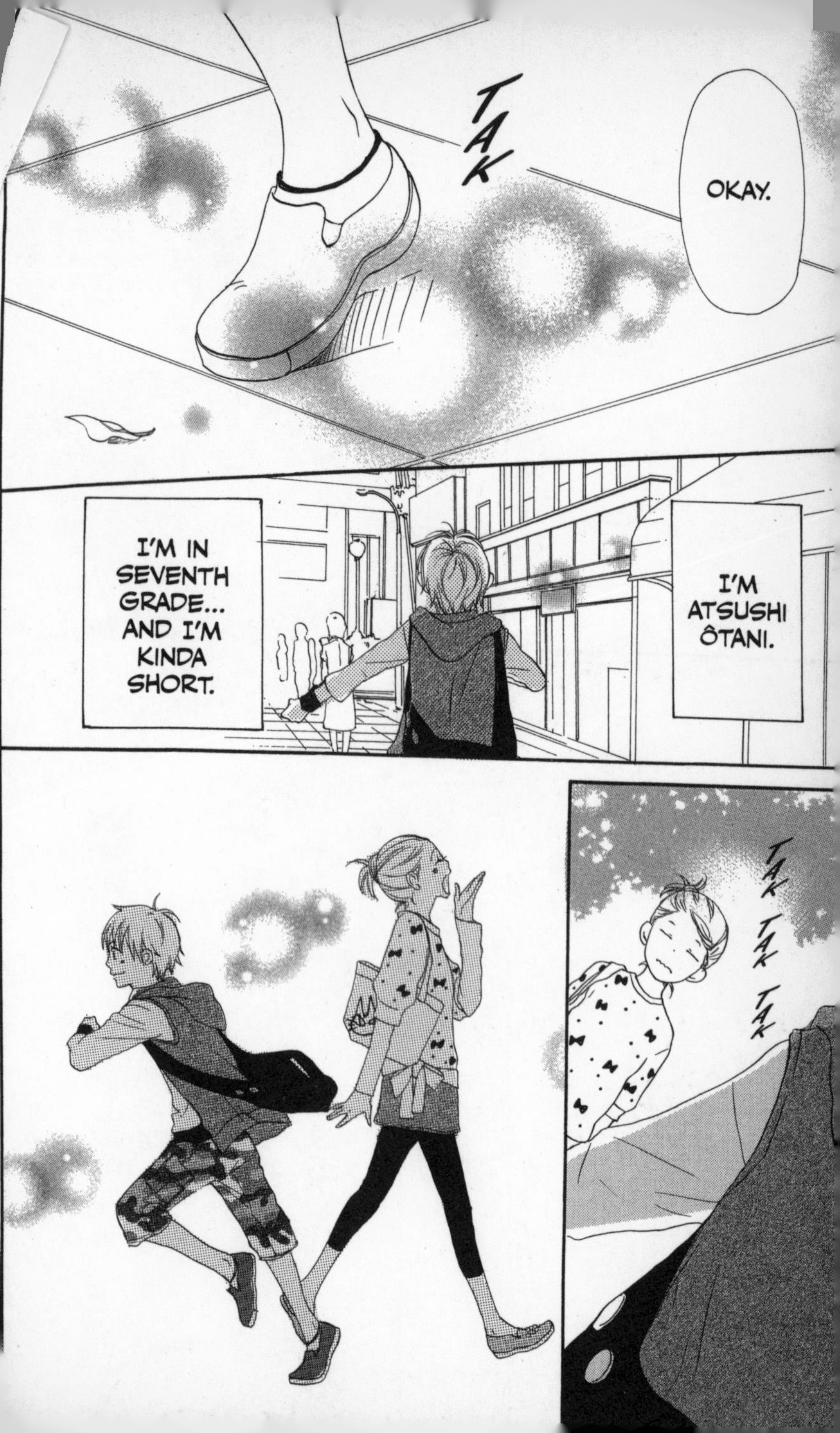
OKAY.
TAK
I'M ATSUSHI ÔTANI.
I'M IN SEVENTH GRADE... AND I'M KINDA SHORT.
TAK TAK TAK TAK

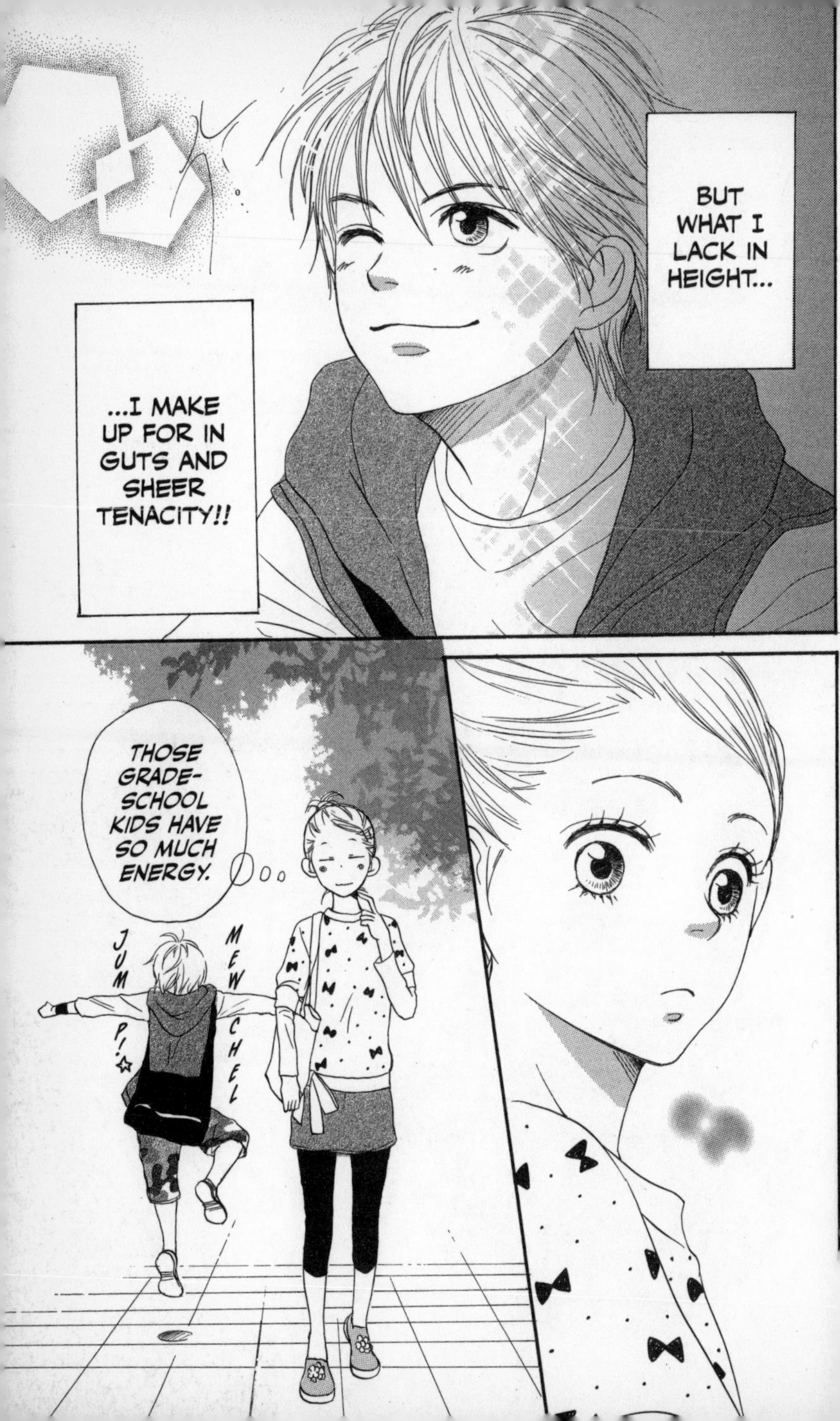
BUT WHAT I LACK IN HEIGHT...
...I MAKE UP FOR IN GUTS AND SHEER TENACITY!!
THOSE GRADE-SCHOOL KIDS HAVE SO MUCH ENERGY.
MEWCHEL
JUMP!☆

LOVE ☆ COM FACTOIDS ♥

Here are some little bits of useless data about Love ✿ Com!

✶ Height ✶

At first I planned to make Risa about the size of an ordinary tallish girl you might see around town. But while I was thinking about the balance between the two leads, I happened to see the comedy duo Ninety-Nine on television. I thought, "That height difference is perfect!" So Risa and Ôtani have the same height difference as Ninety-Nine. Exactly.

✶ Names ✶

When I began this manga, Prime Minister Koizumi had just formed his cabinet. Koizumi, Ishihara, Tanaka and Suzuki were all named after cabinet members. Ôtani was originally named Nakatani. But my editor said, "Since Koizumi's name has the character for 'small,' the guy should have a name with the character for 'big.'" I'm glad I went with "Ôtani."

✶ Ôtani ✶

I had trouble visualizing Ôtani's character. One day I was downtown and saw a grade-schooler doing a street performance. He was so cute I took a photo of him and used it for reference when I drew Ôtani. So if Ôtani looks like he's in grade school, there's a good reason.

✶ Maido Academy ✶

The school's name was chosen from suggestions submitted by the readers. I never imagined I'd end up using it so much. Thank you!

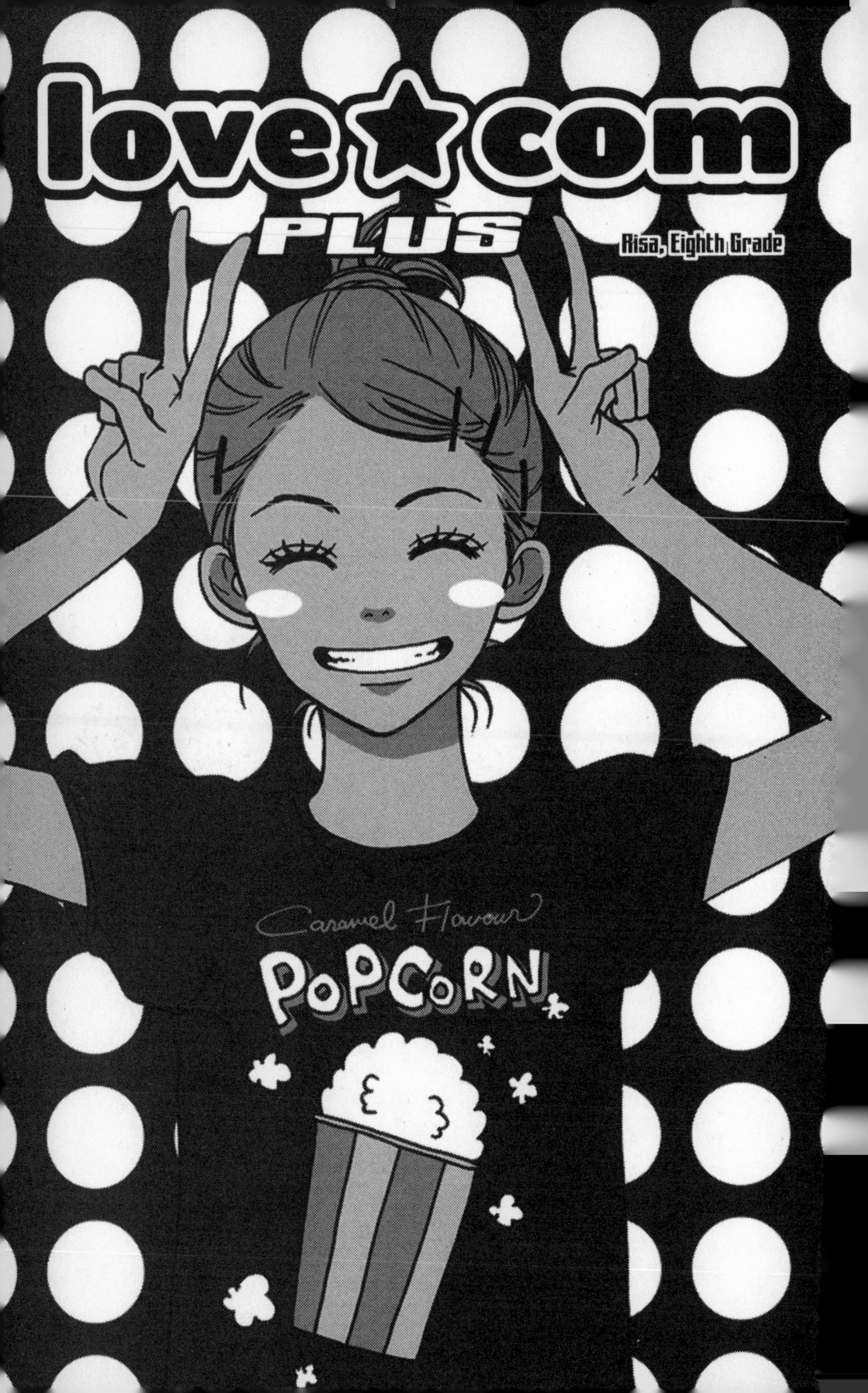
love★com
PLUS
Risa, Eighth Grade
Caramel Flavour
POPCORN

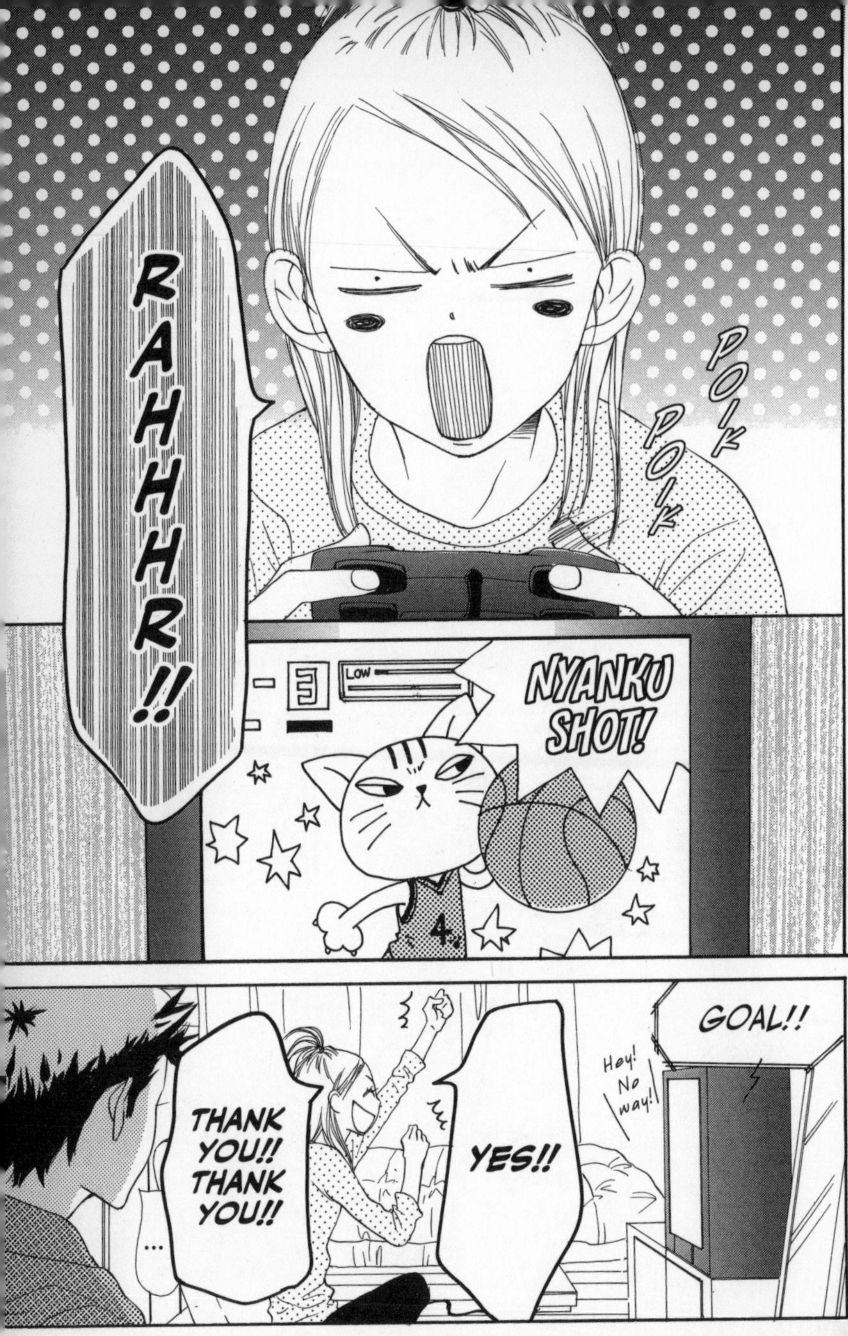
POIK POIK
RAHHHR!!
NYANKU SHOT!
LOW
GOAL!!
Hey! No way!
YES!!
THANK YOU!! THANK YOU!!
...

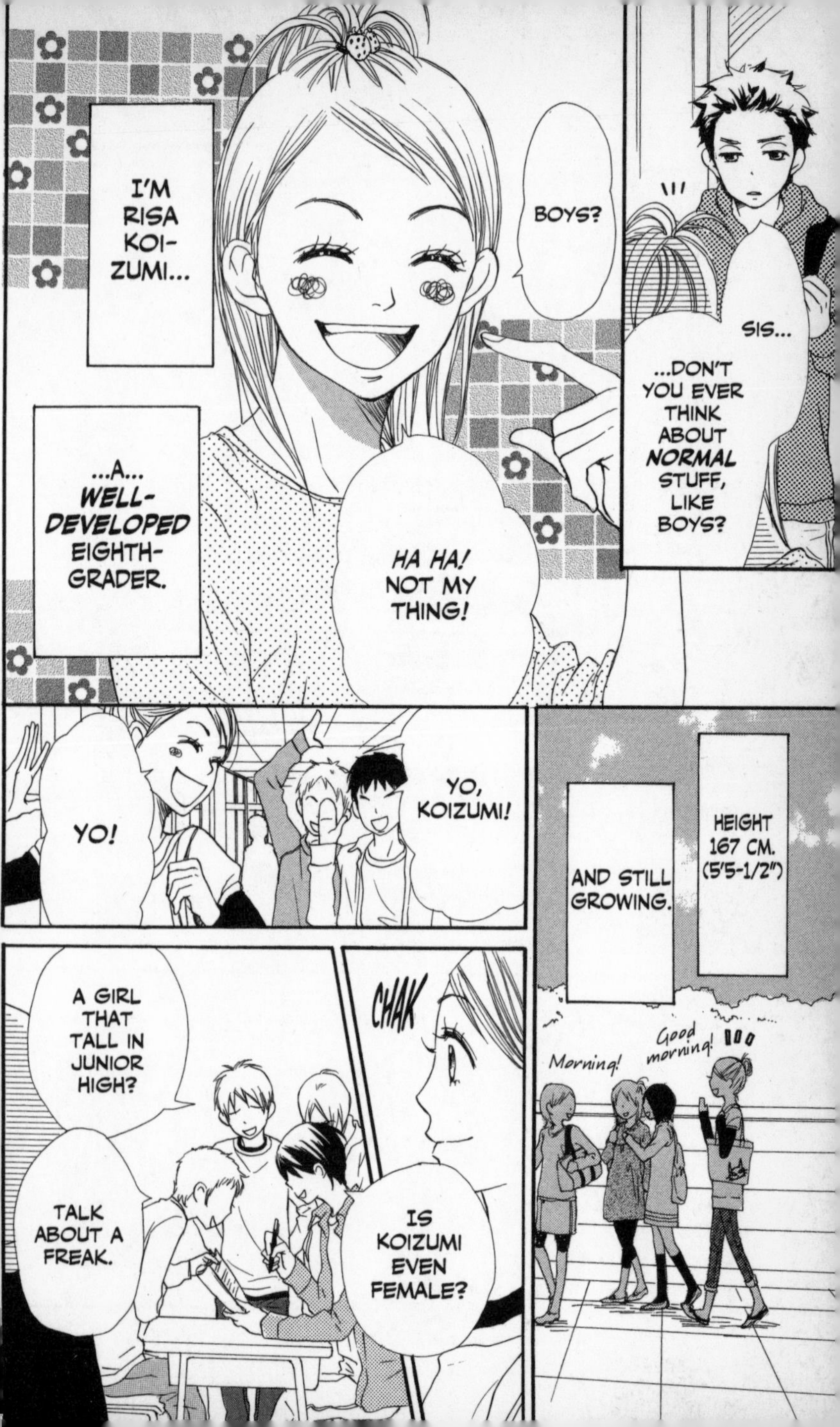

SIS...
...DON'T YOU EVER THINK ABOUT NORMAL STUFF, LIKE BOYS?
BOYS?
I'M RISA KOI-ZUMI...
HA HA! NOT MY THING!
...A... WELL-DEVELOPED EIGHTH-GRADER.
HEIGHT 167 CM. (5'5-1/2")
AND STILL GROWING.
Good morning!
Morning!
YO, KOIZUMI!
YO!
CHAK
IS KOIZUMI EVEN FEMALE?
A GIRL THAT TALL IN JUNIOR HIGH?
TALK ABOUT A FREAK.

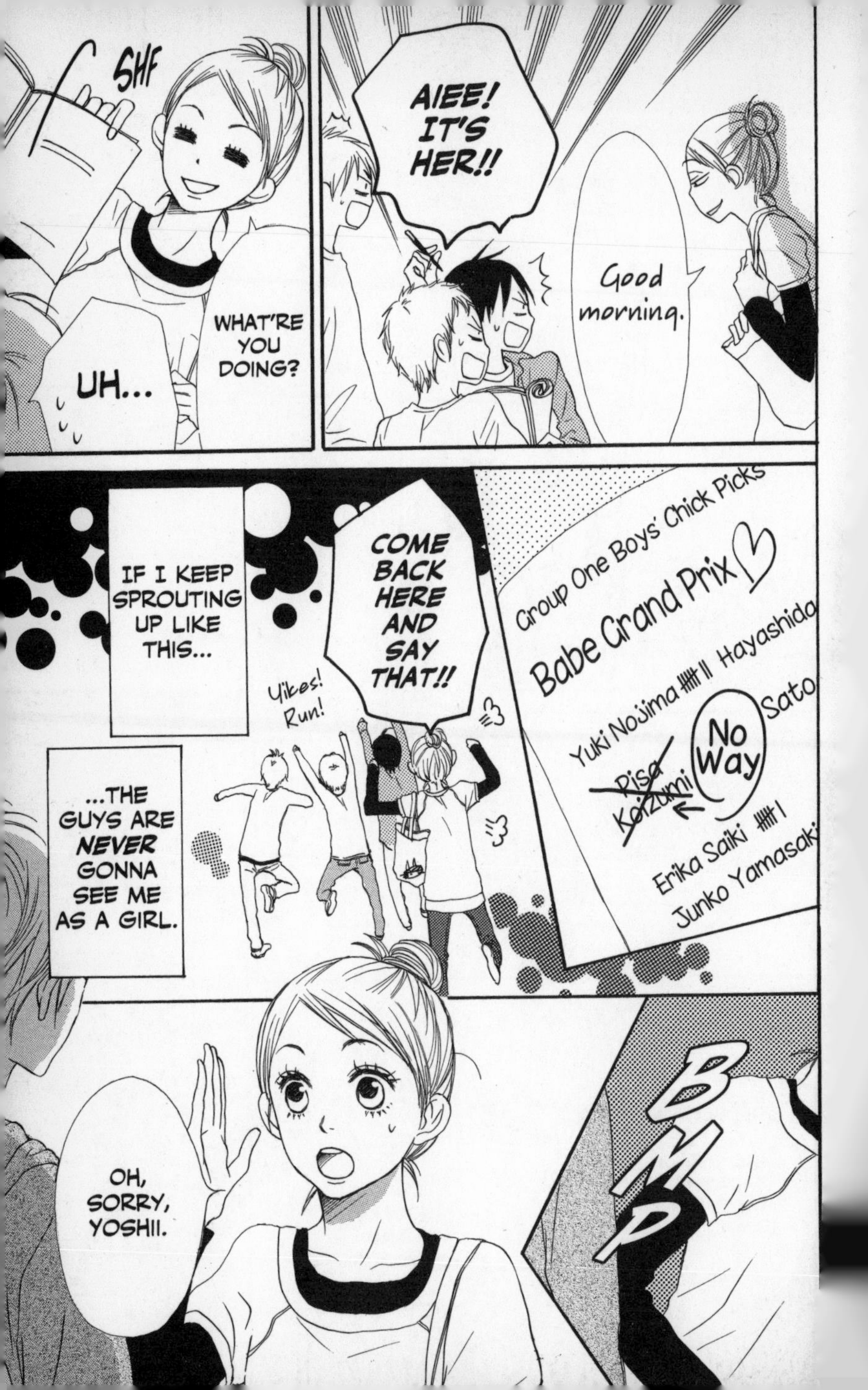

Good morning.
AIEE! IT'S HER!!
SHF
WHAT'RE YOU DOING?
UH...
Group One Boys' Chick Picks
Babe Grand Prix
Yuki Nojima
Hayashida
Sato
No Way
Risa Koizumi
Erika Saiki
Junko Yamasaki
COME BACK HERE AND SAY THAT!!
Yikes! Run!
IF I KEEP SPROUTING UP LIKE THIS...
...THE GUYS ARE NEVER GONNA SEE ME AS A GIRL.
BMP
OH, SORRY, YOSHII.

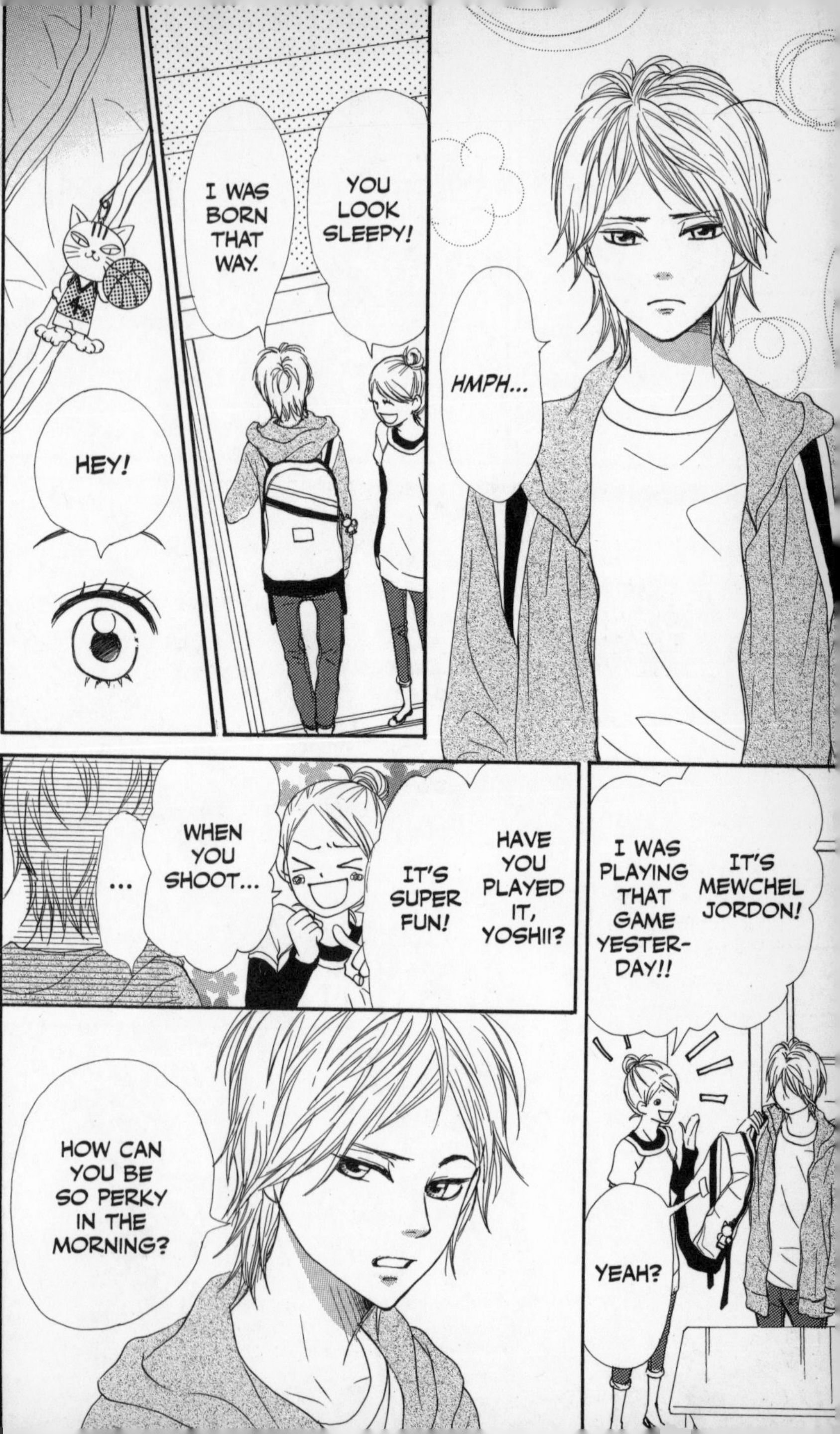
HMPH...
YOU LOOK SLEEPY!
I WAS BORN THAT WAY.
HEY!
IT'S MEWCHEL JORDON!
I WAS PLAYING THAT GAME YESTER-DAY!!
YEAH?
HAVE YOU PLAYED IT, YOSHII?
IT'S SUPER FUN!
WHEN YOU SHOOT...
...
HOW CAN YOU BE SO PERKY IN THE MORNING?

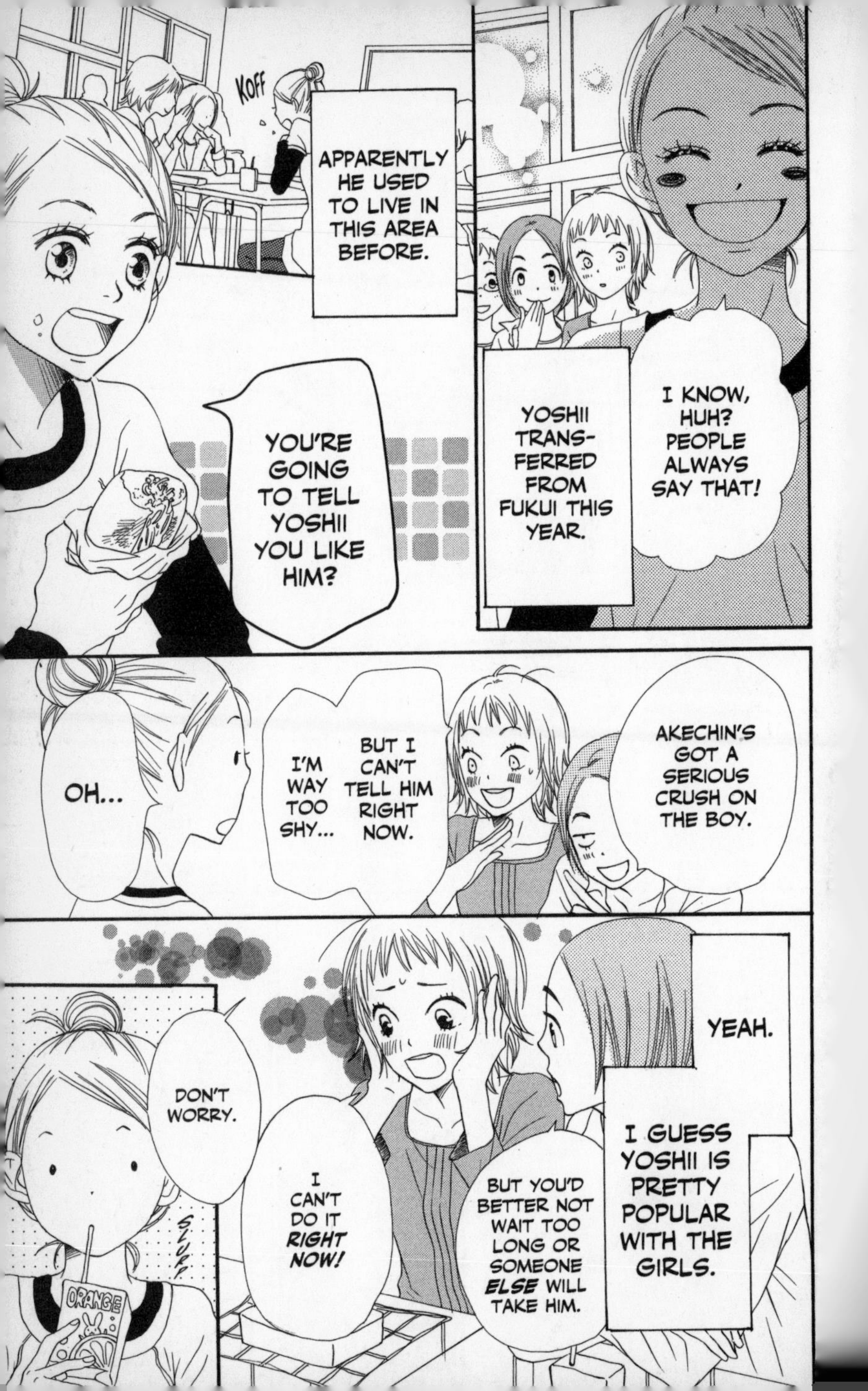
I KNOW, HUH? PEOPLE ALWAYS SAY THAT!
YOSHII TRANSFERRED FROM FUKUI THIS YEAR.
APPARENTLY HE USED TO LIVE IN THIS AREA BEFORE.
KOFF
YOU'RE GOING TO TELL YOSHII YOU LIKE HIM?
AKECHIN'S GOT A SERIOUS CRUSH ON THE BOY.
BUT I CAN'T TELL HIM RIGHT NOW.
I'M WAY TOO SHY...
OH...
YEAH.
I GUESS YOSHII IS PRETTY POPULAR WITH THE GIRLS.
BUT YOU'D BETTER NOT WAIT TOO LONG OR SOMEONE *ELSE* WILL TAKE HIM.
I CAN'T DO IT *RIGHT NOW!*
DON'T WORRY.
SLURP
ORANGE

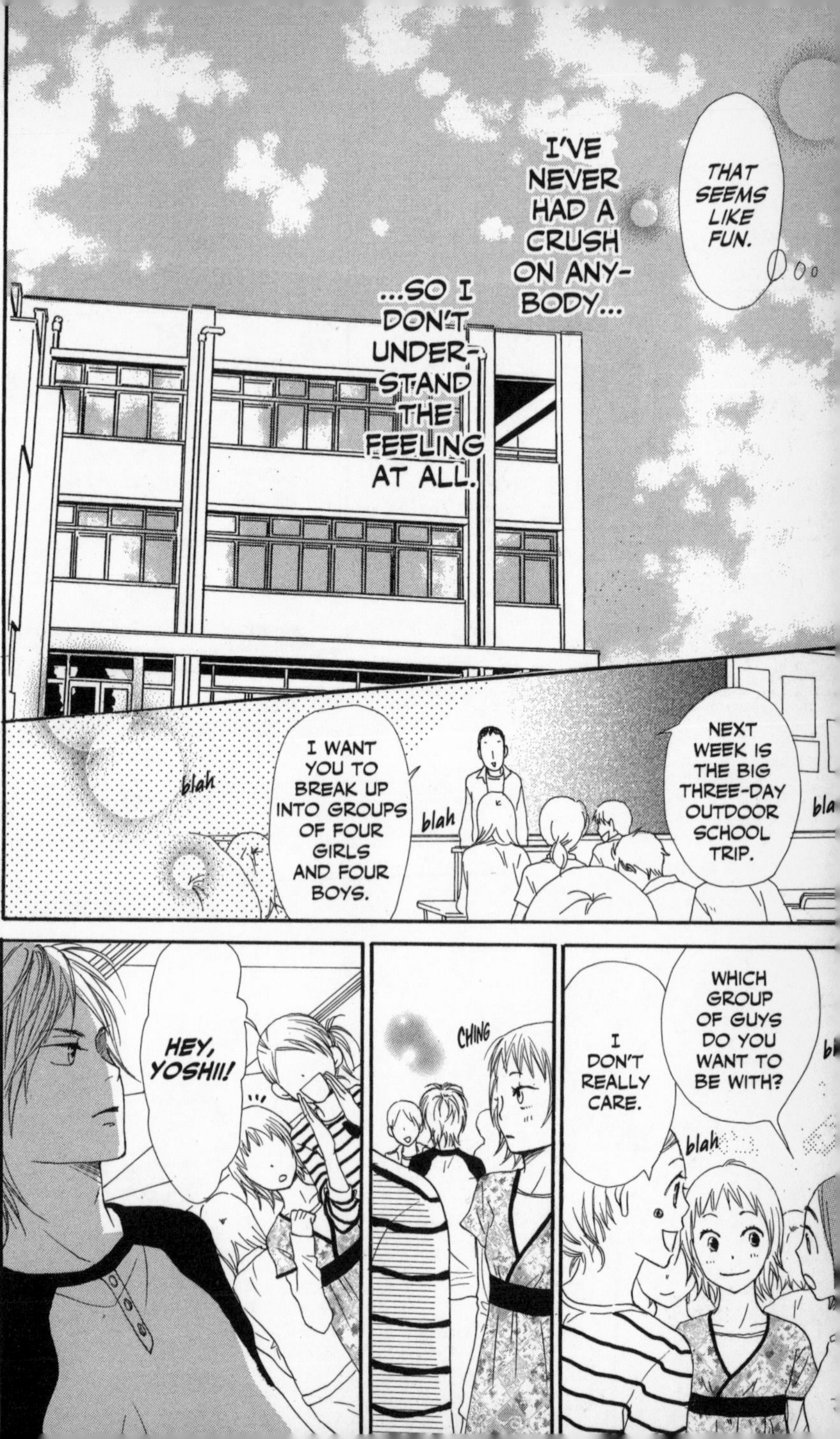
THAT SEEMS LIKE FUN.
I'VE NEVER HAD A CRUSH ON ANYBODY...
...SO I DON'T UNDERSTAND THE FEELING AT ALL.
NEXT WEEK IS THE BIG THREE-DAY OUTDOOR SCHOOL TRIP.
I WANT YOU TO BREAK UP INTO GROUPS OF FOUR GIRLS AND FOUR BOYS.
blah
blah
WHICH GROUP OF GUYS DO YOU WANT TO BE WITH?
blah
I DON'T REALLY CARE.
CHING
HEY, YOSHII!

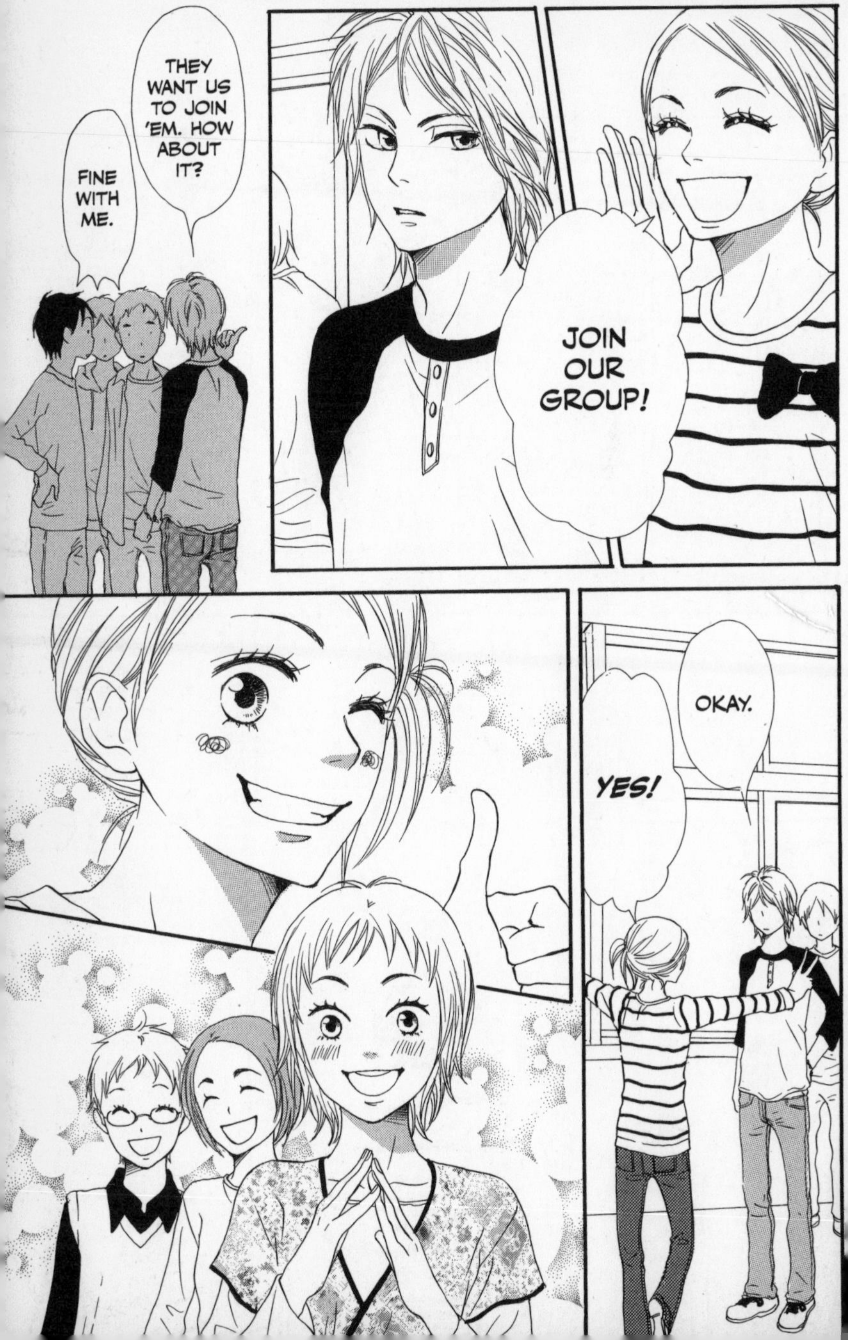
JOIN OUR GROUP!
THEY WANT US TO JOIN 'EM. HOW ABOUT IT?
FINE WITH ME.
OKAY.
YES!

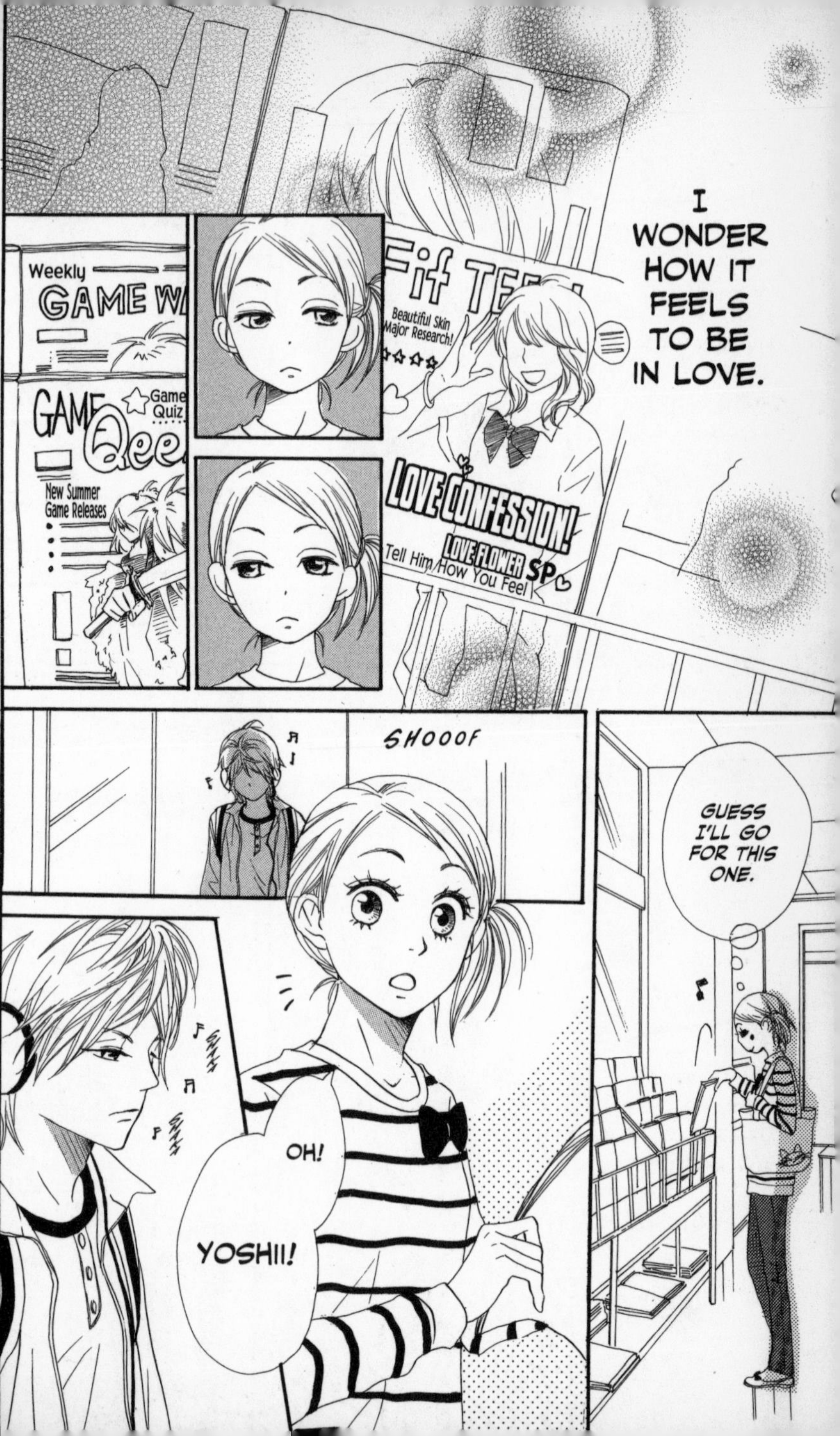
I WONDER HOW IT FEELS TO BE IN LOVE.
Fif TEE
Beautiful Skin Major Research!
LOVE CONFESSION!
LOVE FLOWER SP
Tell Him How You Feel
Weekly GAME W
GAME Qee
Game Quiz
New Summer Game Releases
GUESS I'LL GO FOR THIS ONE.
SHOOOF
OH!
YOSHII!

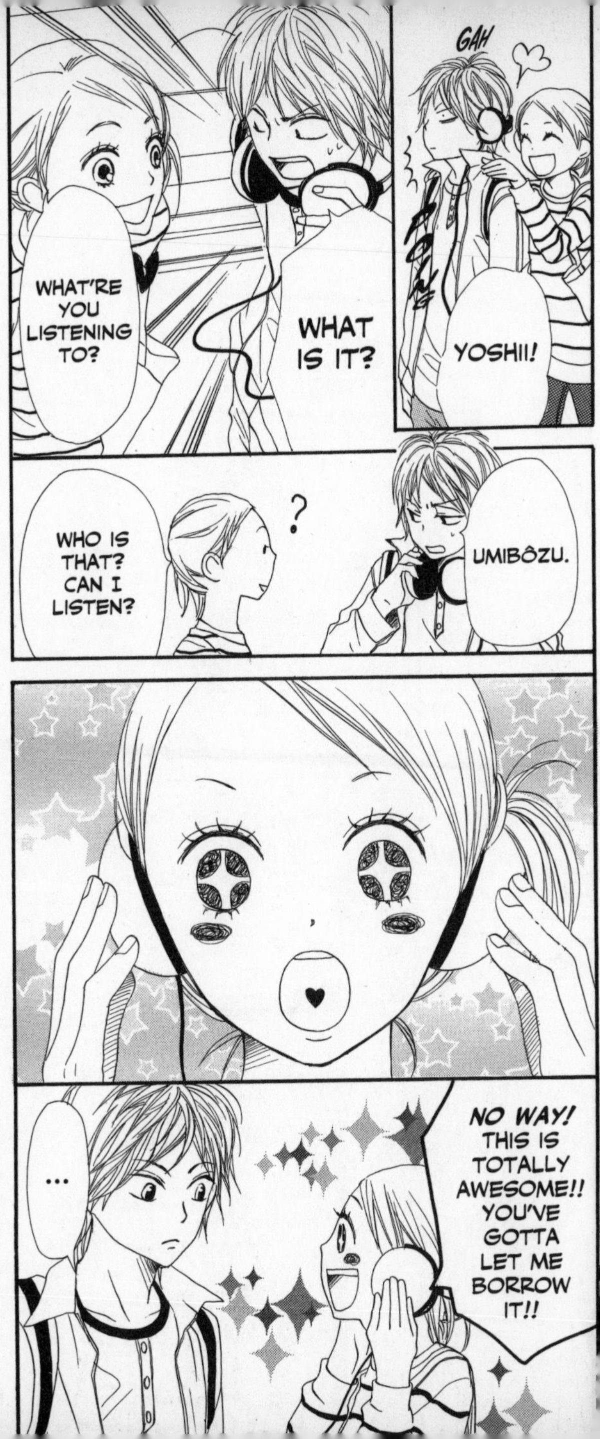
GAH
YOSHII!
WHAT IS IT?
WHAT'RE YOU LISTENING TO?
UMIBÔZU.
?
WHO IS THAT? CAN I LISTEN?
NO WAY! THIS IS TOTALLY AWESOME!! YOU'VE GOTTA LET ME BORROW IT!!
...

2

I visited the anime set several times. The love and enthusiasm they put into their work made me think they care about *Love★Com* even more than I do. Truly, tears came to my eyes.

SNIFFLE

They even used scenes from these bonus stories, which I'd just completed. They went over lines and tried them this way and that to get the dialogue perfect.

Skill is important in creating something, but more than anything, it's the love you put into it! It was a great learning experience for me.

Love is beautiful!! ♡ From now on, I'll always remember to put love into all my creations.

Let's all do our best!! ♡

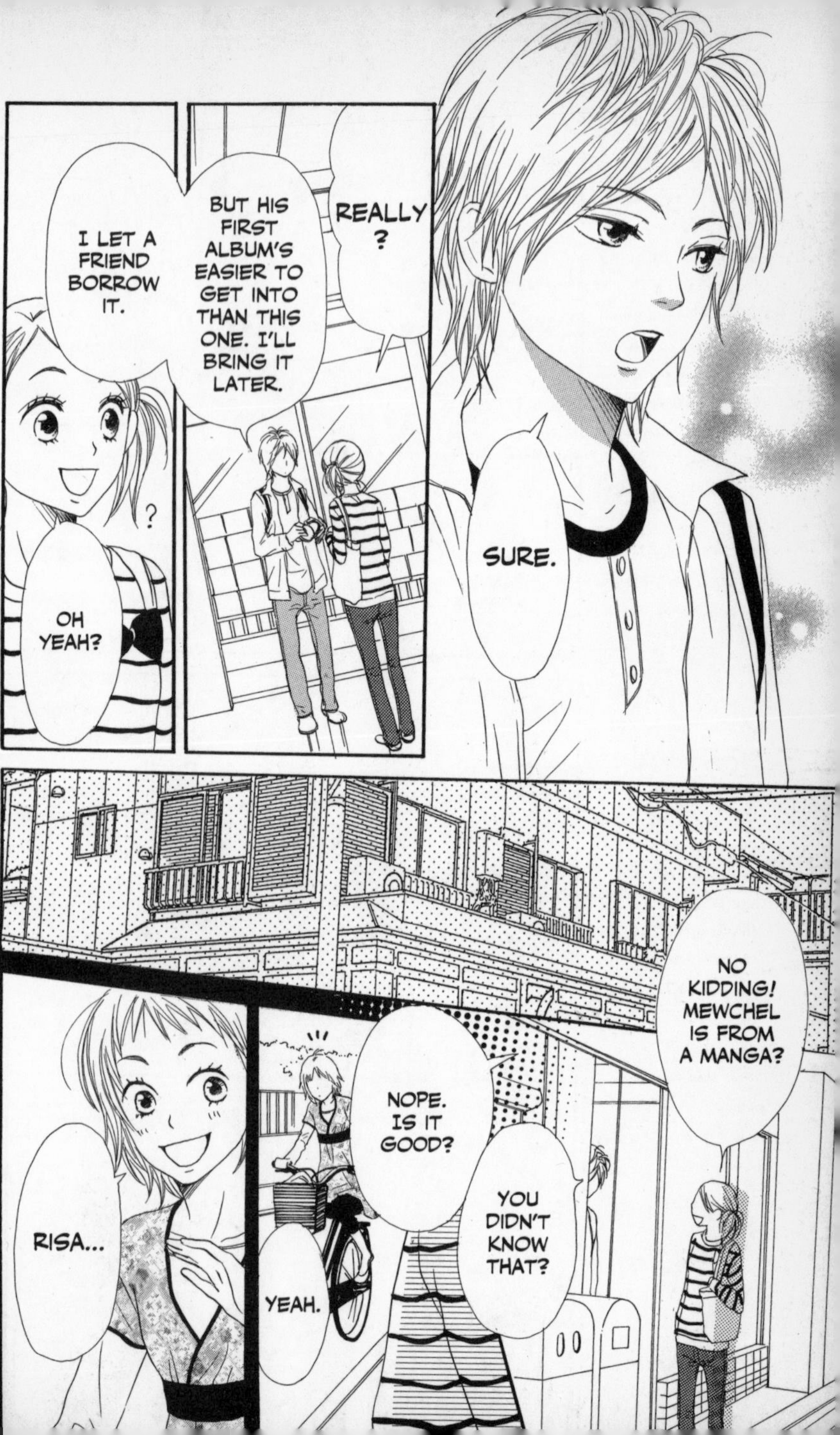
SURE.
REALLY?
BUT HIS FIRST ALBUM'S EASIER TO GET INTO THAN THIS ONE. I'LL BRING IT LATER.
I LET A FRIEND BORROW IT.
?
OH YEAH?
NO KIDDING! MEWCHEL IS FROM A MANGA?
NOPE. IS IT GOOD?
YOU DIDN'T KNOW THAT?
YEAH.
RISA...

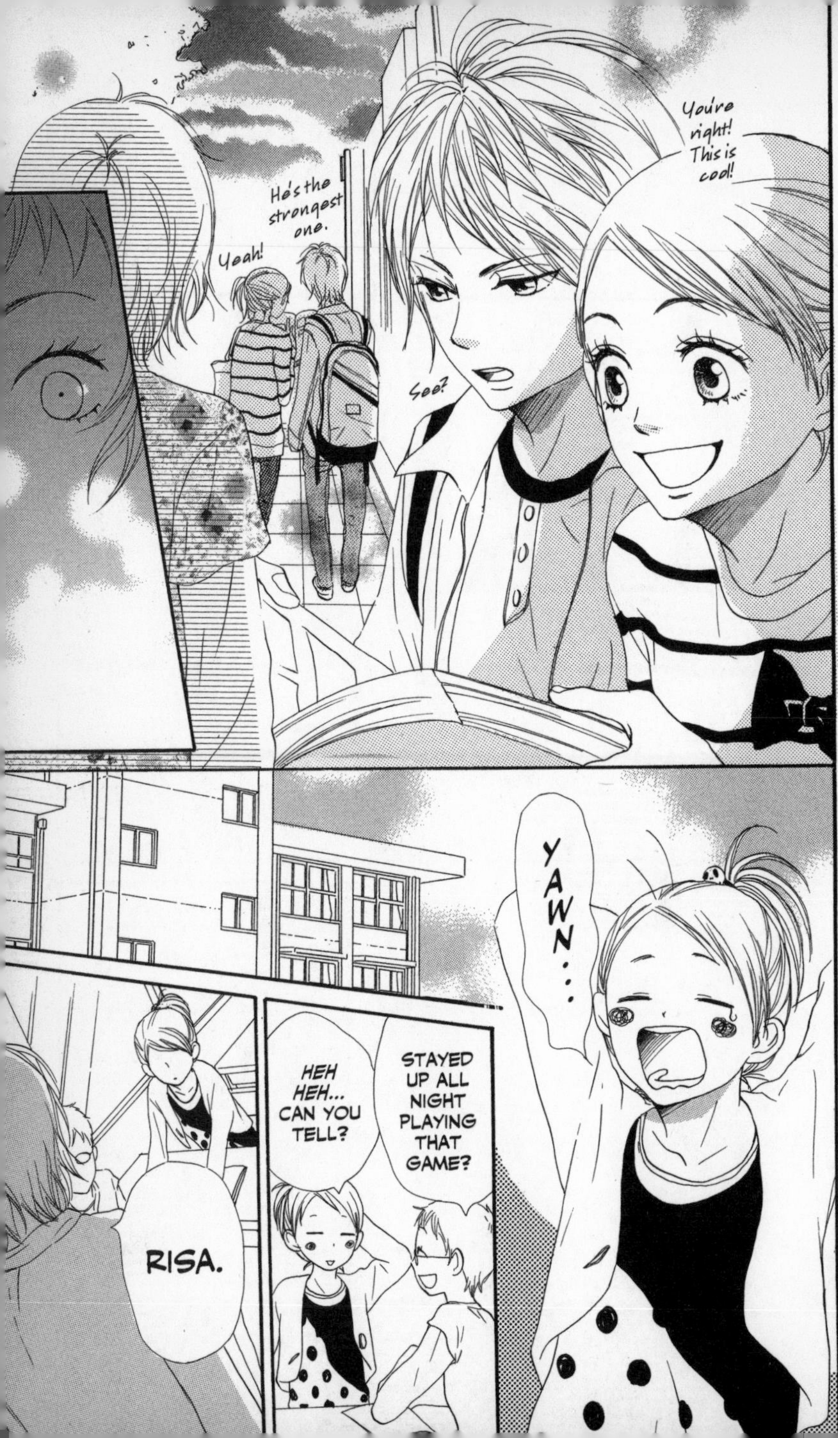
You're right! This is cool!
He's the strongest one.
Yeah!
See?
YAWN...
STAYED UP ALL NIGHT PLAYING THAT GAME?
HEH HEH... CAN YOU TELL?
RISA.

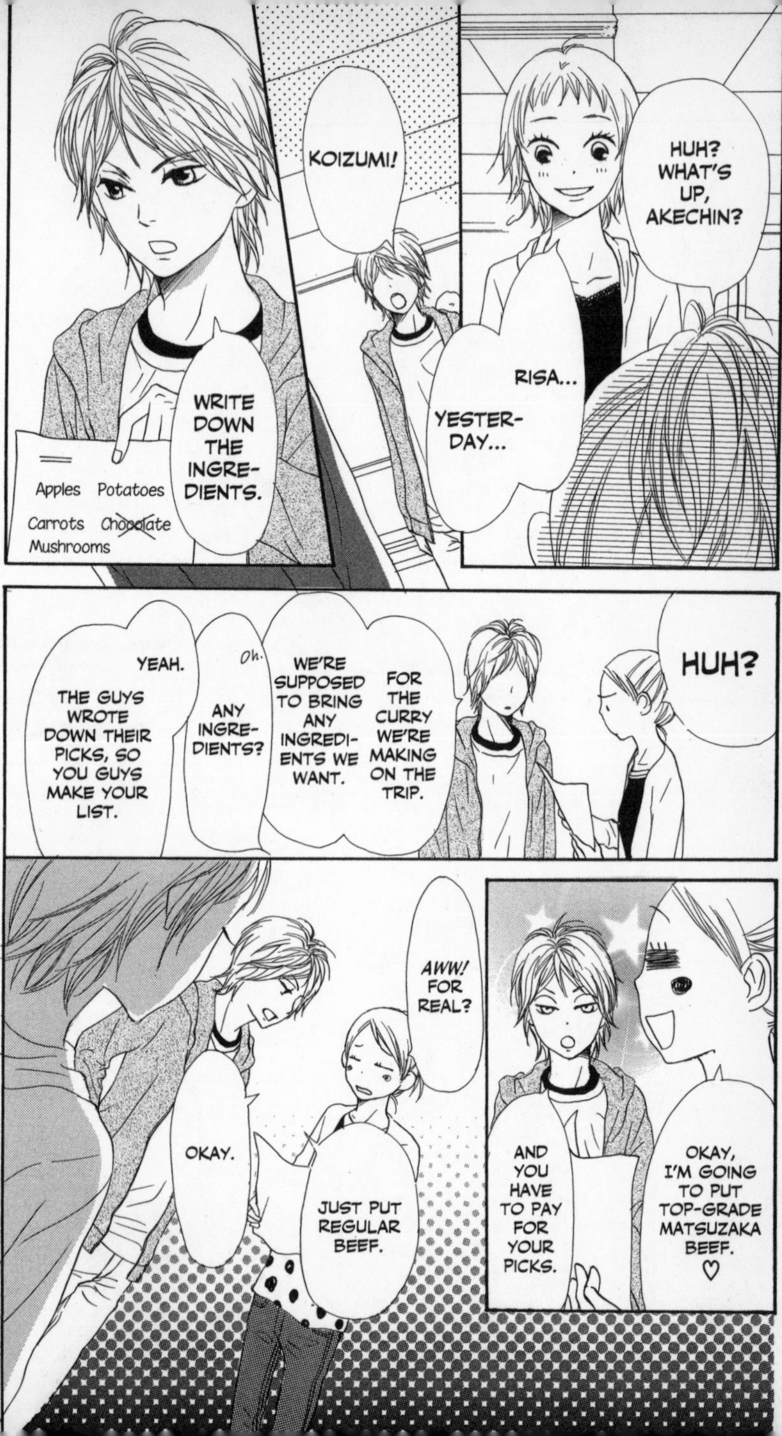
HUH? WHAT'S UP, AKECHIN?
RISA... YESTER-DAY...
KOIZUMI!
WRITE DOWN THE INGRE-DIENTS.
Apples Potatoes
Carrots Chocolate
Mushrooms
HUH?
FOR THE CURRY WE'RE MAKING ON THE TRIP.
WE'RE SUPPOSED TO BRING ANY INGREDI-ENTS WE WANT.
Oh.
ANY INGRE-DIENTS?
YEAH.
THE GUYS WROTE DOWN THEIR PICKS, SO YOU GUYS MAKE YOUR LIST.
OKAY, I'M GOING TO PUT TOP-GRADE MATSUZAKA BEEF. ♡
AND YOU HAVE TO PAY FOR YOUR PICKS.
AWW! FOR REAL?
JUST PUT REGULAR BEEF.
OKAY.

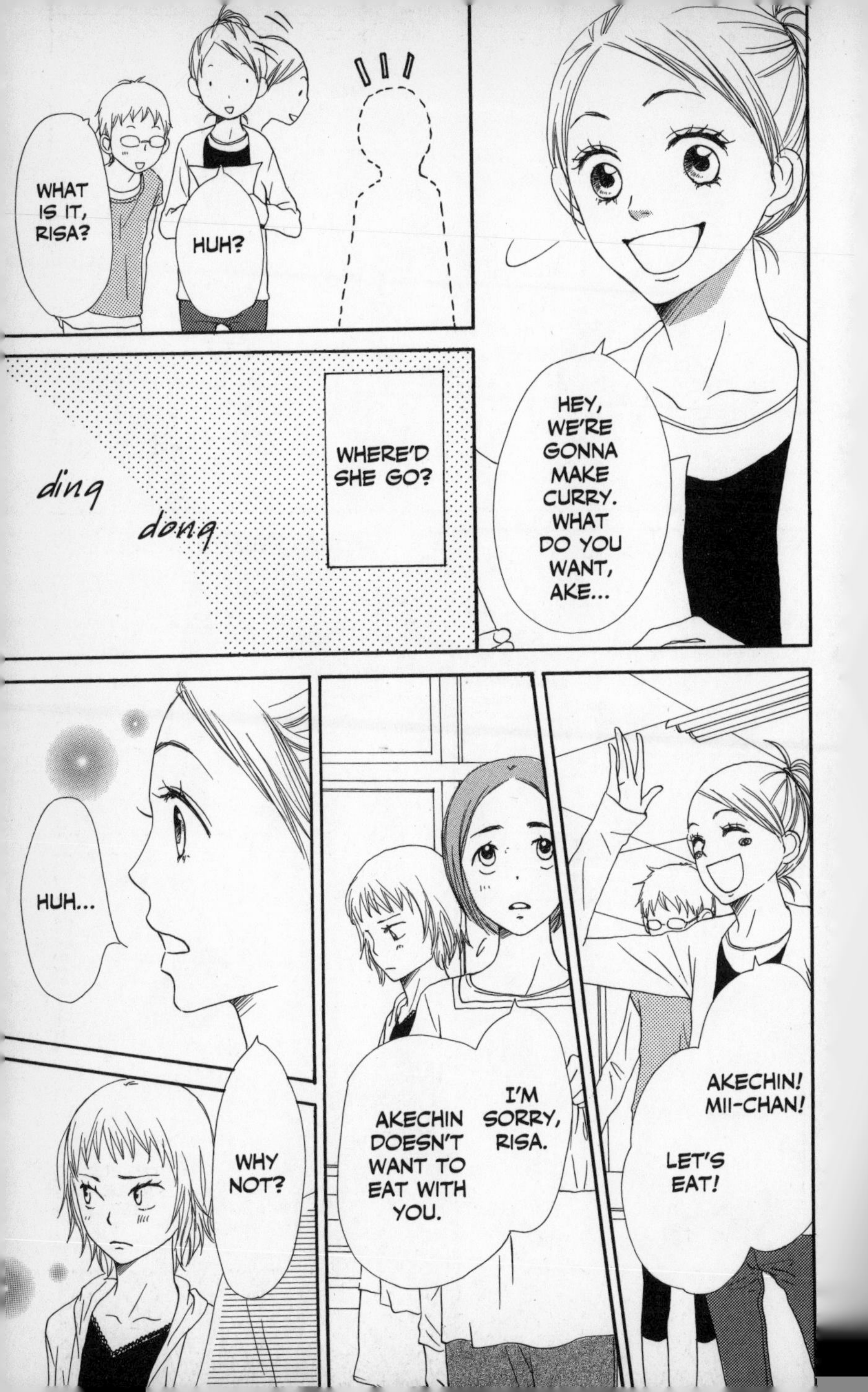
HEY, WE'RE GONNA MAKE CURRY. WHAT DO YOU WANT, AKE...
HUH?
WHAT IS IT, RISA?
WHERE'D SHE GO?
ding
dong
AKECHIN! MII-CHAN!
LET'S EAT!
I'M SORRY, RISA.
AKECHIN DOESN'T WANT TO EAT WITH YOU.
HUH...
WHY NOT?

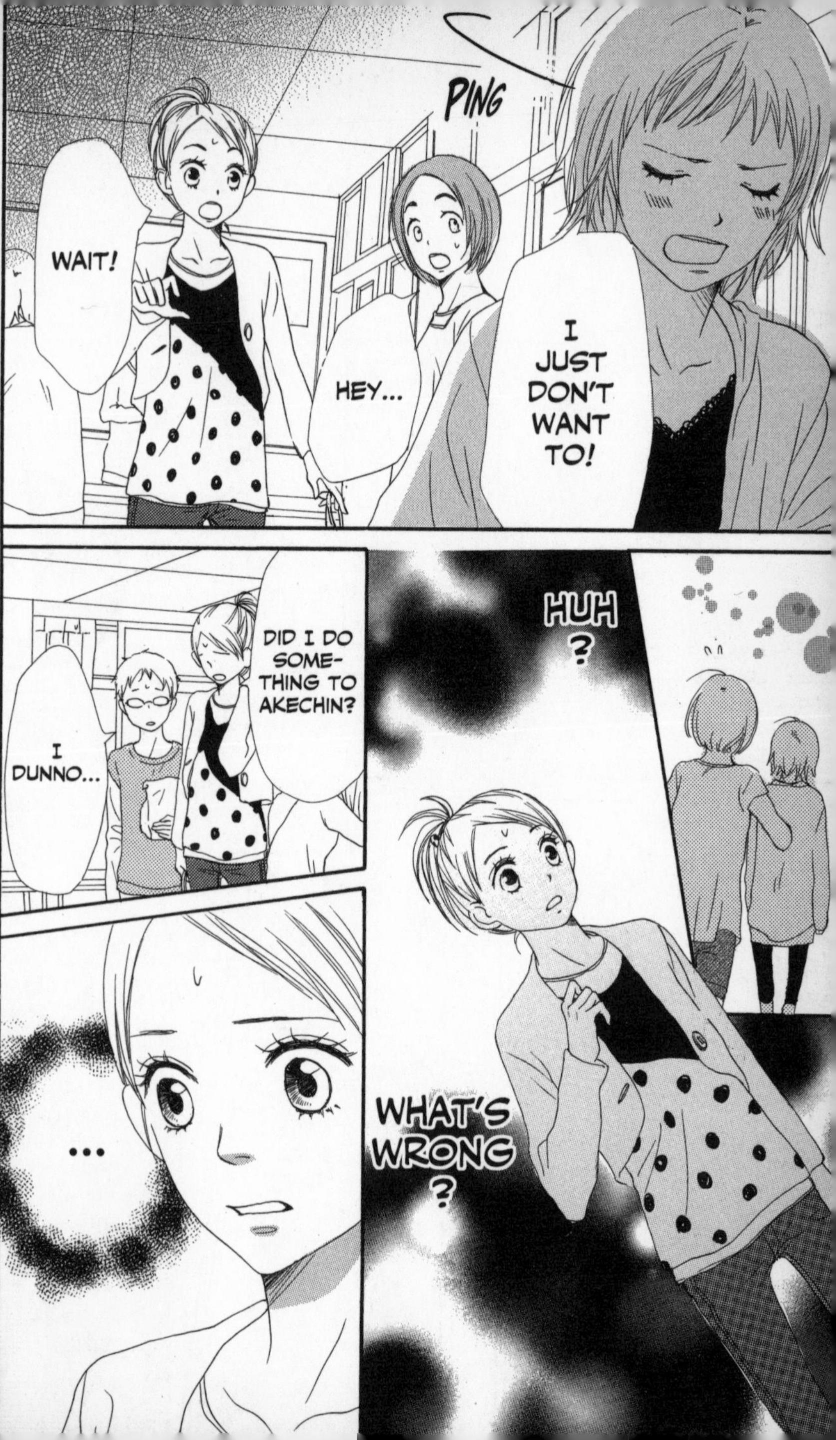
PING
I JUST DON'T WANT TO!
HEY...
WAIT!
HUH ?
WHAT'S WRONG ?
DID I DO SOME-THING TO AKECHIN?
I DUNNO...
...

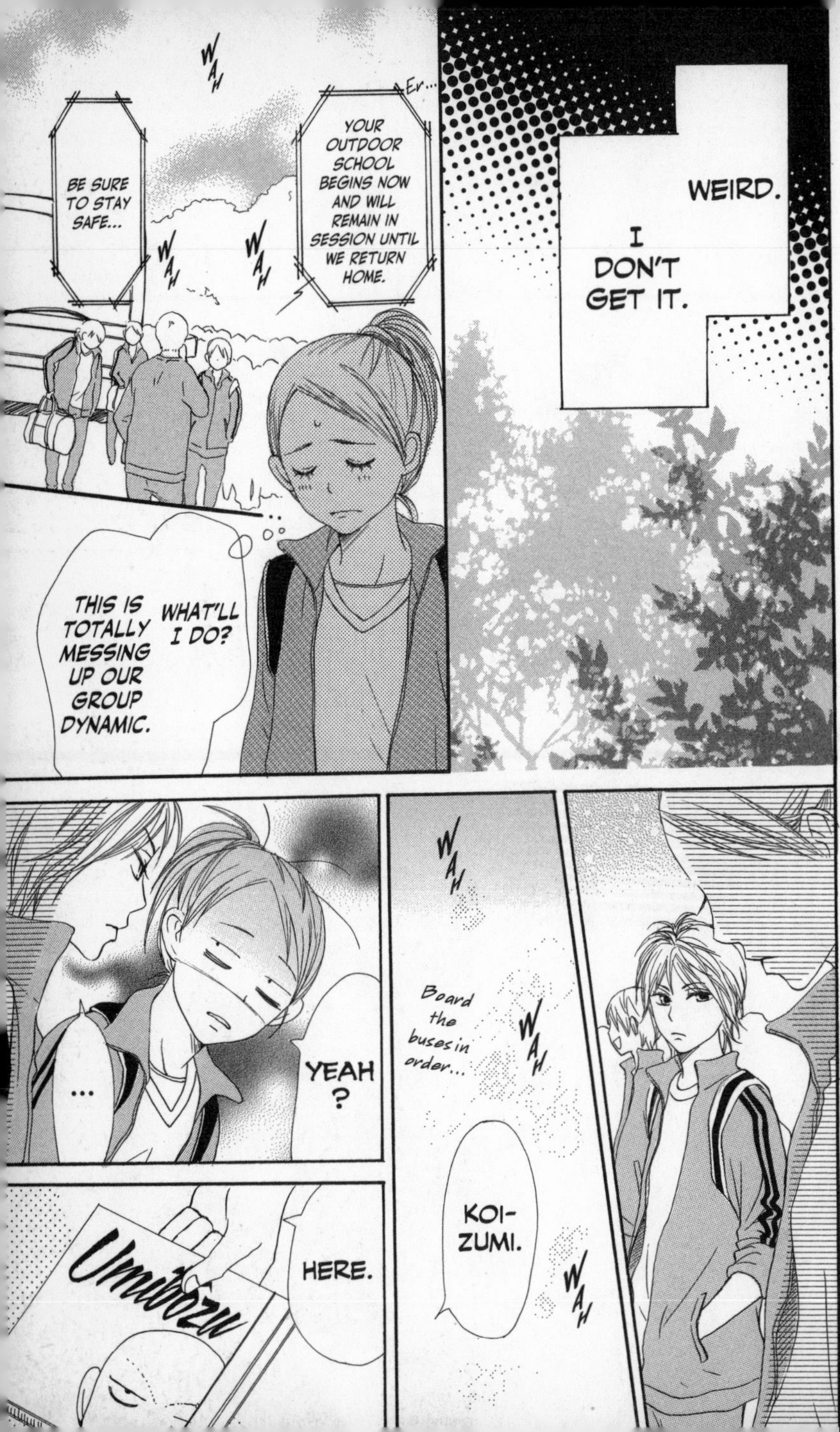
WEIRD.
I DON'T GET IT.
Er...
YOUR OUTDOOR SCHOOL BEGINS NOW AND WILL REMAIN IN SESSION UNTIL WE RETURN HOME.
WAH
WAH
WAH
BE SURE TO STAY SAFE...
WHAT'LL I DO?
THIS IS TOTALLY MESSING UP OUR GROUP DYNAMIC.
WAH
Board the buses in order...
WAH
KOI-ZUMI.
WAH
YEAH?
...
HERE.
Umibozu

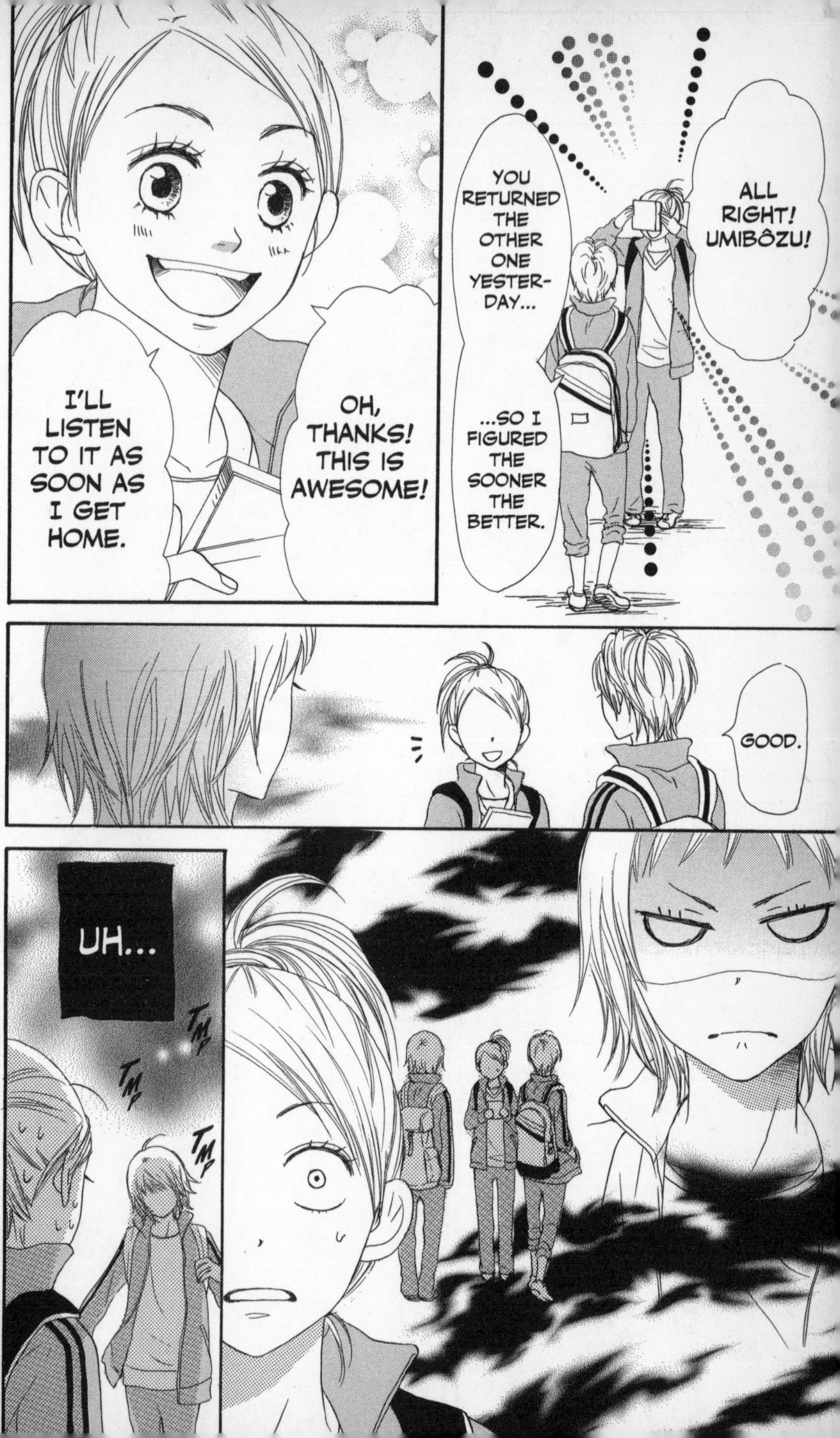
ALL RIGHT! UMIBÔZU!
YOU RETURNED THE OTHER ONE YESTERDAY...
...SO I FIGURED THE SOONER THE BETTER.
OH, THANKS! THIS IS AWESOME!
I'LL LISTEN TO IT AS SOON AS I GET HOME.
GOOD.
TMP
TMP
TMP
UH...

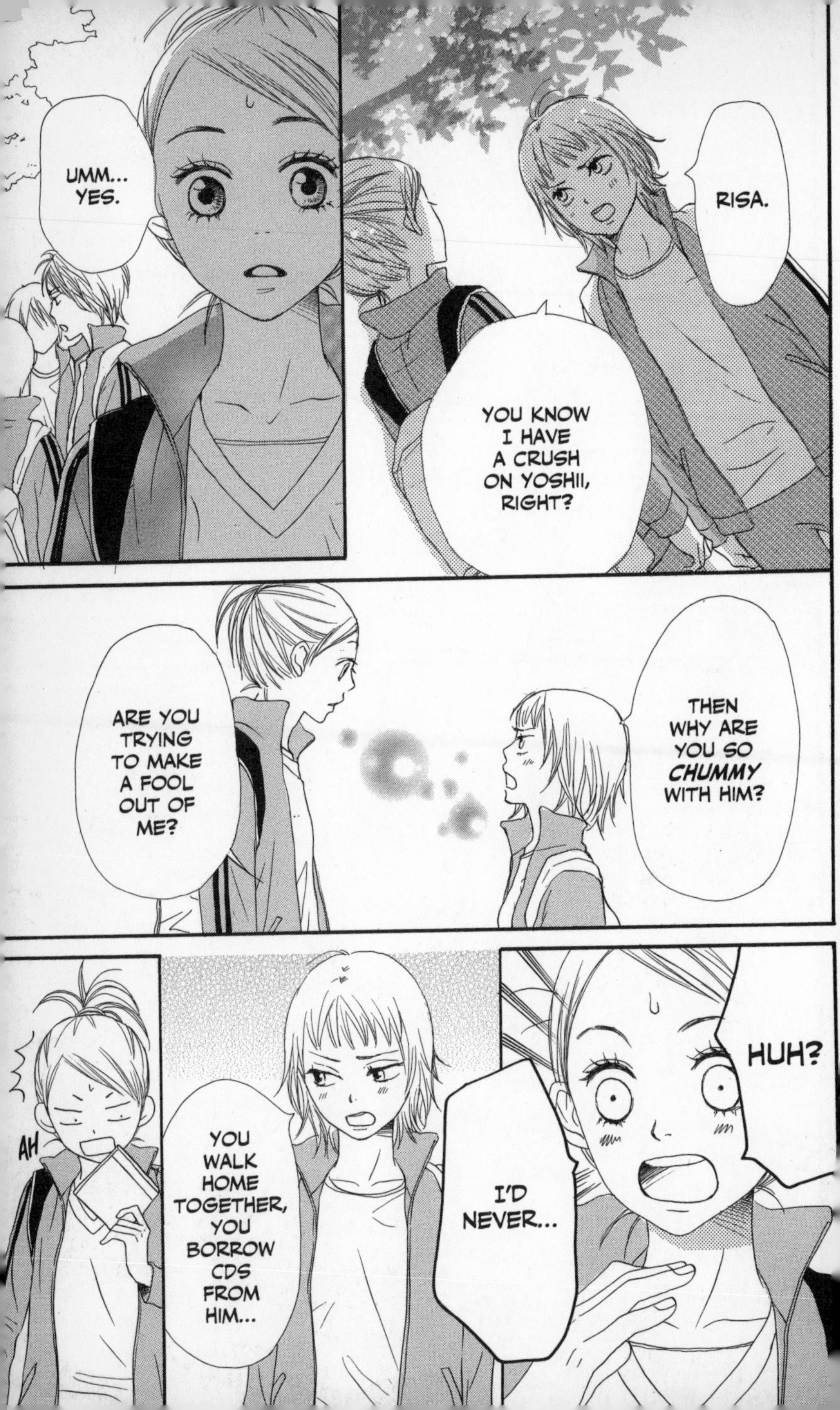
RISA.
YOU KNOW I HAVE A CRUSH ON YOSHII, RIGHT?
UMM... YES.
THEN WHY ARE YOU SO *CHUMMY* WITH HIM?
ARE YOU TRYING TO MAKE A FOOL OUT OF ME?
HUH?
I'D NEVER...
YOU WALK HOME TOGETHER, YOU BORROW CDS FROM HIM...
AH

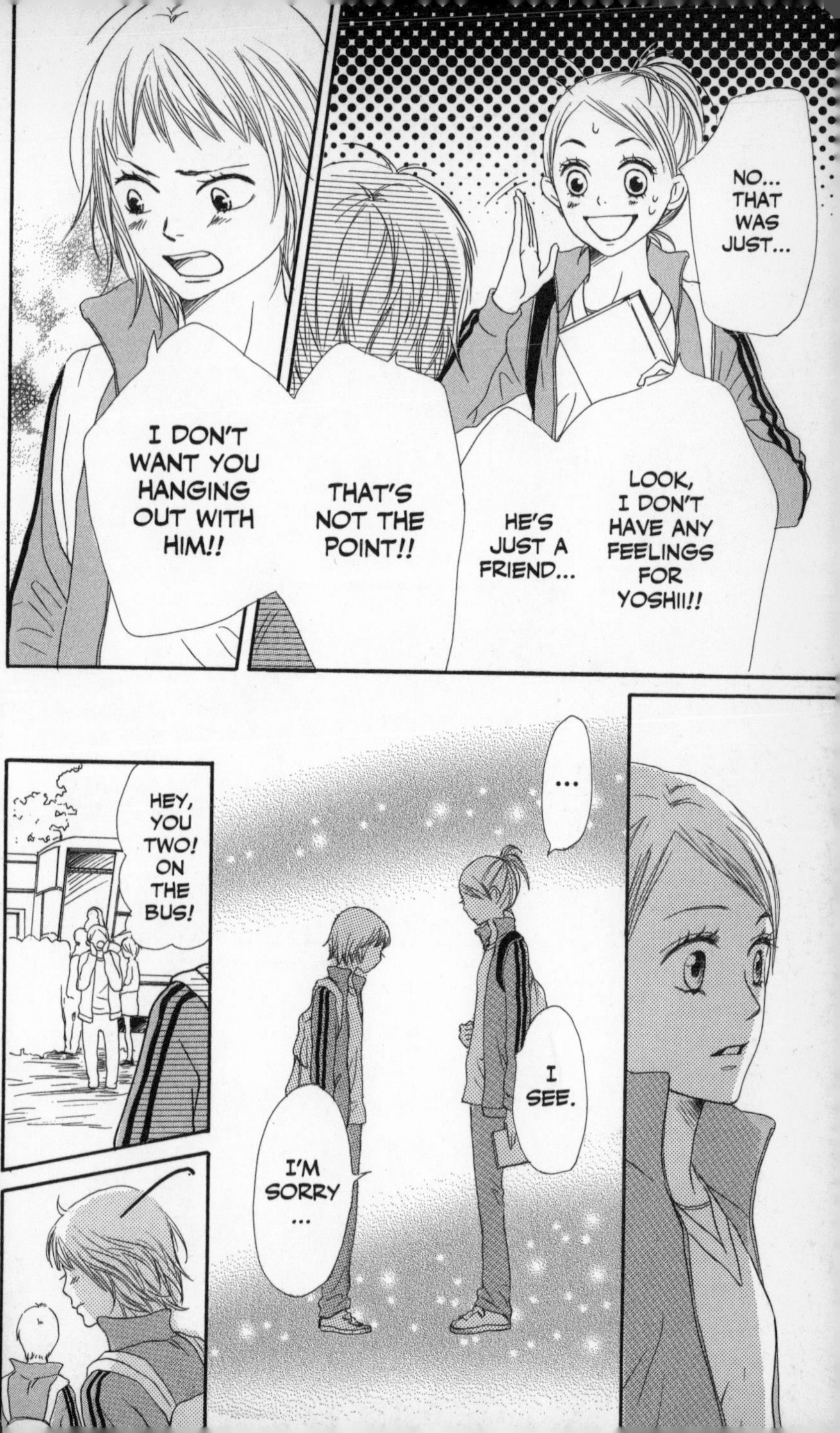
NO... THAT WAS JUST...
LOOK, I DON'T HAVE ANY FEELINGS FOR YOSHII!!
HE'S JUST A FRIEND...
THAT'S NOT THE POINT!!
I DON'T WANT YOU HANGING OUT WITH HIM!!
...
I SEE.
I'M SORRY ...
HEY, YOU TWO! ON THE BUS!

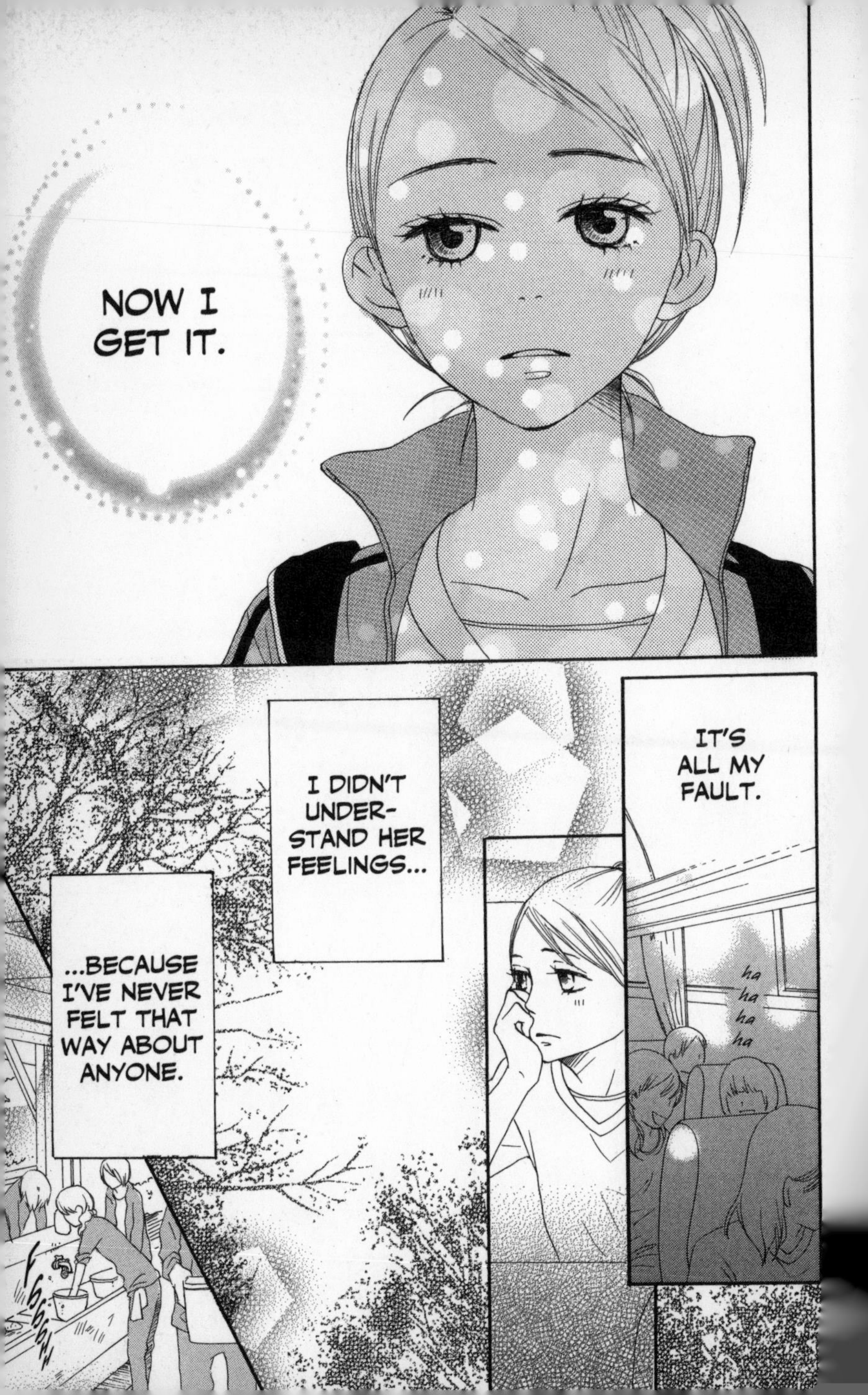
NOW I GET IT.
IT'S ALL MY FAULT.
ha ha ha ha
I DIDN'T UNDER-STAND HER FEELINGS...
...BECAUSE I'VE NEVER FELT THAT WAY ABOUT ANYONE.

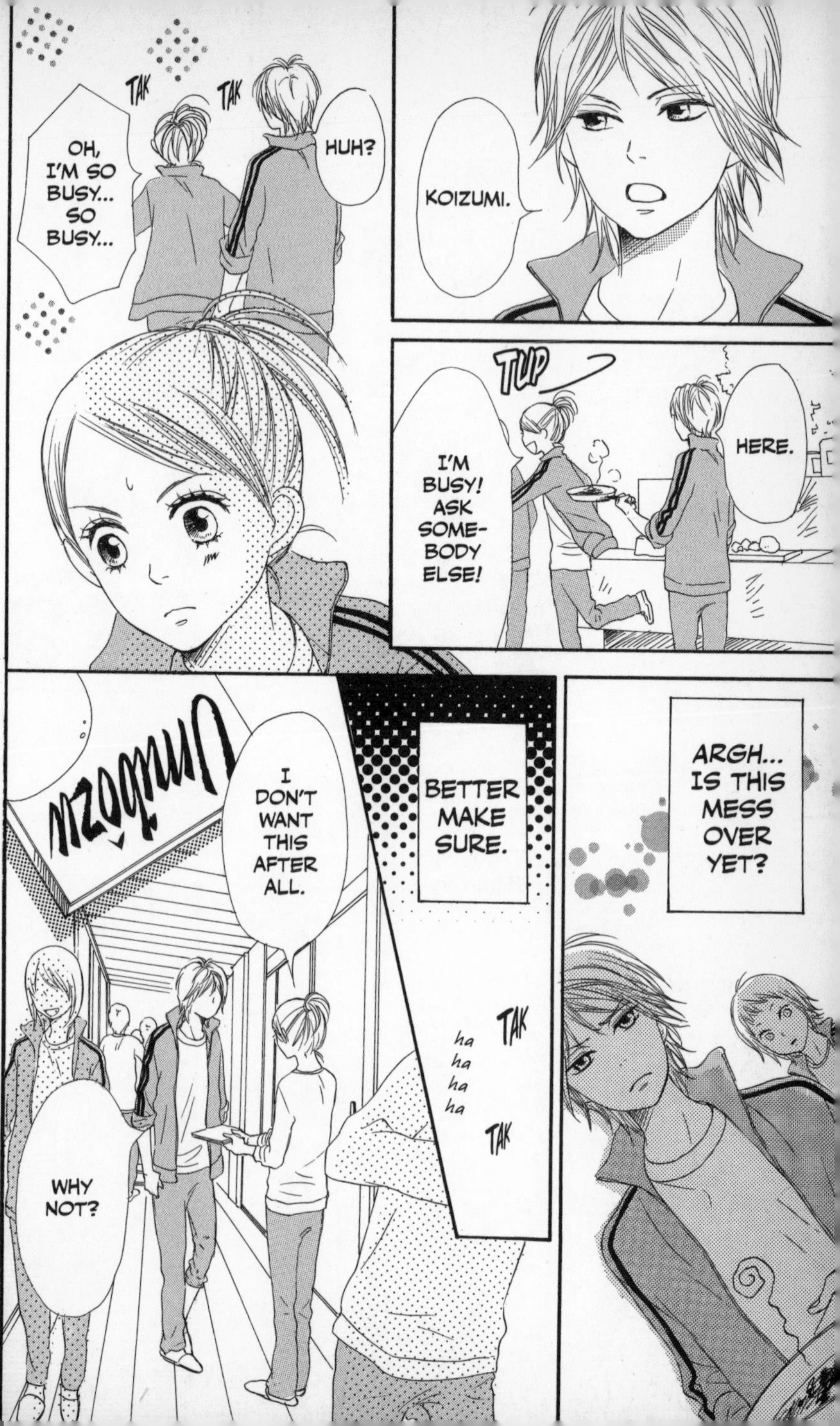
KOIZUMI.
TAK
TAK
HUH?
OH, I'M SO BUSY... SO BUSY...
HERE.
TUP
I'M BUSY! ASK SOMEBODY ELSE!
ARGH... IS THIS MESS OVER YET?
BETTER MAKE SURE.
TAK
ha ha ha ha
TAK
I DON'T WANT THIS AFTER ALL.
WHY NOT?

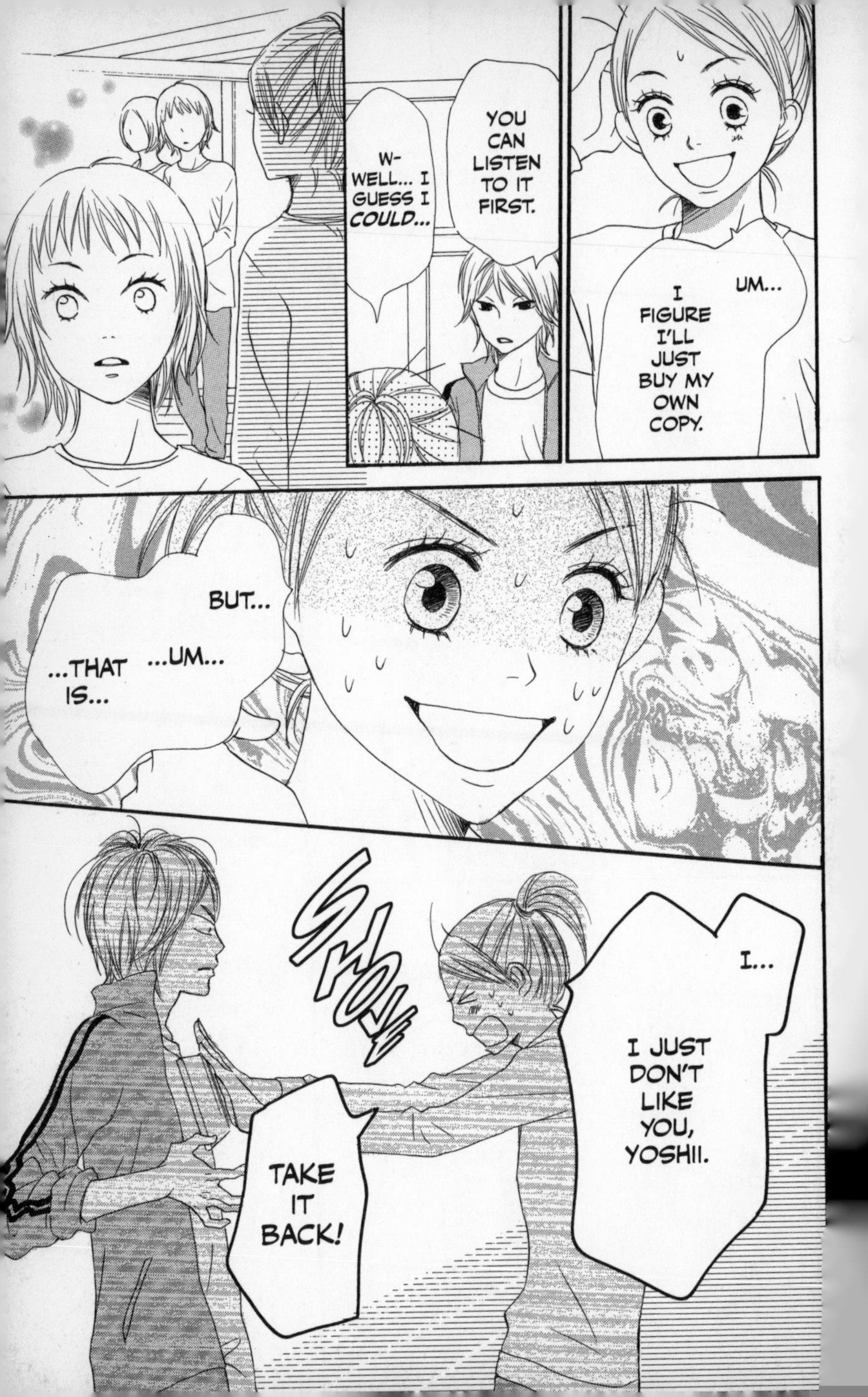
UM...
I FIGURE I'LL JUST BUY MY OWN COPY.
YOU CAN LISTEN TO IT FIRST.
W-WELL... I GUESS I COULD...
BUT...
...UM...
...THAT IS...
I...
I JUST DON'T LIKE YOU, YOSHII.
TAKE IT BACK!

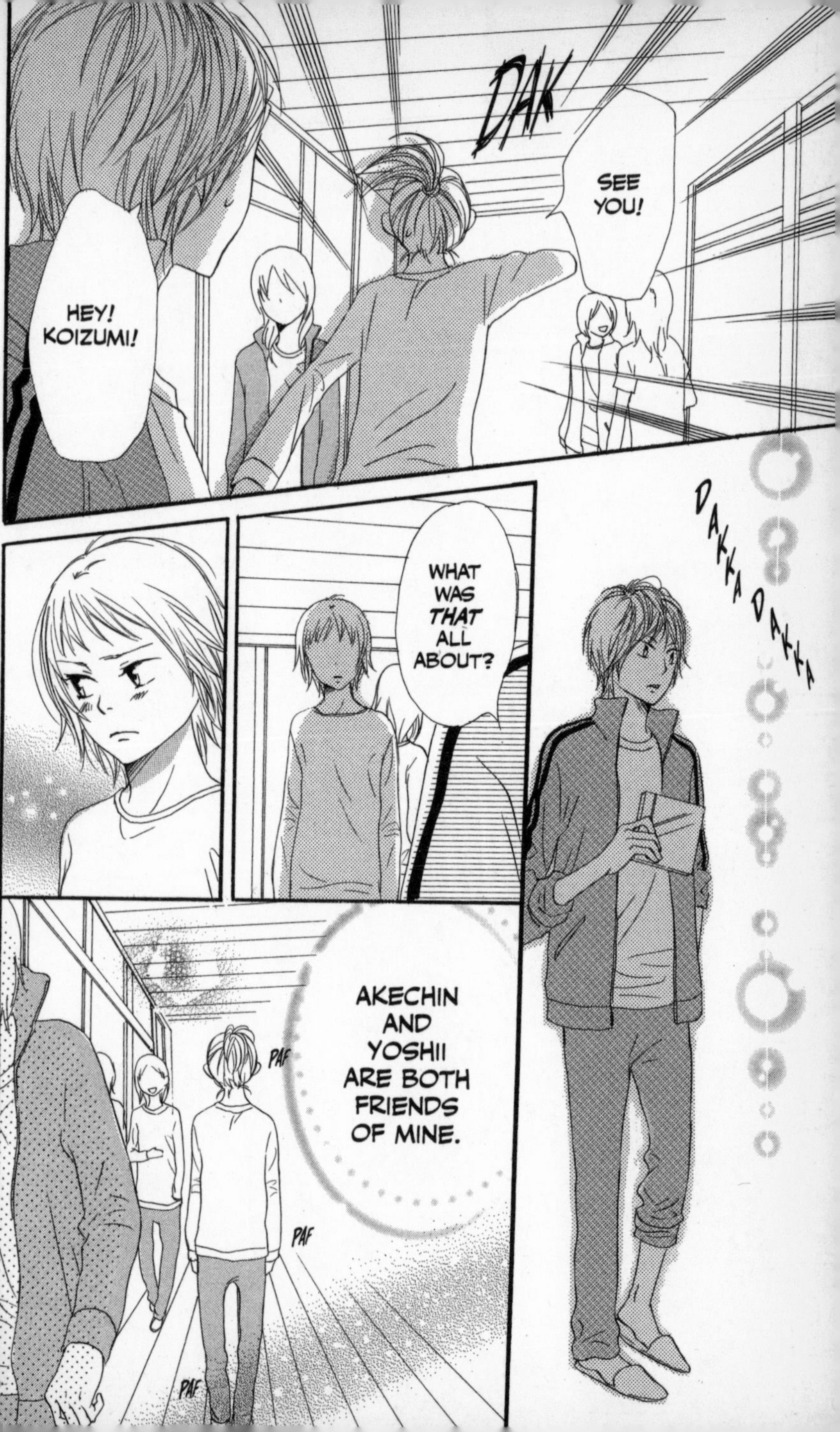
DAK
SEE YOU!
HEY! KOIZUMI!
DAKKA DAKKA
WHAT WAS *THAT* ALL ABOUT?
AKECHIN AND YOSHII ARE BOTH FRIENDS OF MINE.
PAF
PAF
PAF

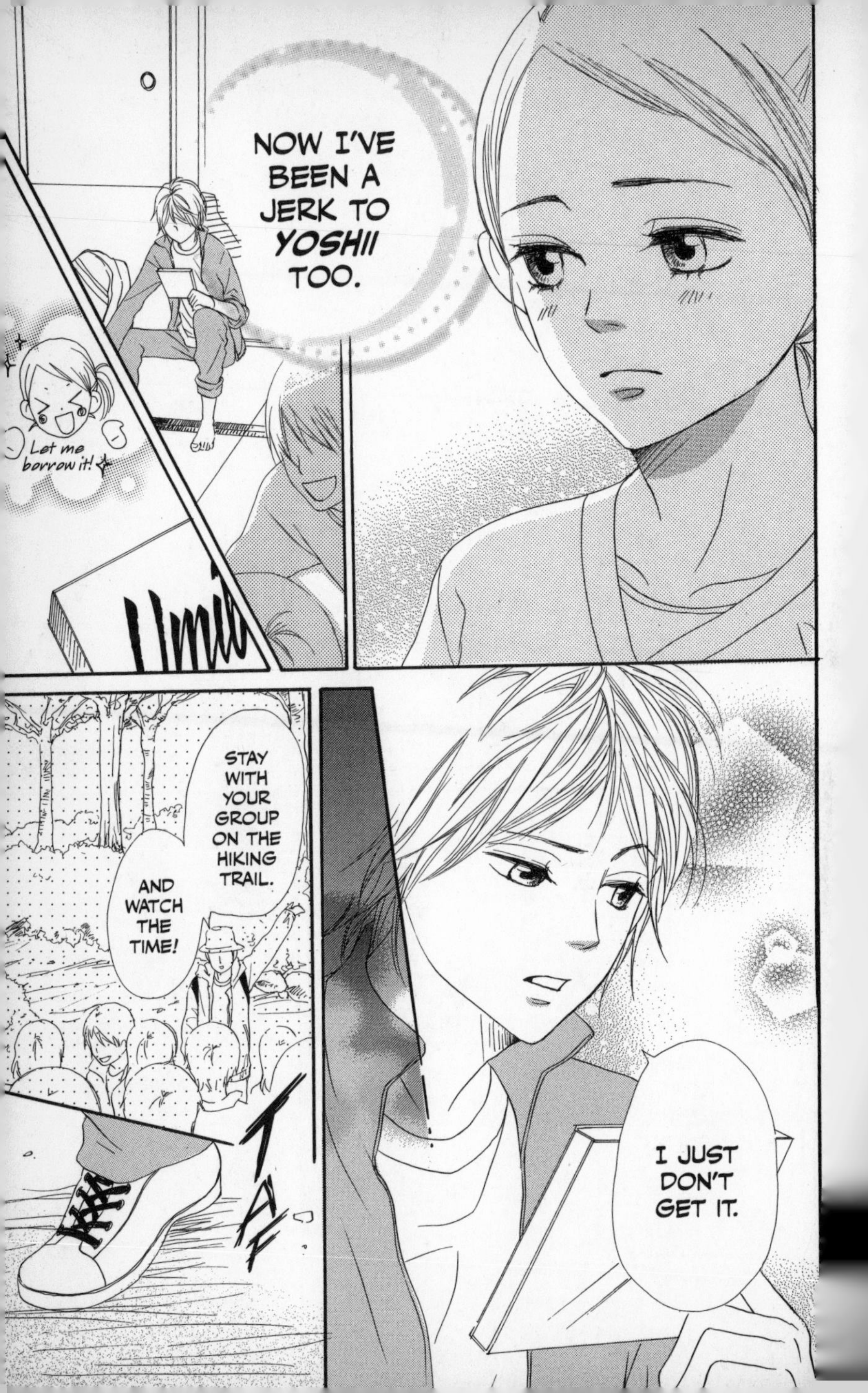
NOW I'VE BEEN A JERK TO YOSHII TOO.
Let me borrow it!
I JUST DON'T GET IT.
STAY WITH YOUR GROUP ON THE HIKING TRAIL.
AND WATCH THE TIME!

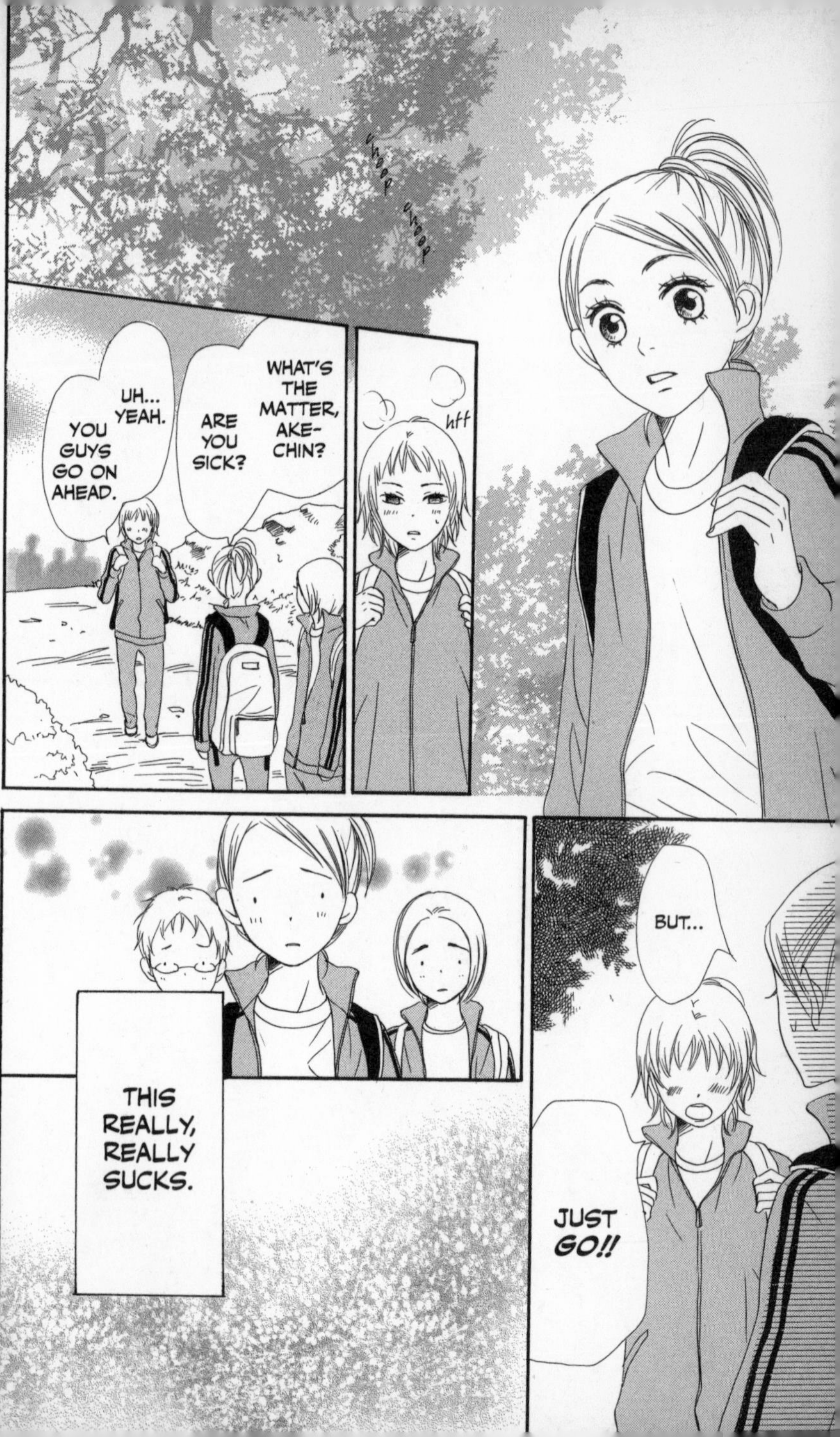
whoop whoop
hff
WHAT'S THE MATTER, AKE-CHIN?
ARE YOU SICK?
UH... YEAH.
YOU GUYS GO ON AHEAD.
BUT...
JUST GO!!
THIS REALLY, REALLY SUCKS.

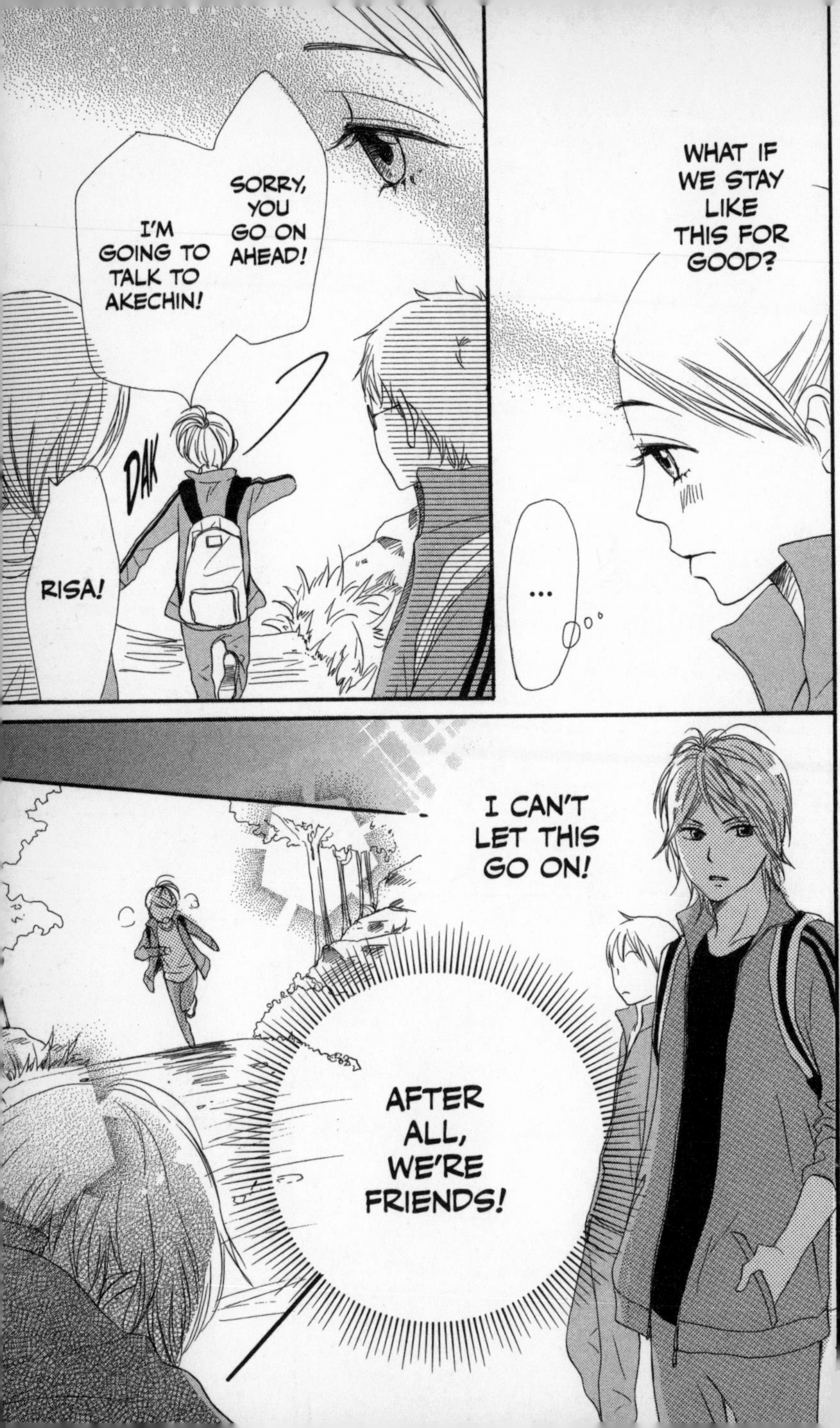
WHAT IF WE STAY LIKE THIS FOR GOOD?
...
SORRY, YOU GO ON AHEAD!
I'M GOING TO TALK TO AKECHIN!
DAK
RISA!
I CAN'T LET THIS GO ON!
AFTER ALL, WE'RE FRIENDS!

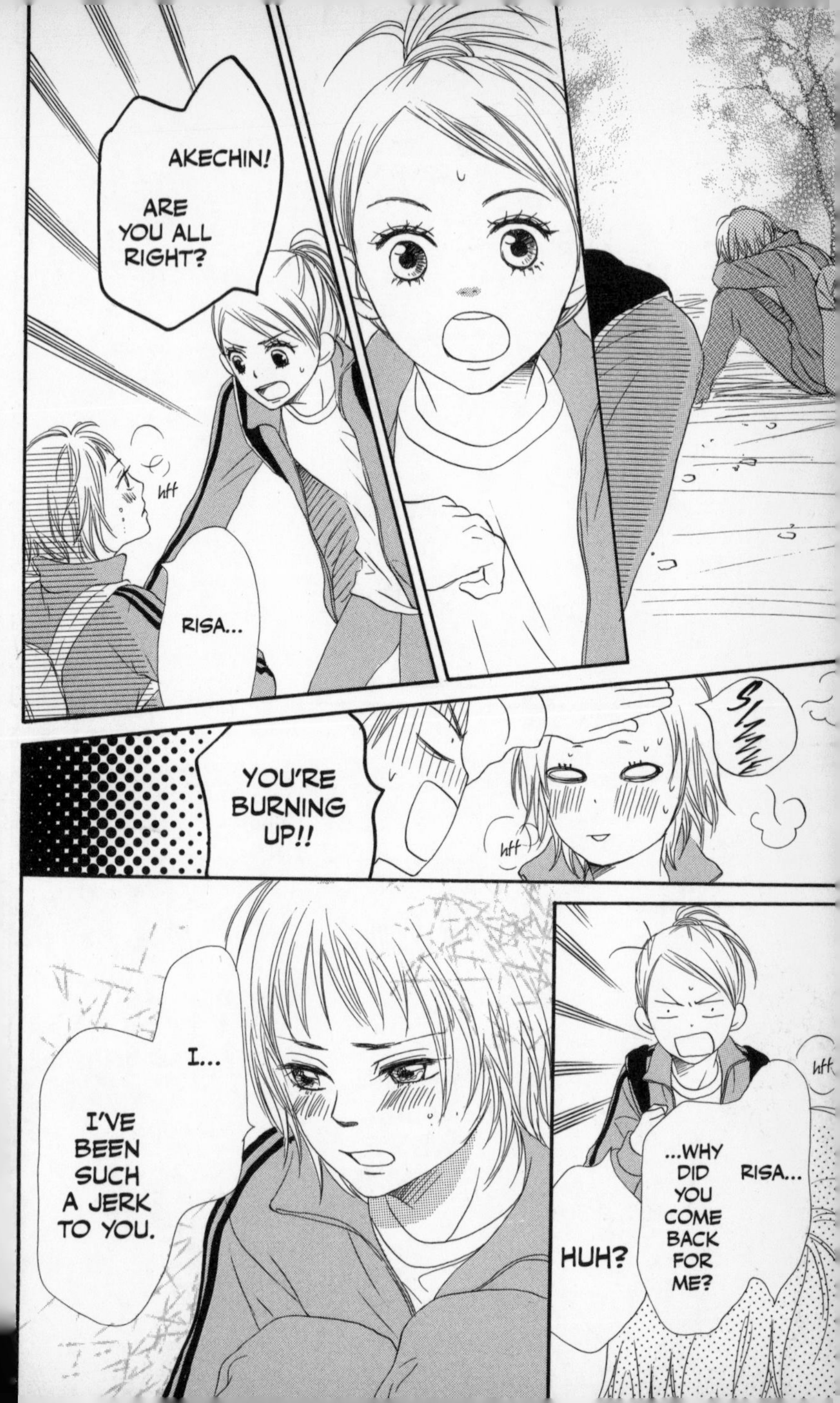
AKECHIN!
ARE YOU ALL RIGHT?
hff
RISA...
hff
YOU'RE BURNING UP!!
hff
RISA...
...WHY DID YOU COME BACK FOR ME?
HUH?
I...
I'VE BEEN SUCH A JERK TO YOU.

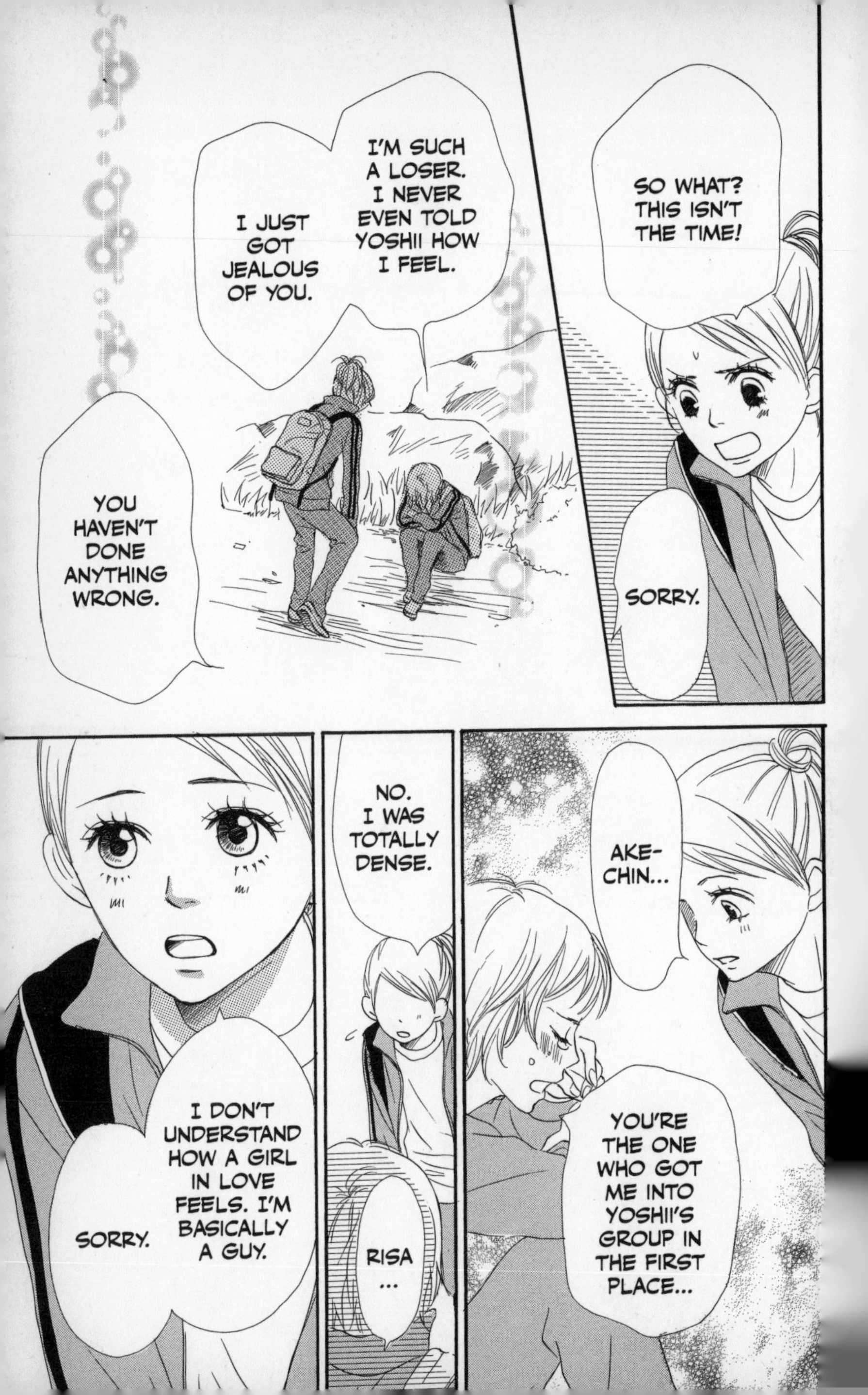
SO WHAT? THIS ISN'T THE TIME!
SORRY.
I'M SUCH A LOSER. I NEVER EVEN TOLD YOSHII HOW I FEEL.
I JUST GOT JEALOUS OF YOU.
YOU HAVEN'T DONE ANYTHING WRONG.
AKE-CHIN...
YOU'RE THE ONE WHO GOT ME INTO YOSHII'S GROUP IN THE FIRST PLACE...
NO. I WAS TOTALLY DENSE.
RISA ...
I DON'T UNDERSTAND HOW A GIRL IN LOVE FEELS. I'M BASICALLY A GUY.
SORRY.

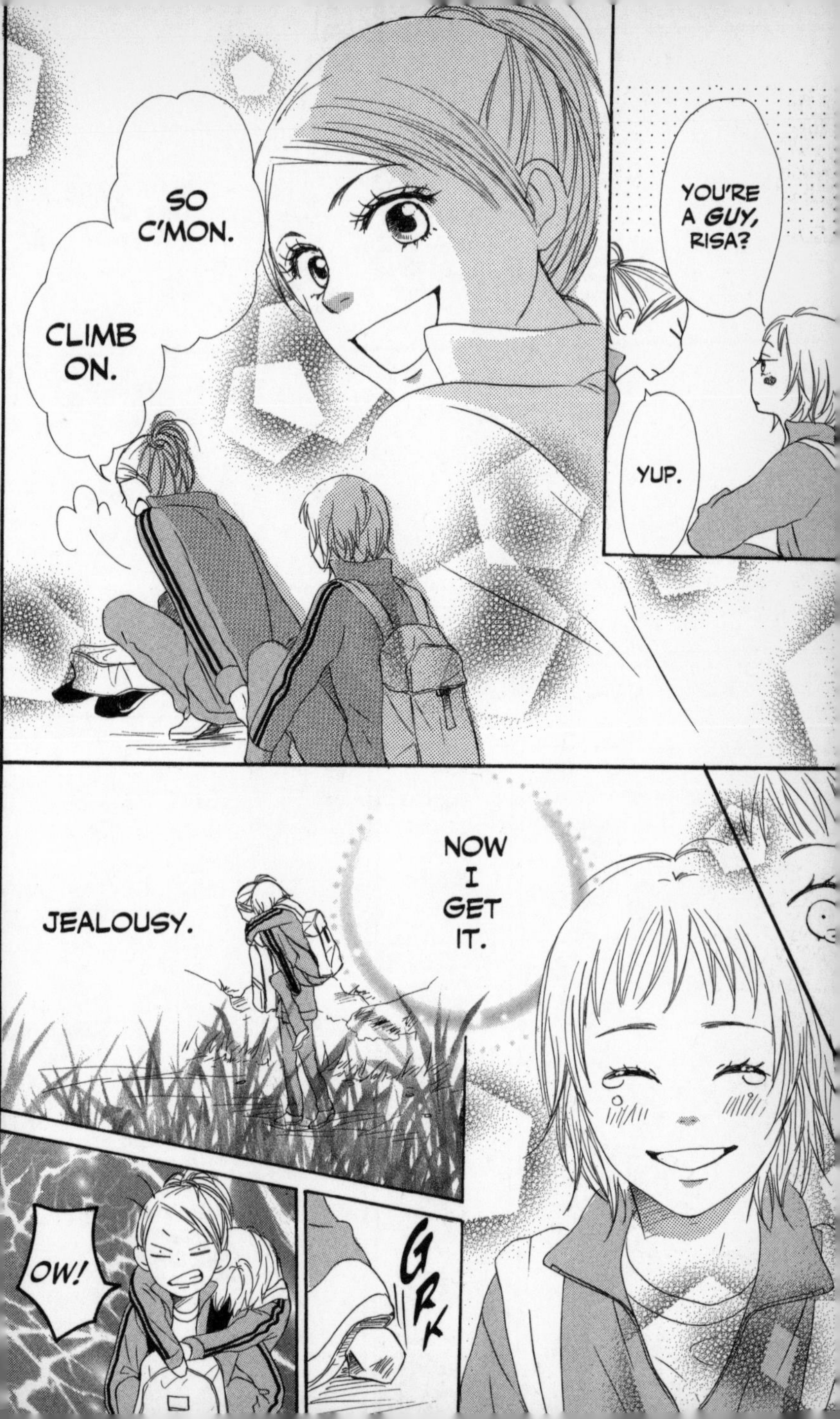
YOU'RE A GUY, RISA?
YUP.
SO C'MON.
CLIMB ON.
NOW I GET IT.
JEALOUSY.
GRK
OW!

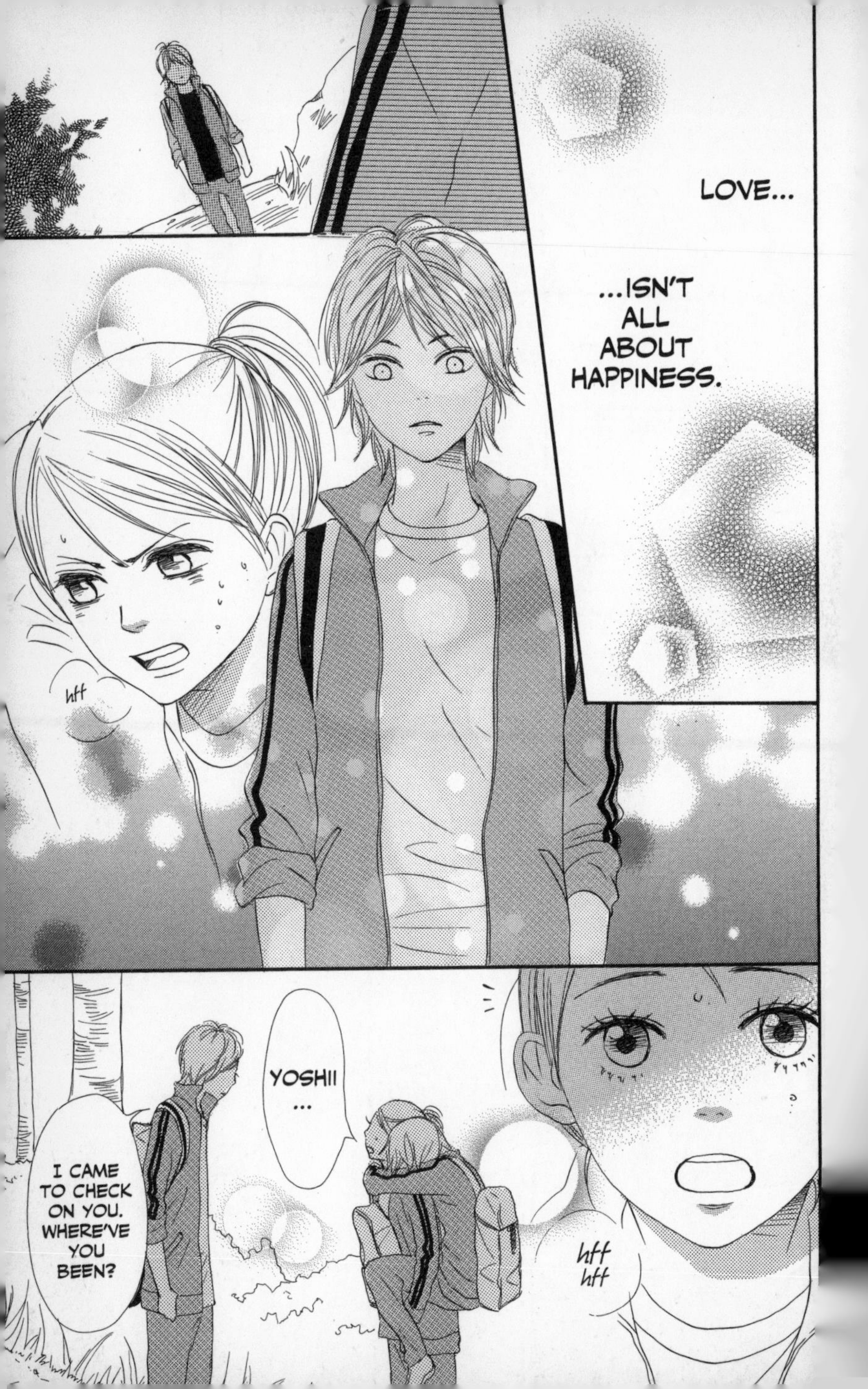
LOVE...
...ISN'T ALL ABOUT HAPPINESS.
hff
hff hff
YOSHII ...
I CAME TO CHECK ON YOU. WHERE'VE YOU BEEN?

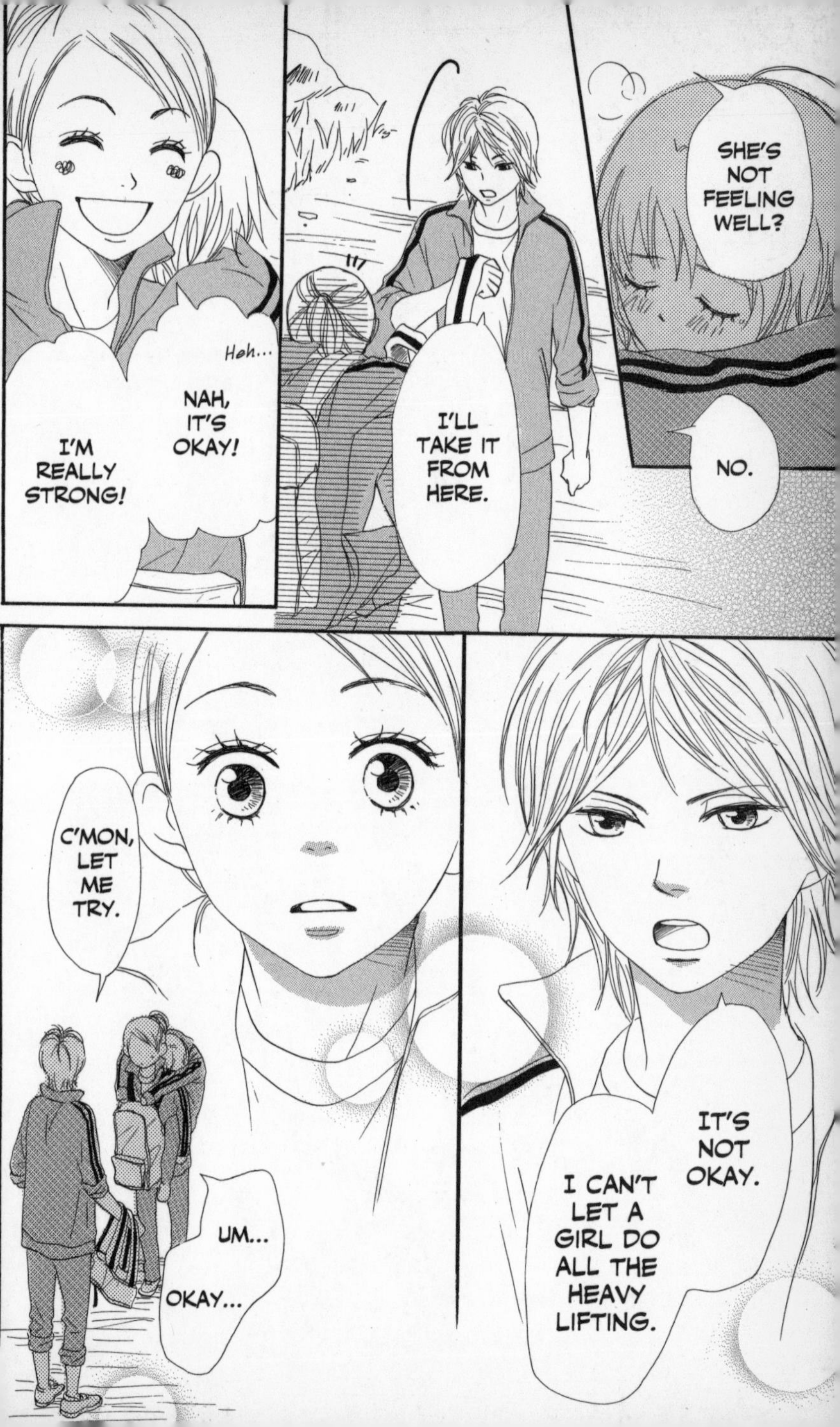
SHE'S NOT FEELING WELL?
NO.
I'LL TAKE IT FROM HERE.
Heh...
NAH, IT'S OKAY!
I'M REALLY STRONG!
IT'S NOT OKAY.
I CAN'T LET A GIRL DO ALL THE HEAVY LIFTING.
C'MON, LET ME TRY.
UM...
OKAY...

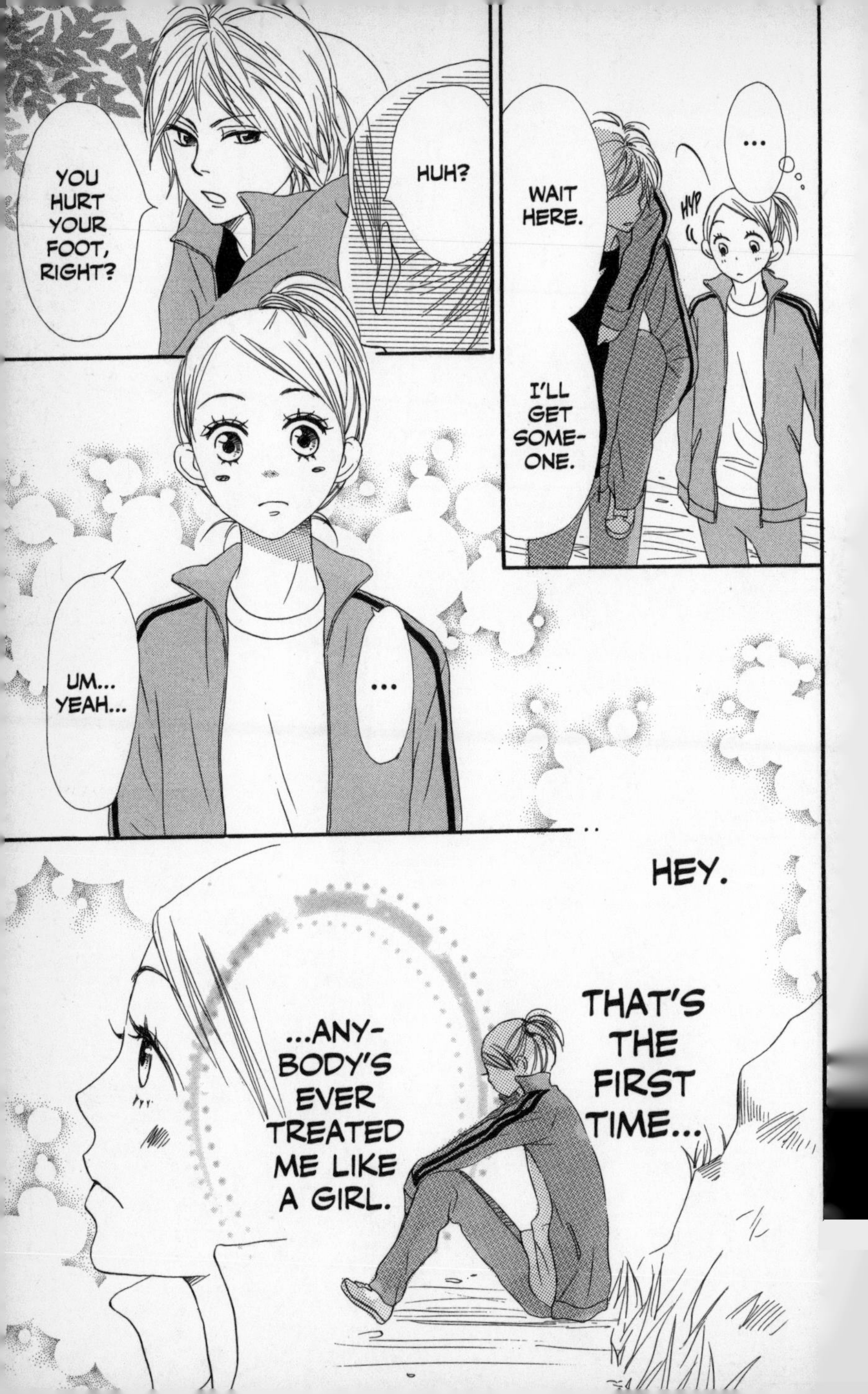
...
HYP
WAIT HERE.
I'LL GET SOME-ONE.
HUH?
YOU HURT YOUR FOOT, RIGHT?
...
UM... YEAH...
HEY.
THAT'S THE FIRST TIME...
...ANY-BODY'S EVER TREATED ME LIKE A GIRL.

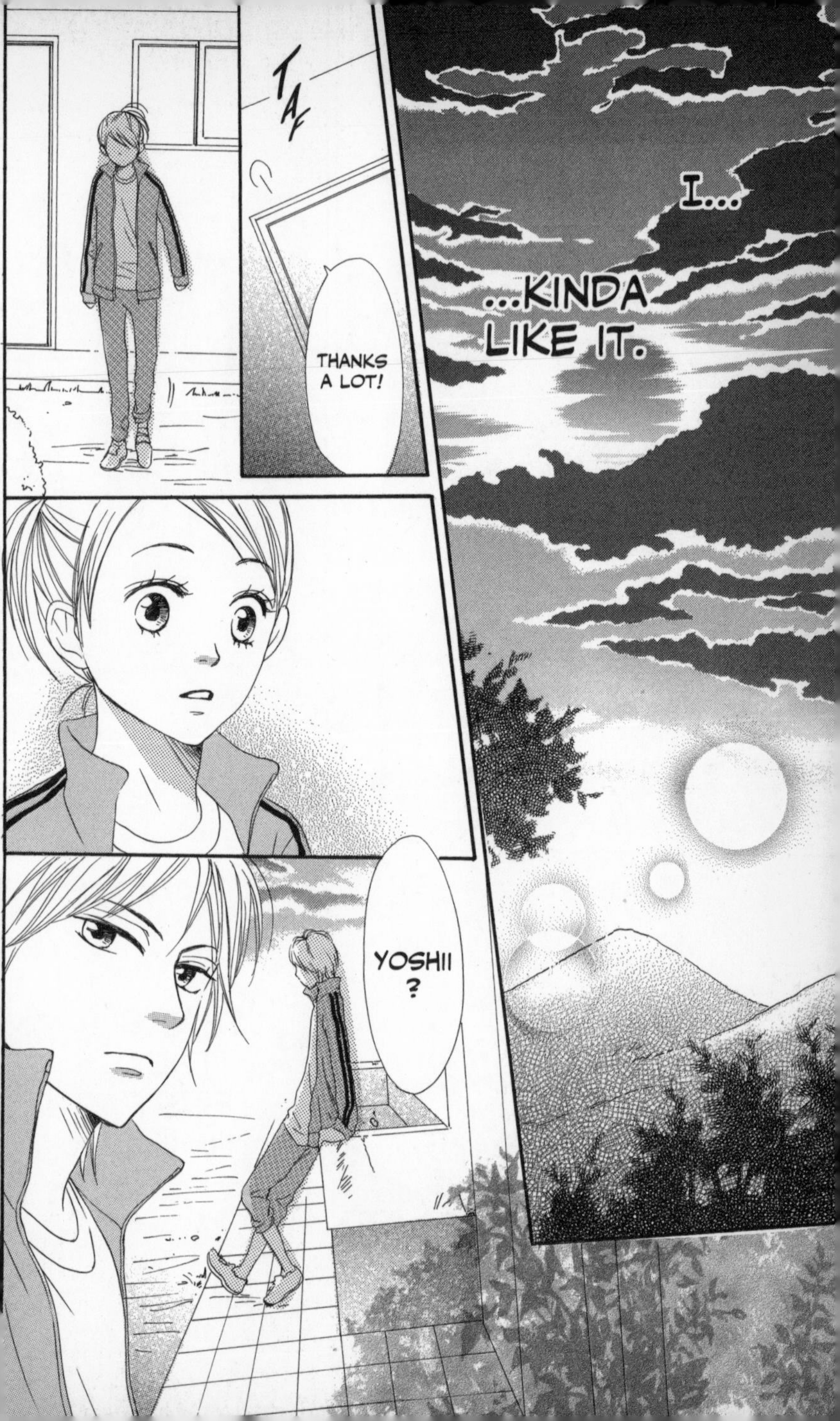
I...
...KINDA LIKE IT.
TAF
THANKS A LOT!
YOSHII ?

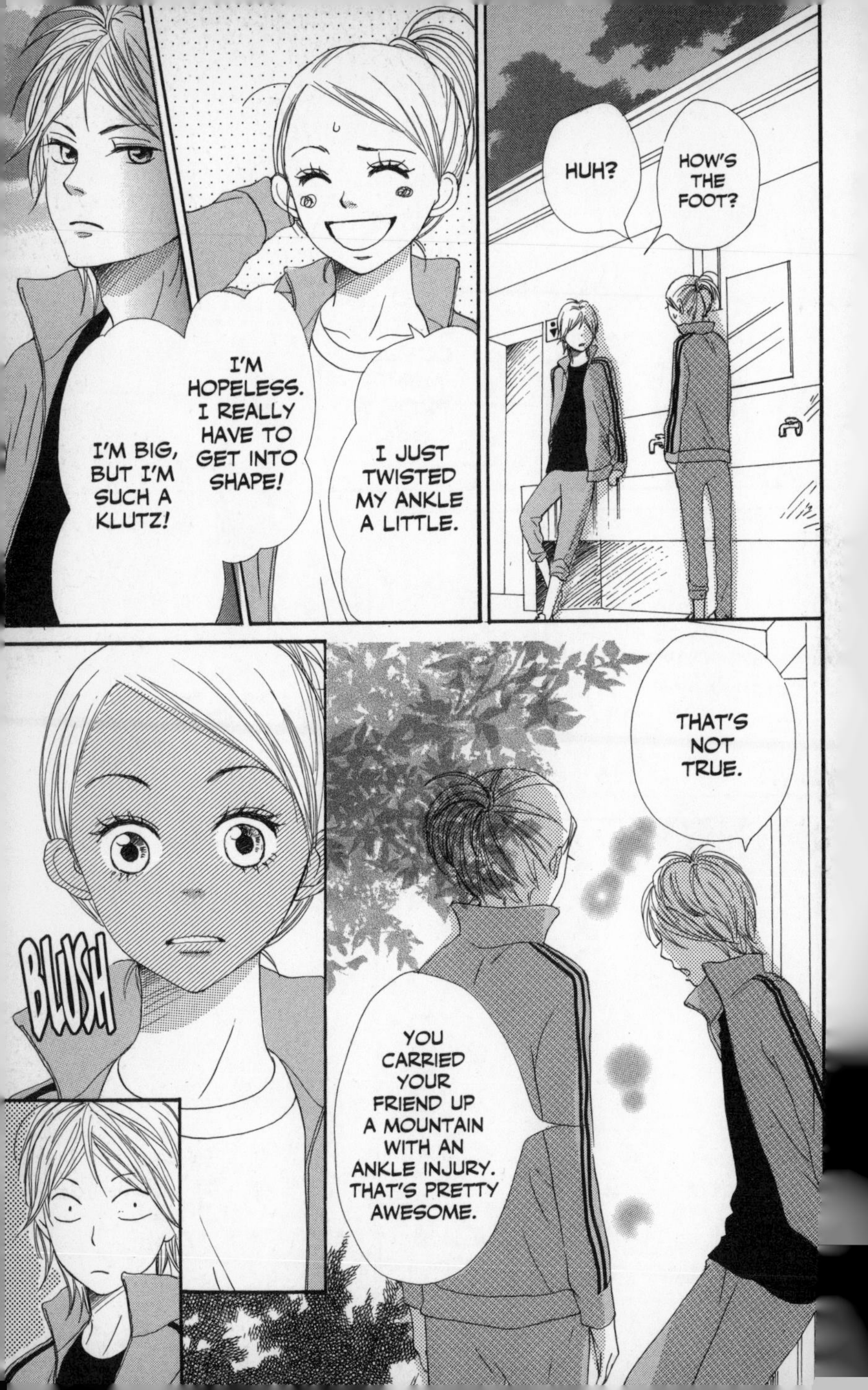
HOW'S THE FOOT?
HUH?
I JUST TWISTED MY ANKLE A LITTLE.
I'M HOPELESS. I REALLY HAVE TO GET INTO SHAPE!
I'M BIG, BUT I'M SUCH A KLUTZ!
THAT'S NOT TRUE.
YOU CARRIED YOUR FRIEND UP A MOUNTAIN WITH AN ANKLE INJURY. THAT'S PRETTY AWESOME.
BLUSH

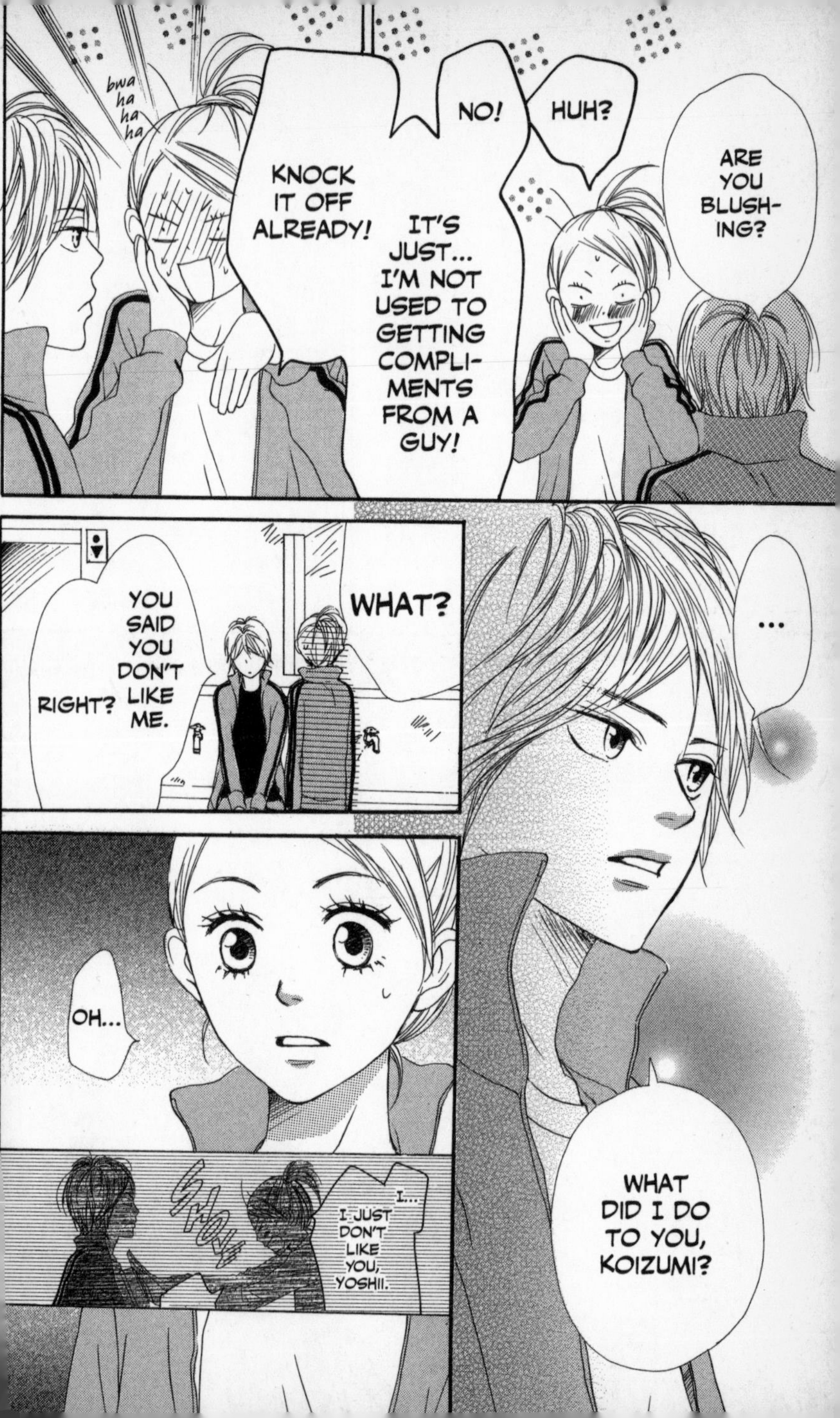
ARE YOU BLUSHING?
HUH?
NO!
IT'S JUST... I'M NOT USED TO GETTING COMPLIMENTS FROM A GUY!
KNOCK IT OFF ALREADY!
bwa ha ha ha
...
WHAT DID I DO TO YOU, KOIZUMI?
WHAT?
YOU SAID YOU DON'T LIKE ME. RIGHT?
OH...
I...
I JUST DON'T LIKE YOU, YOSHII.

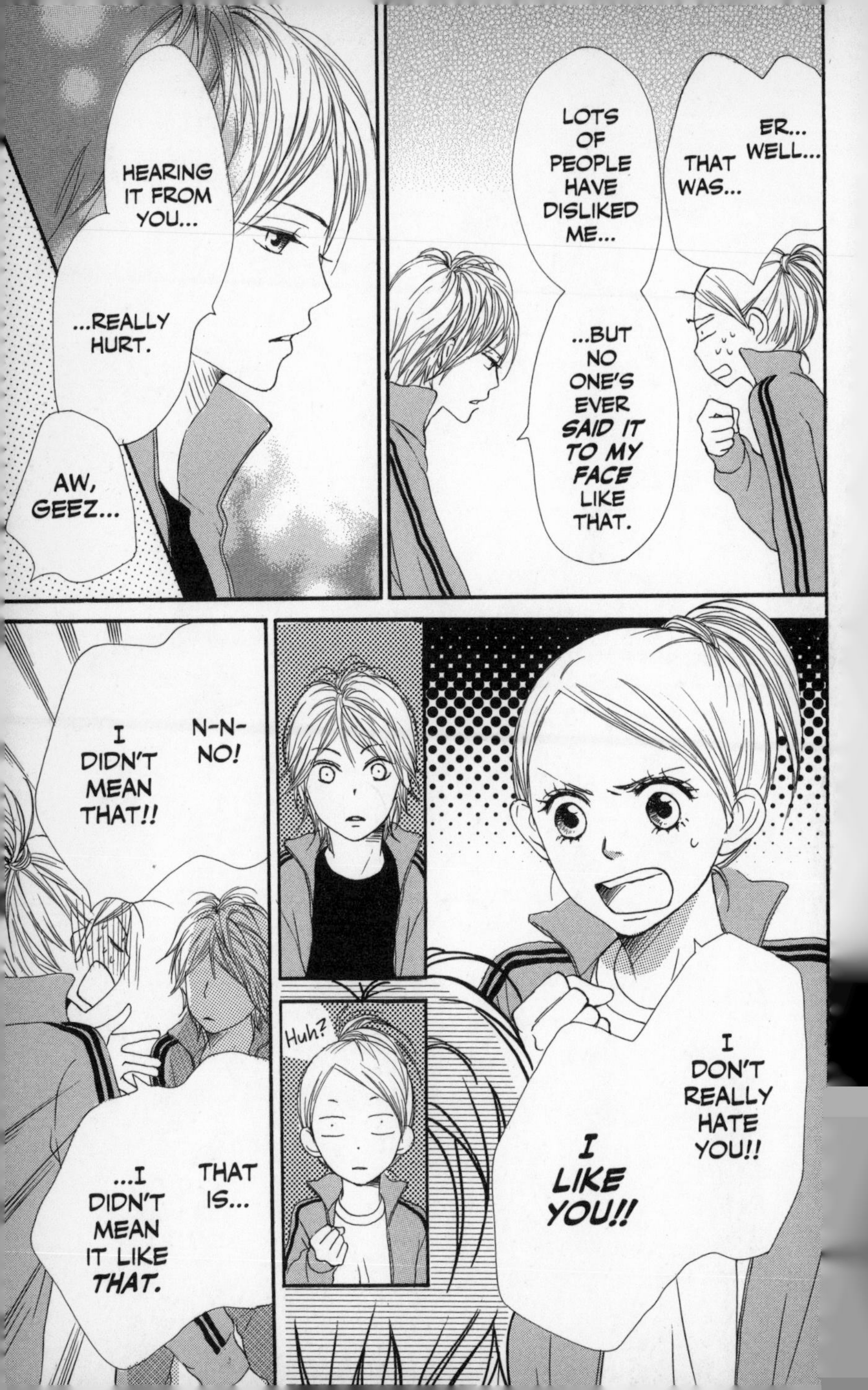
ER... WELL...
THAT WAS...
LOTS OF PEOPLE HAVE DISLIKED ME...
...BUT NO ONE'S EVER SAID IT TO MY FACE LIKE THAT.
HEARING IT FROM YOU...
...REALLY HURT.
AW, GEEZ...
I DON'T REALLY HATE YOU!!
I LIKE YOU!!
Huh?
N-N-NO!
I DIDN'T MEAN THAT!!
THAT IS...
...I DIDN'T MEAN IT LIKE THAT.

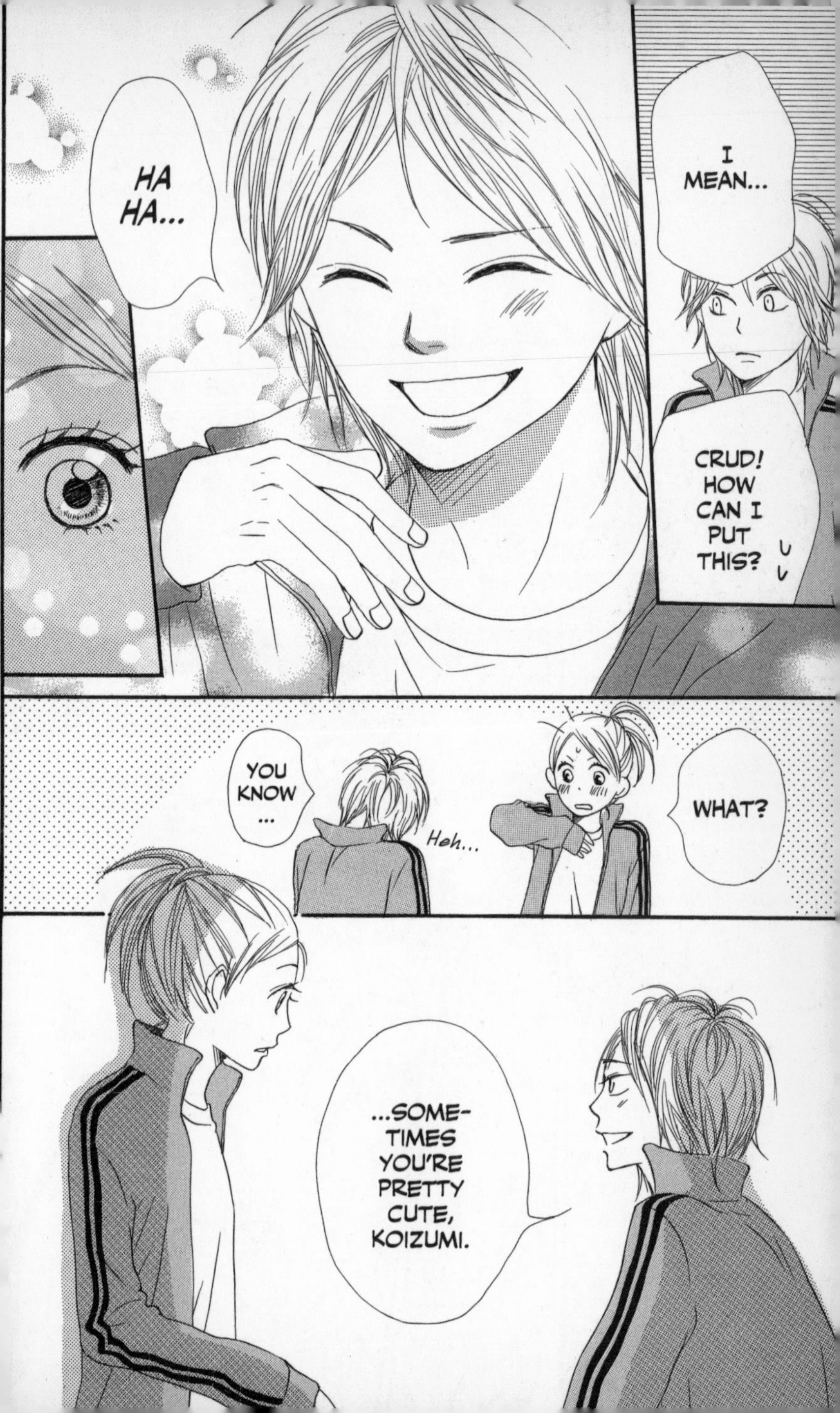
I MEAN...
CRUD! HOW CAN I PUT THIS?
HA HA...
WHAT?
Heh...
YOU KNOW ...
...SOME-TIMES YOU'RE PRETTY CUTE, KOIZUMI.

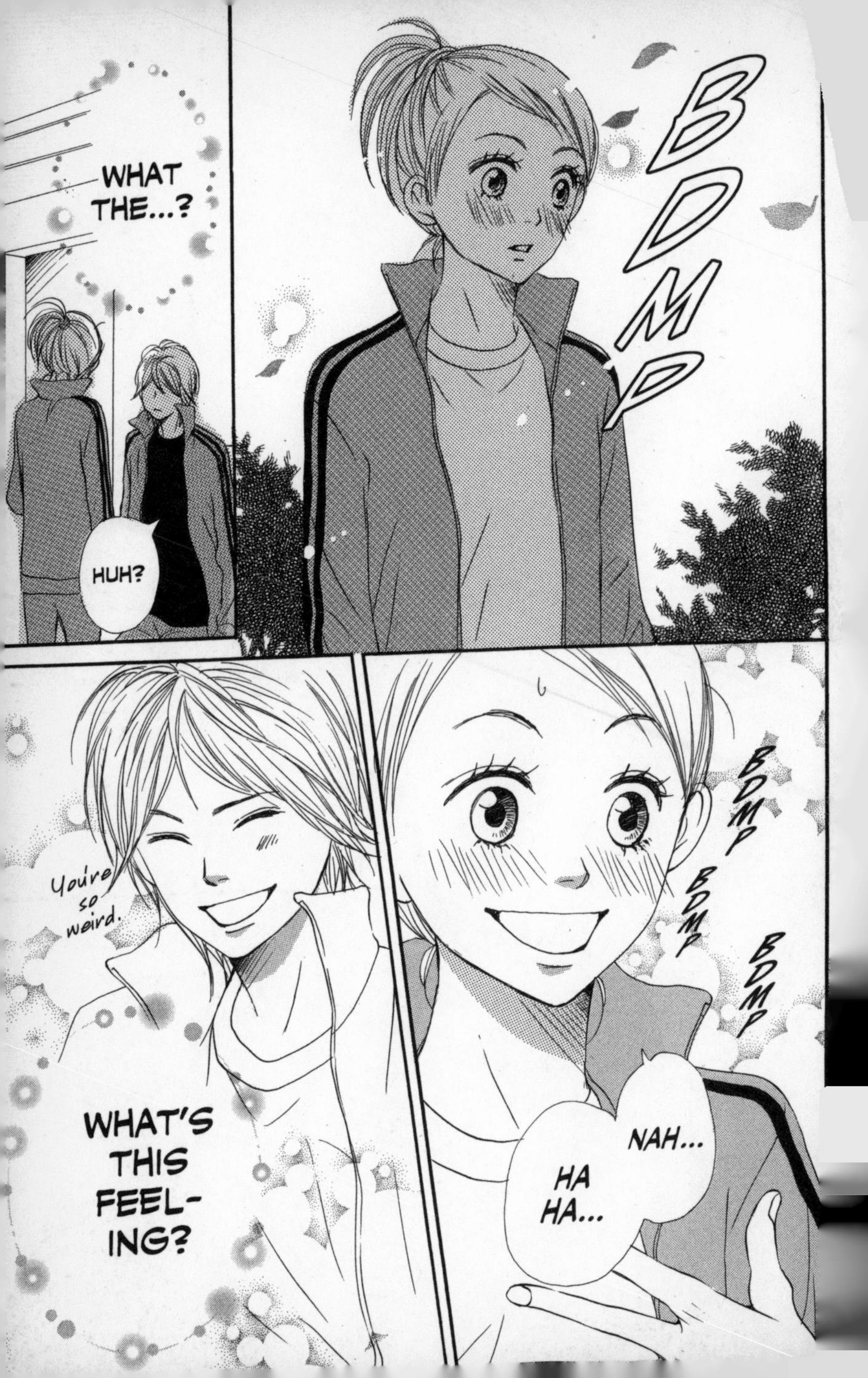
BDMP
WHAT THE...?
HUH?
BDMP
BDMP
BDMP
NAH...
HA HA...
You're so weird.
WHAT'S THIS FEEL- ING?

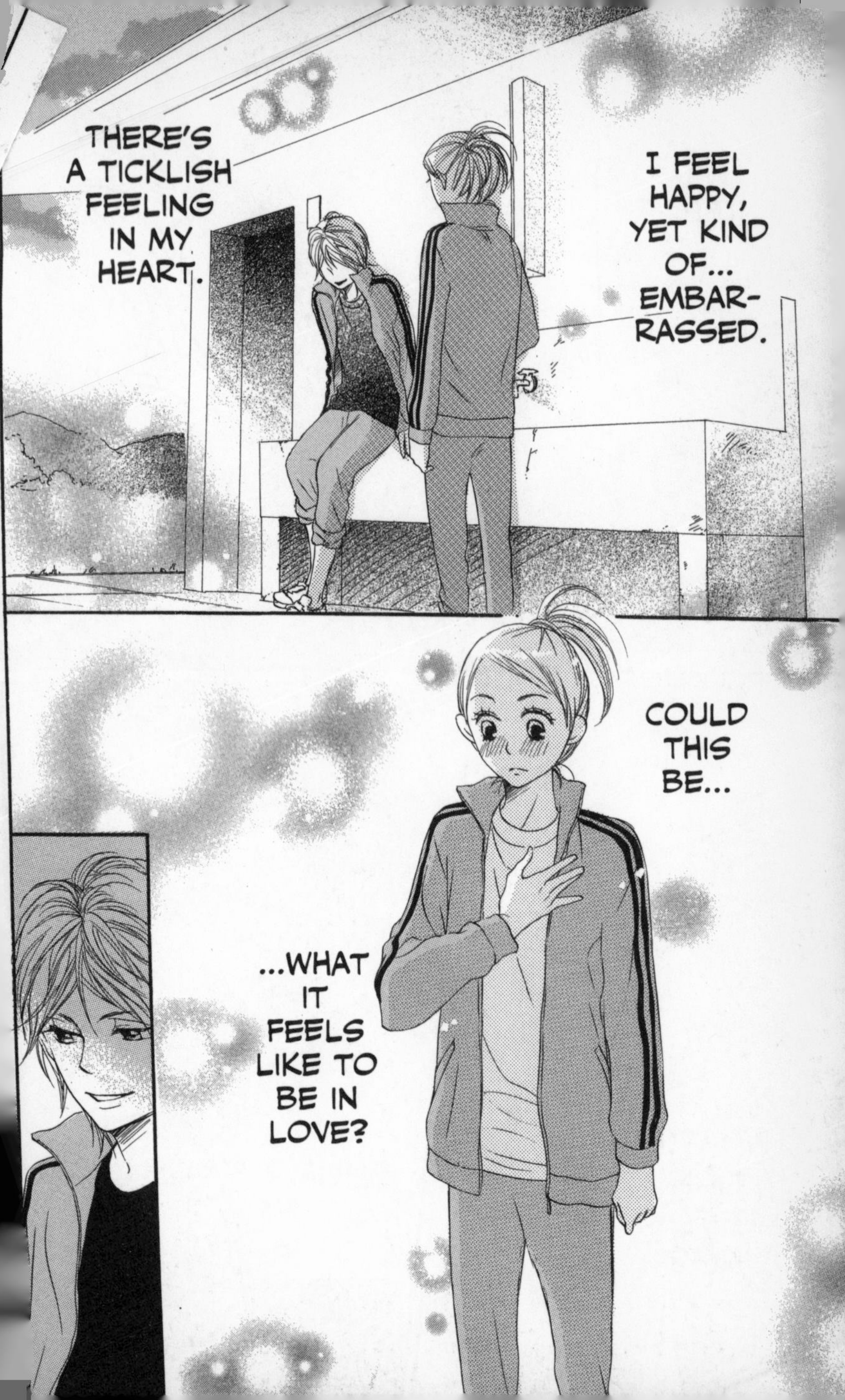
I FEEL HAPPY, YET KIND OF... EMBARRASSED.
THERE'S A TICKLISH FEELING IN MY HEART.
COULD THIS BE...
...WHAT IT FEELS LIKE TO BE IN LOVE?

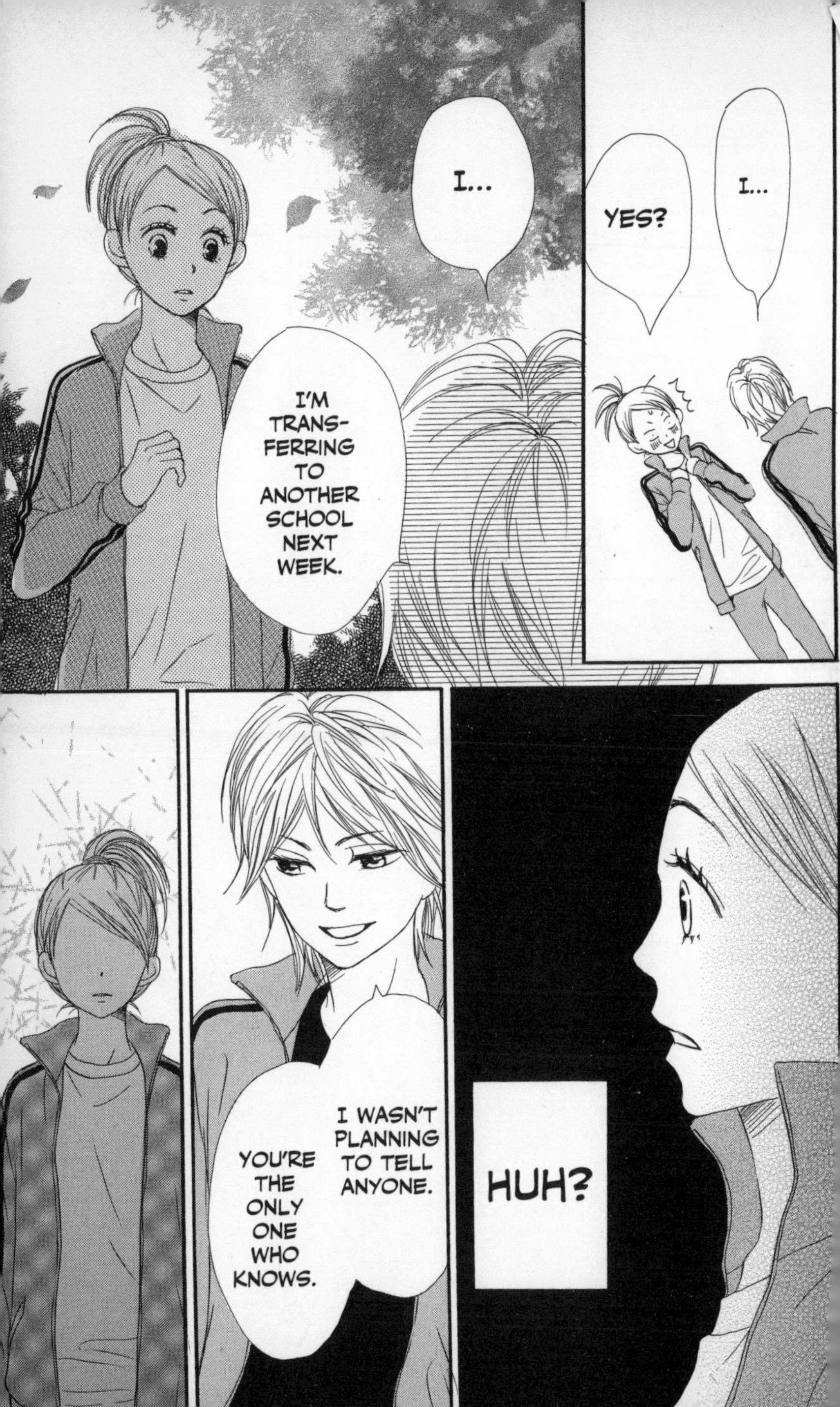
I...
YES?
I...
I'M TRANS-FERRING TO ANOTHER SCHOOL NEXT WEEK.
HUH?
I WASN'T PLANNING TO TELL ANYONE.
YOU'RE THE ONLY ONE WHO KNOWS.

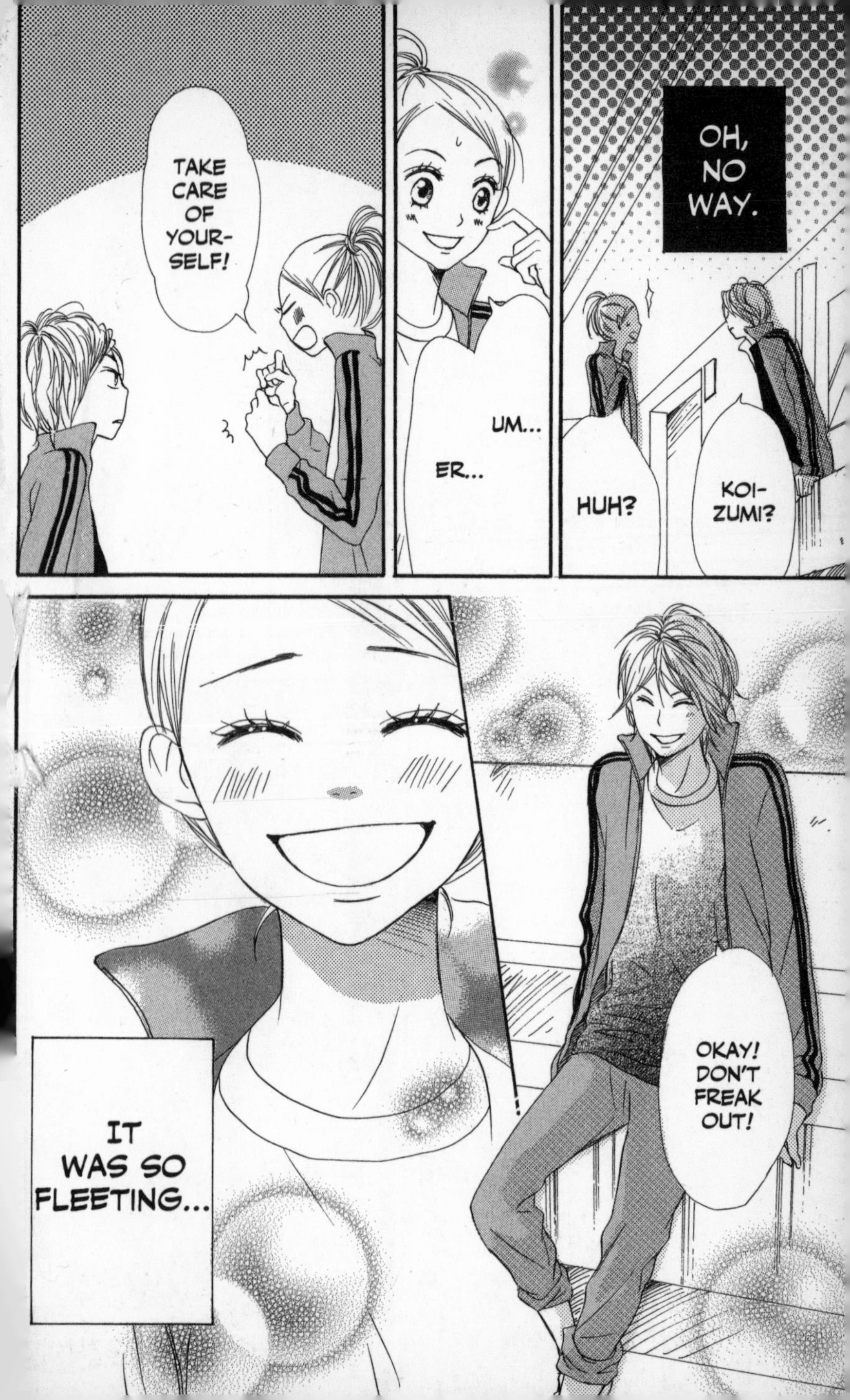
OH, NO WAY.
KOI-ZUMI?
HUH?
UM...
ER...
TAKE CARE OF YOUR-SELF!
OKAY! DON'T FREAK OUT!
IT WAS SO FLEETING...

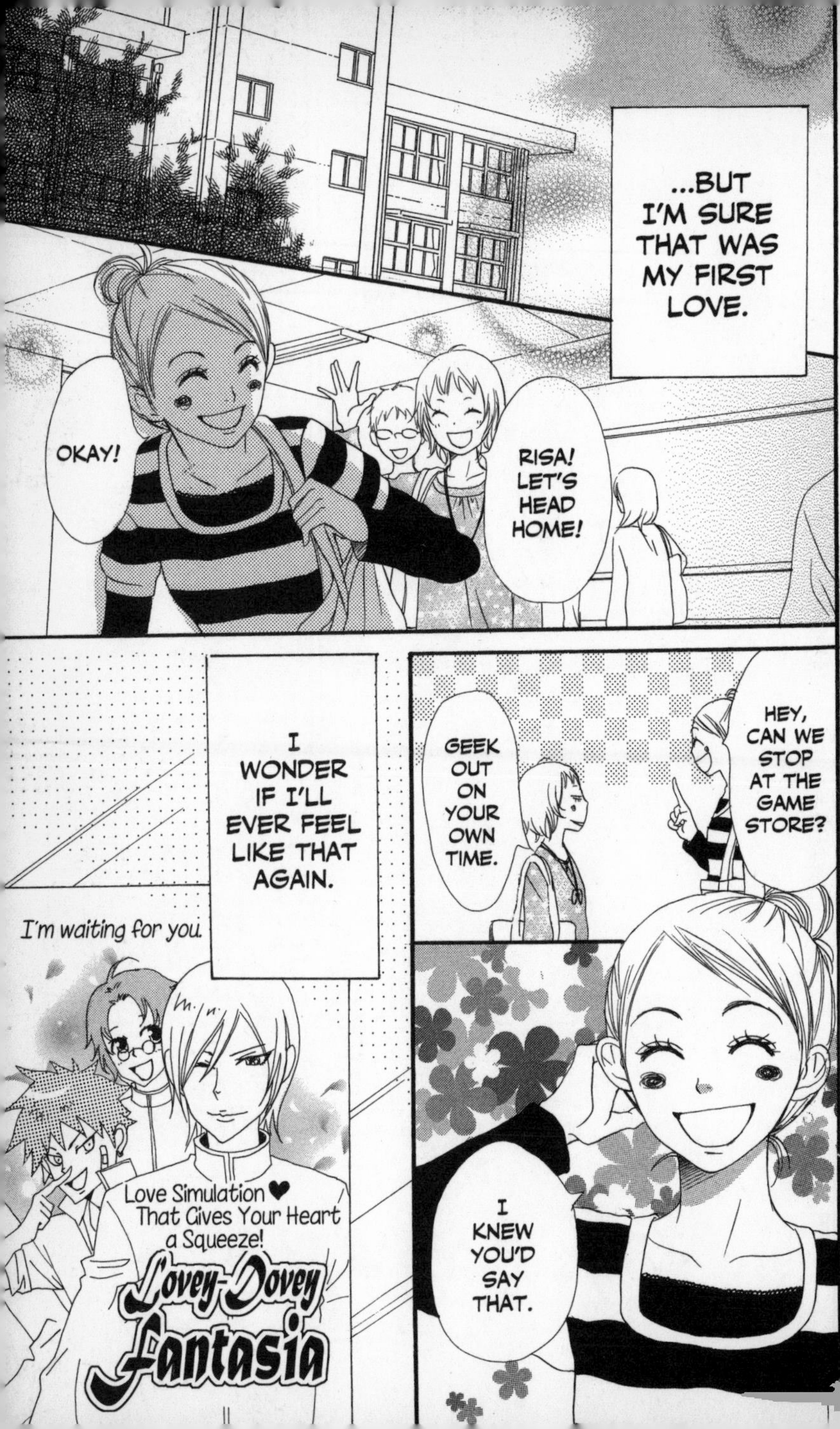
...BUT I'M SURE THAT WAS MY FIRST LOVE.
RISA! LET'S HEAD HOME!
OKAY!
HEY, CAN WE STOP AT THE GAME STORE?
GEEK OUT ON YOUR OWN TIME.
I KNEW YOU'D SAY THAT.
I WONDER IF I'LL EVER FEEL LIKE THAT AGAIN.
I'm waiting for you.
Love Simulation ♥ That Gives Your Heart a Squeeze!
Lovey-Dovey Fantasia

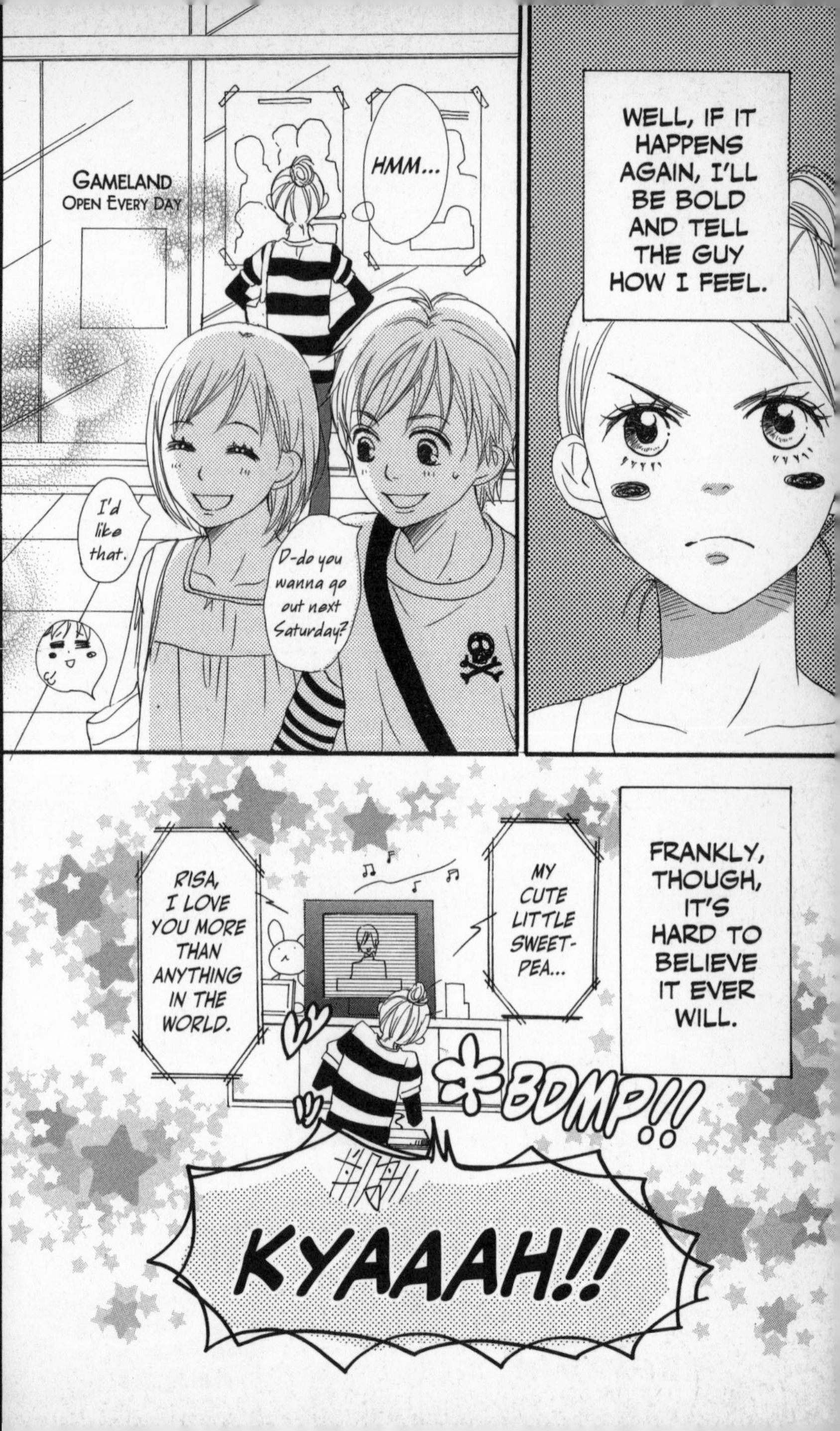
WELL, IF IT HAPPENS AGAIN, I'LL BE BOLD AND TELL THE GUY HOW I FEEL.
HMM...
GAMELAND
OPEN EVERY DAY
D-do you wanna go out next Saturday?
I'd like that.
FRANKLY, THOUGH, IT'S HARD TO BELIEVE IT EVER WILL.
MY CUTE LITTLE SWEET-PEA...
RISA, I LOVE YOU MORE THAN ANYTHING IN THE WORLD.
BDMP!!
KYAAAH!!

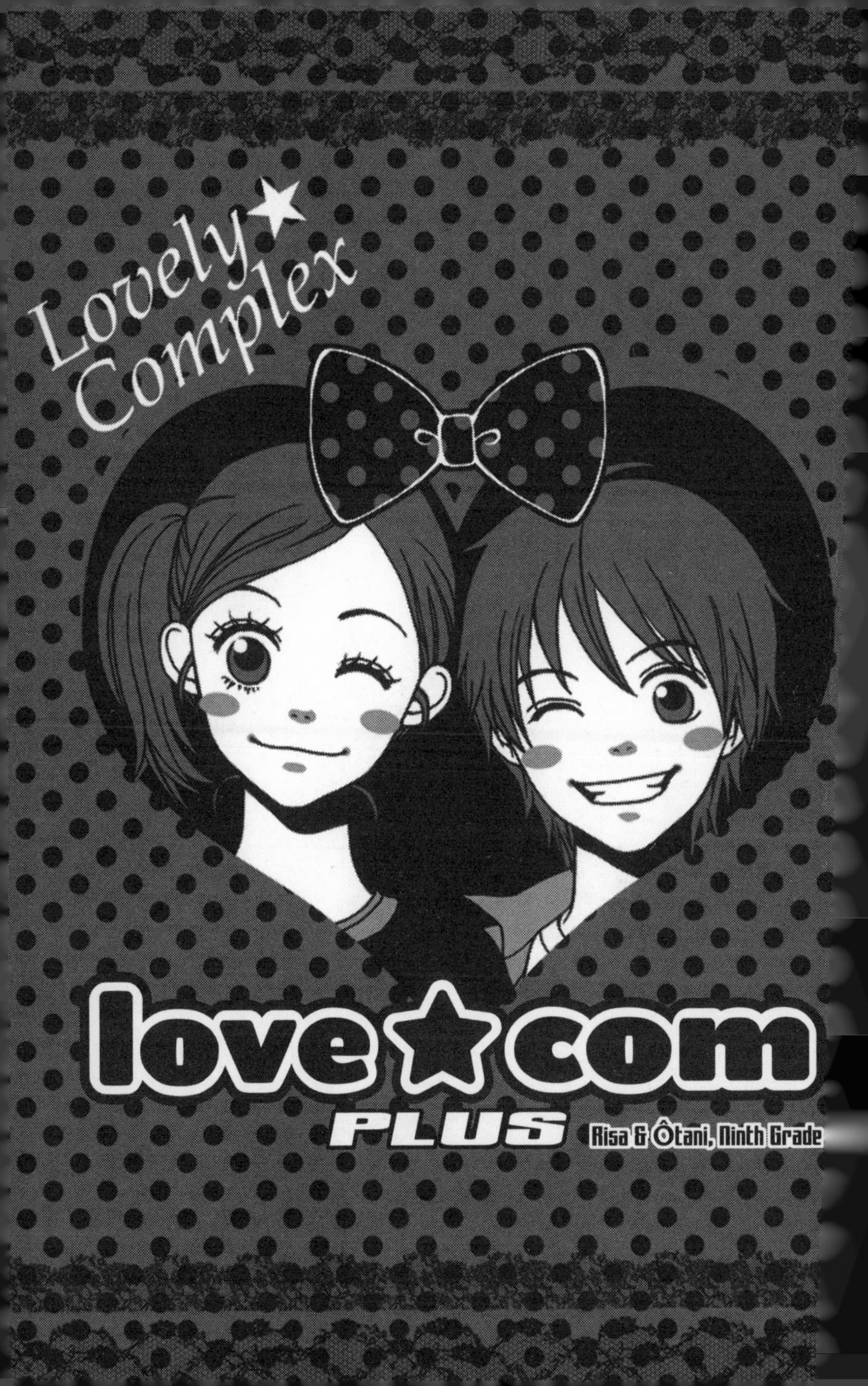
Lovely★Complex
love★com
PLUS
Risa & Ôtani, Ninth Grade

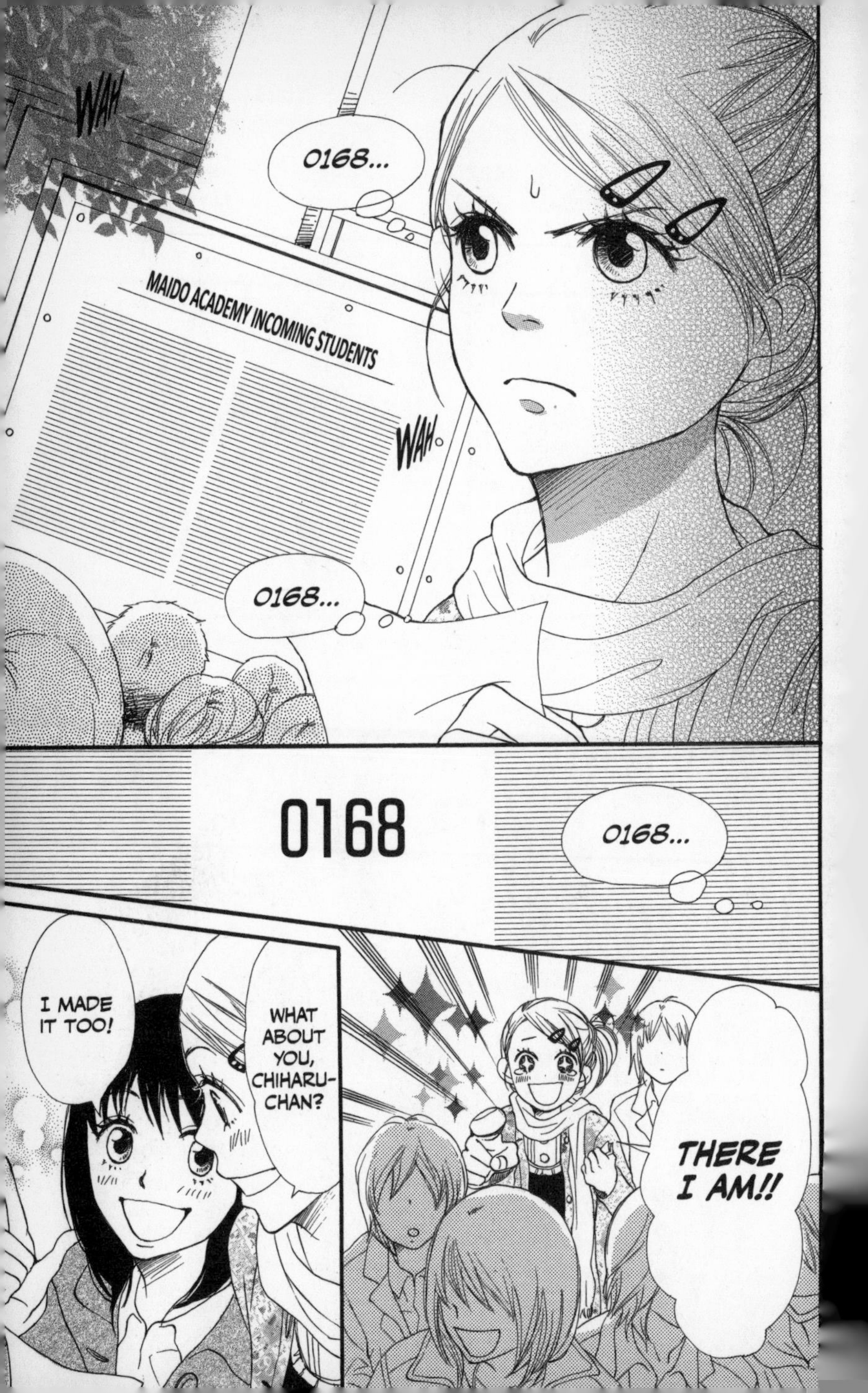
0168...
WAH
MAIDO ACADEMY INCOMING STUDENTS
WAH
0168...
0168...
0168
THERE I AM!!
WHAT ABOUT YOU, CHIHARU-CHAN?
I MADE IT TOO!

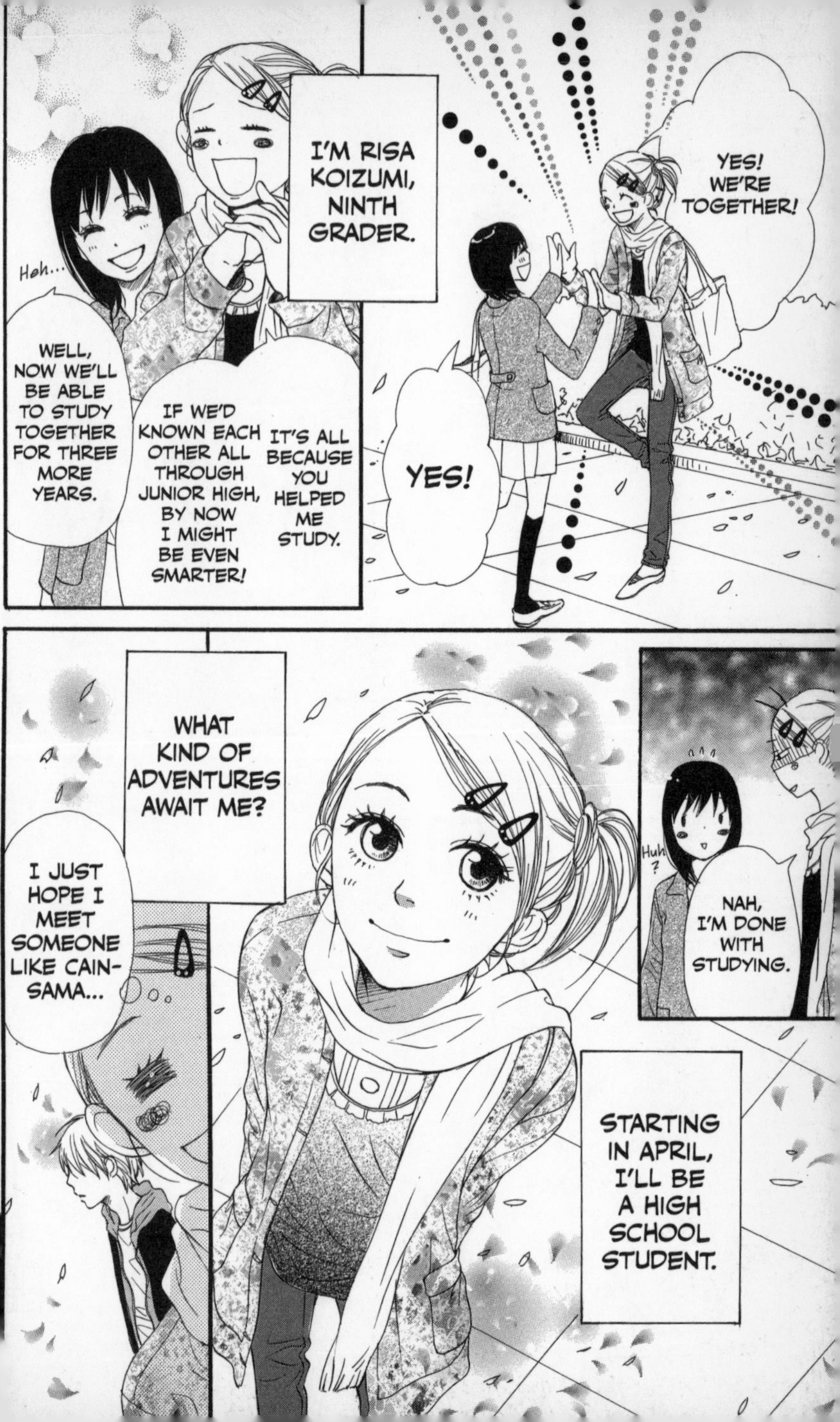
YES! WE'RE TOGETHER!
YES!
I'M RISA KOIZUMI, NINTH GRADER.
IT'S ALL BECAUSE YOU HELPED ME STUDY.
IF WE'D KNOWN EACH OTHER ALL THROUGH JUNIOR HIGH, BY NOW I MIGHT BE EVEN SMARTER!
Heh...
WELL, NOW WE'LL BE ABLE TO STUDY TOGETHER FOR THREE MORE YEARS.
Huh?
NAH, I'M DONE WITH STUDYING.
STARTING IN APRIL, I'LL BE A HIGH SCHOOL STUDENT.
WHAT KIND OF ADVENTURES AWAIT ME?
I JUST HOPE I MEET SOMEONE LIKE CAIN-SAMA...

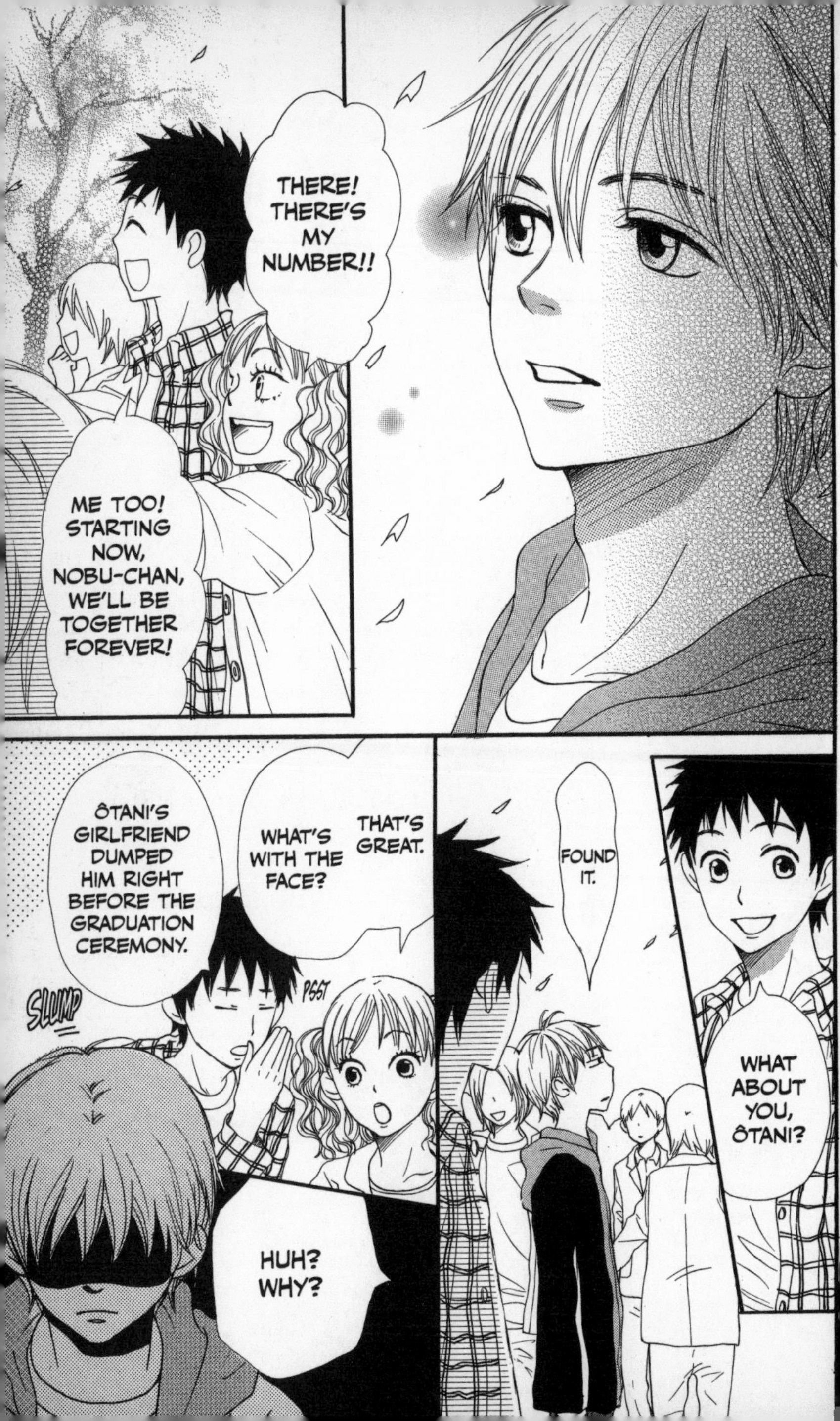
THERE! THERE'S MY NUMBER!!
ME TOO! STARTING NOW, NOBU-CHAN, WE'LL BE TOGETHER FOREVER!
FOUND IT.
WHAT ABOUT YOU, ŌTANI?
THAT'S GREAT.
WHAT'S WITH THE FACE?
ŌTANI'S GIRLFRIEND DUMPED HIM RIGHT BEFORE THE GRADUATION CEREMONY.
PSST
SLUMP
HUH? WHY?

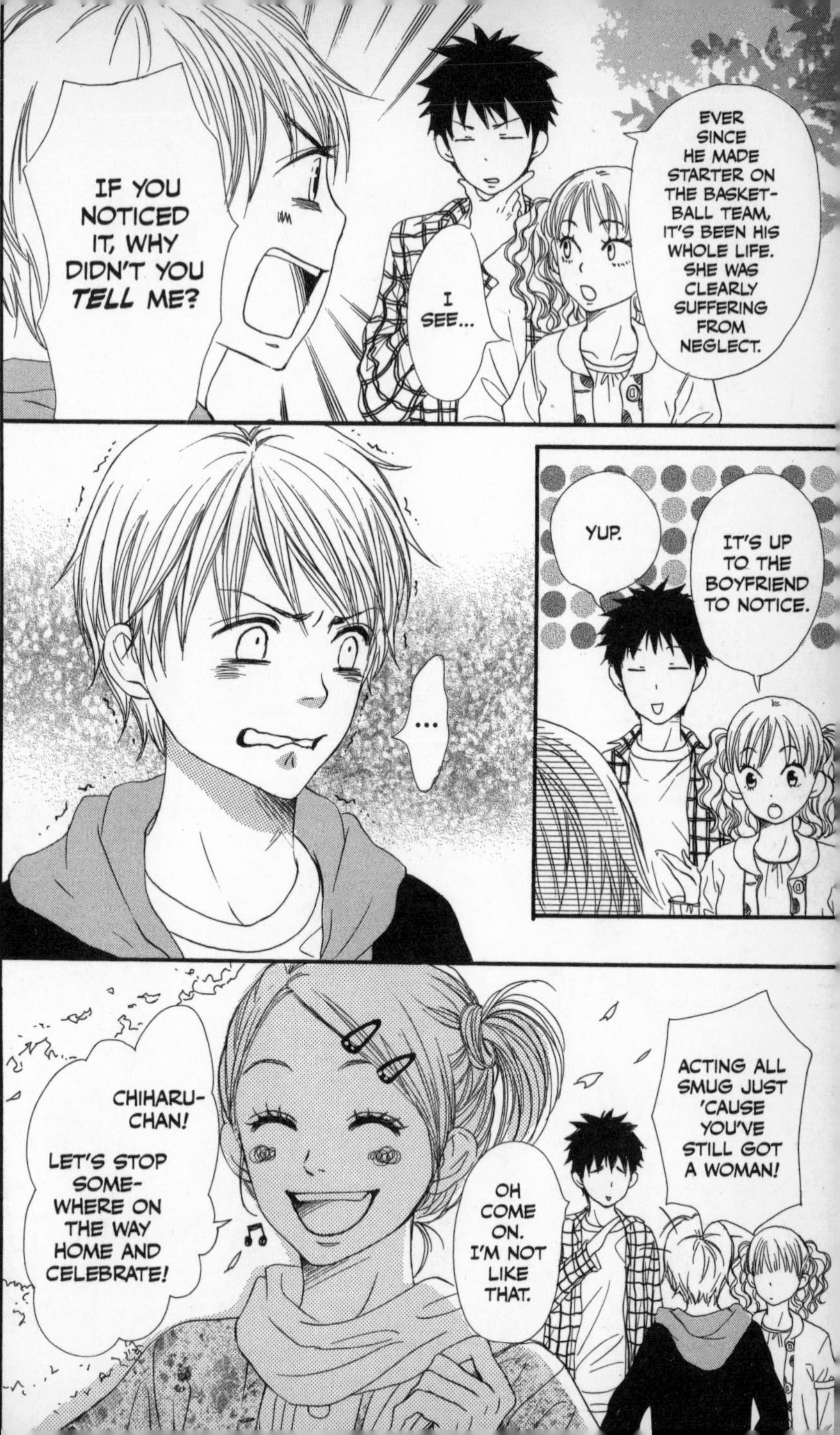
EVER SINCE HE MADE STARTER ON THE BASKET-BALL TEAM, IT'S BEEN HIS WHOLE LIFE. SHE WAS CLEARLY SUFFERING FROM NEGLECT.
I SEE...
IF YOU NOTICED IT, WHY DIDN'T YOU *TELL* ME?
IT'S UP TO THE BOYFRIEND TO NOTICE.
YUP.
...
ACTING ALL SMUG JUST 'CAUSE YOU'VE STILL GOT A WOMAN!
OH COME ON. I'M NOT LIKE THAT.
CHIHARU-CHAN!
LET'S STOP SOME-WHERE ON THE WAY HOME AND CELEBRATE!

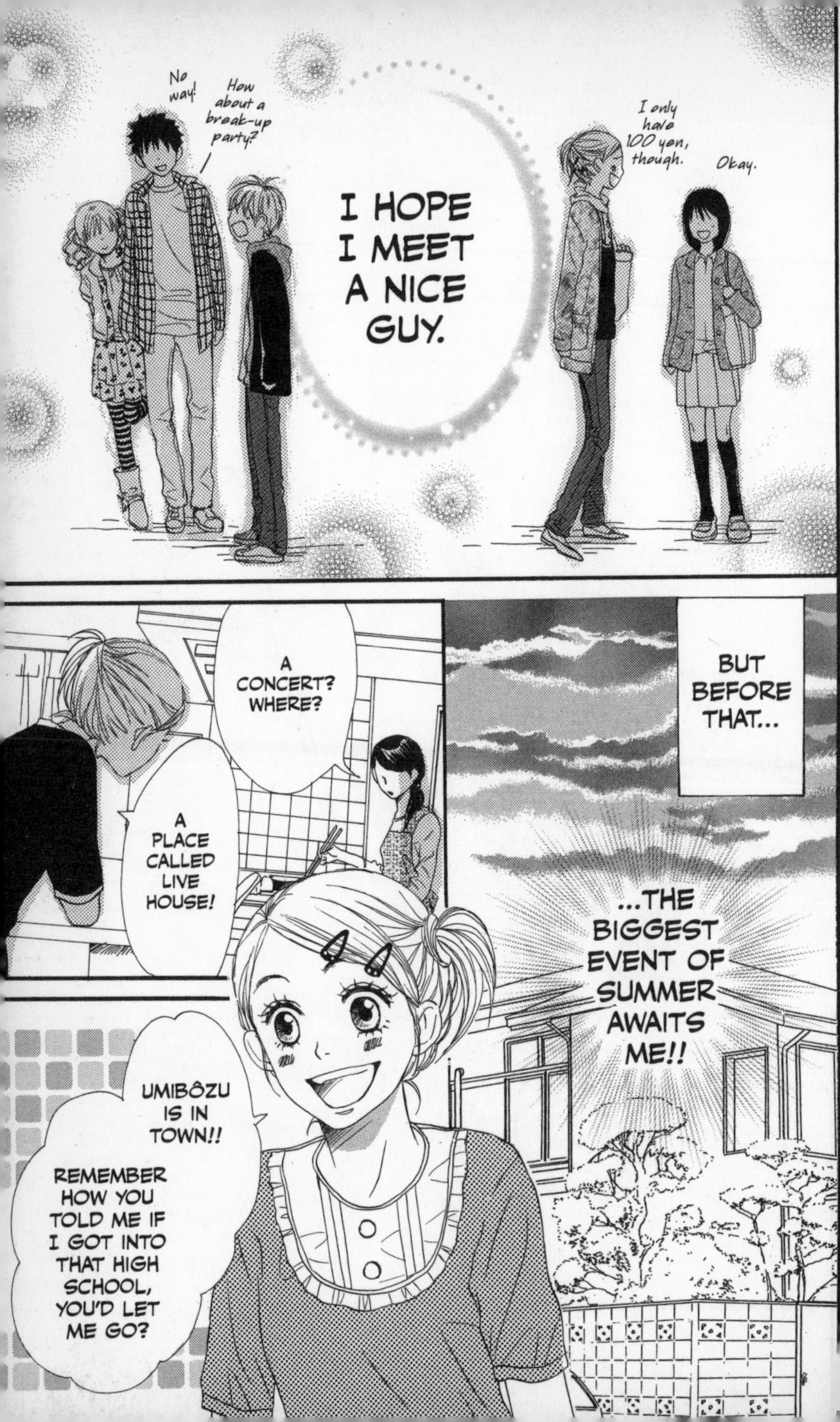
Okay.
I only have 100 yen, though.
I HOPE I MEET A NICE GUY.
How about a break-up party?
No way!
BUT BEFORE THAT...
...THE BIGGEST EVENT OF SUMMER AWAITS ME!!
A CONCERT? WHERE?
A PLACE CALLED LIVE HOUSE!
UMIBÔZU IS IN TOWN!!
REMEMBER HOW YOU TOLD ME IF I GOT INTO THAT HIGH SCHOOL, YOU'D LET ME GO?

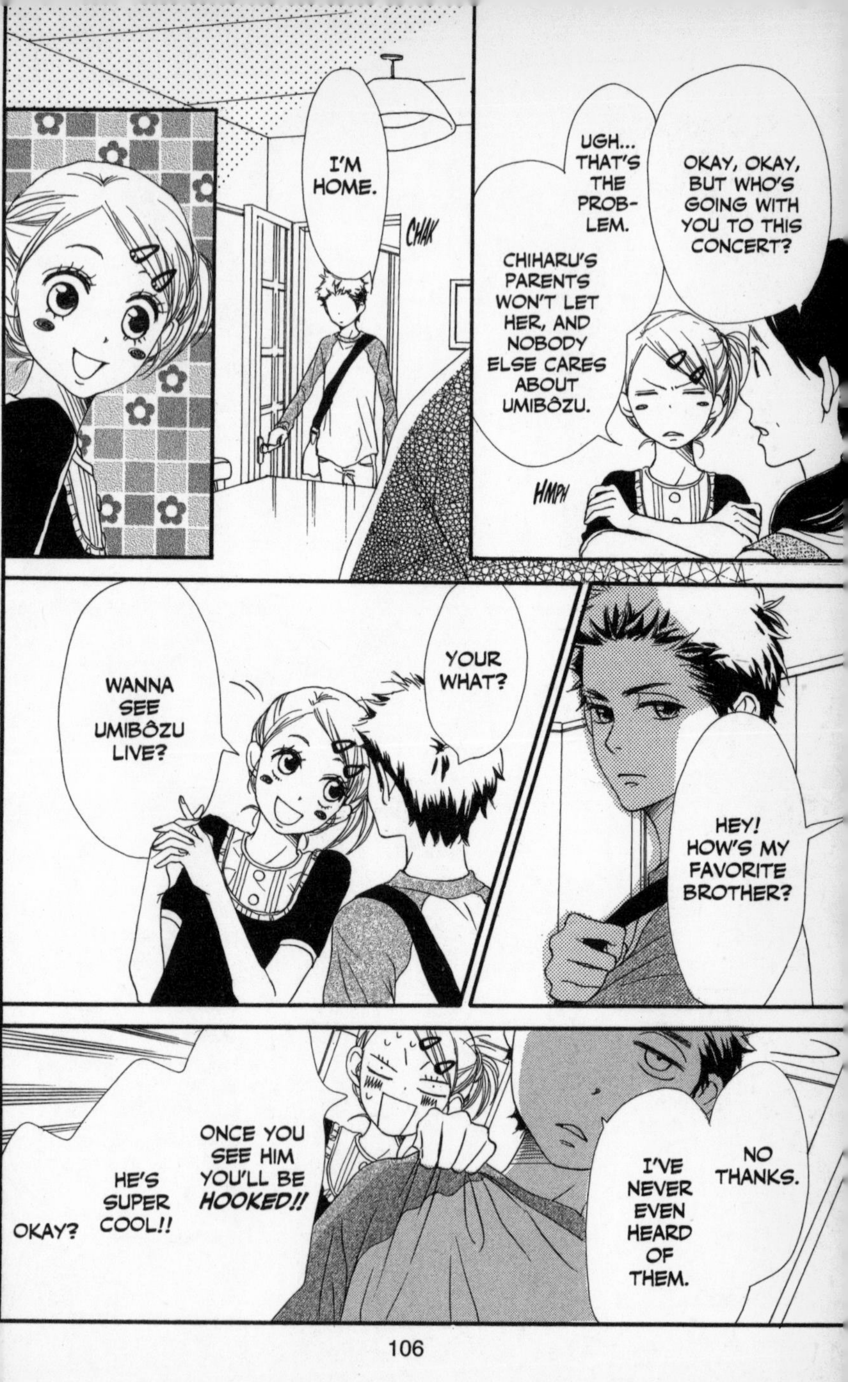
OKAY, OKAY, BUT WHO'S GOING WITH YOU TO THIS CONCERT?
UGH... THAT'S THE PROB-LEM.
CHIHARU'S PARENTS WON'T LET HER, AND NOBODY ELSE CARES ABOUT UMIBÔZU.
HMPH
I'M HOME.
CHAK
HEY! HOW'S MY FAVORITE BROTHER?
YOUR WHAT?
WANNA SEE UMIBÔZU LIVE?
NO THANKS.
I'VE NEVER EVEN HEARD OF THEM.
ONCE YOU SEE HIM YOU'LL BE HOOKED!!
HE'S SUPER COOL!!
OKAY?

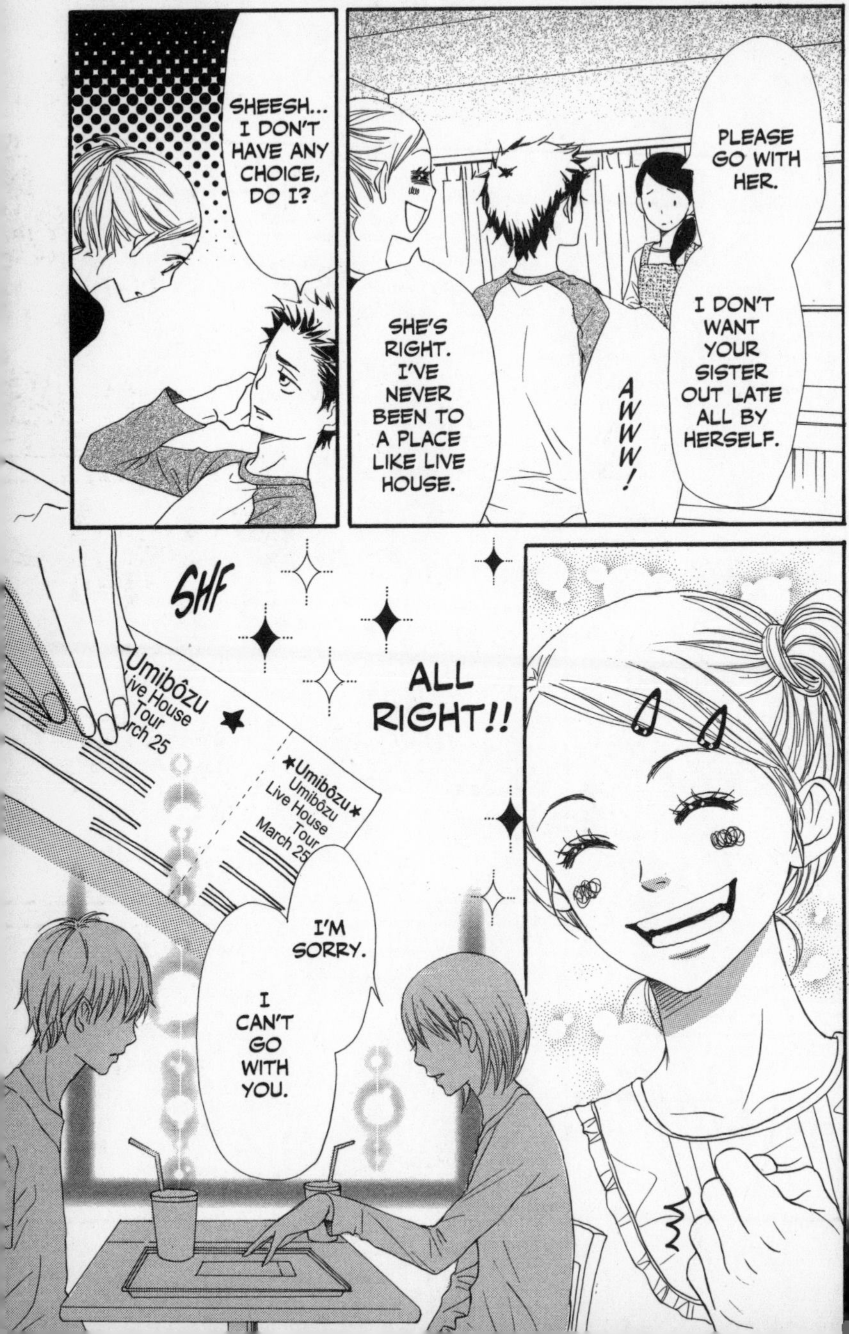
PLEASE GO WITH HER.
I DON'T WANT YOUR SISTER OUT LATE ALL BY HERSELF.
AWWW!
SHE'S RIGHT. I'VE NEVER BEEN TO A PLACE LIKE LIVE HOUSE.
SHEESH... I DON'T HAVE ANY CHOICE, DO I?
ALL RIGHT!!
SHF
★Umibôzu★
Umibôzu
Live House
Tour
March 25
I'M SORRY.
I CAN'T GO WITH YOU.

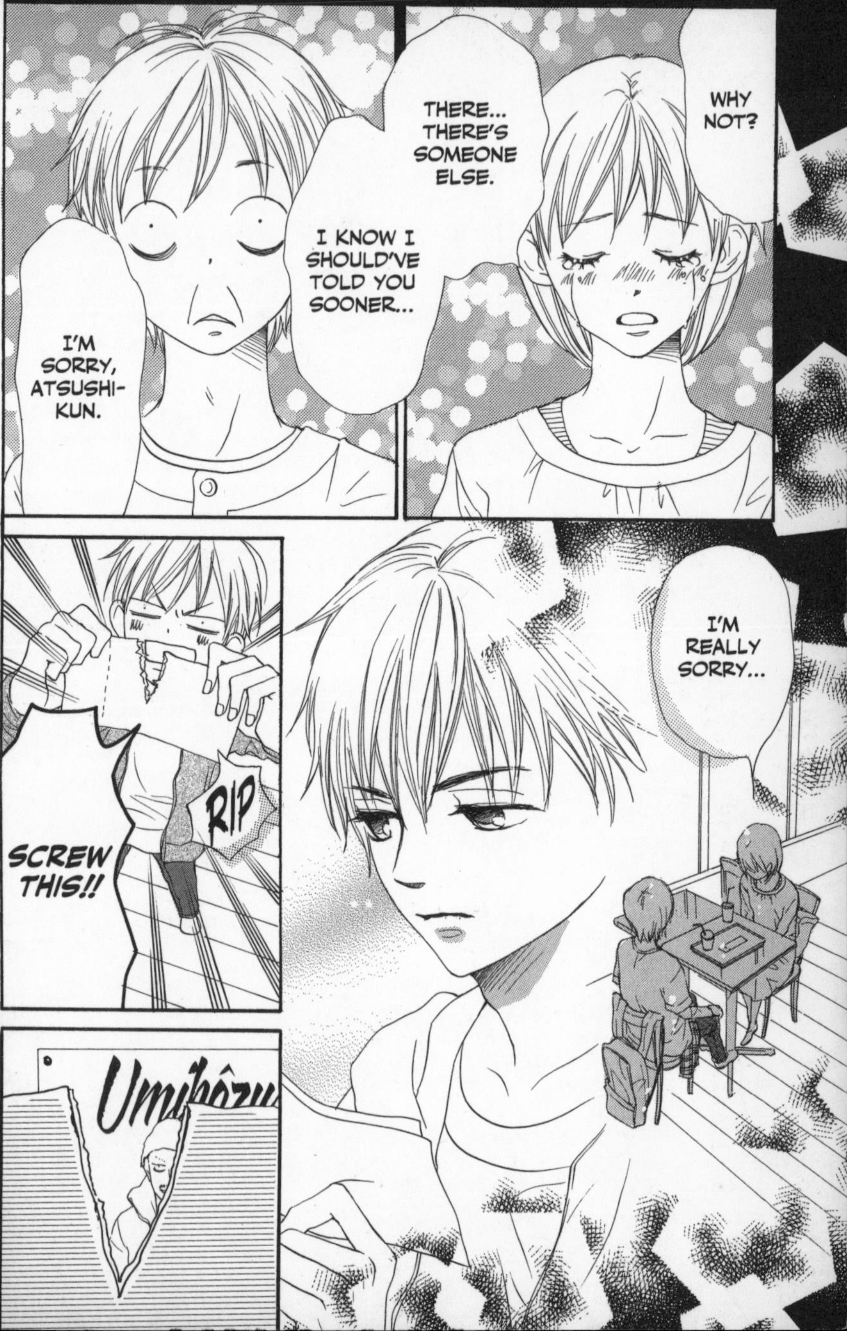
WHY NOT?
THERE... THERE'S SOMEONE ELSE.
I KNOW I SHOULD'VE TOLD YOU SOONER...
I'M SORRY, ATSUSHI-KUN.
I'M REALLY SORRY...
RIP
SCREW THIS!!
Umibôzu

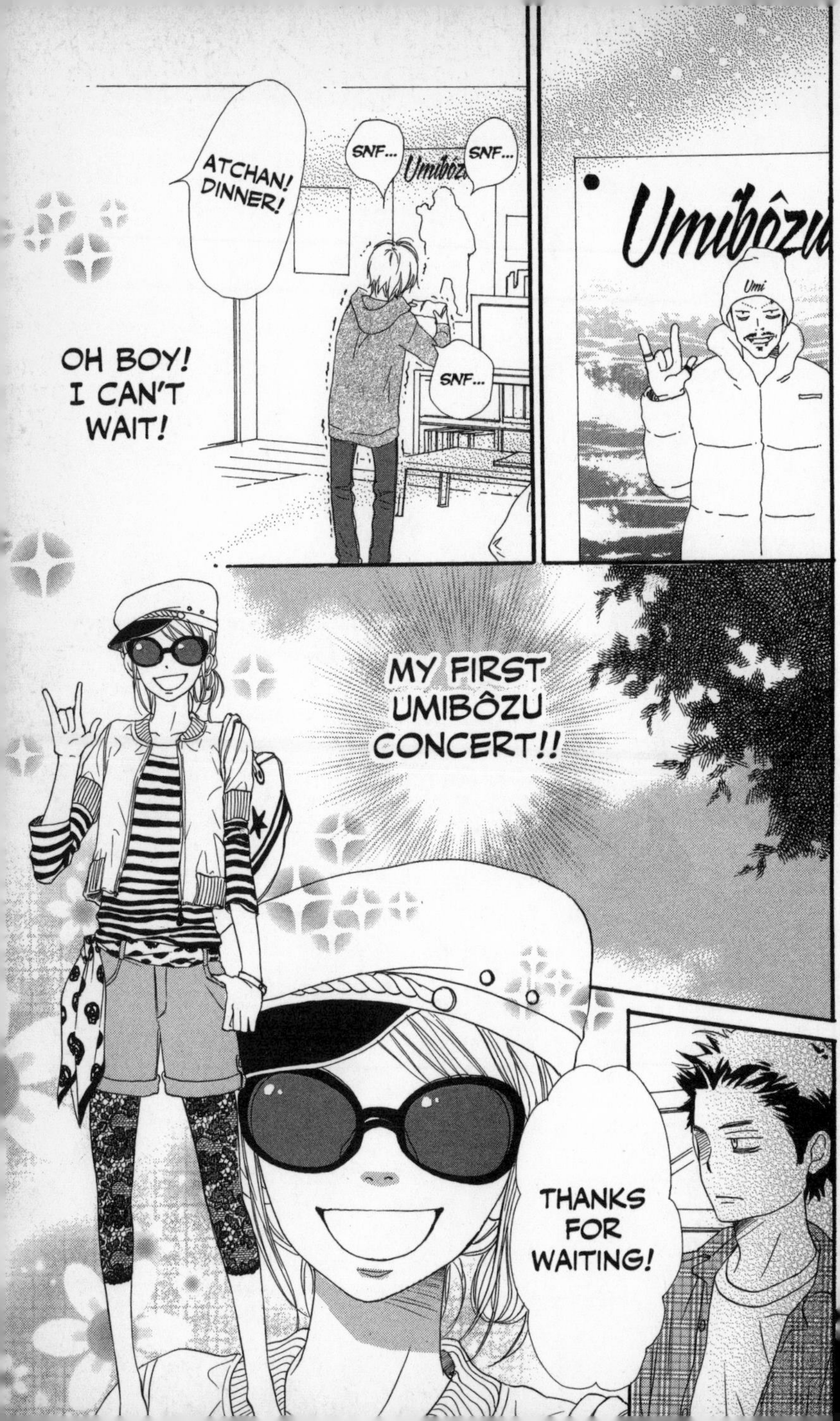
Umibôzu
Umi
SNF...
SNF...
ATCHAN! DINNER!
SNF...
OH BOY! I CAN'T WAIT!
MY FIRST UMIBÔZU CONCERT!!
THANKS FOR WAITING!

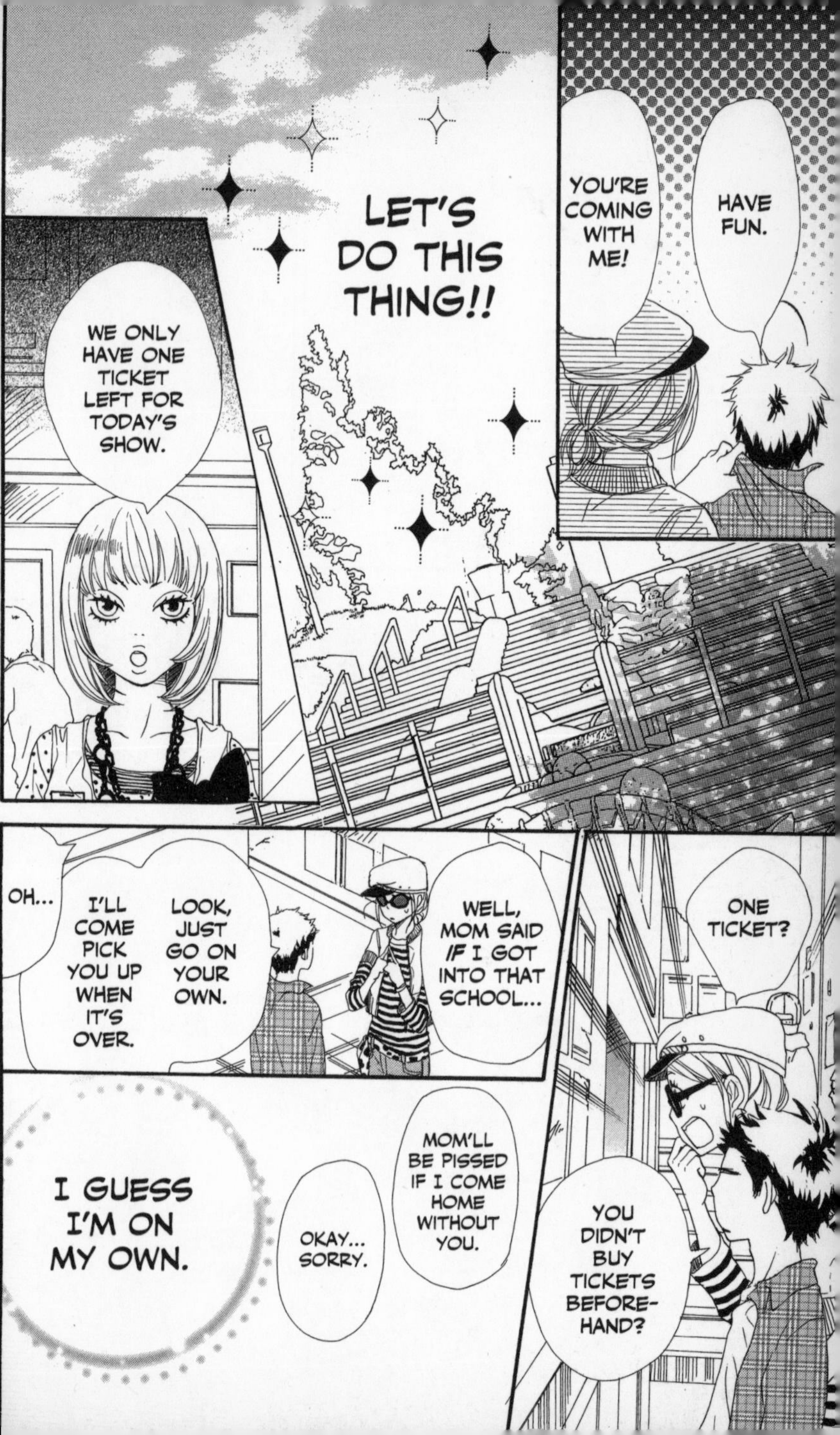
HAVE FUN.
YOU'RE COMING WITH ME!
LET'S DO THIS THING!!
WE ONLY HAVE ONE TICKET LEFT FOR TODAY'S SHOW.
ONE TICKET?
WELL, MOM SAID *IF* I GOT INTO THAT SCHOOL...
LOOK, JUST GO ON YOUR OWN.
I'LL COME PICK YOU UP WHEN IT'S OVER.
OH...
YOU DIDN'T BUY TICKETS BEFORE-HAND?
MOM'LL BE PISSED IF I COME HOME WITHOUT YOU.
OKAY... SORRY.
I GUESS I'M ON MY OWN.

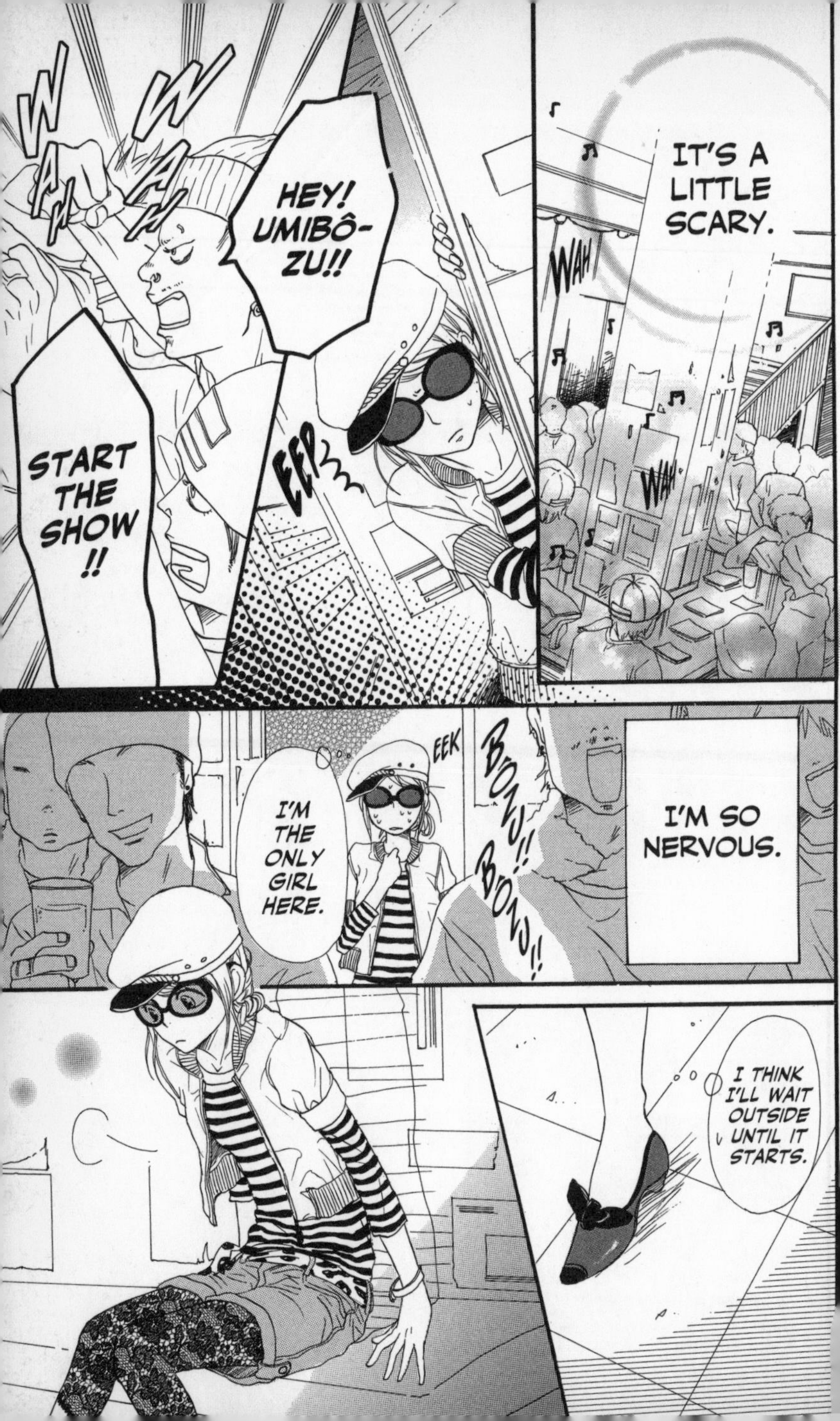
IT'S A LITTLE SCARY.
WAH
WAH
HEY! UMIBÔ-ZU!!
WAH
WAH
EEP
START THE SHOW!!
I'M SO NERVOUS.
BONG!!
BONG!!
EEK
I'M THE ONLY GIRL HERE.
I THINK I'LL WAIT OUTSIDE UNTIL IT STARTS.

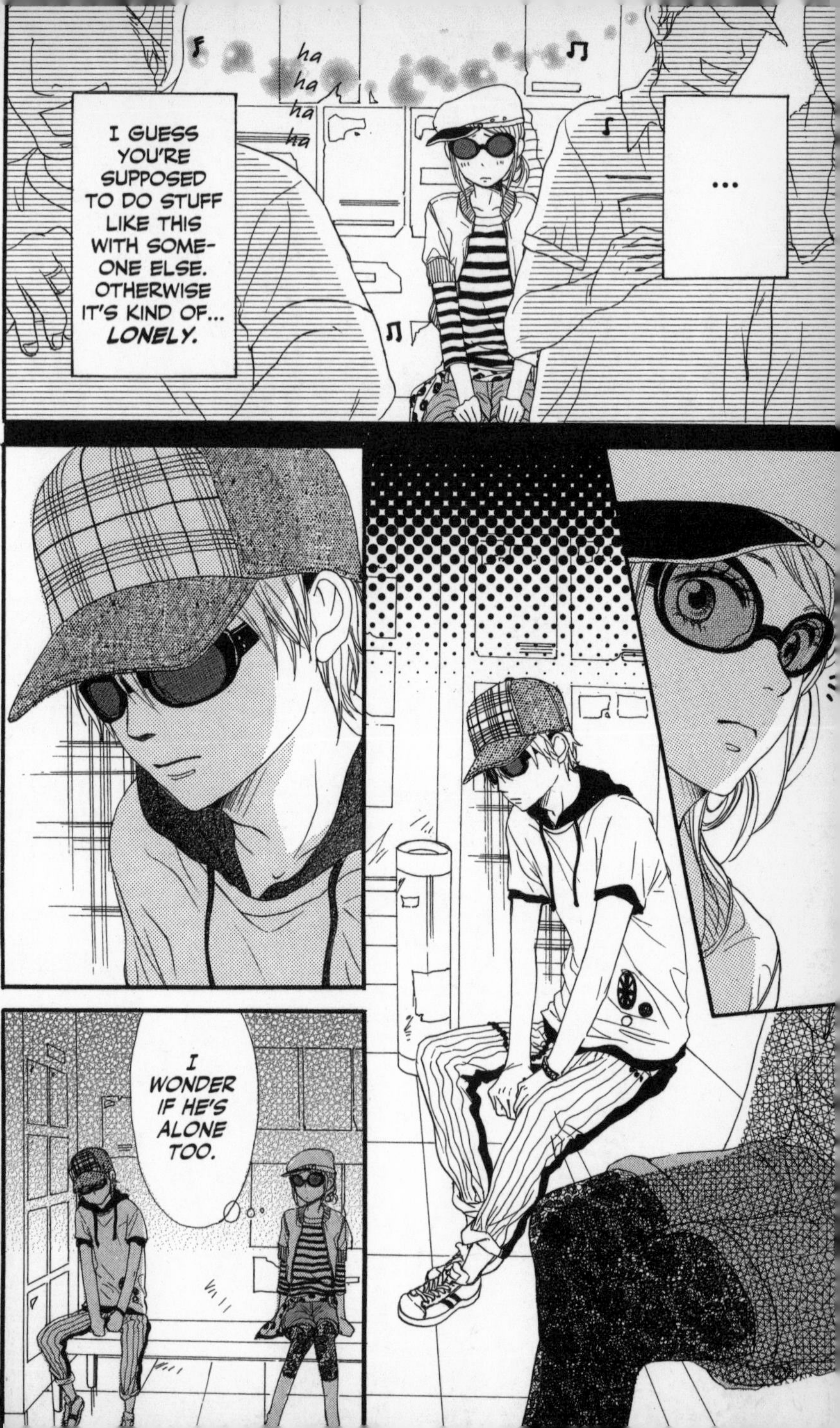
...
I GUESS YOU'RE SUPPOSED TO DO STUFF LIKE THIS WITH SOME-ONE ELSE. OTHERWISE IT'S KIND OF... ***LONELY.***
ha ha ha ha
I WONDER IF HE'S ALONE TOO.

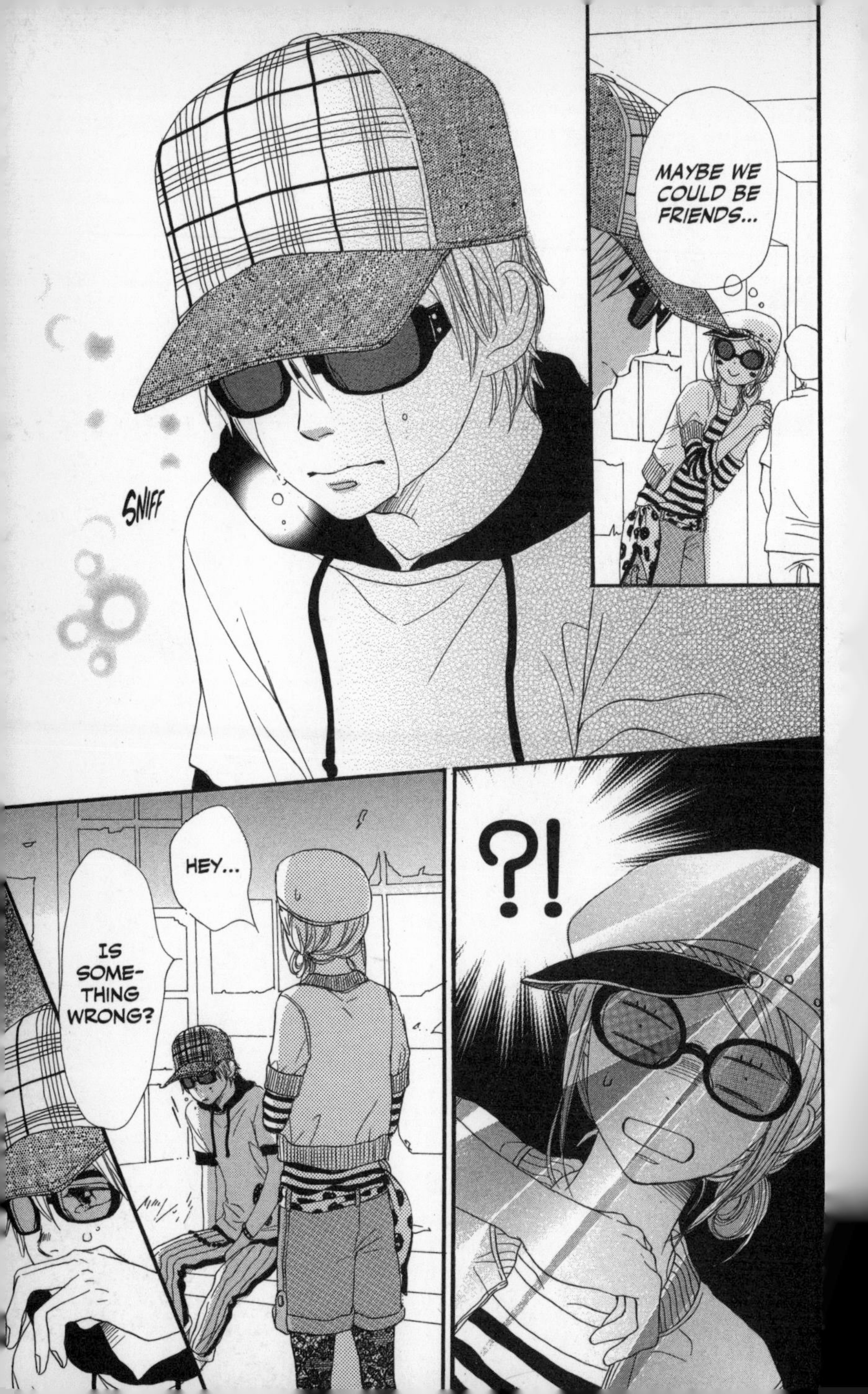
MAYBE WE COULD BE FRIENDS...
SNIFF
?!
HEY...
IS SOME-THING WRONG?

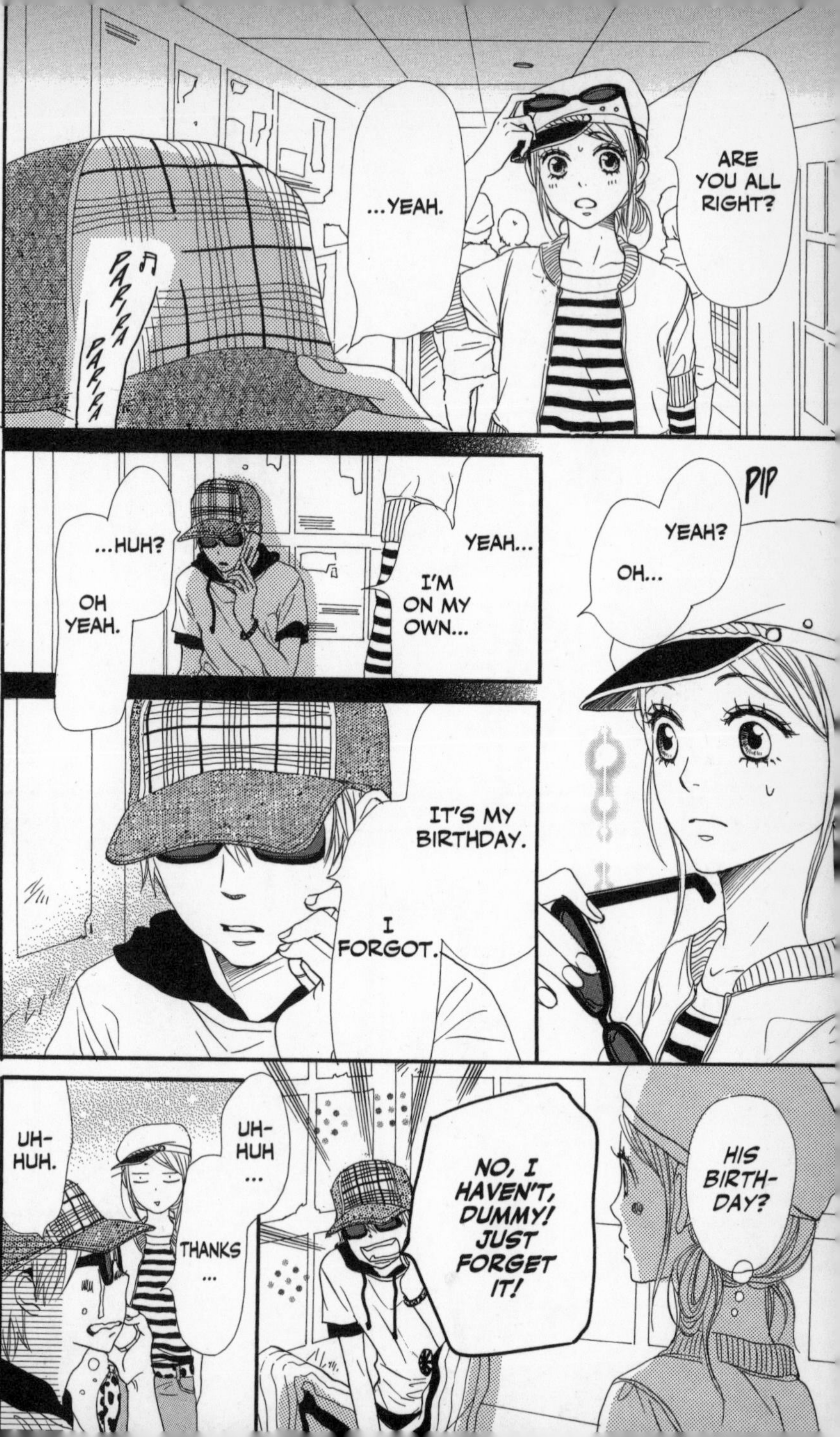
ARE YOU ALL RIGHT?
...YEAH.
PARIRA PARIRA
PIP
YEAH?
OH...
YEAH... I'M ON MY OWN...
...HUH?
OH YEAH.
IT'S MY BIRTHDAY.
I FORGOT.
HIS BIRTH-DAY?
NO, I HAVEN'T, DUMMY! JUST FORGET IT!
UH-HUH...
THANKS...
UH-HUH.

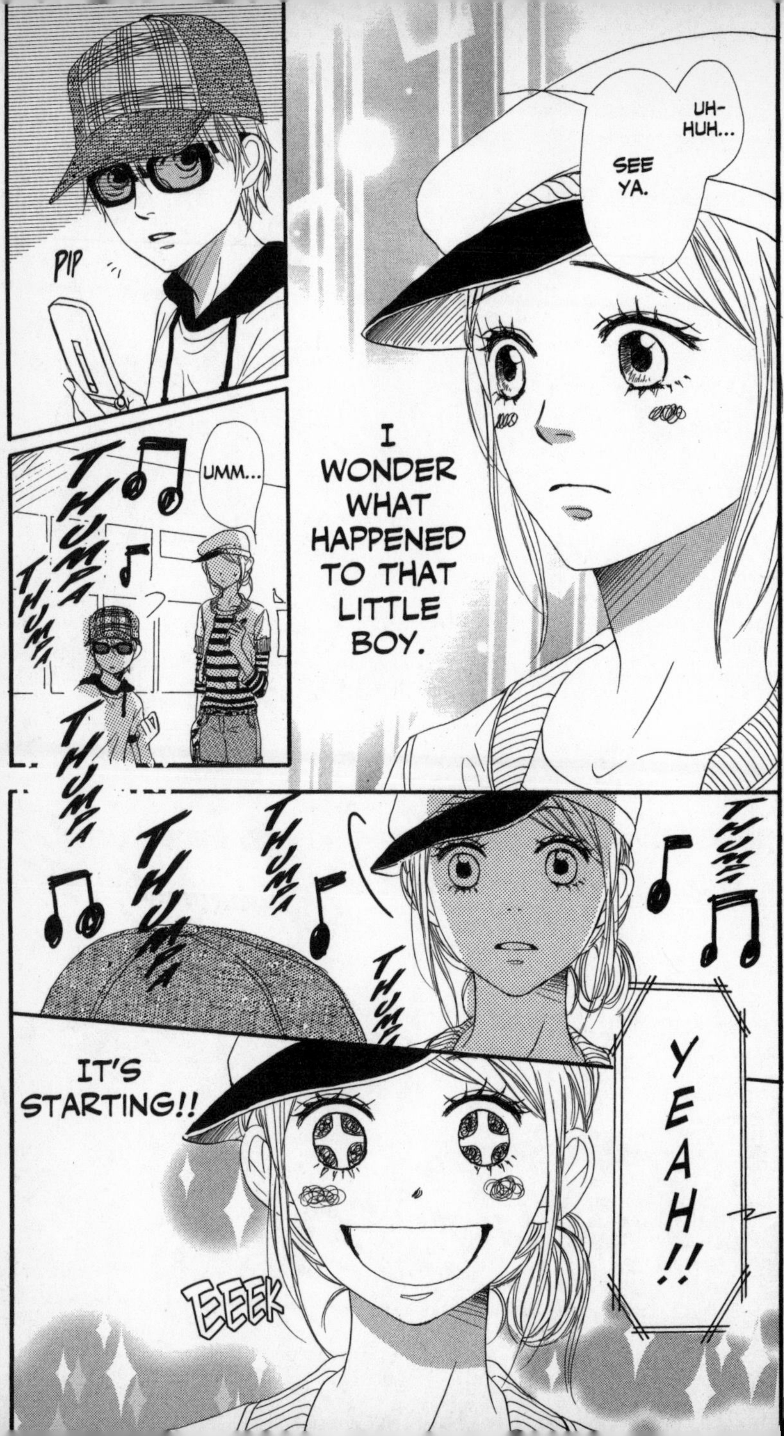
UH-HUH...
SEE YA.
I WONDER WHAT HAPPENED TO THAT LITTLE BOY.
PIP
UMM...
THUMPA
THUMPA
THUMPA
THUMPA
THUMPA
THUMPA
THUMPA
YEAH!!
IT'S STARTING!!
EEEK

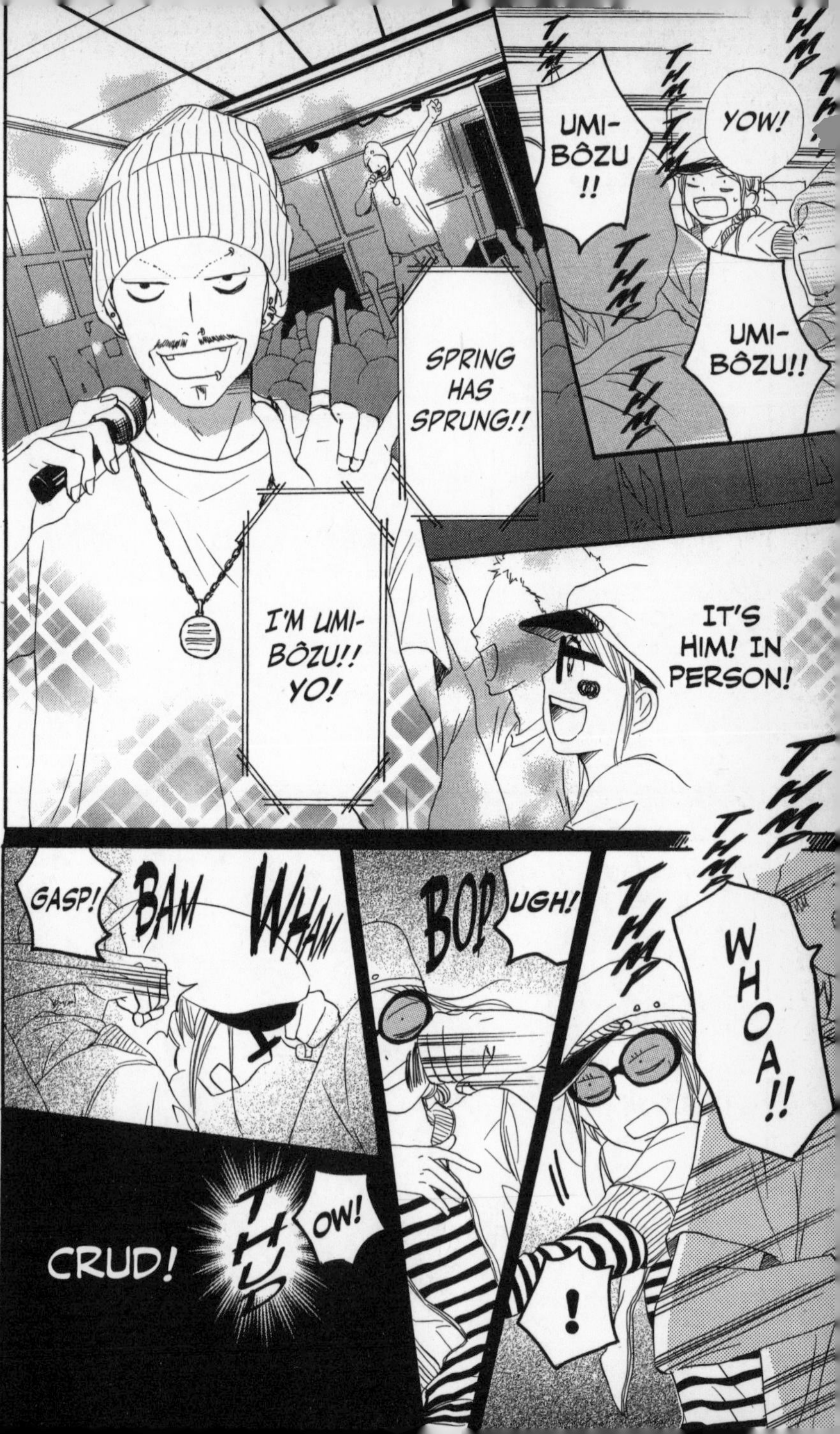
THMP
THMP
YOW!
UMI-BÔZU!!
THMP
THMP
UMI-BÔZU!!
IT'S HIM! IN PERSON!
SPRING HAS SPRUNG!!
I'M UMI-BÔZU!! YO!
THMP
THMP
THMP
WHOA!!
!
UGH!
BOP
WHAM
BAM
GASP!
OW!
THUD
CRUD!

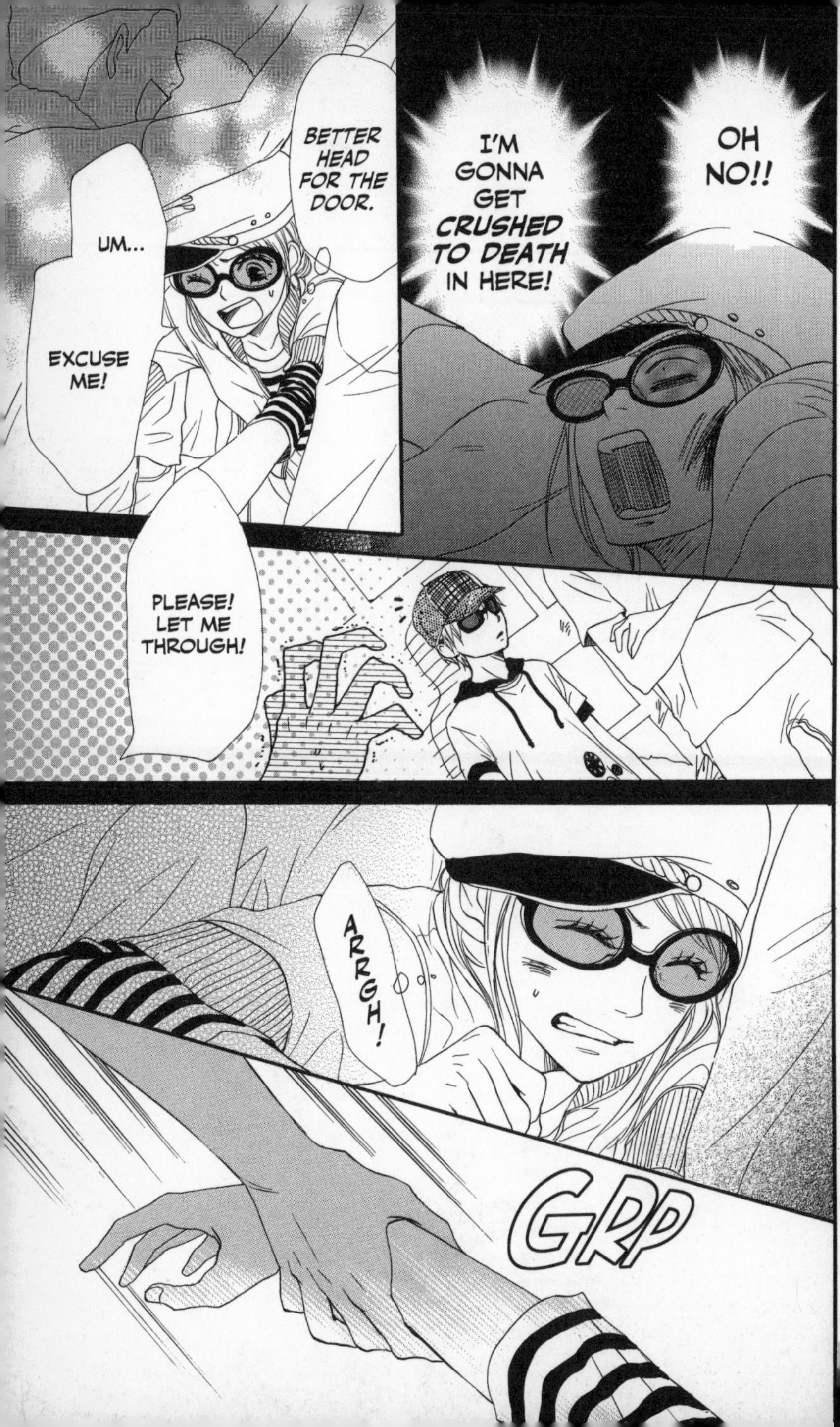
OH NO!!
I'M GONNA GET CRUSHED TO DEATH IN HERE!
BETTER HEAD FOR THE DOOR.
UM...
EXCUSE ME!
PLEASE! LET ME THROUGH!
ARRGH!
GRP

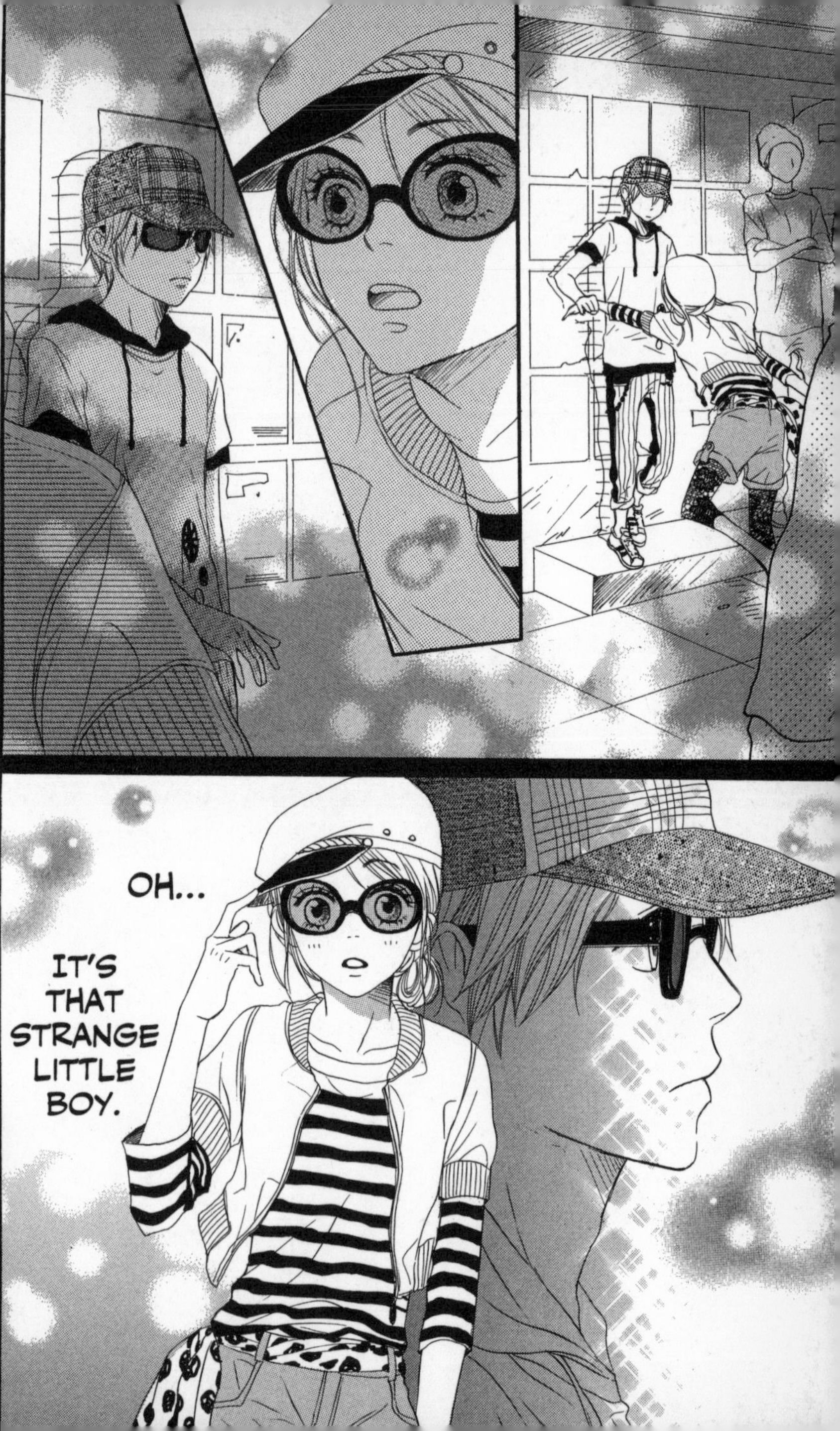
OH...
IT'S THAT STRANGE LITTLE BOY.

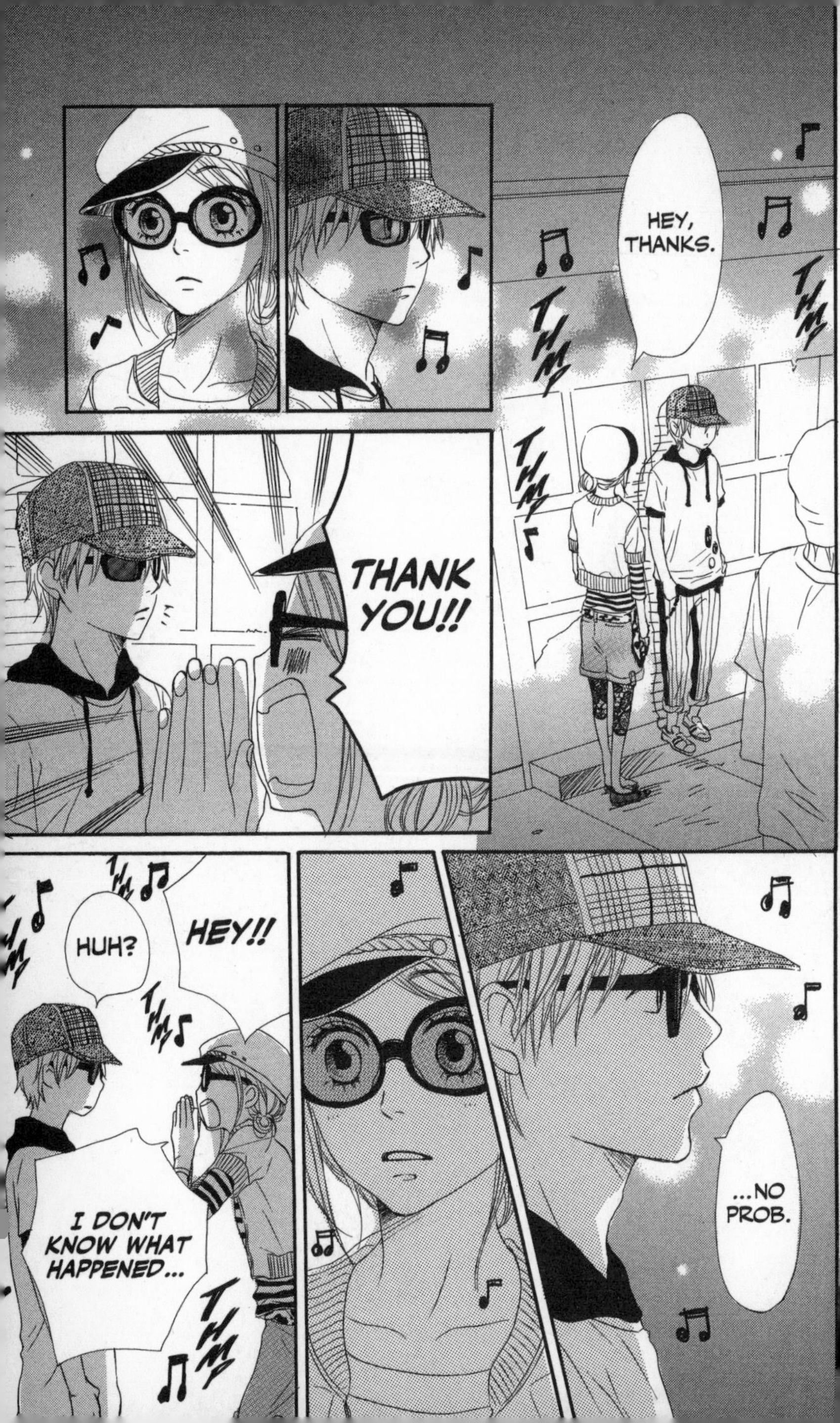
HEY, THANKS.
THMP
THMP
THMP
THANK YOU!!
...NO PROB.
THMP
HUH?
HEY!!
THMP
I DON'T KNOW WHAT HAPPENED...
THMP

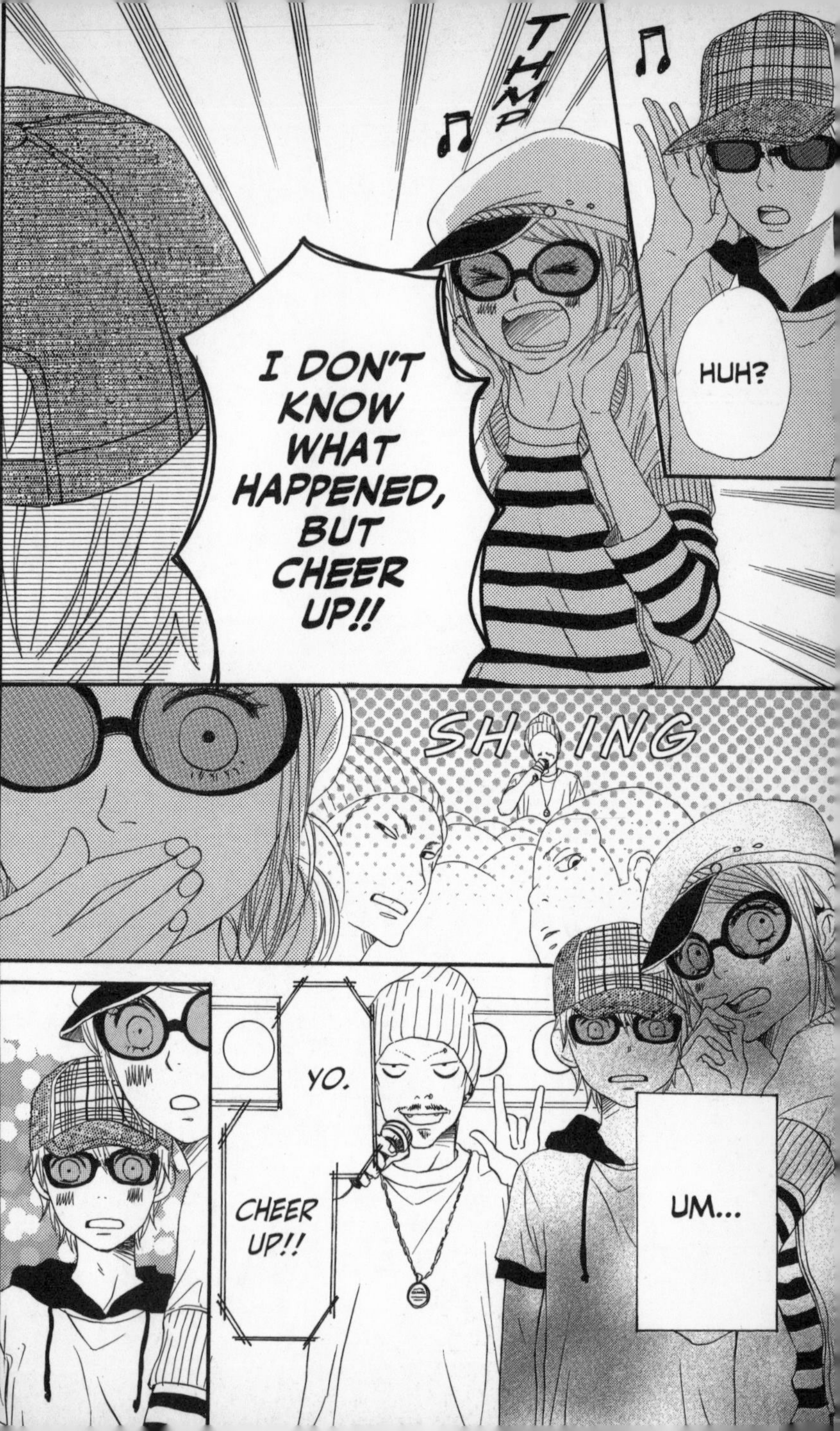
HUH?
THMP
I DON'T KNOW WHAT HAPPENED, BUT CHEER UP!!
SH ING
UM...
YO.
CHEER UP!!

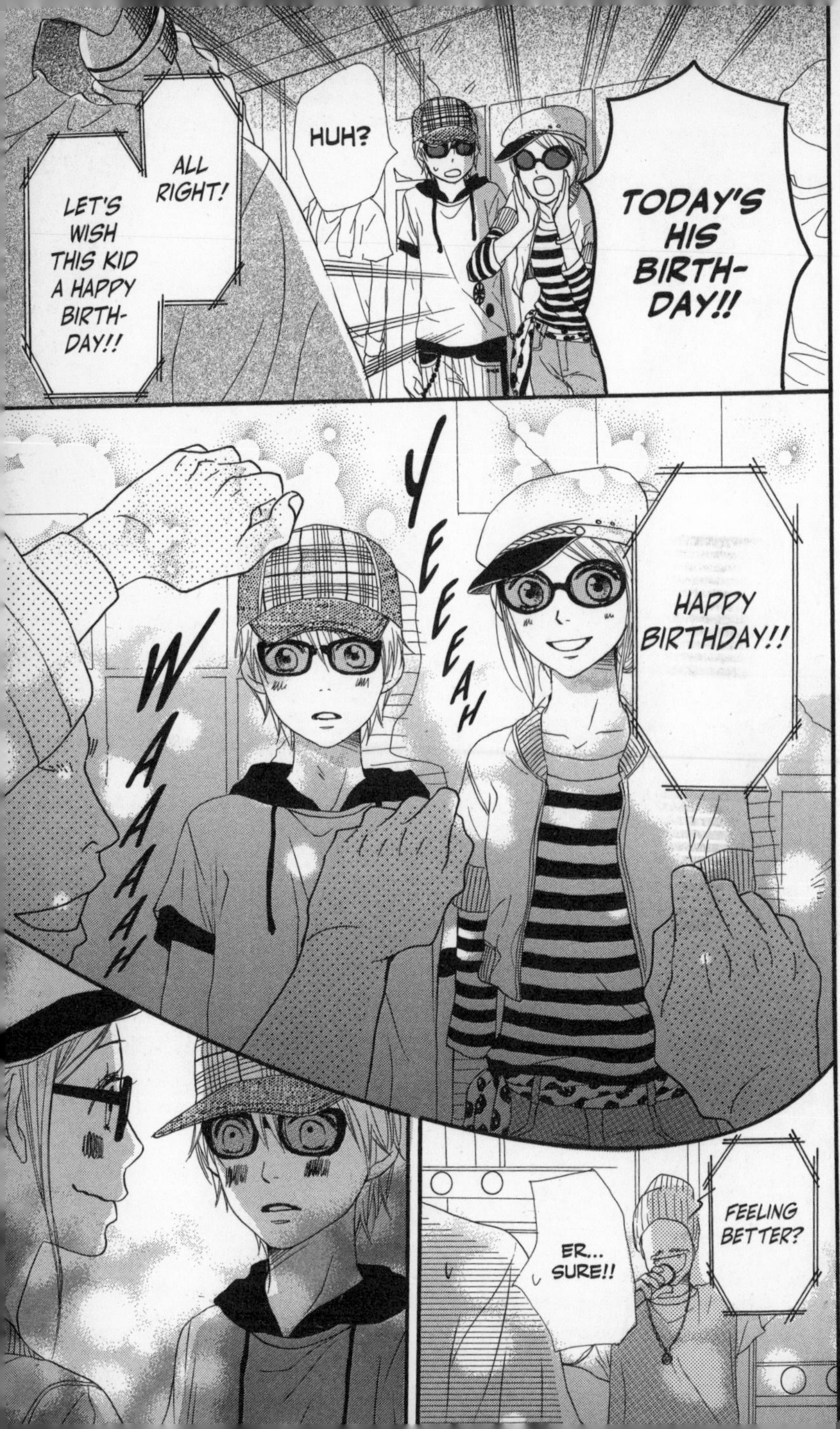
TODAY'S HIS BIRTH-DAY!!
HUH?
ALL RIGHT!
LET'S WISH THIS KID A HAPPY BIRTH-DAY!!
HAPPY BIRTHDAY!!
YEEEEAH
WAAAAAAAH
FEELING BETTER?
ER... SURE!!

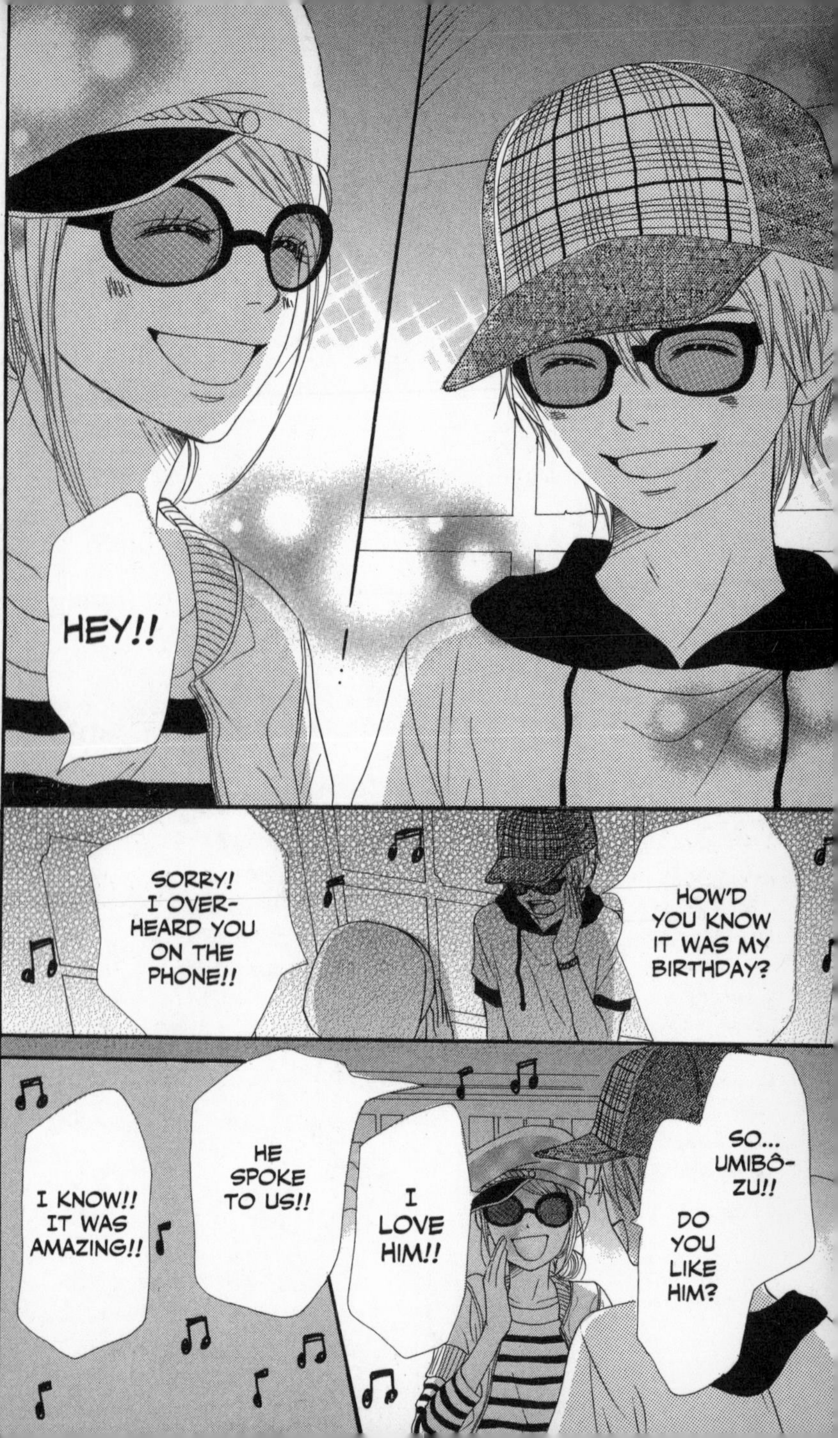
HEY!!
HOW'D YOU KNOW IT WAS MY BIRTHDAY?
SORRY! I OVER-HEARD YOU ON THE PHONE!!
SO... UMIBÔ-ZU!! DO YOU LIKE HIM?
I LOVE HIM!!
HE SPOKE TO US!!
I KNOW!! IT WAS AMAZING!!

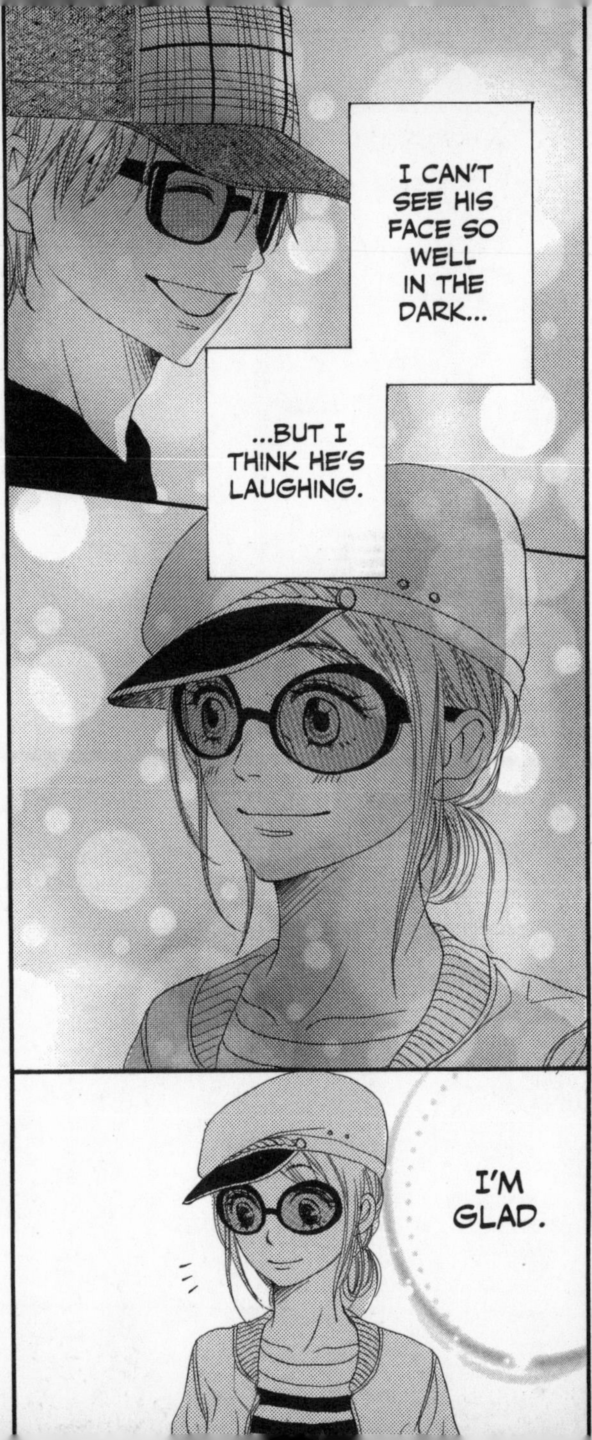
I CAN'T SEE HIS FACE SO WELL IN THE DARK...
...BUT I THINK HE'S LAUGHING.
I'M GLAD.

So much came out of Love♣Com. I felt the love from so many places. The anime, the live-action movie, the CD, the games and all the merchandise... I met so many people and have been truly blessed. This would not have been possible without the manga. And I've been forced to think about things I never thought about before, and I've been influenced in ways that have changed my life. Really, truly.

I'm a very lucky person. I never dreamed I'd walk a path like this. Nope. And I owe it all to you readers for encouraging and supporting me. I promise to take all the love that's been bestowed upon me and put it into doing my best as a manga artist.

heh heh

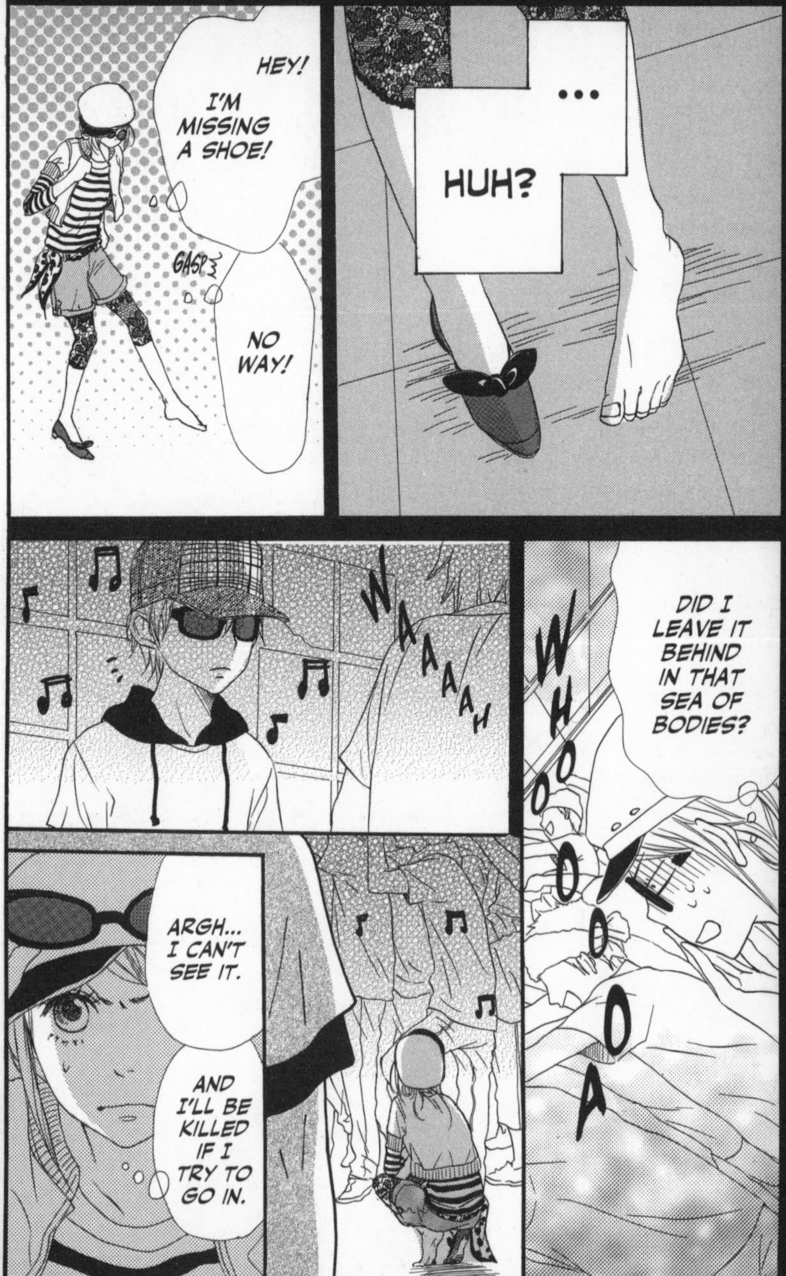
...
HUH?
HEY!
I'M MISSING A SHOE!
GASP
NO WAY!
WHOOOOOOA
DID I LEAVE IT BEHIND IN THAT SEA OF BODIES?
WAAAAAH
ARGH... I CAN'T SEE IT.
AND I'LL BE KILLED IF I TRY TO GO IN.

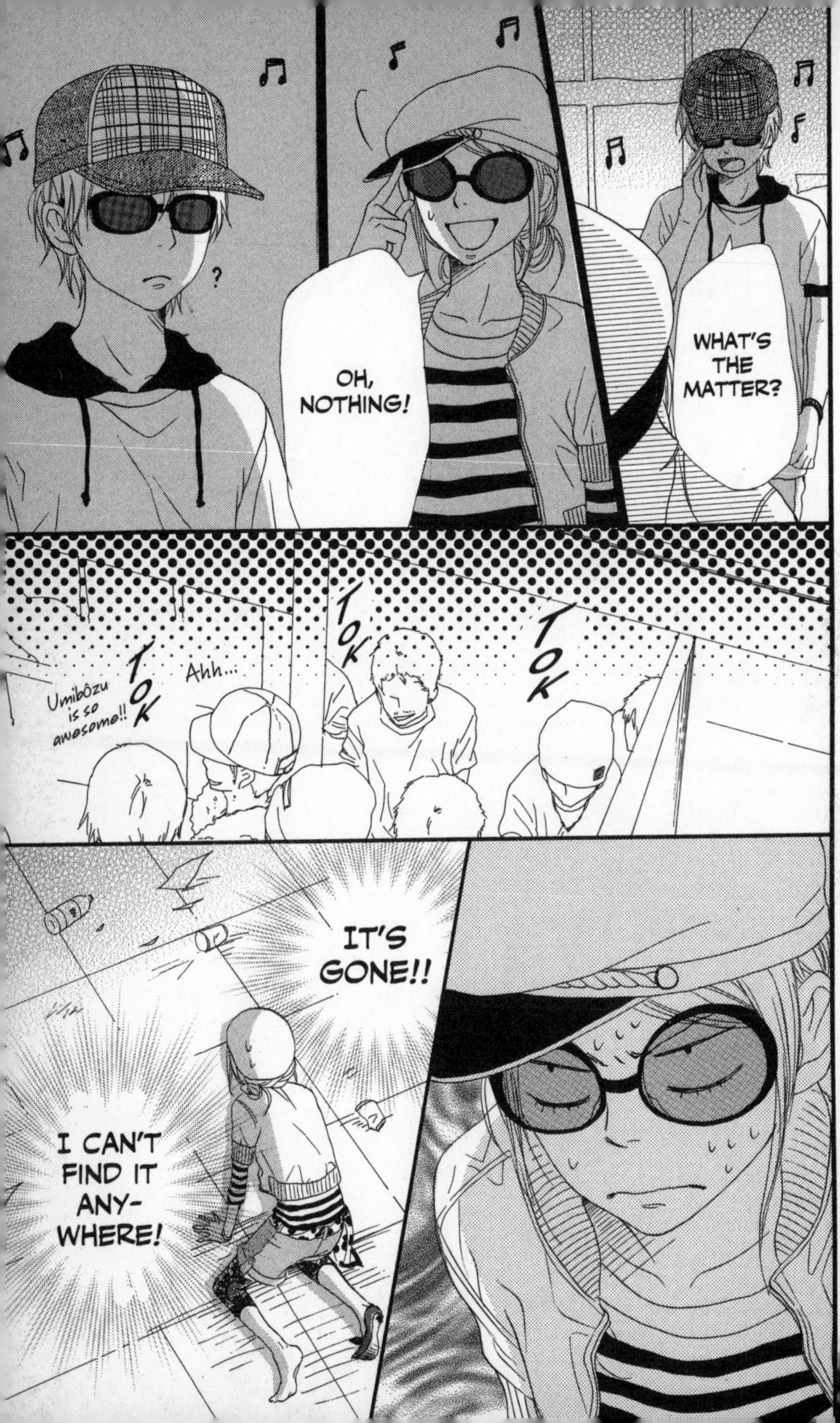
WHAT'S THE MATTER?
OH, NOTHING!
?
TOK
TOK
TOK
Ahh...
Umibôzu is so awesome!!
IT'S GONE!!
I CAN'T FIND IT ANY-WHERE!

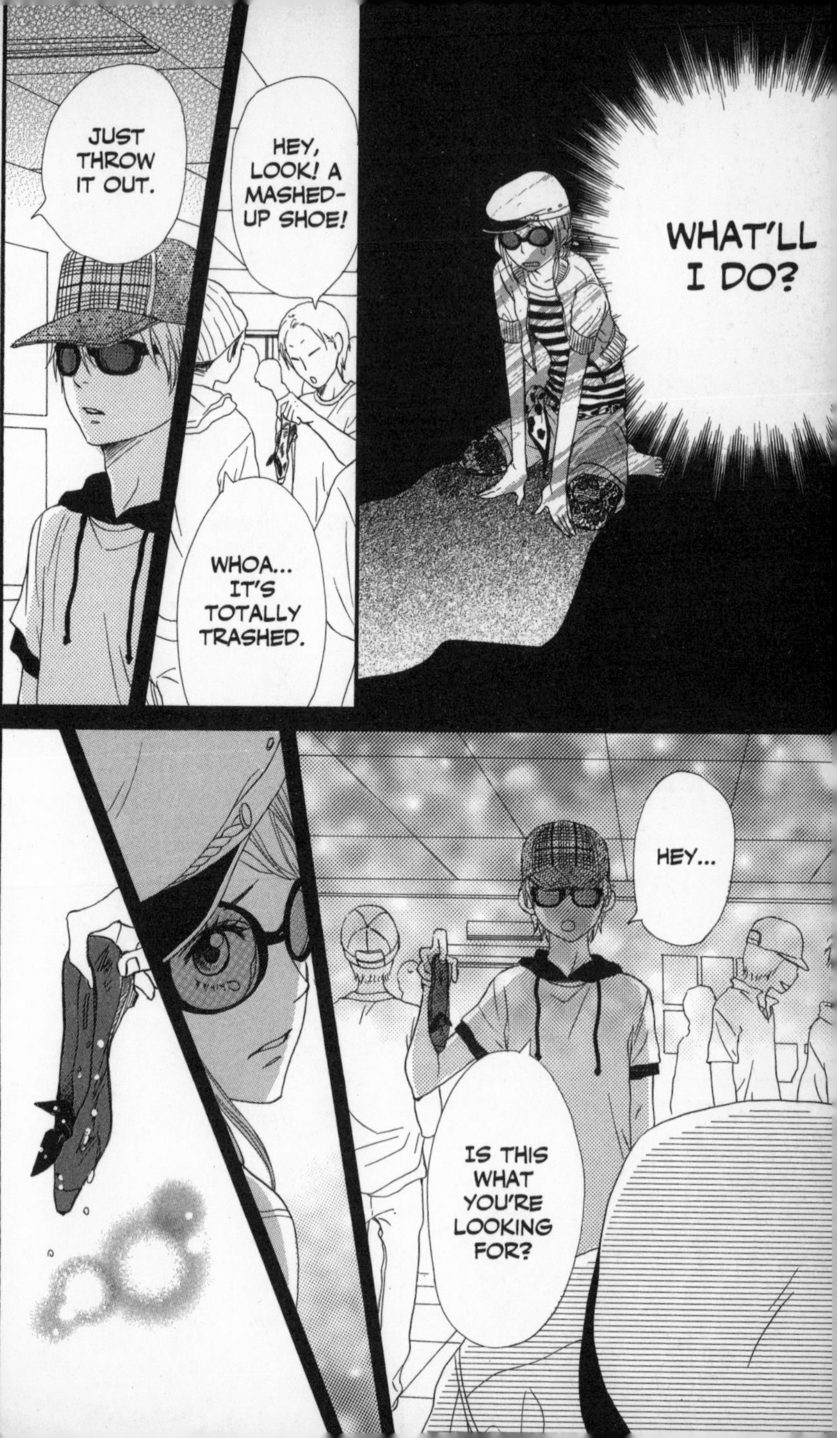
WHAT'LL I DO?
HEY, LOOK! A MASHED-UP SHOE!
WHOA... IT'S TOTALLY TRASHED.
JUST THROW IT OUT.
HEY...
IS THIS WHAT YOU'RE LOOKING FOR?

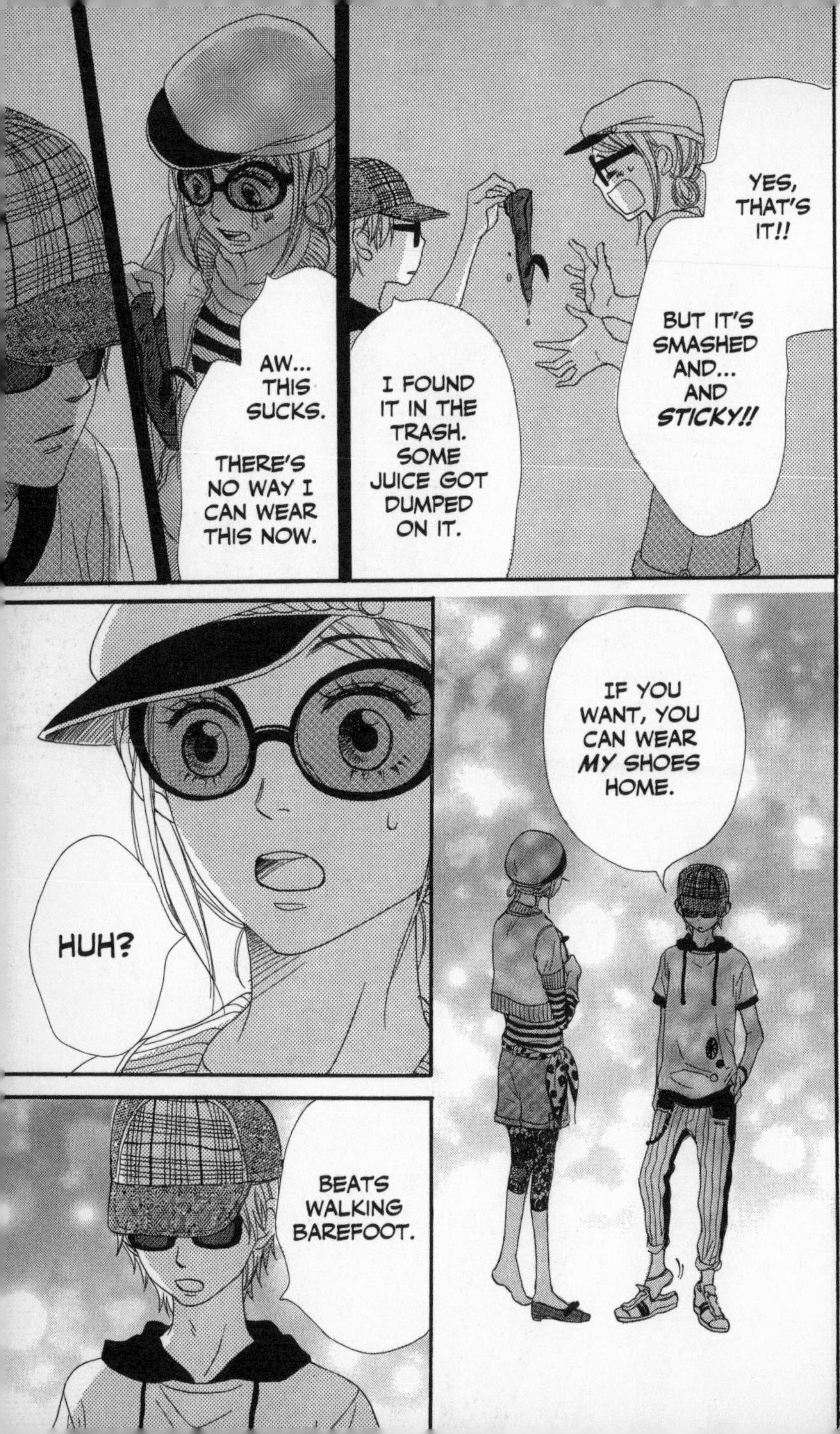

YES, THAT'S IT!!
BUT IT'S SMASHED AND... AND *STICKY!!*
I FOUND IT IN THE TRASH. SOME JUICE GOT DUMPED ON IT.
AW... THIS SUCKS.
THERE'S NO WAY I CAN WEAR THIS NOW.
IF YOU WANT, YOU CAN WEAR *MY* SHOES HOME.
HUH?
BEATS WALKING BAREFOOT.

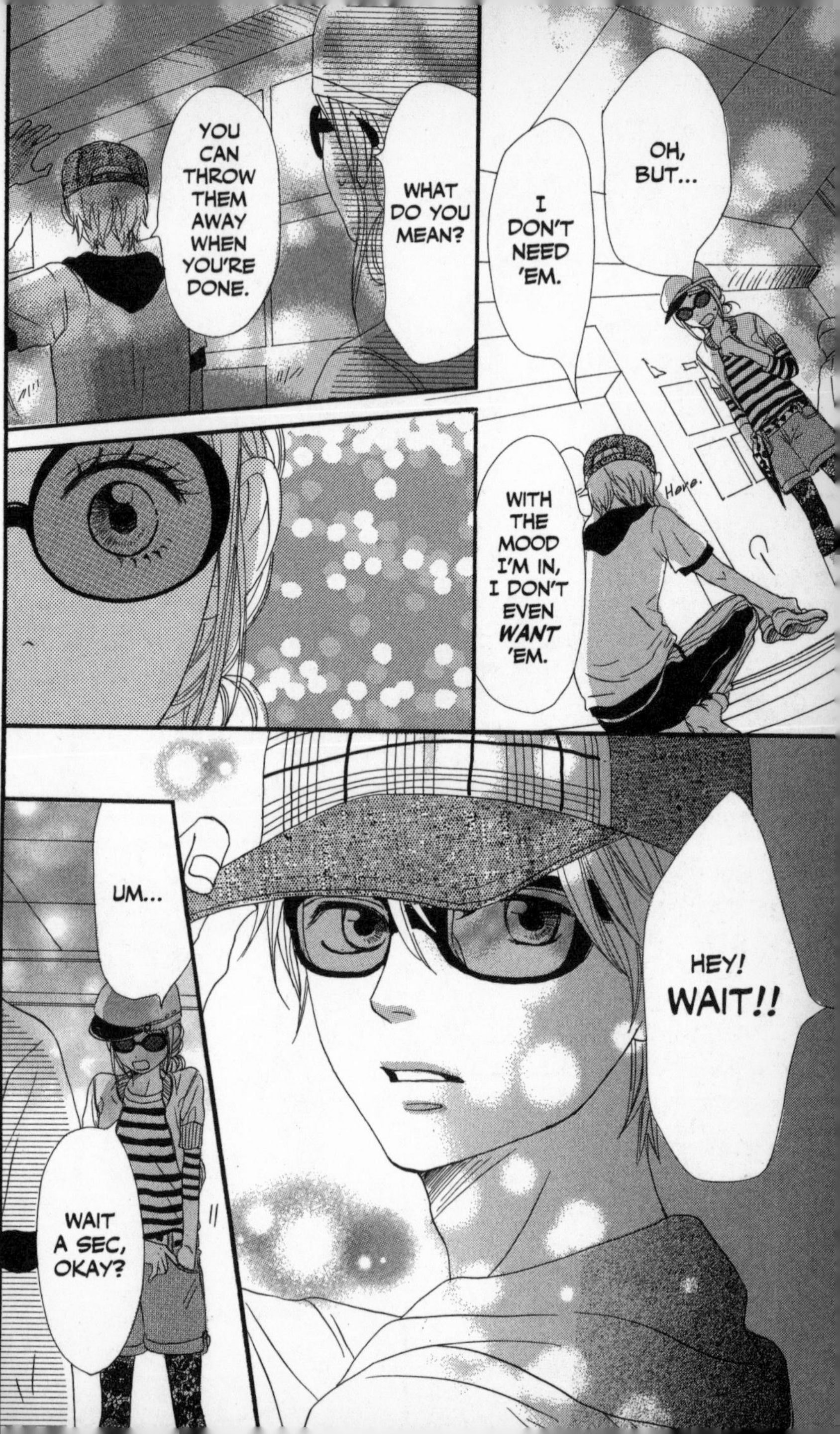
OH, BUT...
I DON'T NEED 'EM.
WITH THE MOOD I'M IN, I DON'T EVEN *WANT* 'EM.
Here.
WHAT DO YOU MEAN?
YOU CAN THROW THEM AWAY WHEN YOU'RE DONE.
HEY! WAIT!!
UM...
WAIT A SEC, OKAY?

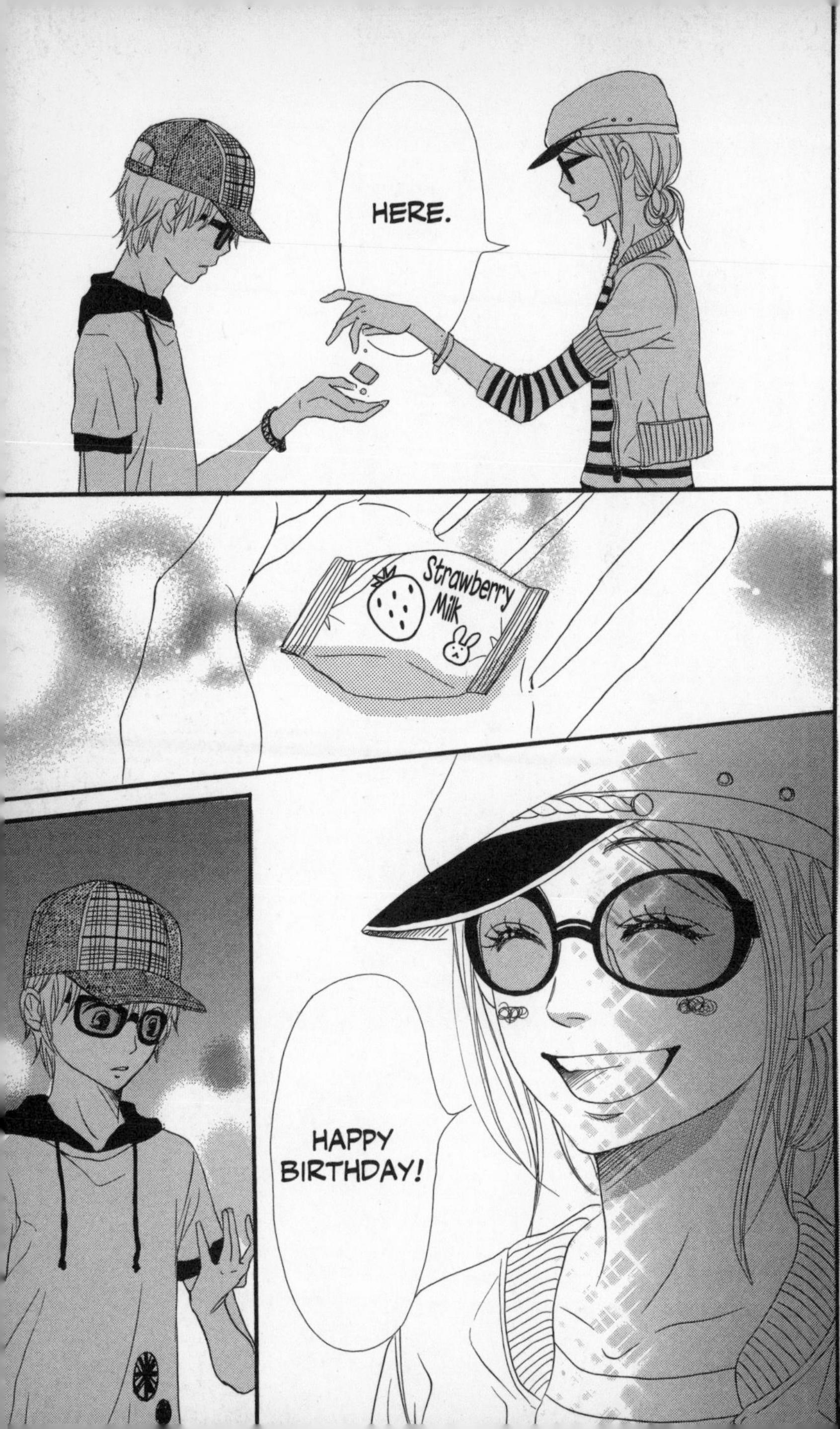
HERE.
Strawberry Milk
HAPPY BIRTHDAY!

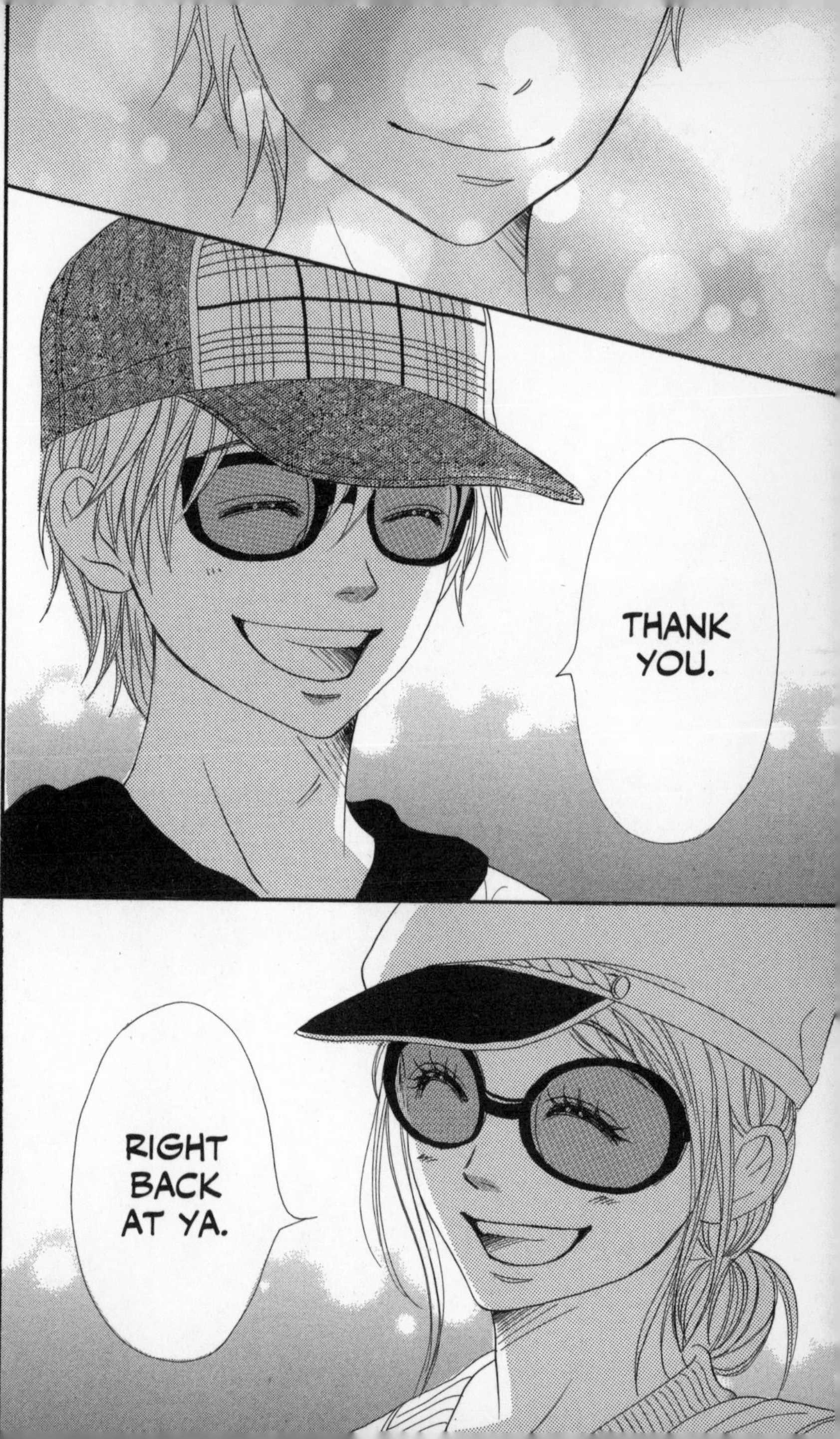
THANK YOU.
RIGHT BACK AT YA.

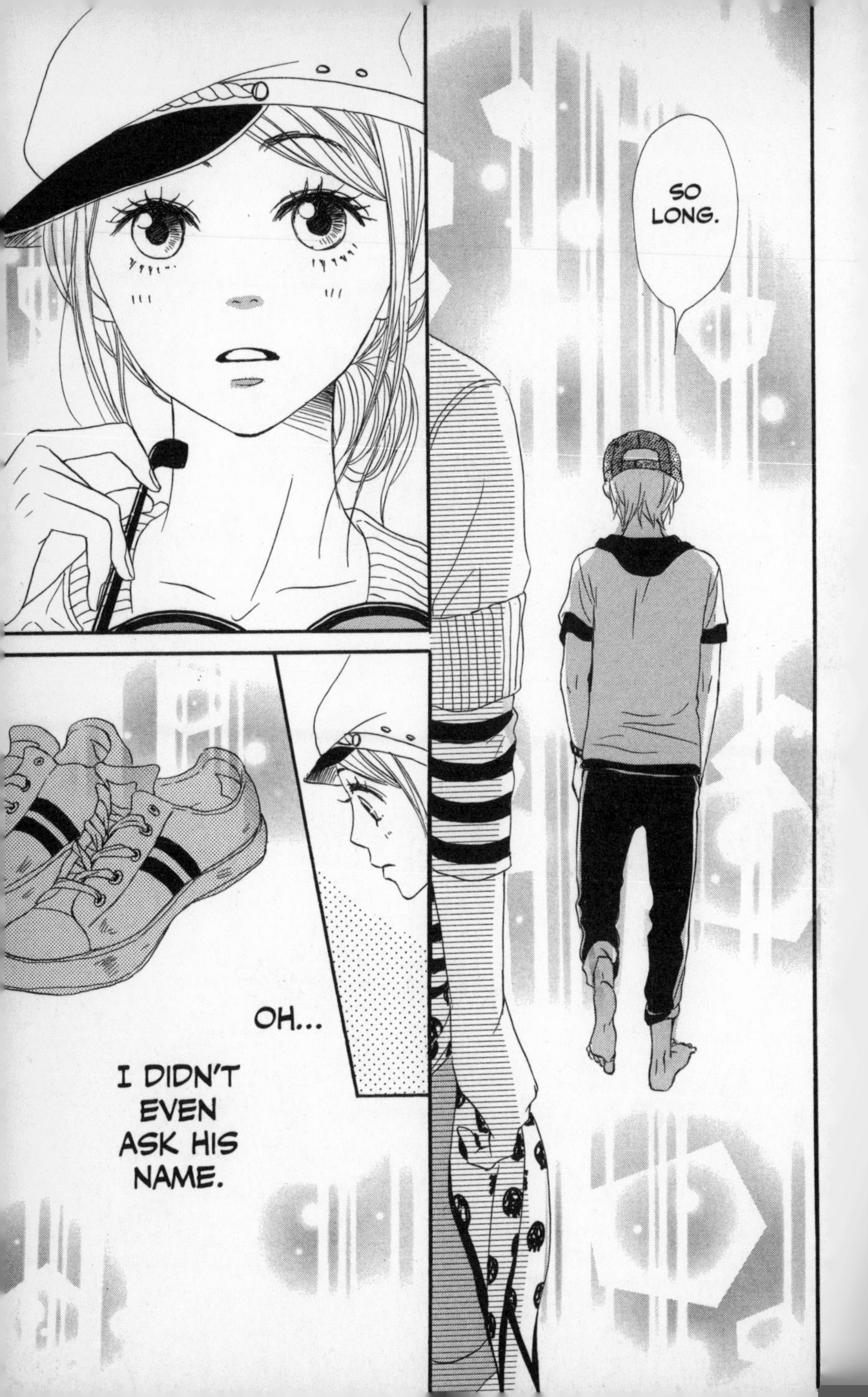
SO LONG.
OH...
I DIDN'T EVEN ASK HIS NAME.

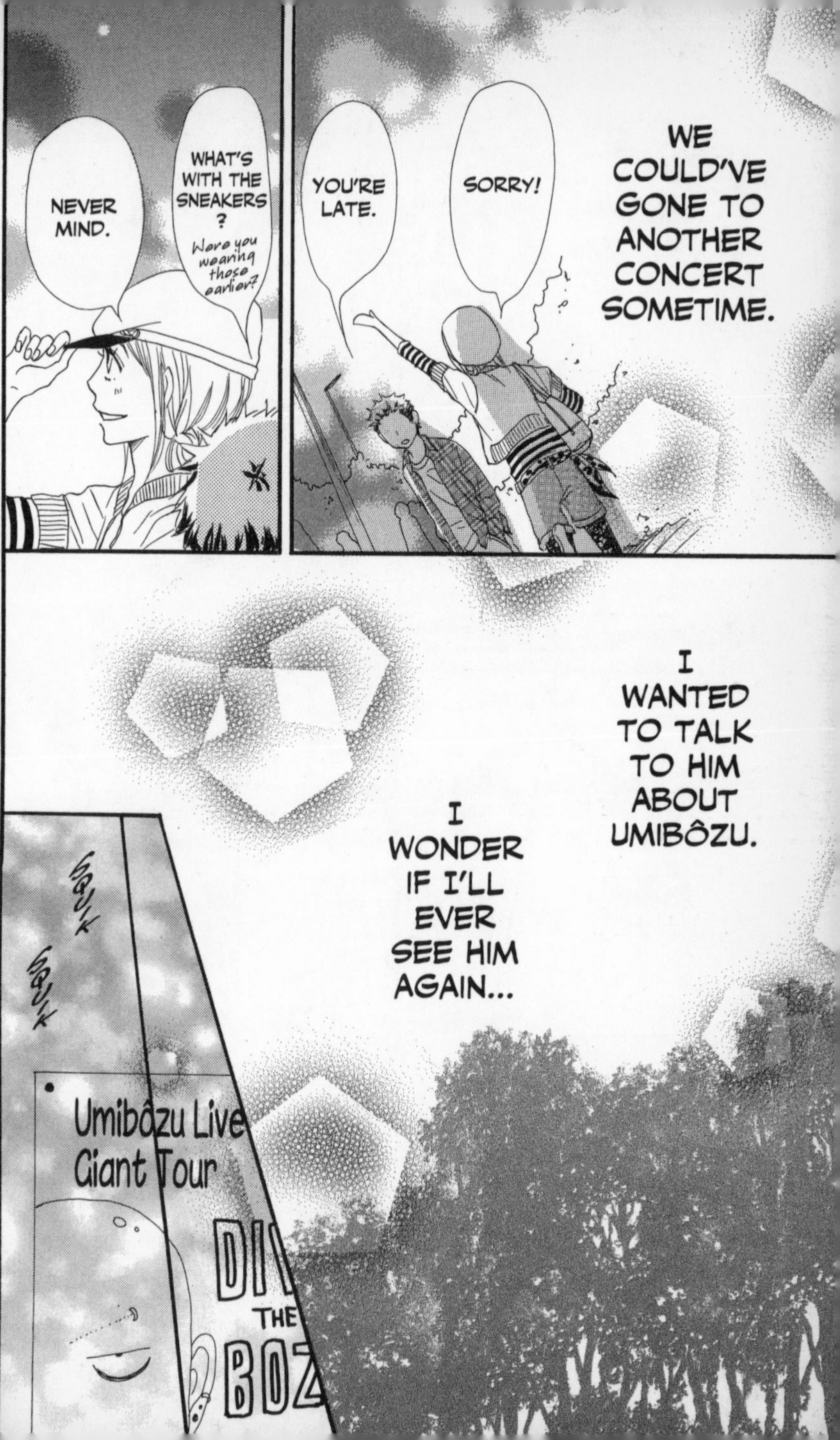
WE COULD'VE GONE TO ANOTHER CONCERT SOMETIME.
SORRY!
YOU'RE LATE.
WHAT'S WITH THE SNEAKERS?
Were you wearing those earlier?
NEVER MIND.
I WANTED TO TALK TO HIM ABOUT UMIBÔZU.
I WONDER IF I'LL EVER SEE HIM AGAIN...
SQUIK
SQUIK
Umibôzu Live Giant Tour
THE

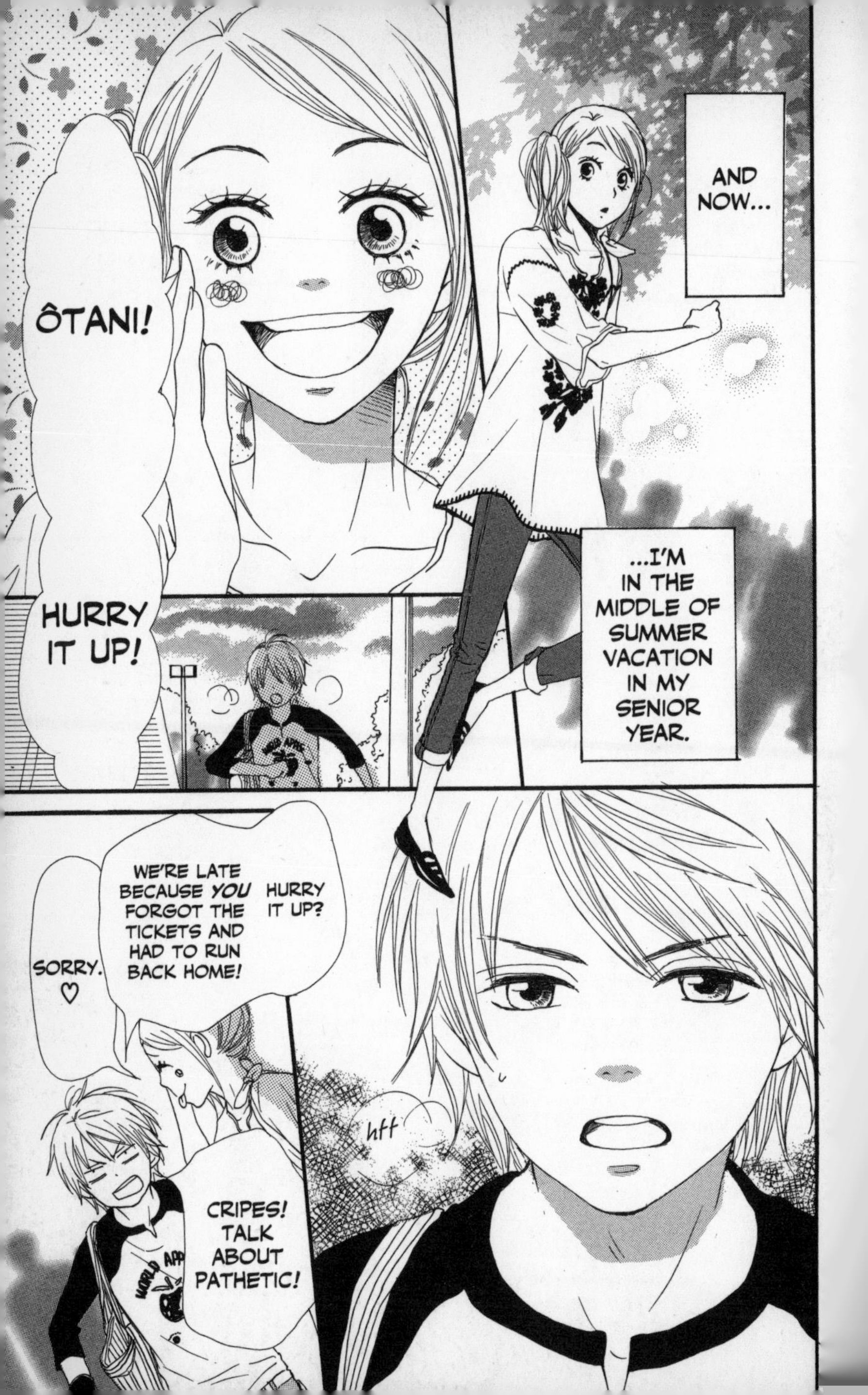
AND NOW...
...I'M IN THE MIDDLE OF SUMMER VACATION IN MY SENIOR YEAR.
ÔTANI!
HURRY IT UP!
HURRY IT UP?
WE'RE LATE BECAUSE *YOU* FORGOT THE TICKETS AND HAD TO RUN BACK HOME!
hff
SORRY. ♡
CRIPES! TALK ABOUT PATHETIC!

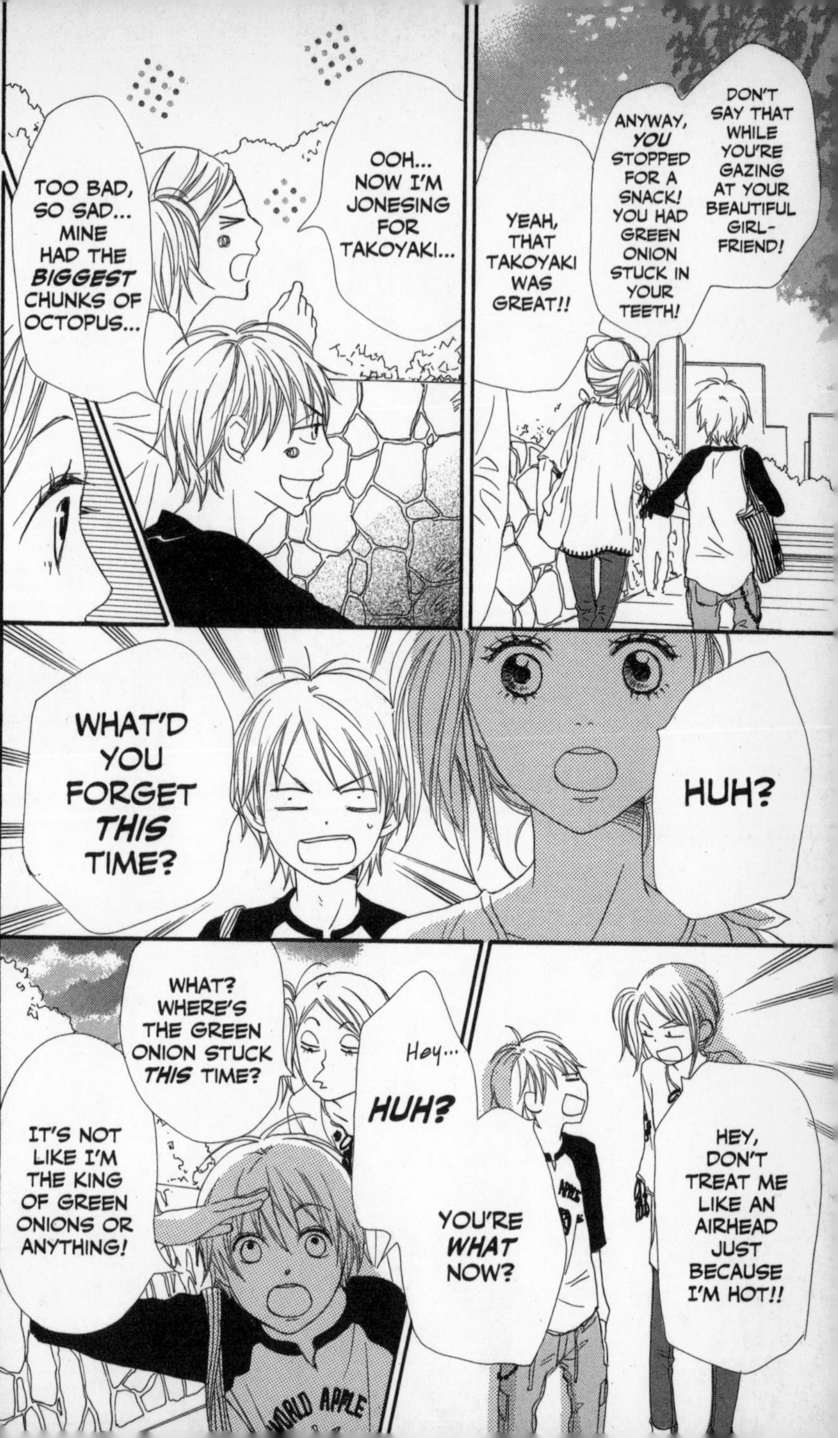
DON'T SAY THAT WHILE YOU'RE GAZING AT YOUR BEAUTIFUL GIRL-FRIEND!
ANYWAY, *YOU* STOPPED FOR A SNACK! YOU HAD GREEN ONION STUCK IN YOUR TEETH!
YEAH, THAT TAKOYAKI WAS GREAT!!
OOH... NOW I'M JONESING FOR TAKOYAKI...
TOO BAD, SO SAD... MINE HAD THE *BIGGEST* CHUNKS OF OCTOPUS...
HUH?
WHAT'D YOU FORGET *THIS* TIME?
HEY, DON'T TREAT ME LIKE AN AIRHEAD JUST BECAUSE I'M HOT!!
YOU'RE *WHAT* NOW?
Hey...
HUH?
WHAT? WHERE'S THE GREEN ONION STUCK *THIS* TIME?
IT'S NOT LIKE I'M THE KING OF GREEN ONIONS OR ANYTHING!

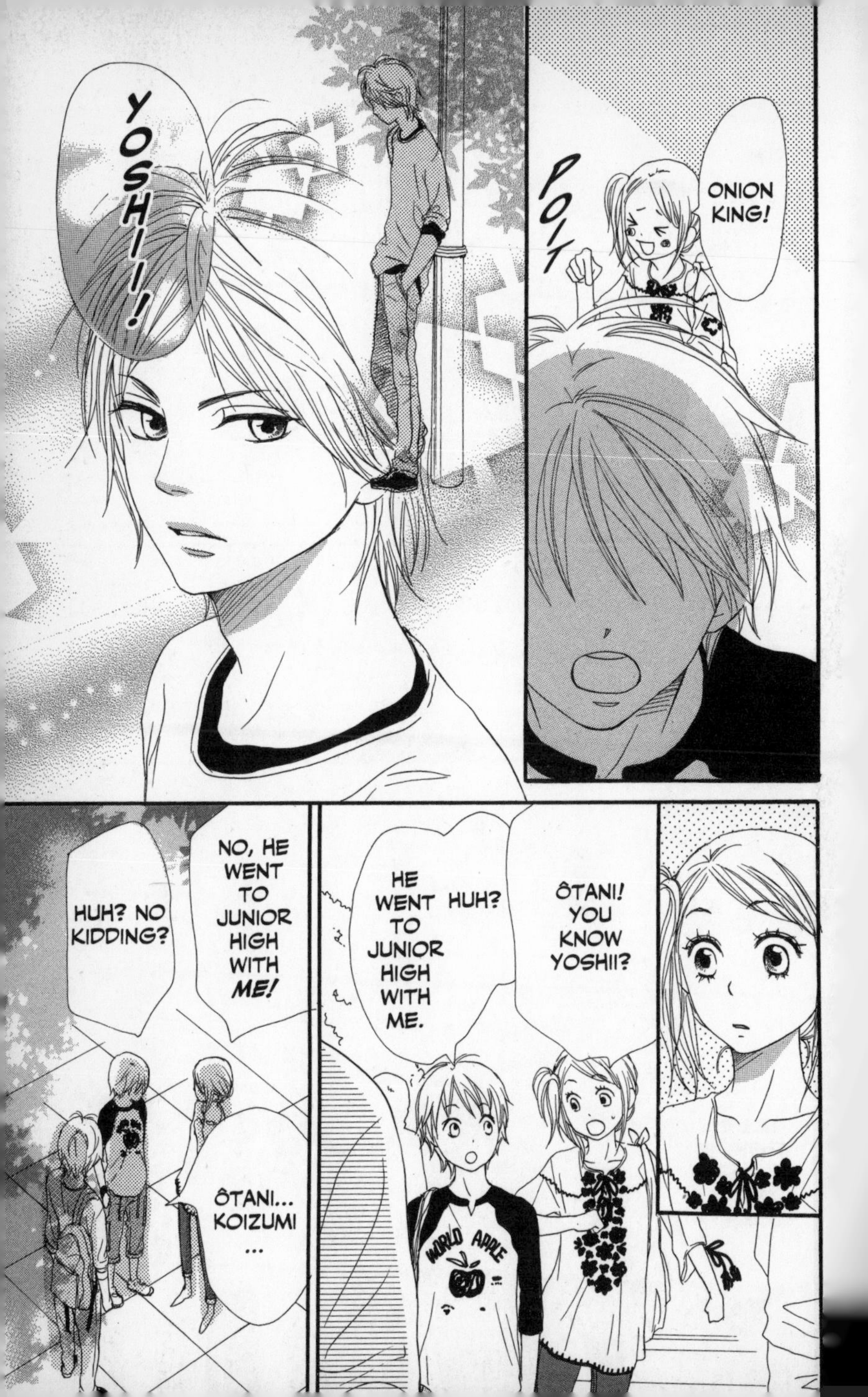

ONION KING!
POI
YOSHII!
ÔTANI! YOU KNOW YOSHII?
HUH?
HE WENT TO JUNIOR HIGH WITH ME.
WORLD APPLE
NO, HE WENT TO JUNIOR HIGH WITH *ME!*
HUH? NO KIDDING?
ÔTANI... KOIZUMI ...

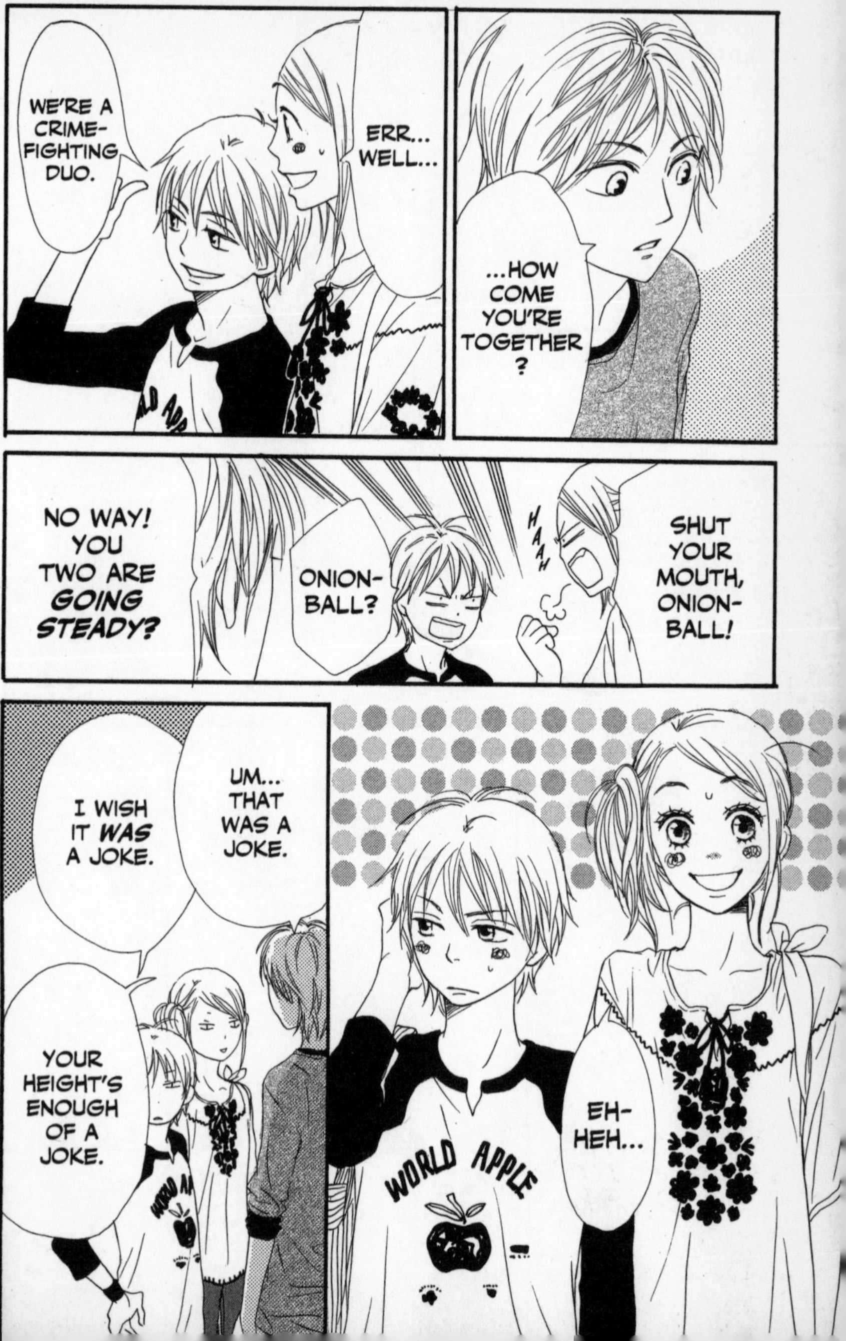
...HOW COME YOU'RE TOGETHER?
ERR... WELL...
WE'RE A CRIME-FIGHTING DUO.
SHUT YOUR MOUTH, ONION-BALL!
HAAH
ONION-BALL?
NO WAY! YOU TWO ARE *GOING STEADY?*
EH-HEH...
UM... THAT WAS A JOKE.
I WISH IT *WAS* A JOKE.
YOUR HEIGHT'S ENOUGH OF A JOKE.

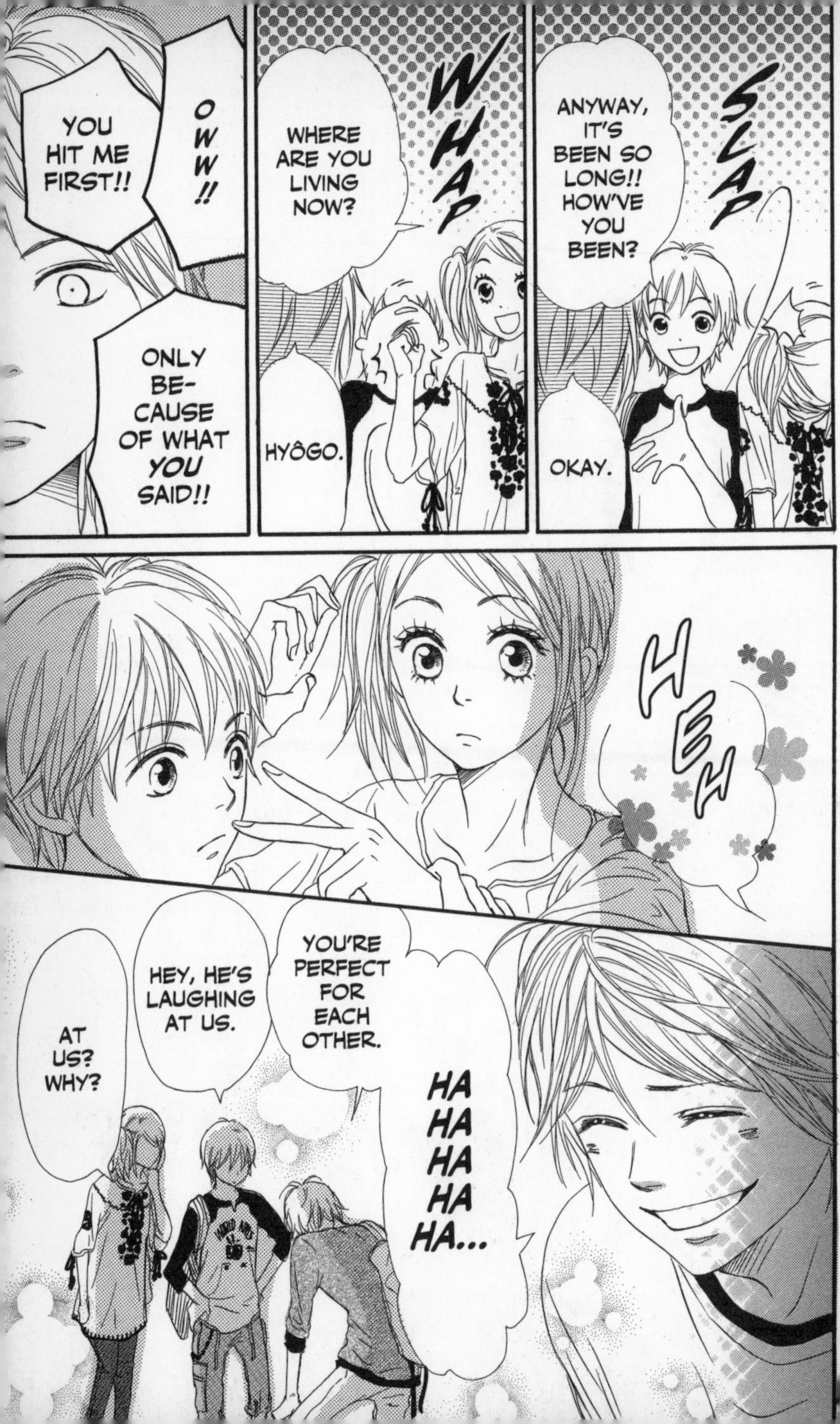
ANYWAY, IT'S BEEN SO LONG!! HOW'VE YOU BEEN?
SLAP
OKAY.
WHERE ARE YOU LIVING NOW?
WHAP
HYÔGO.
OWW!!
YOU HIT ME FIRST!!
ONLY BE-CAUSE OF WHAT *YOU* SAID!!
HEH
YOU'RE PERFECT FOR EACH OTHER.
HA HA HA HA HA HA...
HEY, HE'S LAUGHING AT US.
AT US? WHY?

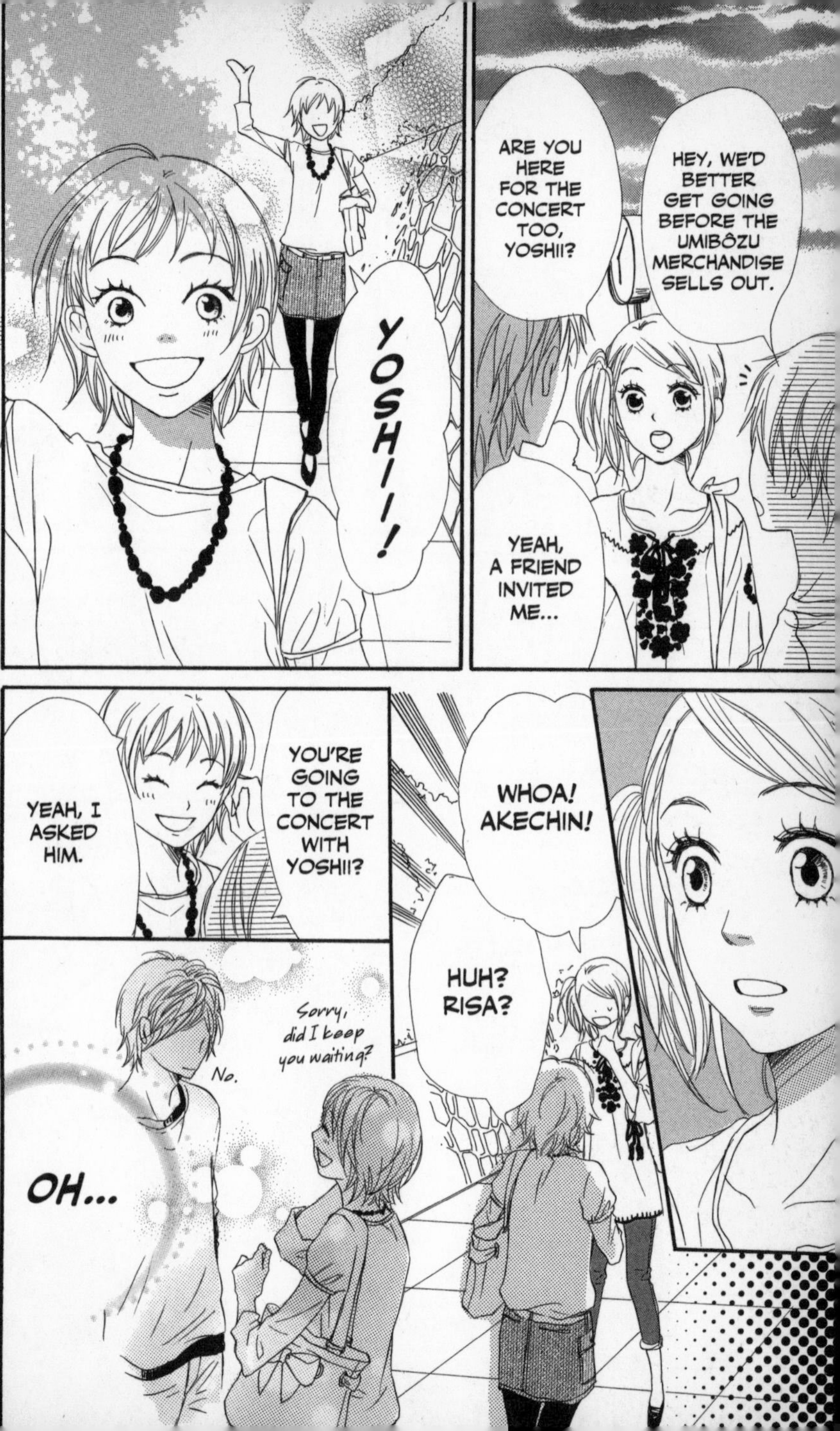
HEY, WE'D BETTER GET GOING BEFORE THE UMIBÔZU MERCHANDISE SELLS OUT.
ARE YOU HERE FOR THE CONCERT TOO, YOSHII?
YEAH, A FRIEND INVITED ME...
YOSHII!
WHOA! AKECHIN!
HUH? RISA?
YOU'RE GOING TO THE CONCERT WITH YOSHII?
YEAH, I ASKED HIM.
Sorry, did I keep you waiting?
No.
OH...

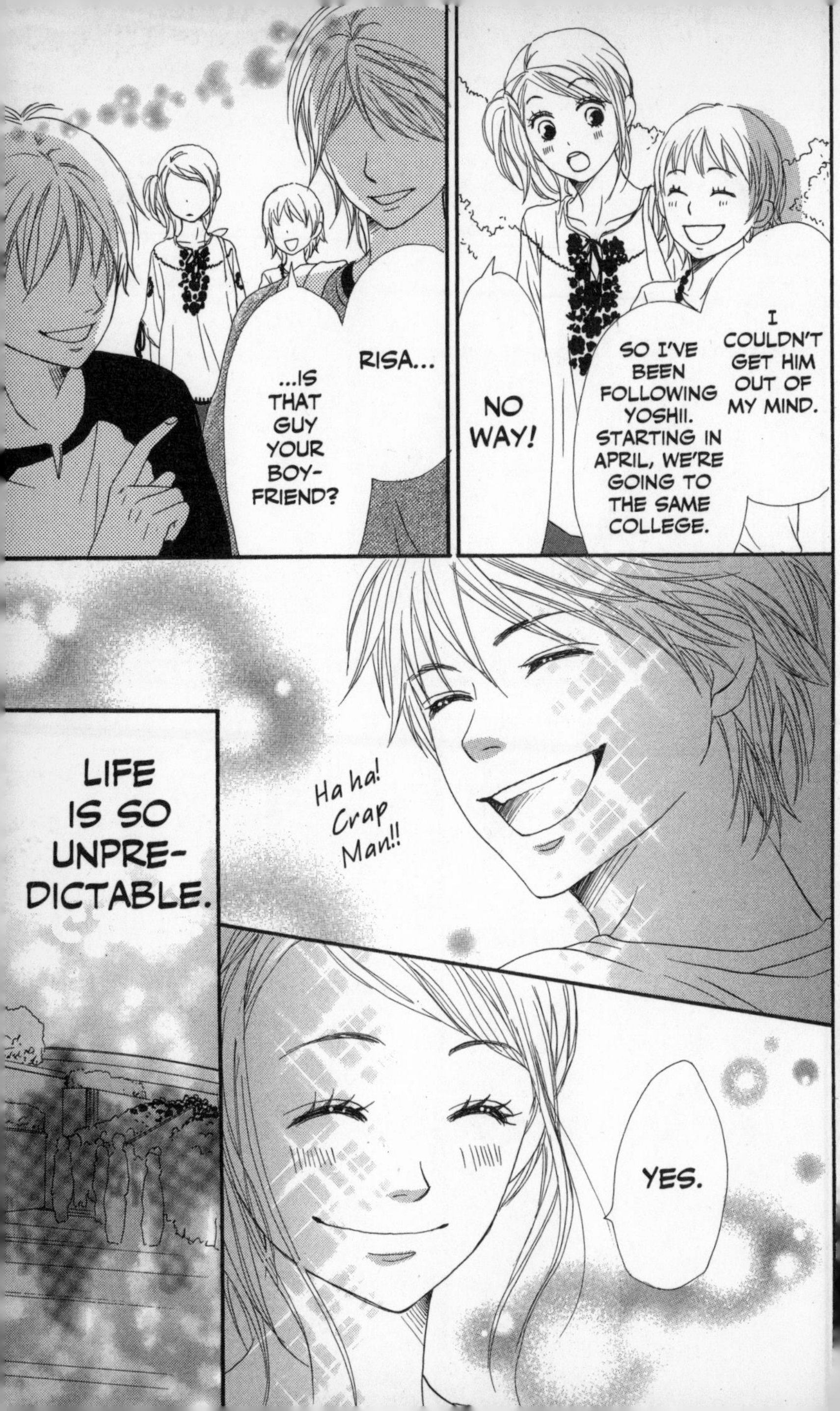

I COULDN'T GET HIM OUT OF MY MIND.
SO I'VE BEEN FOLLOWING YOSHII. STARTING IN APRIL, WE'RE GOING TO THE SAME COLLEGE.
NO WAY!
RISA...
...IS THAT GUY YOUR BOY-FRIEND?
Ha ha! Crap Man!!
YES.
LIFE IS SO UNPRE-DICTABLE.

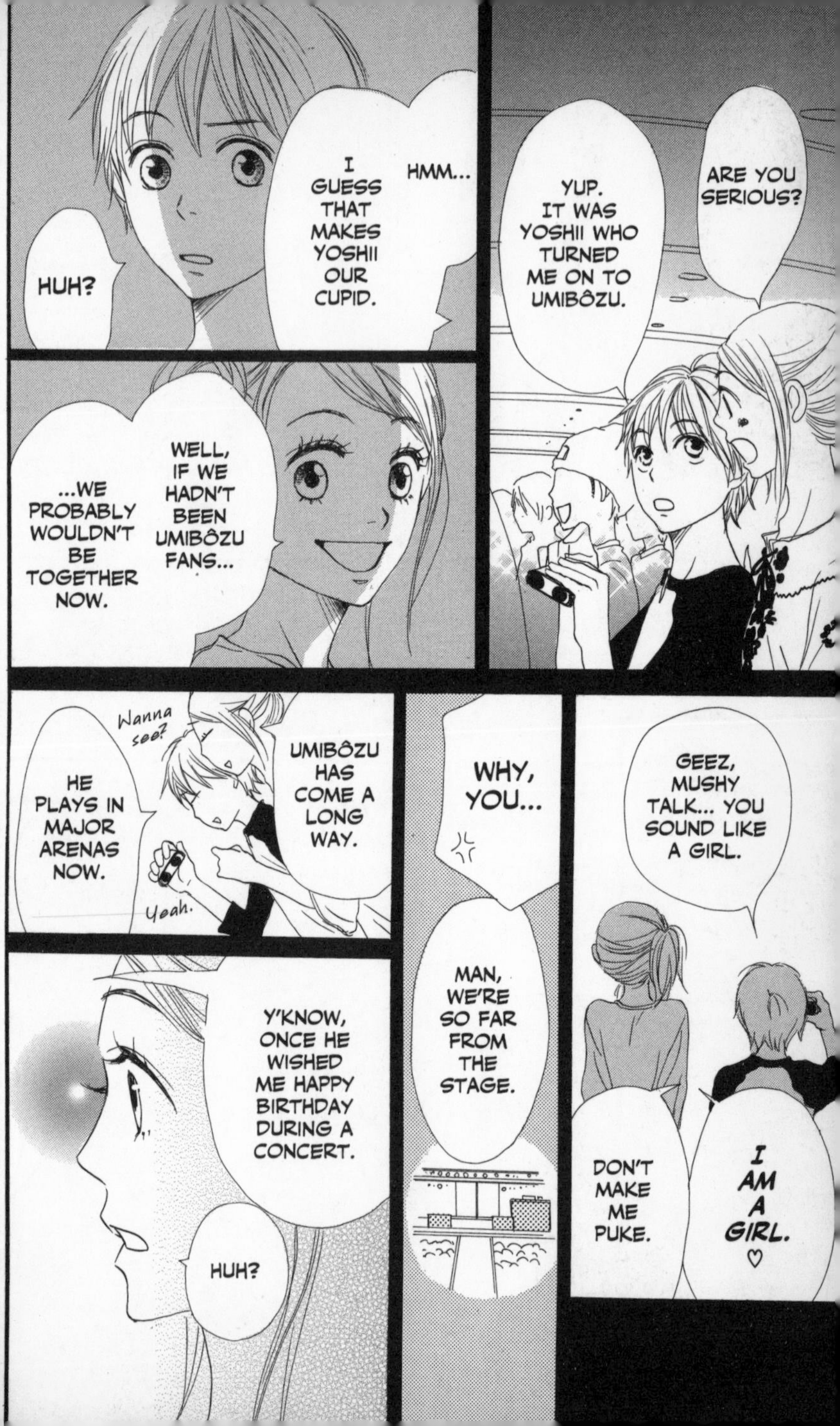
ARE YOU SERIOUS?
YUP. IT WAS YOSHII WHO TURNED ME ON TO UMIBÔZU.
HMM...
I GUESS THAT MAKES YOSHII OUR CUPID.
HUH?
WELL, IF WE HADN'T BEEN UMIBÔZU FANS...
...WE PROBABLY WOULDN'T BE TOGETHER NOW.
GEEZ, MUSHY TALK... YOU SOUND LIKE A GIRL.
I AM A GIRL. ♡
DON'T MAKE ME PUKE.
WHY, YOU...
MAN, WE'RE SO FAR FROM THE STAGE.
UMIBÔZU HAS COME A LONG WAY.
Wanna see?
HE PLAYS IN MAJOR ARENAS NOW.
Yeah.
Y'KNOW, ONCE HE WISHED ME HAPPY BIRTHDAY DURING A CONCERT.
HUH?

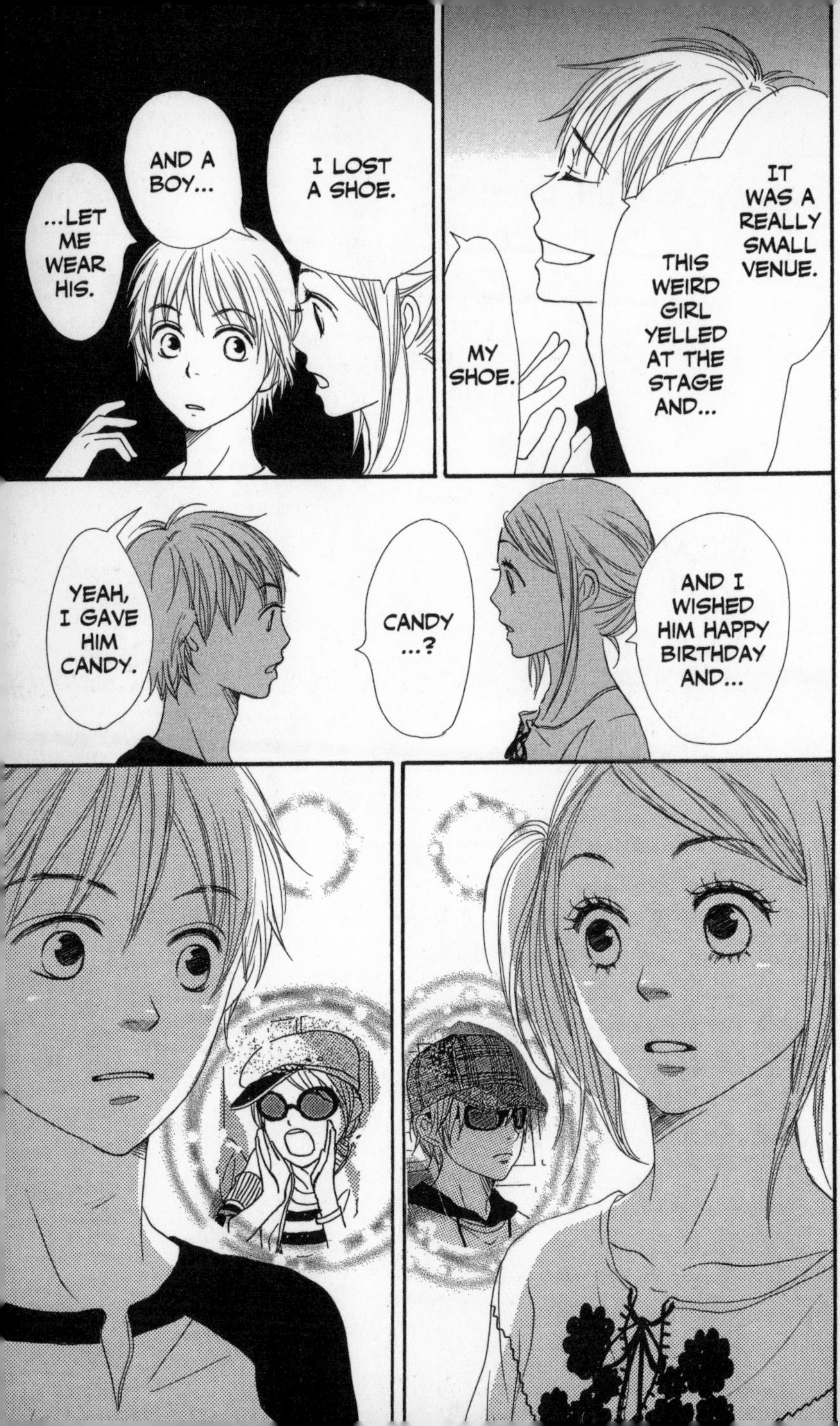
IT WAS A REALLY SMALL VENUE.
THIS WEIRD GIRL YELLED AT THE STAGE AND...
MY SHOE.
I LOST A SHOE.
AND A BOY...
...LET ME WEAR HIS.
AND I WISHED HIM HAPPY BIRTHDAY AND...
CANDY ...?
YEAH, I GAVE HIM CANDY.

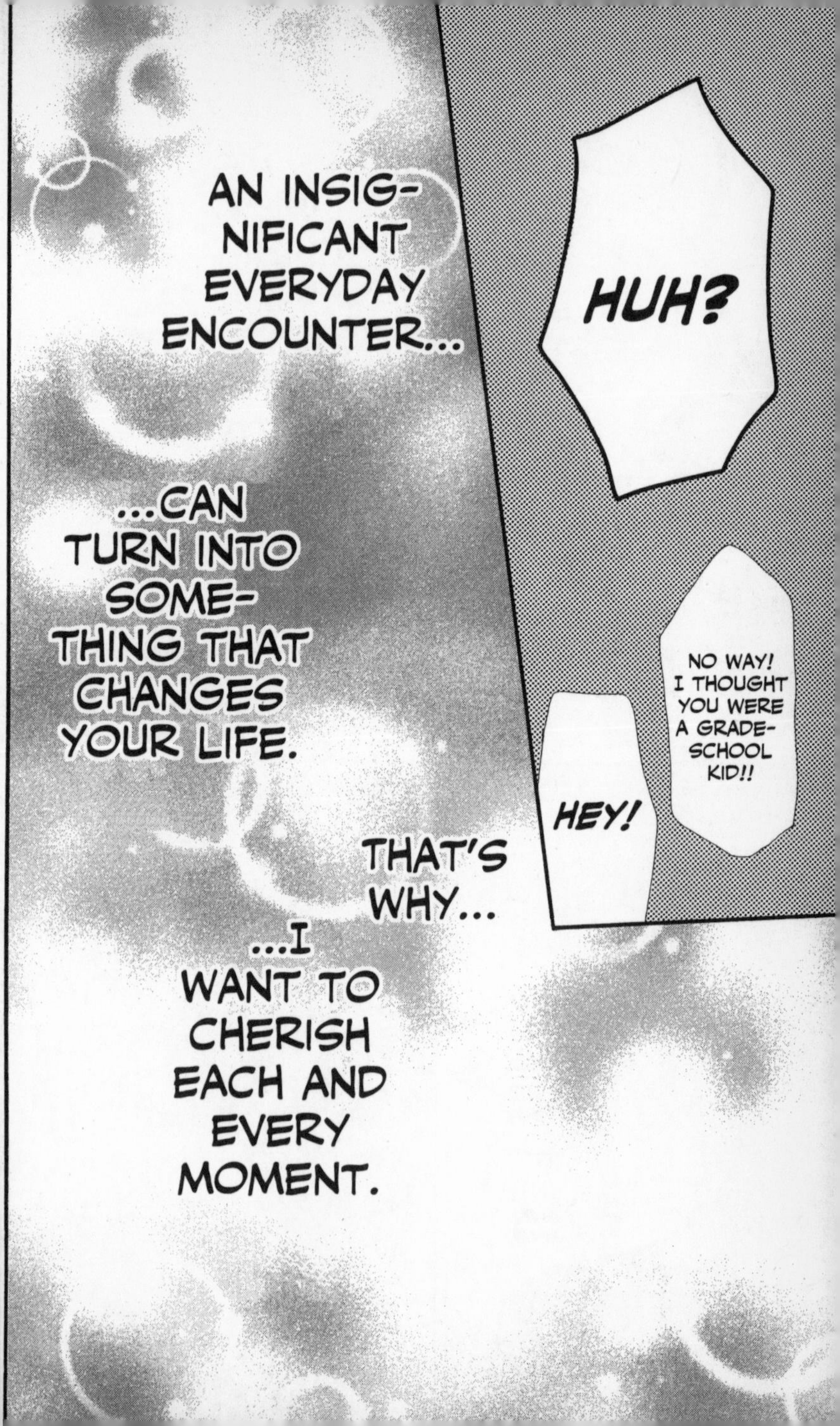
HUH?
NO WAY! I THOUGHT YOU WERE A GRADE-SCHOOL KID!!
HEY!
AN INSIGNIFICANT EVERYDAY ENCOUNTER...
...CAN TURN INTO SOMETHING THAT CHANGES YOUR LIFE.
THAT'S WHY...
...I WANT TO CHERISH EACH AND EVERY MOMENT.

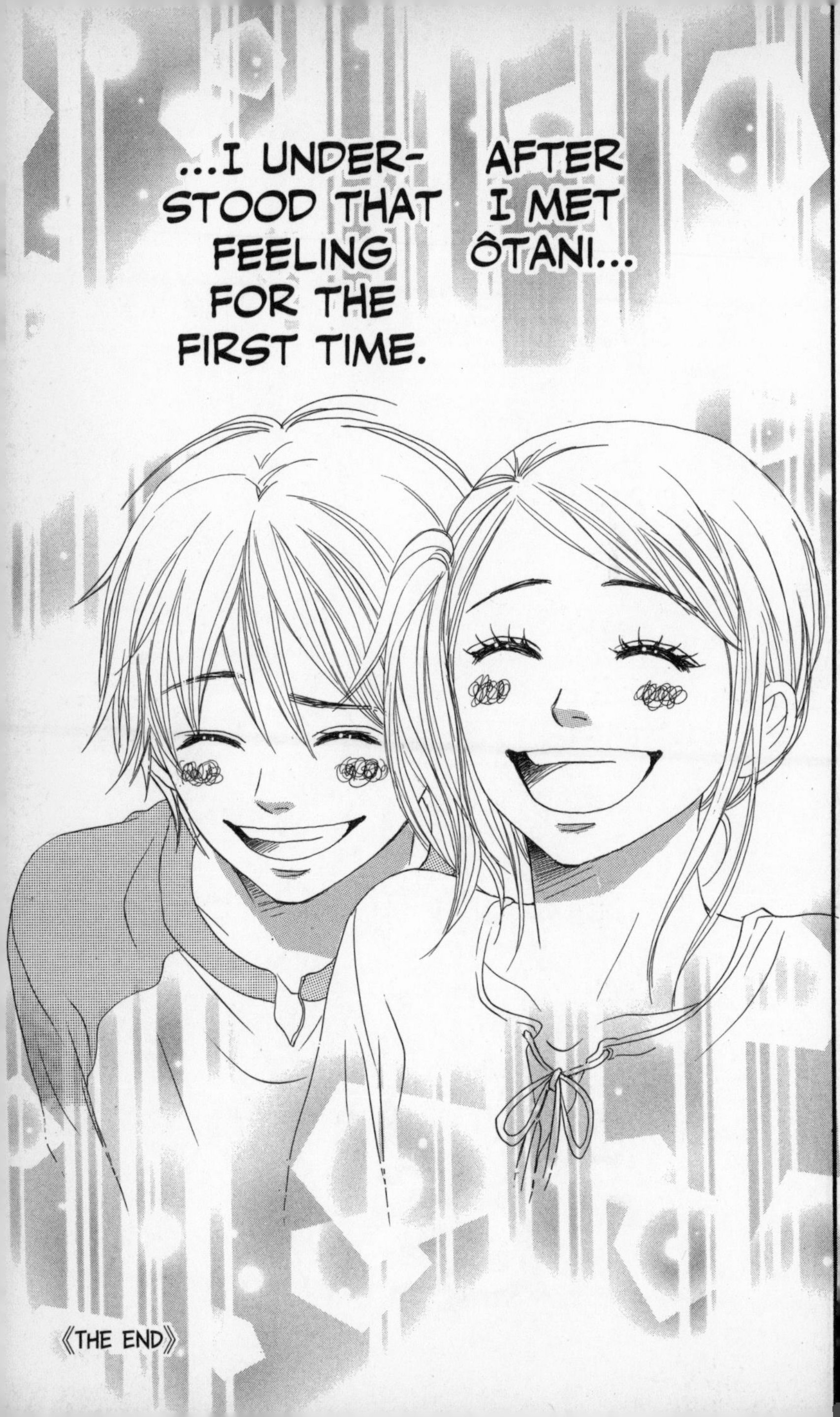
AFTER I MET ÔTANI...
...I UNDER-STOOD THAT FEELING FOR THE FIRST TIME.
《THE END》

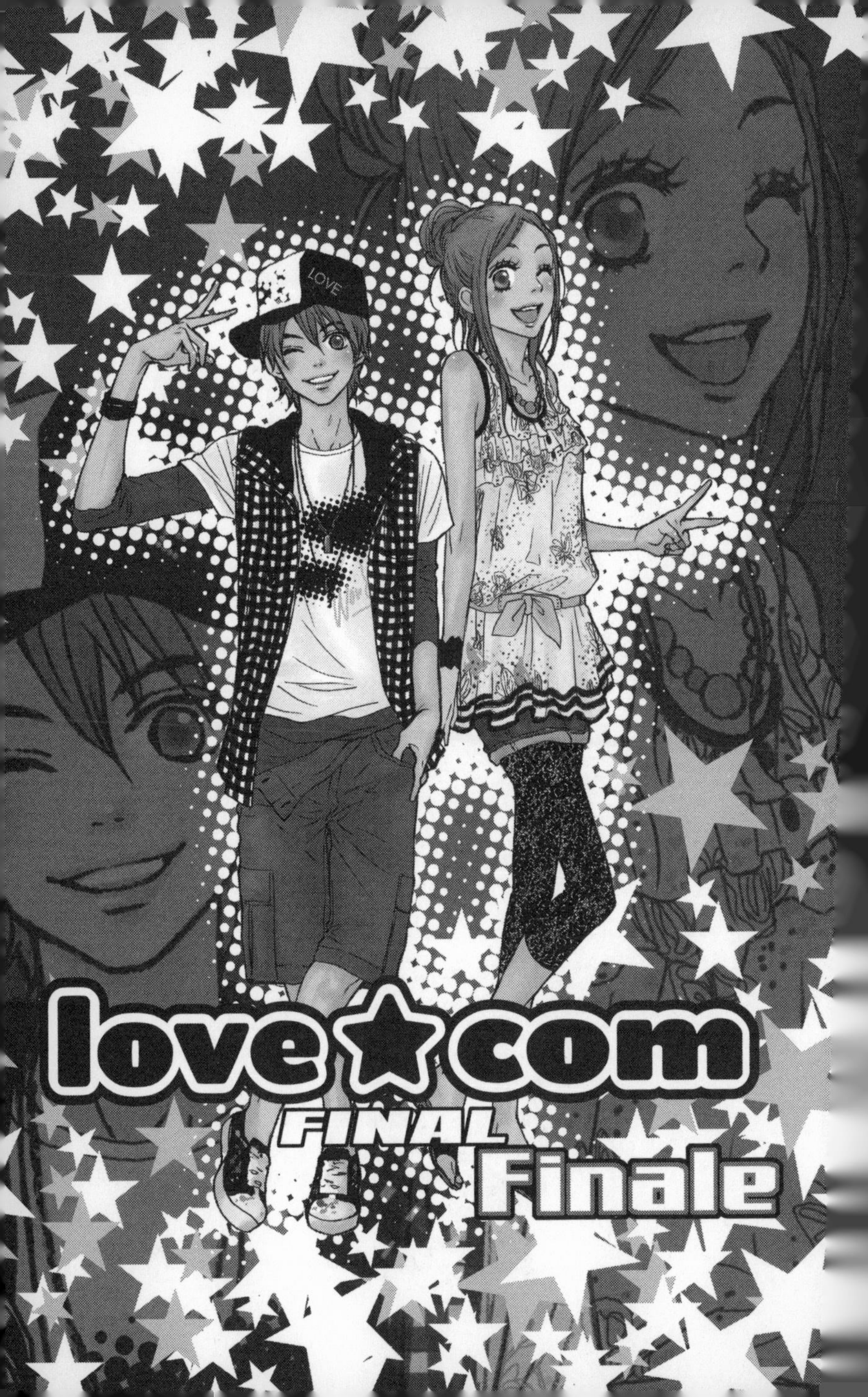
LOVE
love★com
FINAL
Finale

Thank you ♡

To Nana-chan, Mimi-chan, Mambo,
Araki-kun, Et-chan, Hikari-chan,
Ido-chan, Iku-chan, Fuk-kun, Taka-kun,
Ichiro-kun, Pee-chan, Mr. Editor at
Betsucomi, everyone in the Nakahara
family, all my readers and everyone
who supported *Love✻Com...*

Thank you so much! ♡

August 2007 Aya

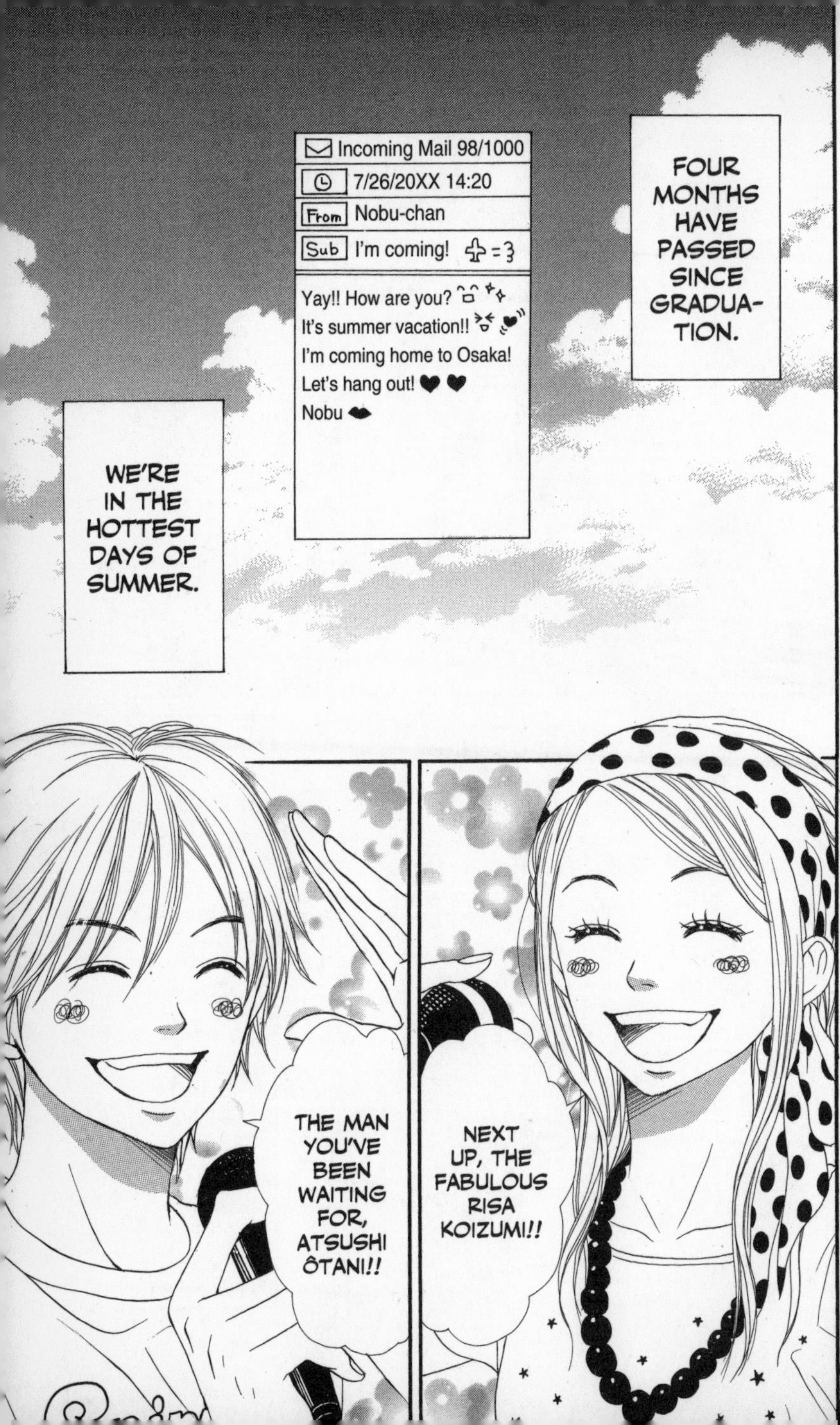
FOUR MONTHS HAVE PASSED SINCE GRADUA-TION.
Incoming Mail 98/1000
7/26/20XX 14:20
From Nobu-chan
Sub I'm coming!
Yay!! How are you?
It's summer vacation!!
I'm coming home to Osaka!
Let's hang out!
Nobu
WE'RE IN THE HOTTEST DAYS OF SUMMER.
NEXT UP, THE FABULOUS RISA KOIZUMI!!
THE MAN YOU'VE BEEN WAITING FOR, ATSUSHI ÔTANI!!

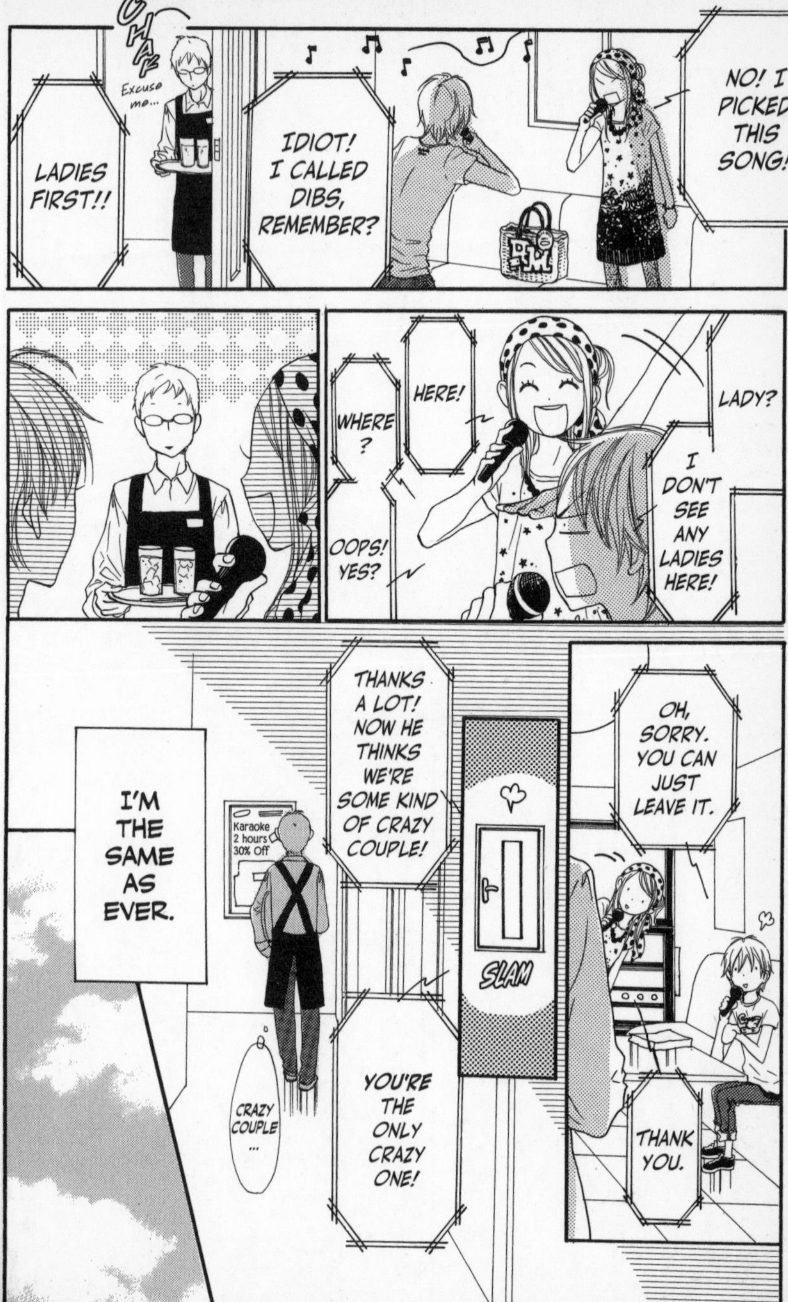
NO! I PICKED THIS SONG!
IDIOT! I CALLED DIBS, REMEMBER?
CHAK
Excuse me...
LADIES FIRST!!
LADY?
I DON'T SEE ANY LADIES HERE!
HERE!
WHERE?
OOPS! YES?
OH, SORRY. YOU CAN JUST LEAVE IT.
THANK YOU.
SLAM
THANKS A LOT! NOW HE THINKS WE'RE SOME KIND OF CRAZY COUPLE!
YOU'RE THE ONLY CRAZY ONE!
Karaoke 2 hours 30% Off
CRAZY COUPLE ...
I'M THE SAME AS EVER.

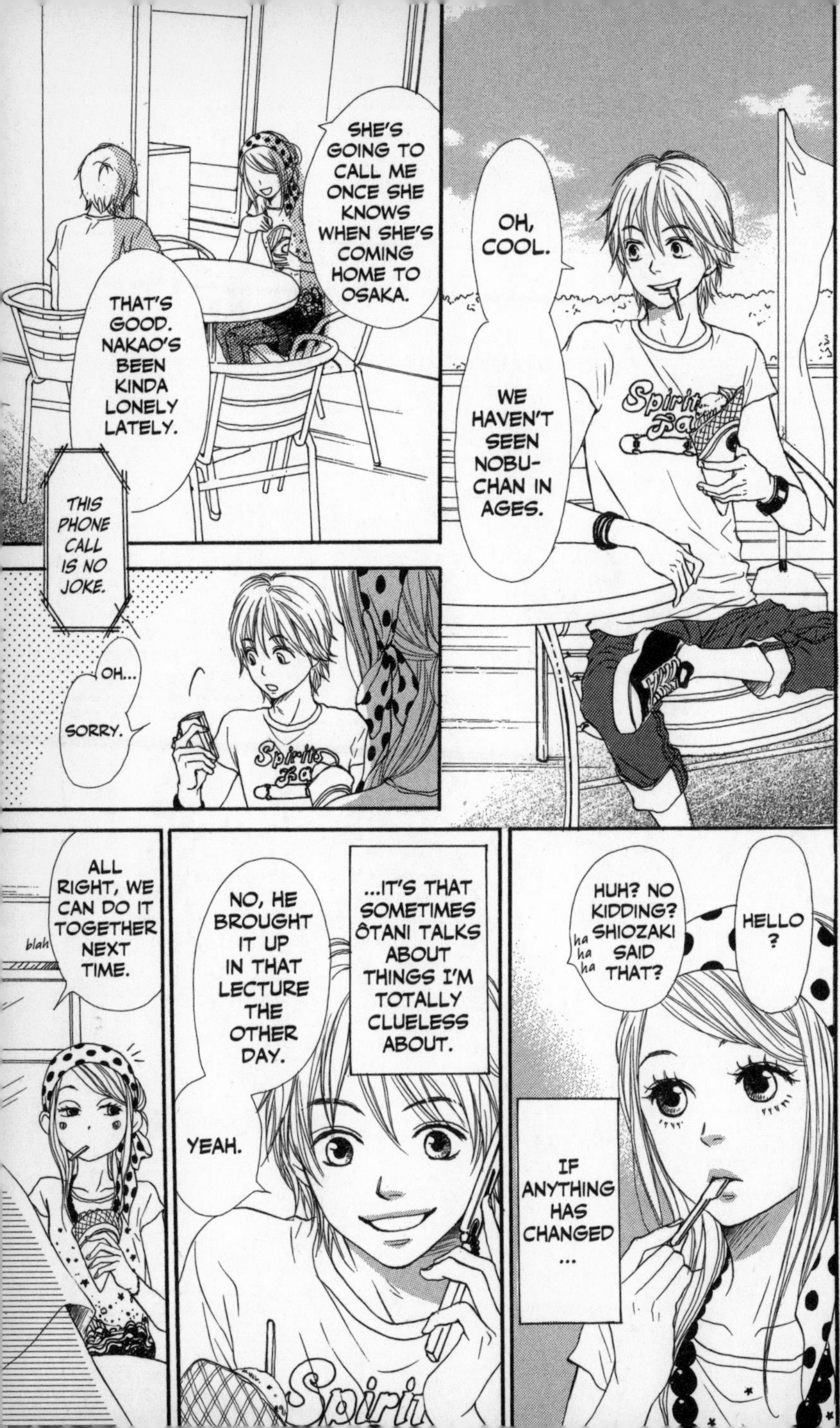
OH, COOL.
WE HAVEN'T SEEN NOBU-CHAN IN AGES.
SHE'S GOING TO CALL ME ONCE SHE KNOWS WHEN SHE'S COMING HOME TO OSAKA.
THAT'S GOOD. NAKAO'S BEEN KINDA LONELY LATELY.
THIS PHONE CALL IS NO JOKE.
OH...
SORRY.
HELLO?
HUH? NO KIDDING? SHIOZAKI SAID THAT?
ha ha ha
IF ANYTHING HAS CHANGED ...
...IT'S THAT SOMETIMES ÔTANI TALKS ABOUT THINGS I'M TOTALLY CLUELESS ABOUT.
NO, HE BROUGHT IT UP IN THAT LECTURE THE OTHER DAY.
YEAH.
ALL RIGHT, WE CAN DO IT TOGETHER NEXT TIME.
blah

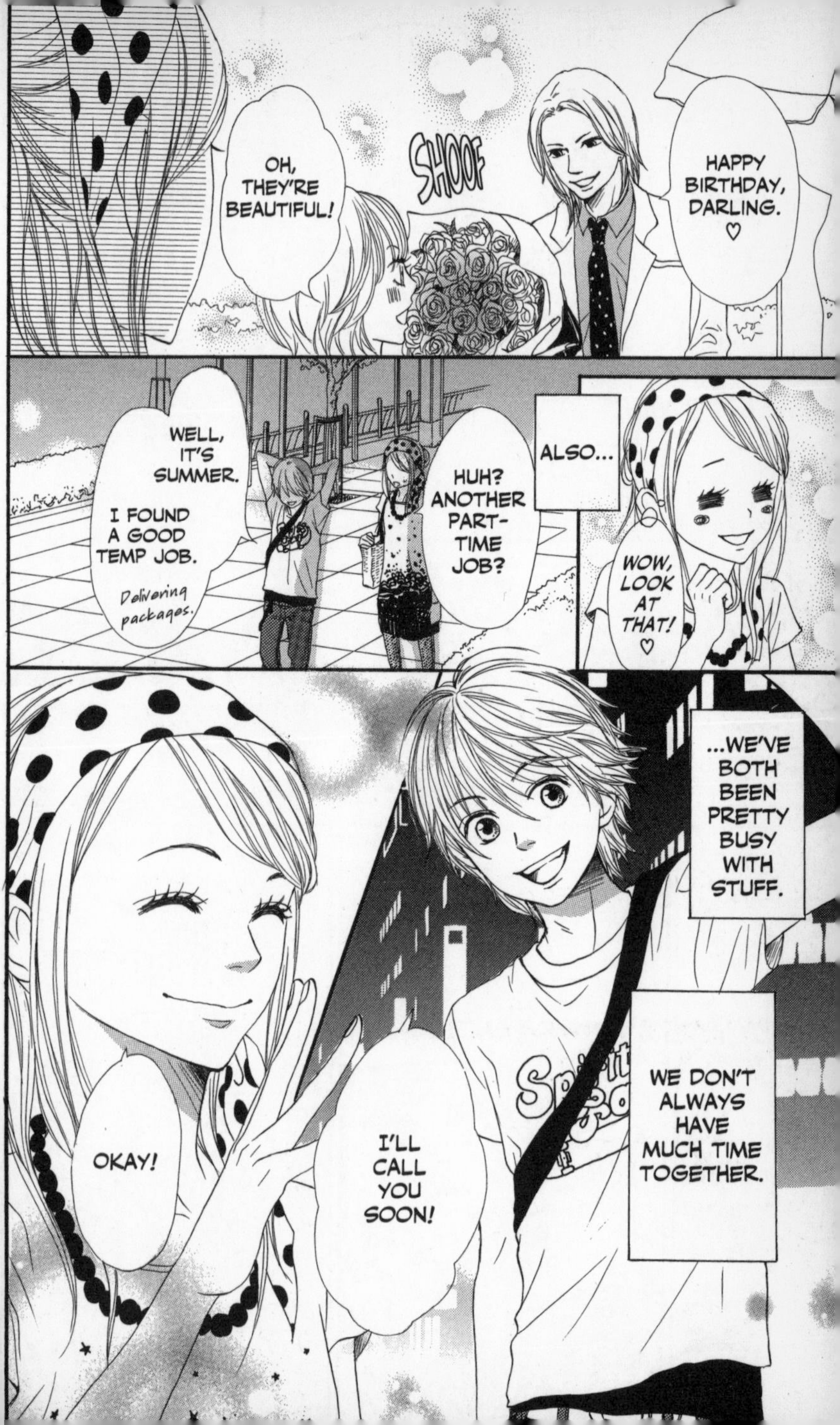
HAPPY BIRTHDAY, DARLING. ♡
SHOOF
OH, THEY'RE BEAUTIFUL!
ALSO...
WOW, LOOK AT THAT! ♡
HUH? ANOTHER PART-TIME JOB?
WELL, IT'S SUMMER.
I FOUND A GOOD TEMP JOB.
Delivering packages.
...WE'VE BOTH BEEN PRETTY BUSY WITH STUFF.
WE DON'T ALWAYS HAVE MUCH TIME TOGETHER.
I'LL CALL YOU SOON!
OKAY!

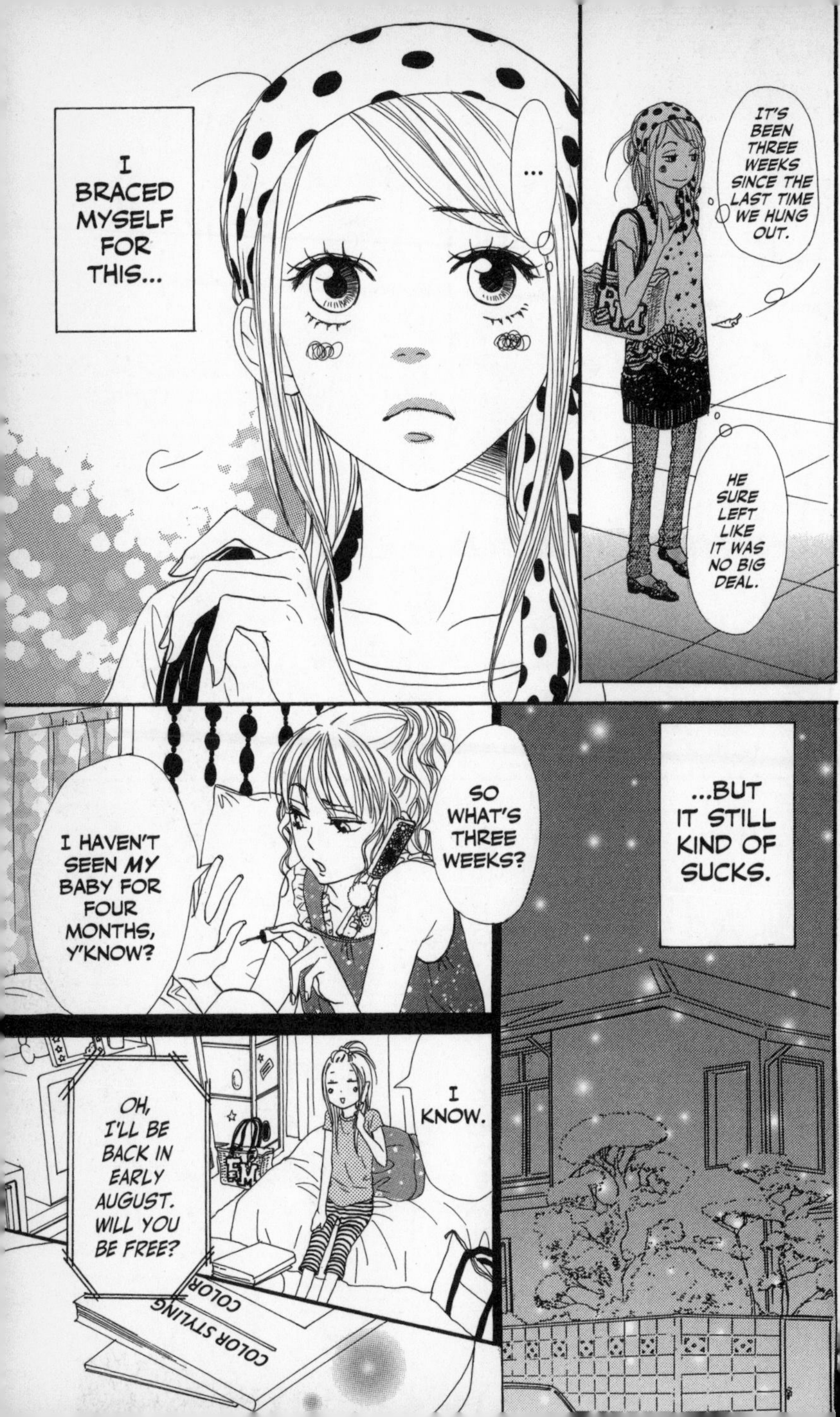

IT'S BEEN THREE WEEKS SINCE THE LAST TIME WE HUNG OUT.
HE SURE LEFT LIKE IT WAS NO BIG DEAL.
...
I BRACED MYSELF FOR THIS...
...BUT IT STILL KIND OF SUCKS.
SO WHAT'S THREE WEEKS?
I HAVEN'T SEEN *MY* BABY FOR FOUR MONTHS, Y'KNOW?
I KNOW.
OH, I'LL BE BACK IN EARLY AUGUST. WILL YOU BE FREE?
COLOR STYLING
COLOR

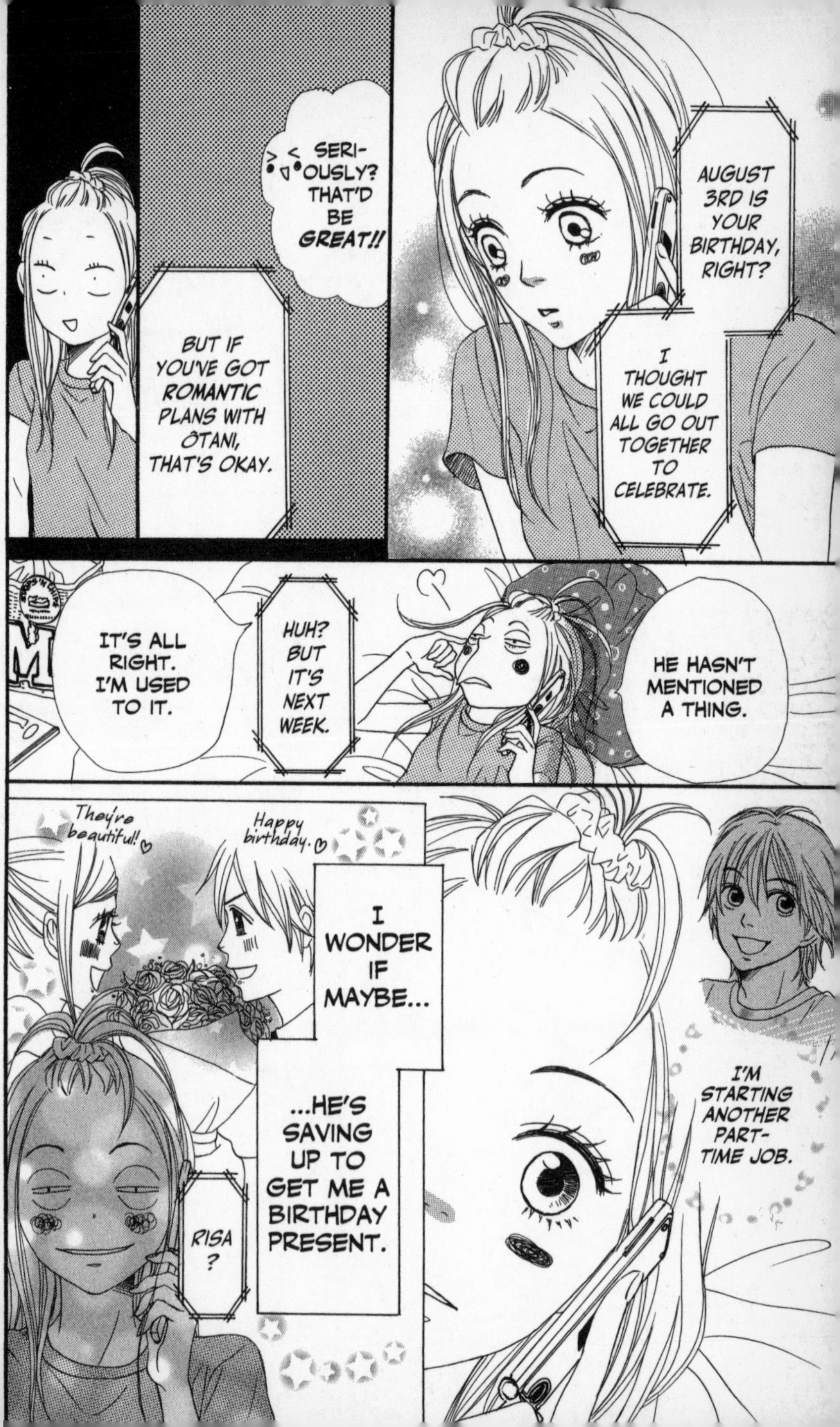
AUGUST 3RD IS YOUR BIRTHDAY, RIGHT?
I THOUGHT WE COULD ALL GO OUT TOGETHER TO CELEBRATE.
SERIOUSLY? THAT'D BE GREAT!!
BUT IF YOU'VE GOT ROMANTIC PLANS WITH ŌTANI, THAT'S OKAY.
HE HASN'T MENTIONED A THING.
HUH? BUT IT'S NEXT WEEK.
IT'S ALL RIGHT. I'M USED TO IT.
I'M STARTING ANOTHER PART-TIME JOB.
I WONDER IF MAYBE...
...HE'S SAVING UP TO GET ME A BIRTHDAY PRESENT.
Happy birthday.
They're beautiful!
RISA?

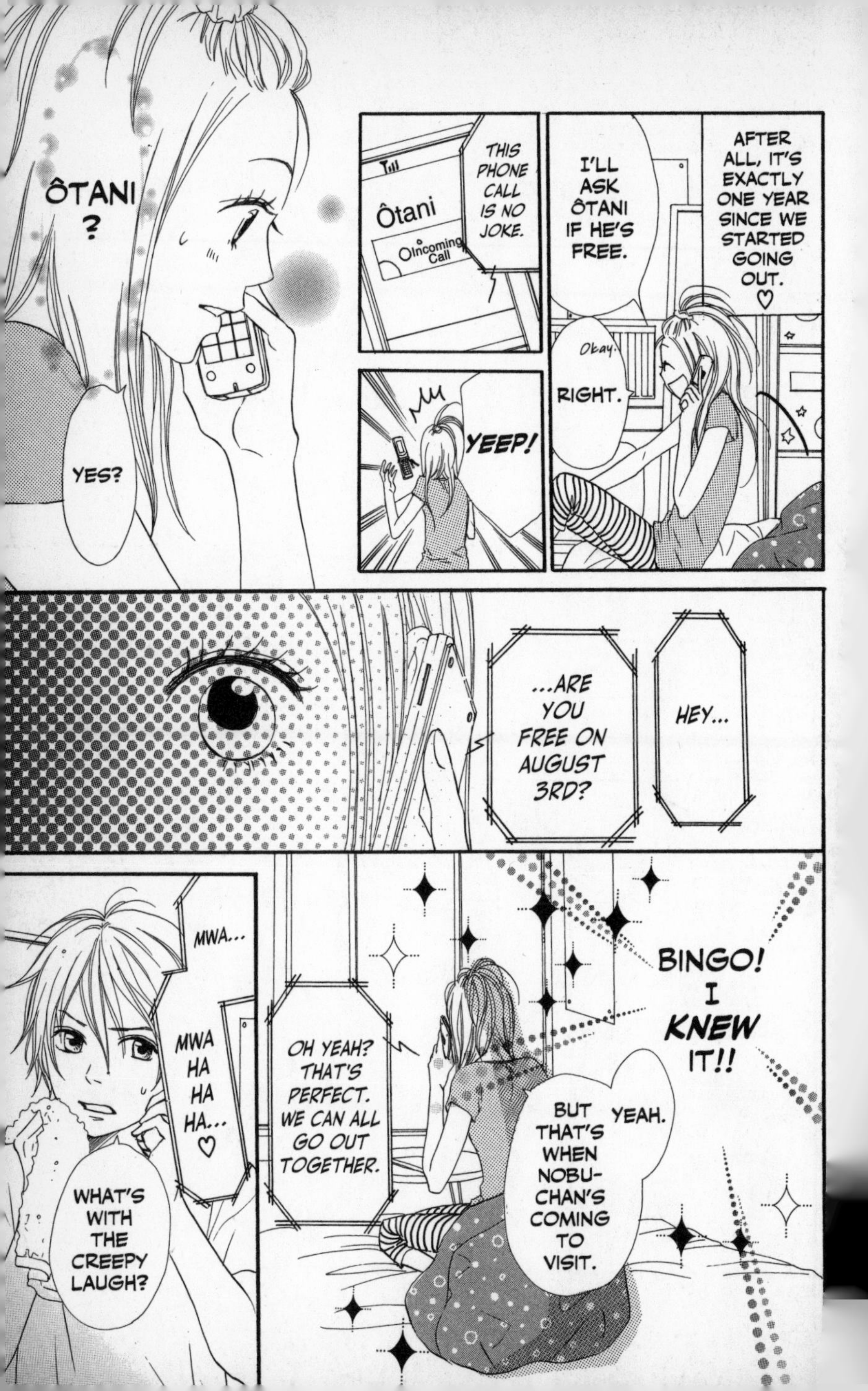
AFTER ALL, IT'S EXACTLY ONE YEAR SINCE WE STARTED GOING OUT. ♡
I'LL ASK ÔTANI IF HE'S FREE.
Okay.
RIGHT.
THIS PHONE CALL IS NO JOKE.
Ôtani
Incoming Call
YEEP!
ÔTANI ?
YES?
HEY...
...ARE YOU FREE ON AUGUST 3RD?
BINGO! I KNEW IT!!
YEAH.
BUT THAT'S WHEN NOBU-CHAN'S COMING TO VISIT.
OH YEAH? THAT'S PERFECT. WE CAN ALL GO OUT TOGETHER.
MWA...
MWA HA HA HA... ♡
WHAT'S WITH THE CREEPY LAUGH?

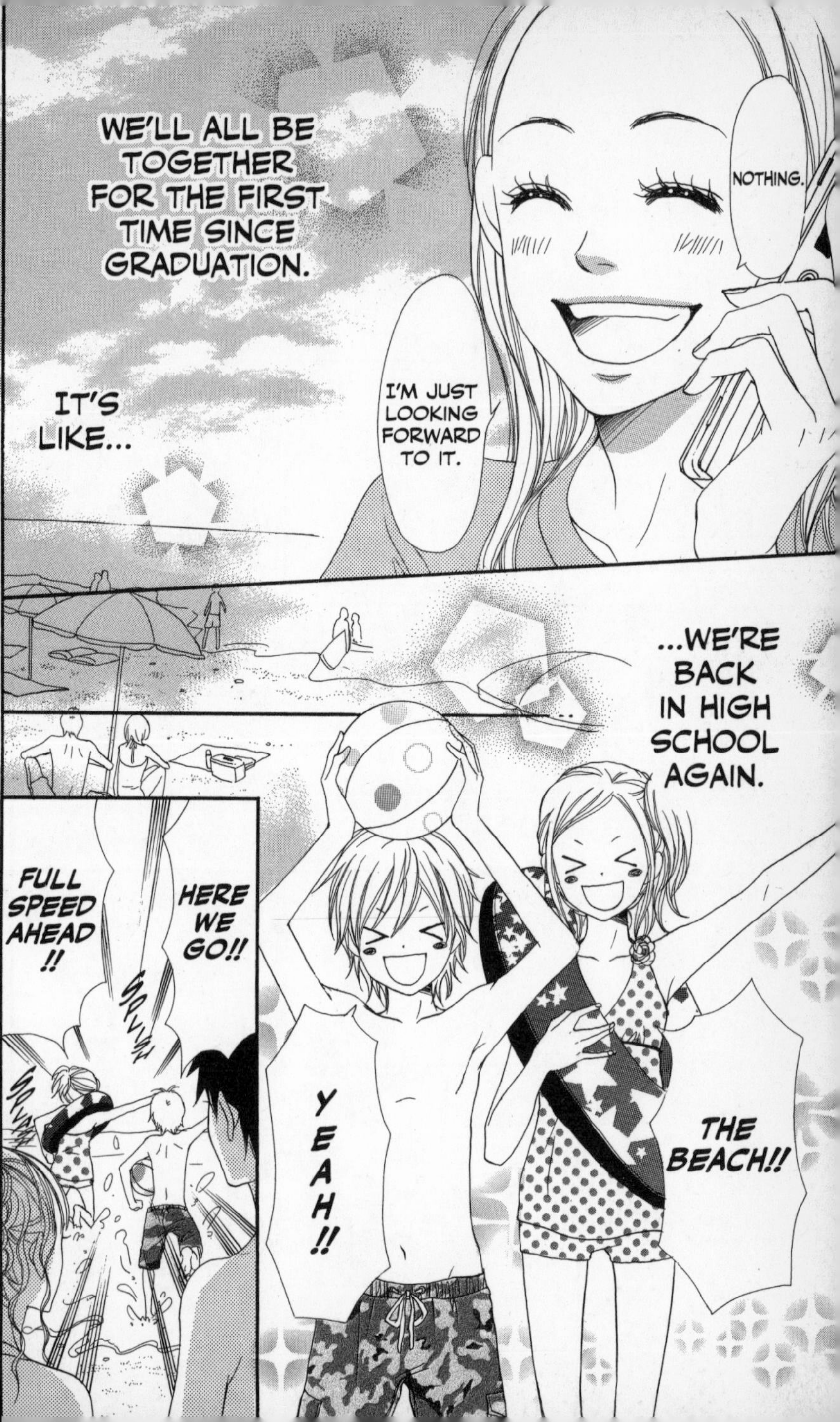
NOTHING.
I'M JUST LOOKING FORWARD TO IT.
WE'LL ALL BE TOGETHER FOR THE FIRST TIME SINCE GRADUATION.
IT'S LIKE...
...WE'RE BACK IN HIGH SCHOOL AGAIN.
THE BEACH!!
YEAH!!
HERE WE GO!!
FULL SPEED AHEAD!!

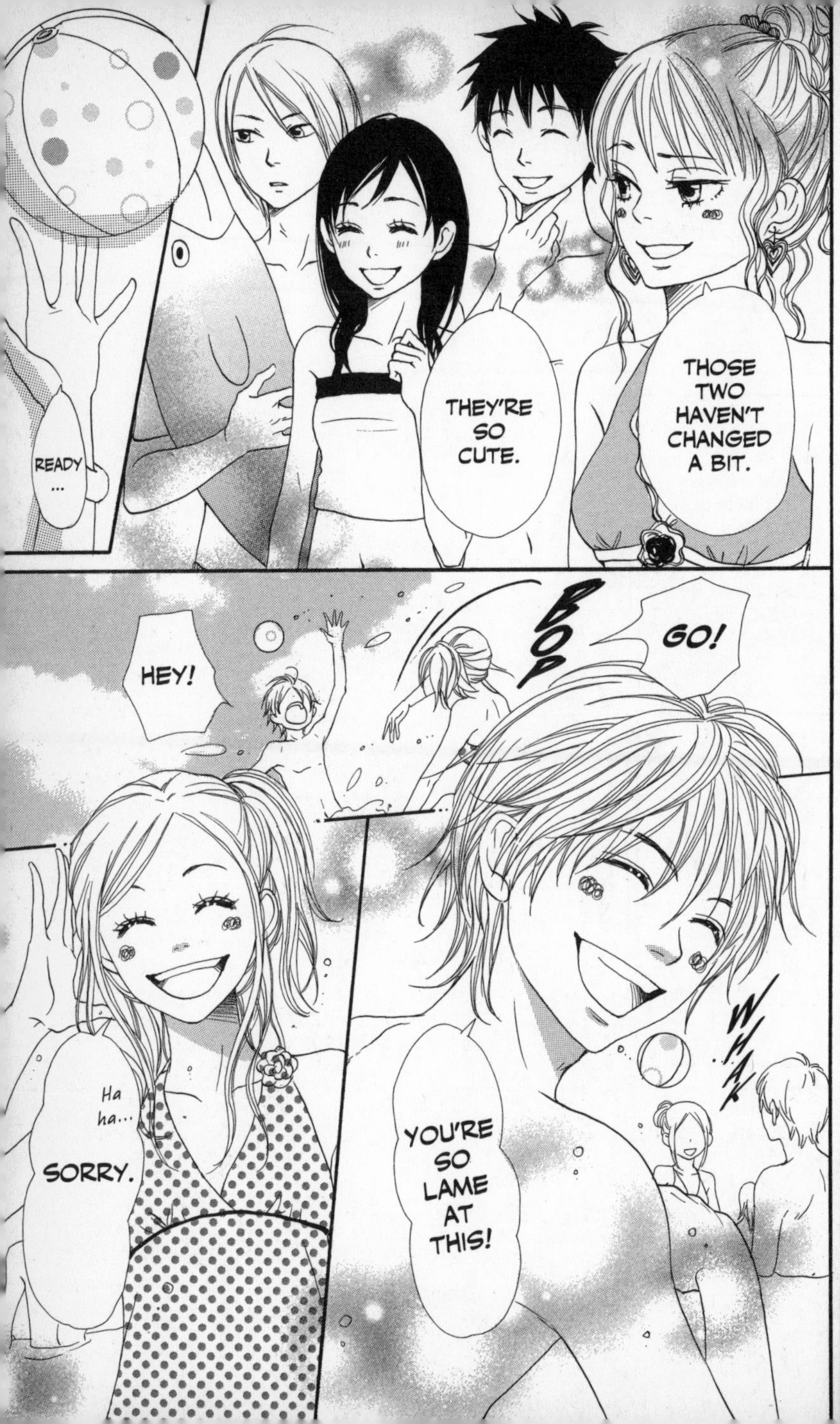
THOSE TWO HAVEN'T CHANGED A BIT.
THEY'RE SO CUTE.
READY...
GO!
BOOP
HEY!
WHAP
YOU'RE SO LAME AT THIS!
Ha ha...
SORRY.

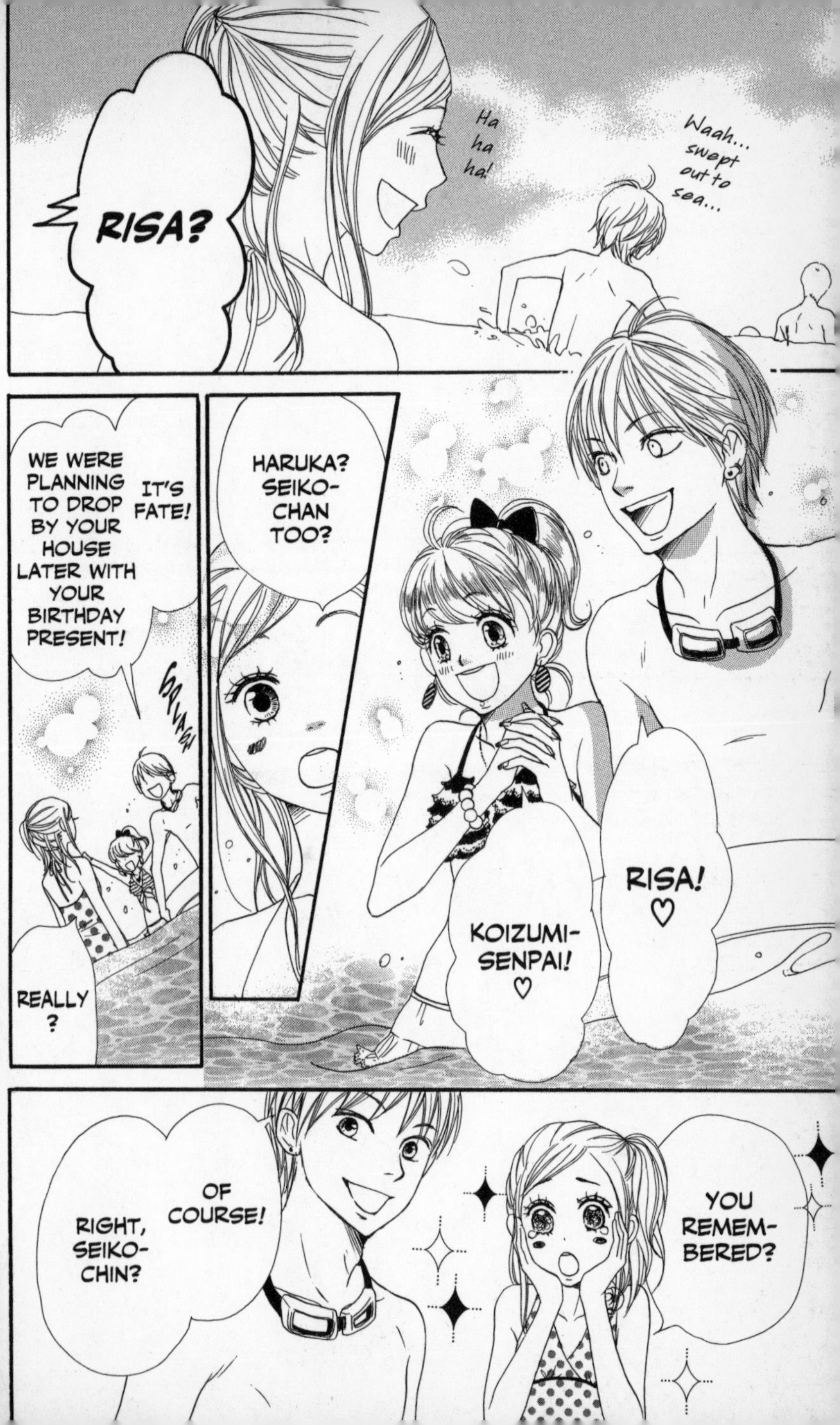
Waah... swept out to sea...
Ha ha ha!
RISA?
RISA! ♡
KOIZUMI-SENPAI! ♡
HARUKA? SEIKO-CHAN TOO?
IT'S FATE!
WE WERE PLANNING TO DROP BY YOUR HOUSE LATER WITH YOUR BIRTHDAY PRESENT!
REALLY?
YOU REMEMBERED?
OF COURSE!
RIGHT, SEIKO-CHIN?

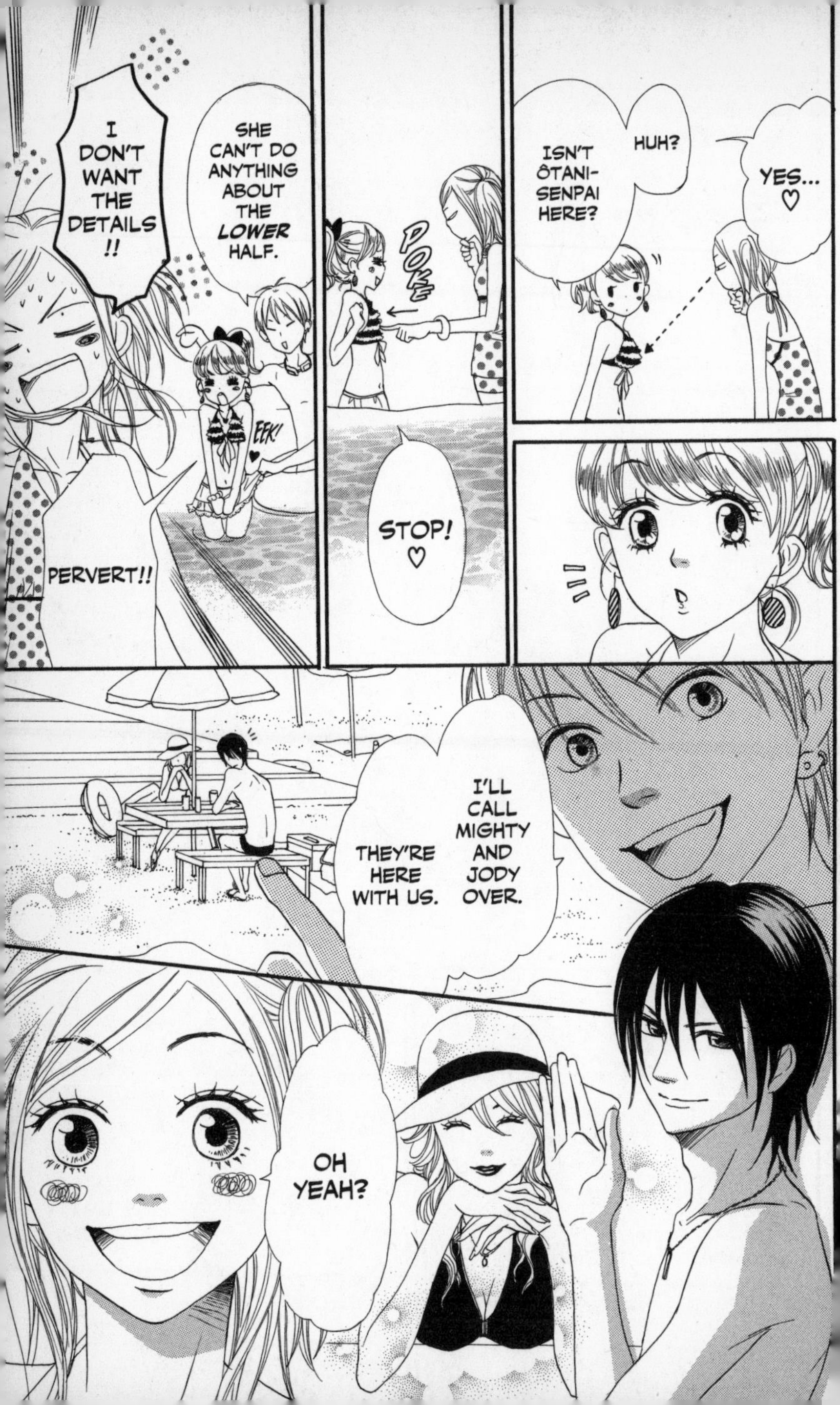
YES... ♡
HUH?
ISN'T ŌTANI-SENPAI HERE?
POKE
STOP! ♡
SHE CAN'T DO ANYTHING ABOUT THE *LOWER* HALF.
I DON'T WANT THE DETAILS!!
EEK!
PERVERT!!
I'LL CALL MIGHTY AND JODY OVER.
THEY'RE HERE WITH US.
OH YEAH?

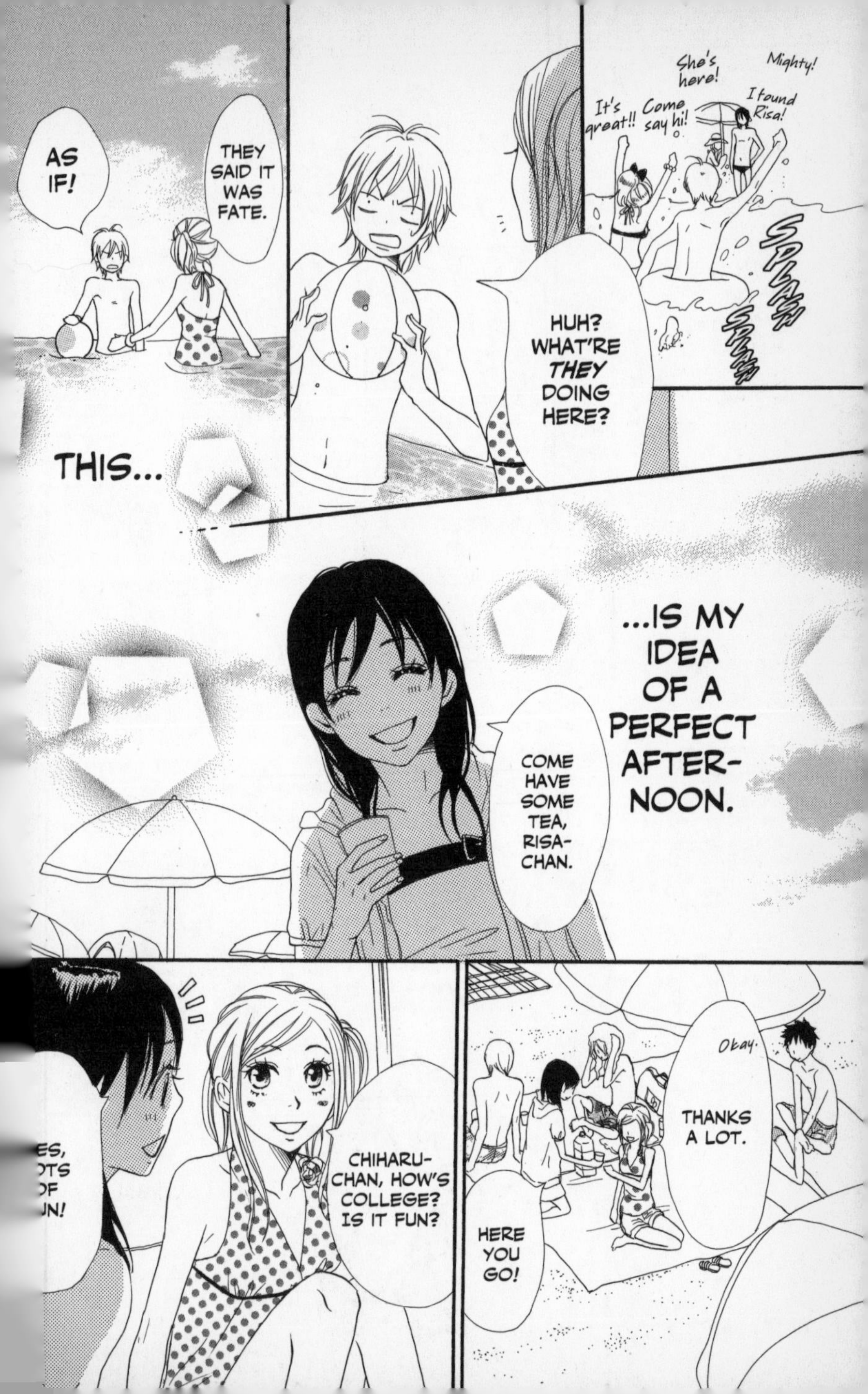
She's here!
Mighty!
I found Risa!
It's great!!
Come say hi!
SPLASH
SPLASH
HUH? WHAT'RE *THEY* DOING HERE?
THEY SAID IT WAS FATE.
AS IF!
THIS...
...IS MY IDEA OF A PERFECT AFTERNOON.
COME HAVE SOME TEA, RISA-CHAN.
Okay.
THANKS A LOT.
HERE YOU GO!
CHIHARU-CHAN, HOW'S COLLEGE? IS IT FUN?
ES, OTS OF UN!

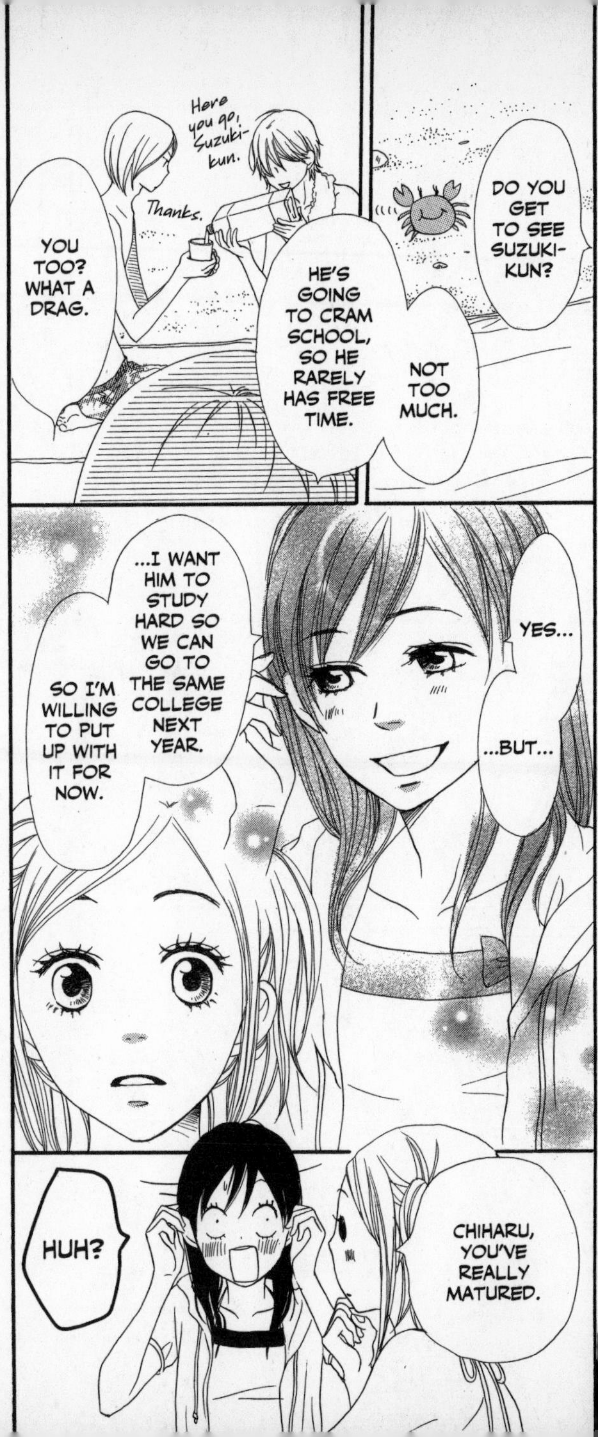
DO YOU GET TO SEE SUZUKI-KUN?
NOT TOO MUCH.
HE'S GOING TO CRAM SCHOOL, SO HE RARELY HAS FREE TIME.
Here you go, Suzuki-kun.
Thanks.
YOU TOO? WHAT A DRAG.
YES...
...BUT...
...I WANT HIM TO STUDY HARD SO WE CAN GO TO THE SAME COLLEGE NEXT YEAR.
SO I'M WILLING TO PUT UP WITH IT FOR NOW.
CHIHARU, YOU'VE REALLY MATURED.
HUH?

Okay! This is it!

I'm really glad I created Love★Com. I'm still learning and making lots of mistakes, but that just means I'll keep working to grow and mature. If you should come upon another Aya Nakahara manga in the future, please read it.

Well, take care!!

August 2008
Aya Nakahara

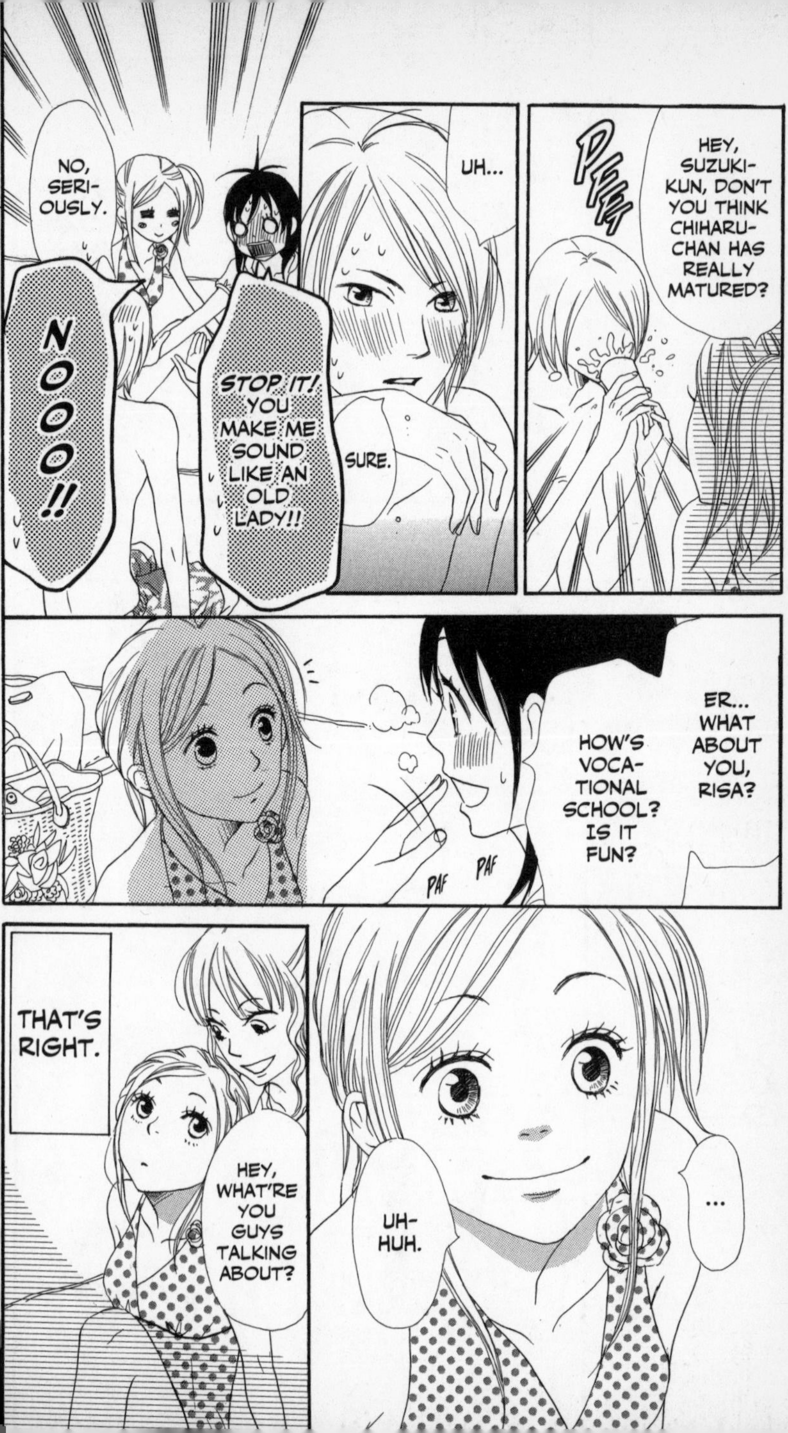
HEY, SUZUKI-KUN, DON'T YOU THINK CHIHARU-CHAN HAS REALLY MATURED?
UH...
SURE.
NO, SERIOUSLY.
NOOOO!!
STOP IT! YOU MAKE ME SOUND LIKE AN OLD LADY!!
ER... WHAT ABOUT YOU, RISA?
HOW'S VOCATIONAL SCHOOL? IS IT FUN?
PAF
PAF
...
UH-HUH.
HEY, WHAT'RE YOU GUYS TALKING ABOUT?
THAT'S RIGHT.

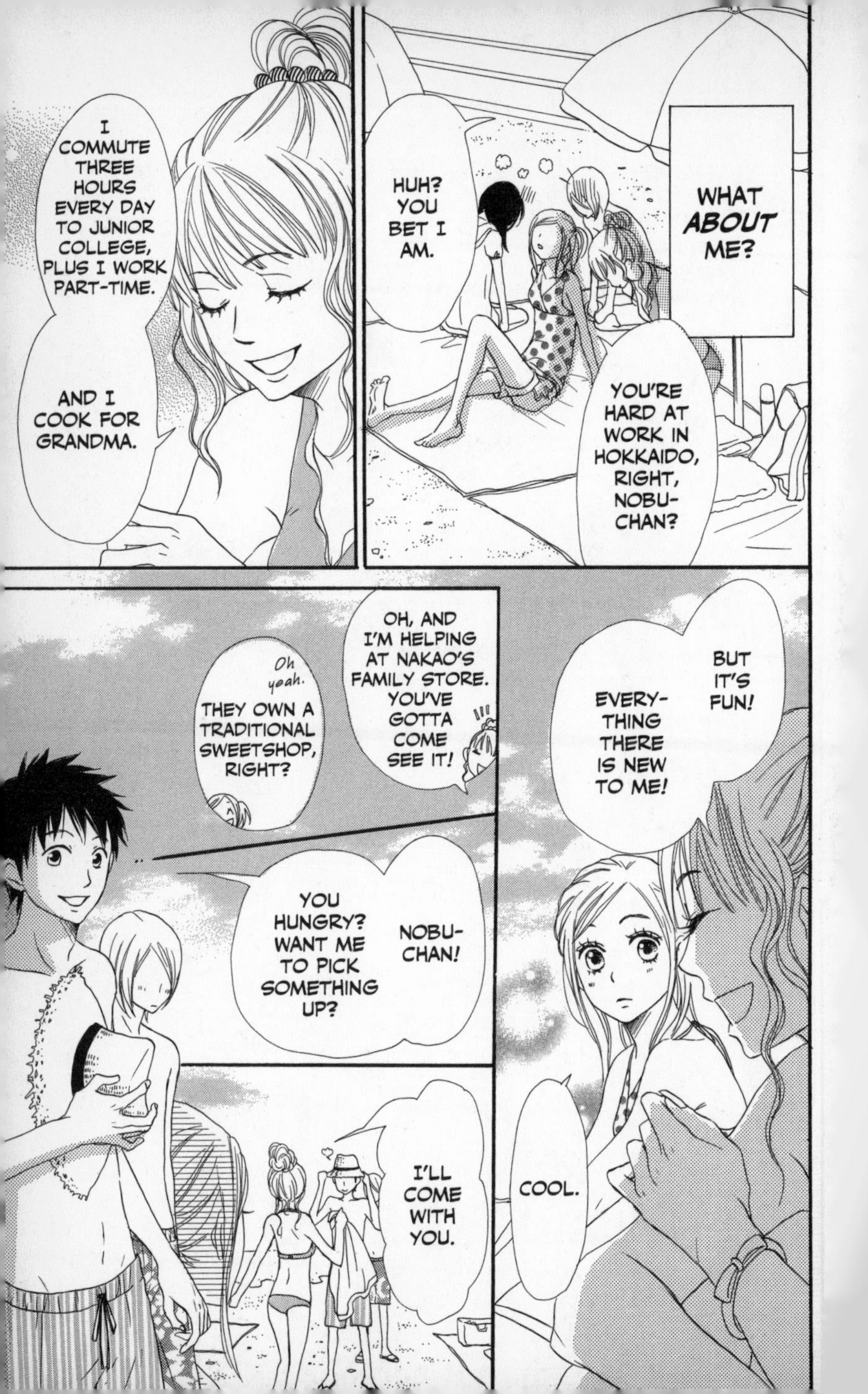
WHAT ABOUT ME?
YOU'RE HARD AT WORK IN HOKKAIDO, RIGHT, NOBU-CHAN?
HUH? YOU BET I AM.
I COMMUTE THREE HOURS EVERY DAY TO JUNIOR COLLEGE, PLUS I WORK PART-TIME.
AND I COOK FOR GRANDMA.
BUT IT'S FUN!
EVERYTHING THERE IS NEW TO ME!
COOL.
OH, AND I'M HELPING AT NAKAO'S FAMILY STORE. YOU'VE GOTTA COME SEE IT!
Oh yeah.
THEY OWN A TRADITIONAL SWEETSHOP, RIGHT?
..
NOBU-CHAN!
YOU HUNGRY? WANT ME TO PICK SOMETHING UP?
I'LL COME WITH YOU.

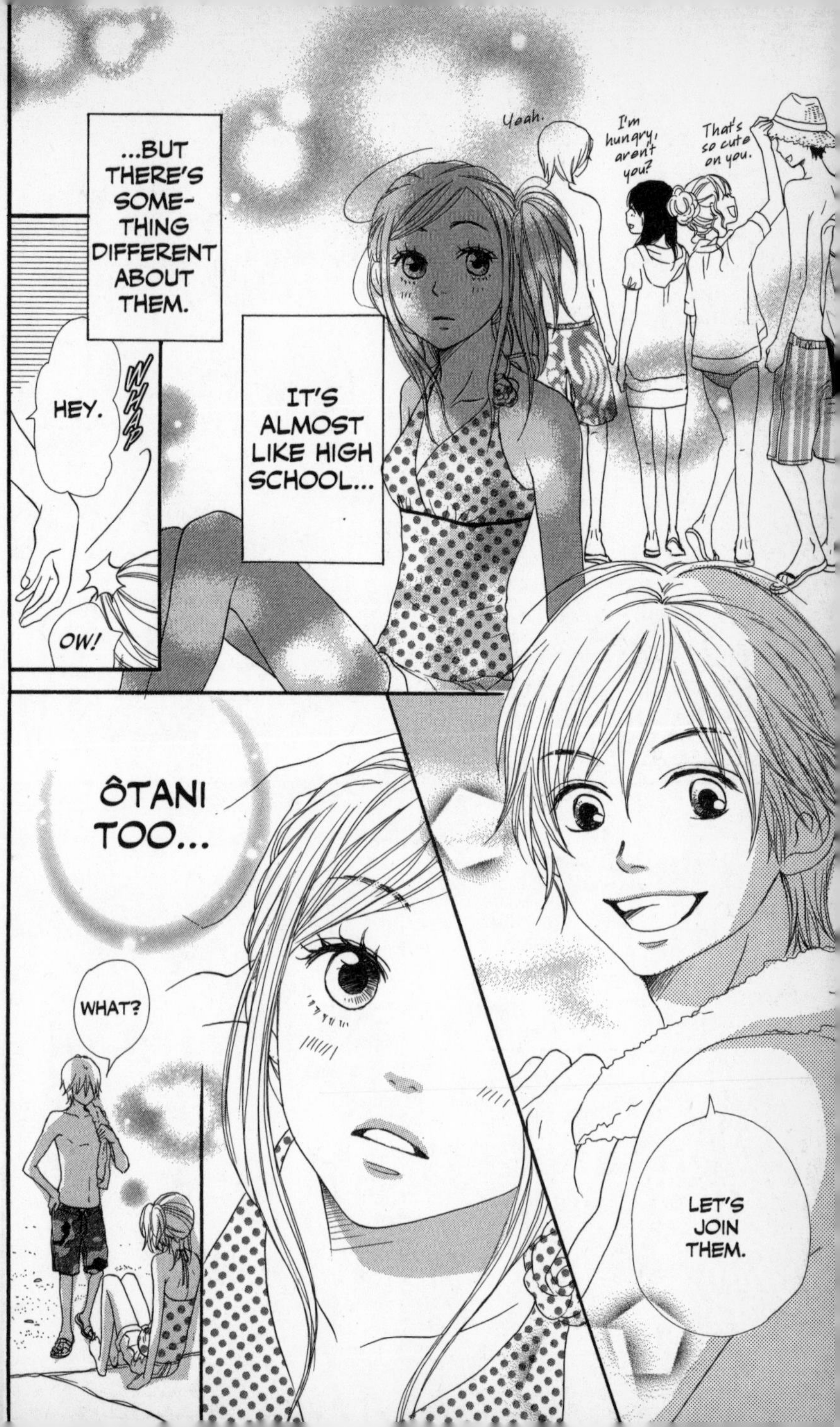
That's so cute on you.
I'm hungry, aren't you?
Yeah.
IT'S ALMOST LIKE HIGH SCHOOL...
...BUT THERE'S SOME-THING DIFFERENT ABOUT THEM.
HEY.
WHAP
OW!
LET'S JOIN THEM.
ÔTANI TOO...
WHAT?

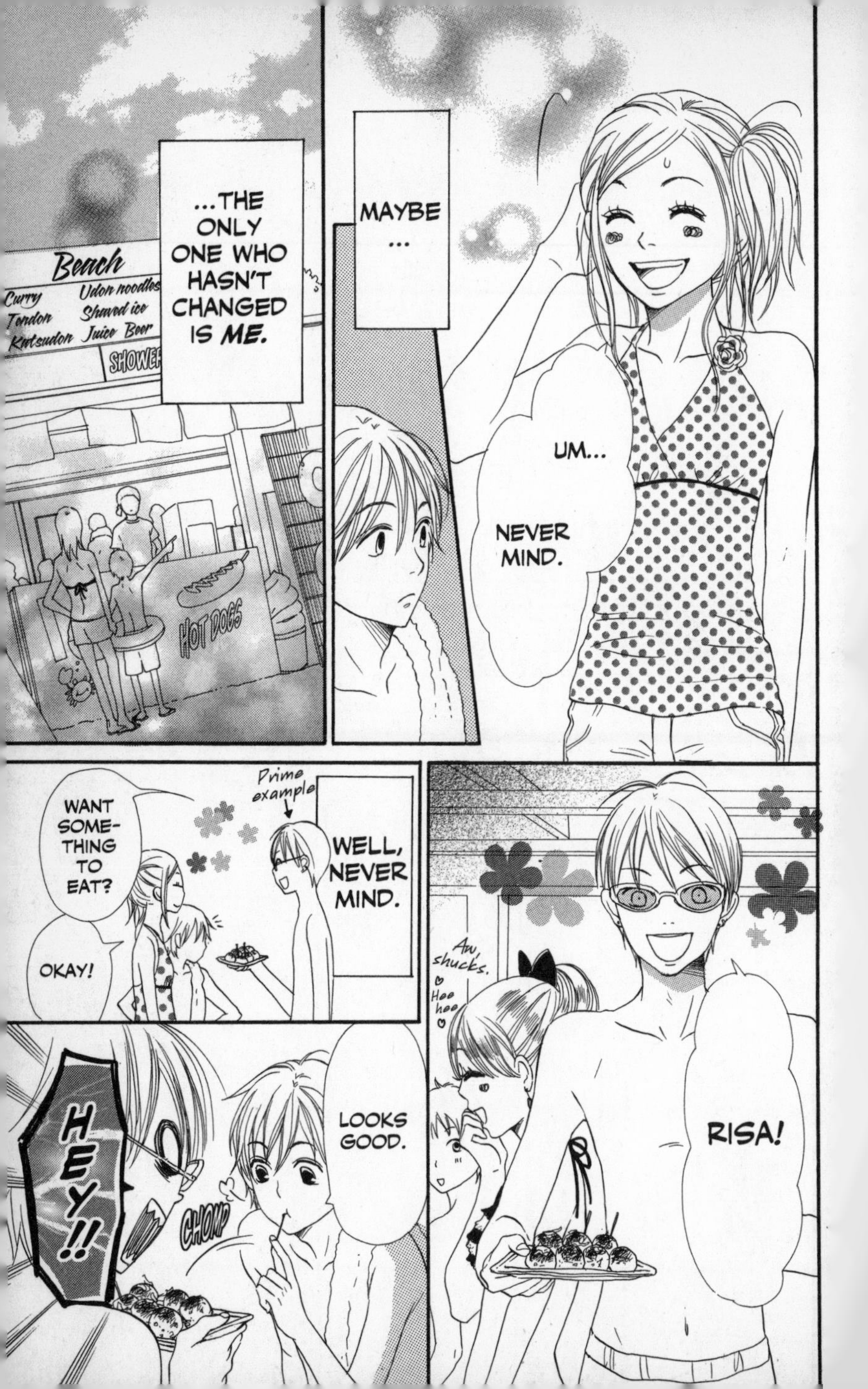
UM...
NEVER MIND.
MAYBE ...
...THE ONLY ONE WHO HASN'T CHANGED IS *ME.*
Beach
Curry
Tendon
Katsudon
Udon noodles
Shaved ice
Juice Beer
SHOWER
HOT DOGS
RISA!
Aw, shucks.
Hee hee
WELL, NEVER MIND.
Prime example
WANT SOME-THING TO EAT?
OKAY!
LOOKS GOOD.
CHOMP
HEY!!

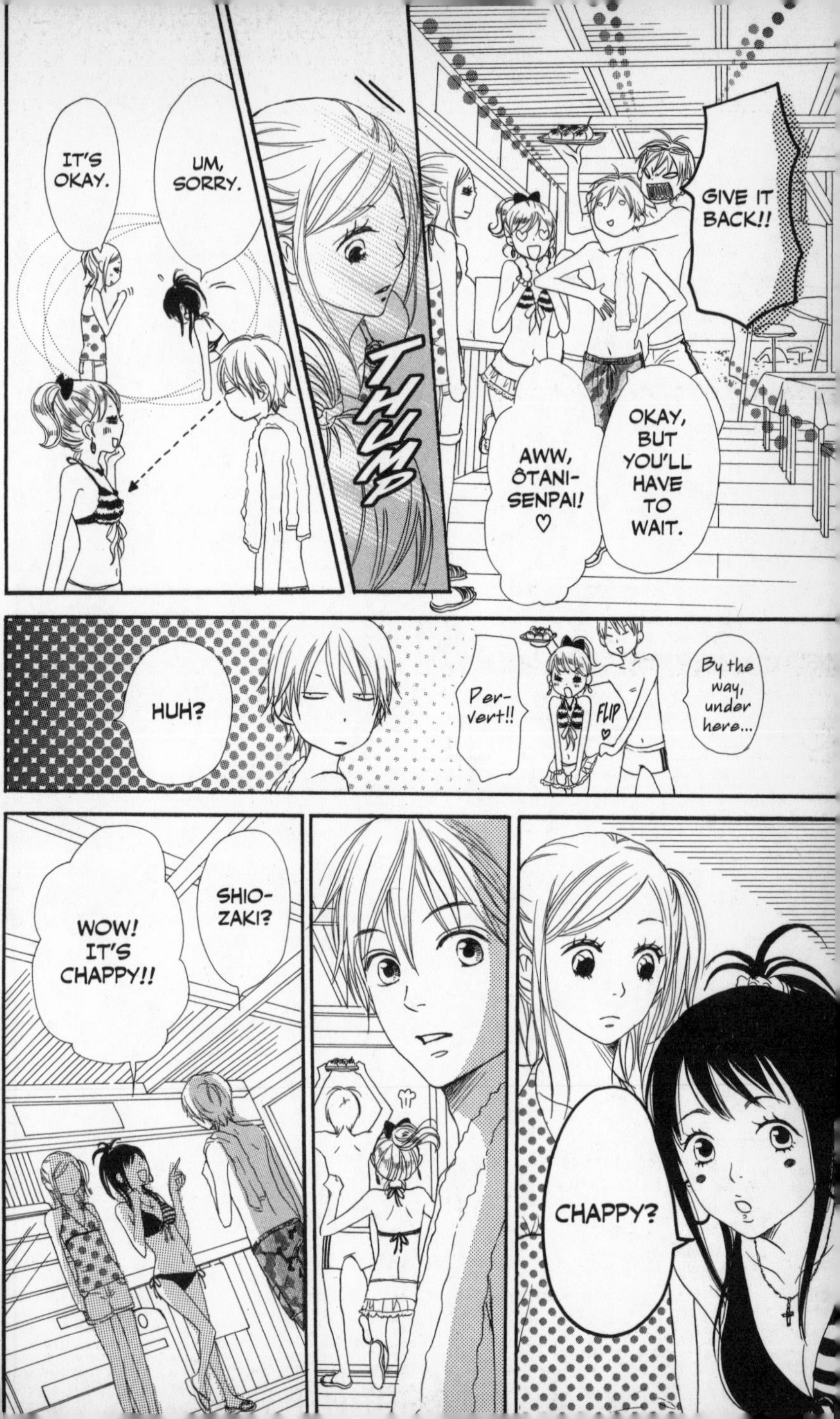
GIVE IT BACK!!
OKAY, BUT YOU'LL HAVE TO WAIT.
AWW, ŌTANI-SENPAI! ♡
THUMP
UM, SORRY.
IT'S OKAY.
By the way, under here...
FLIP ♡
Per-vert!!
HUH?
CHAPPY?
SHIO-ZAKI?
WOW! IT'S CHAPPY!!

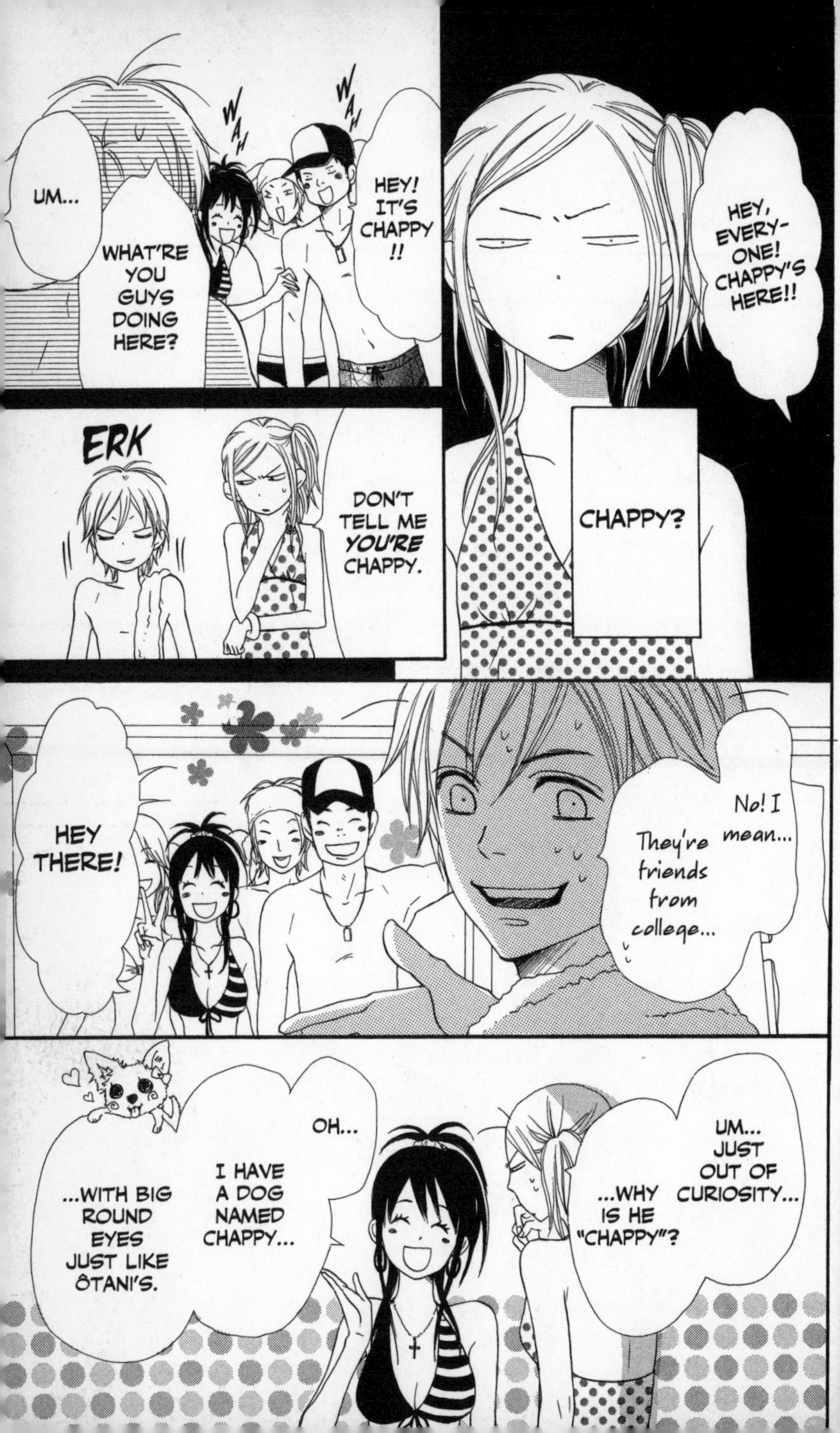
HEY, EVERYONE! CHAPPY'S HERE!!
CHAPPY?
WAH
WAH
HEY! IT'S CHAPPY!!
WHAT'RE YOU GUYS DOING HERE?
UM...
DON'T TELL ME *YOU'RE* CHAPPY.
ERK
No! I mean...
They're friends from college...
HEY THERE!
UM... JUST OUT OF CURIOSITY...
...WHY IS HE "CHAPPY"?
OH...
I HAVE A DOG NAMED CHAPPY...
...WITH BIG ROUND EYES JUST LIKE ŌTANI'S.

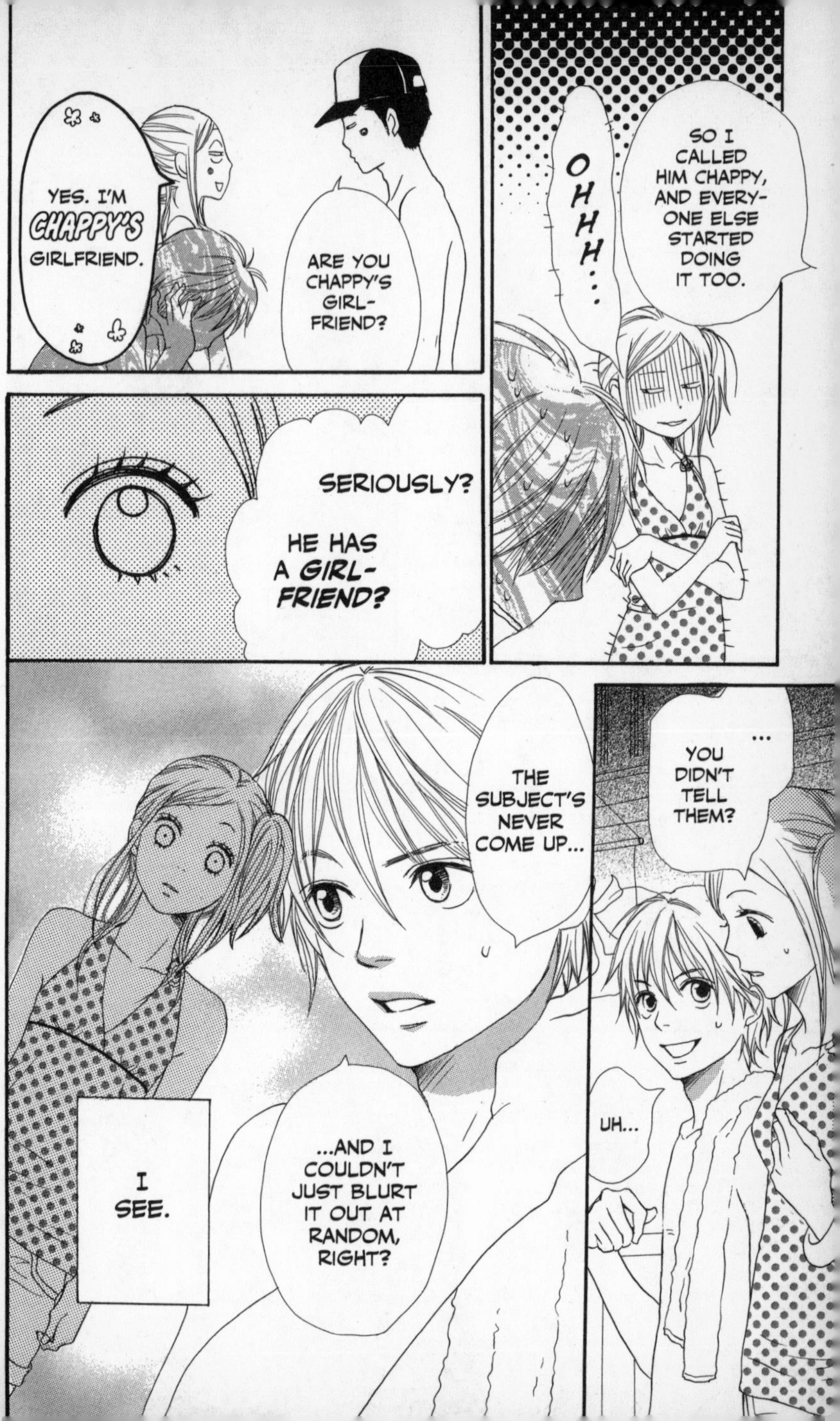

SO I CALLED HIM CHAPPY, AND EVERY-ONE ELSE STARTED DOING IT TOO.
OHHH...
ARE YOU CHAPPY'S GIRL-FRIEND?
YES. I'M CHAPPY'S GIRLFRIEND.
SERIOUSLY?
HE HAS A GIRL-FRIEND?
...
YOU DIDN'T TELL THEM?
UH...
THE SUBJECT'S NEVER COME UP...
...AND I COULDN'T JUST BLURT IT OUT AT RANDOM, RIGHT?
I SEE.

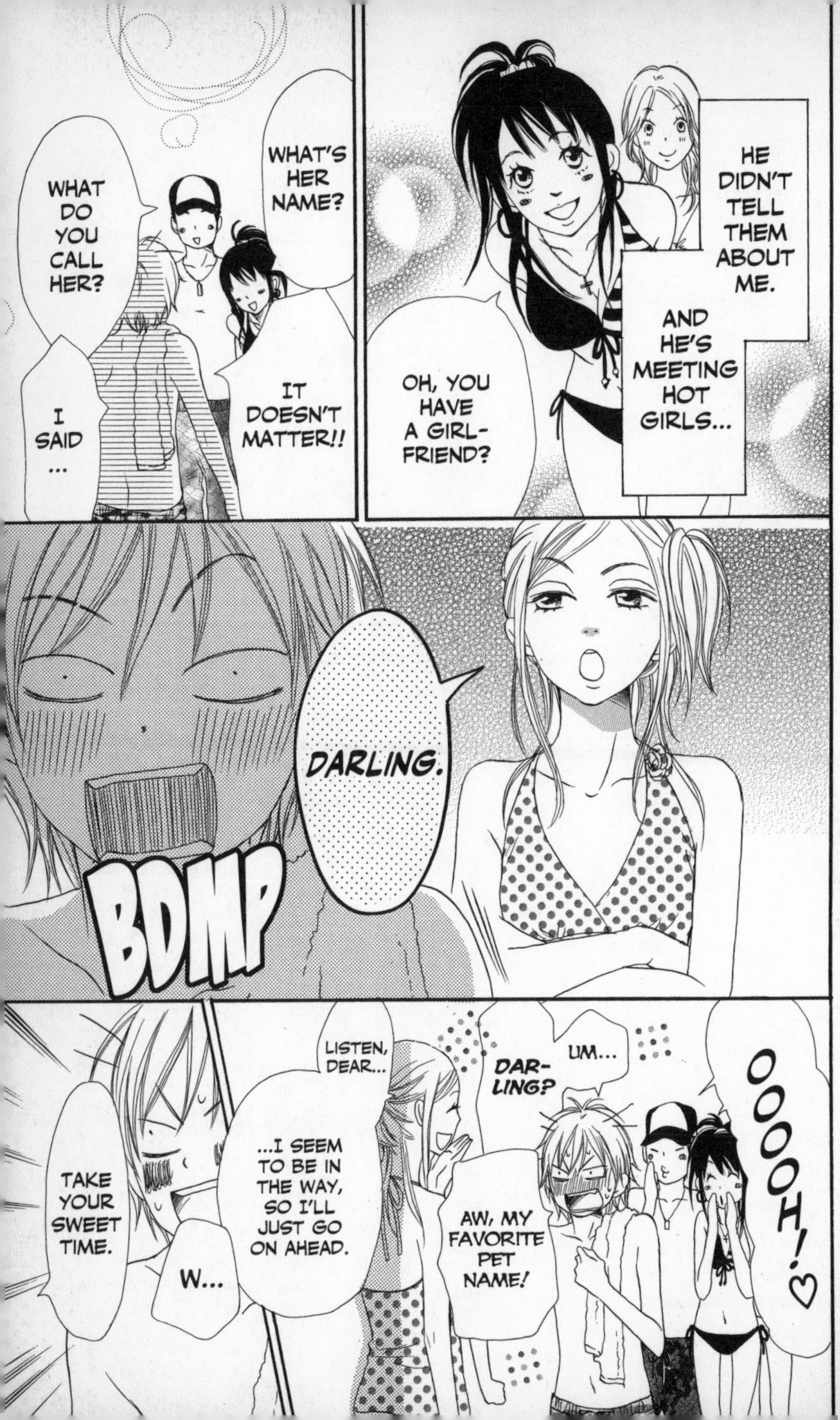
HE DIDN'T TELL THEM ABOUT ME.
AND HE'S MEETING HOT GIRLS...
OH, YOU HAVE A GIRL-FRIEND?
WHAT'S HER NAME?
WHAT DO YOU CALL HER?
IT DOESN'T MATTER!!
I SAID ...
DARLING.
BDMP
OOOOH!♡
UM...
DAR-LING?
AW, MY FAVORITE PET NAME!
LISTEN, DEAR...
...I SEEM TO BE IN THE WAY, SO I'LL JUST GO ON AHEAD.
TAKE YOUR SWEET TIME.
W...

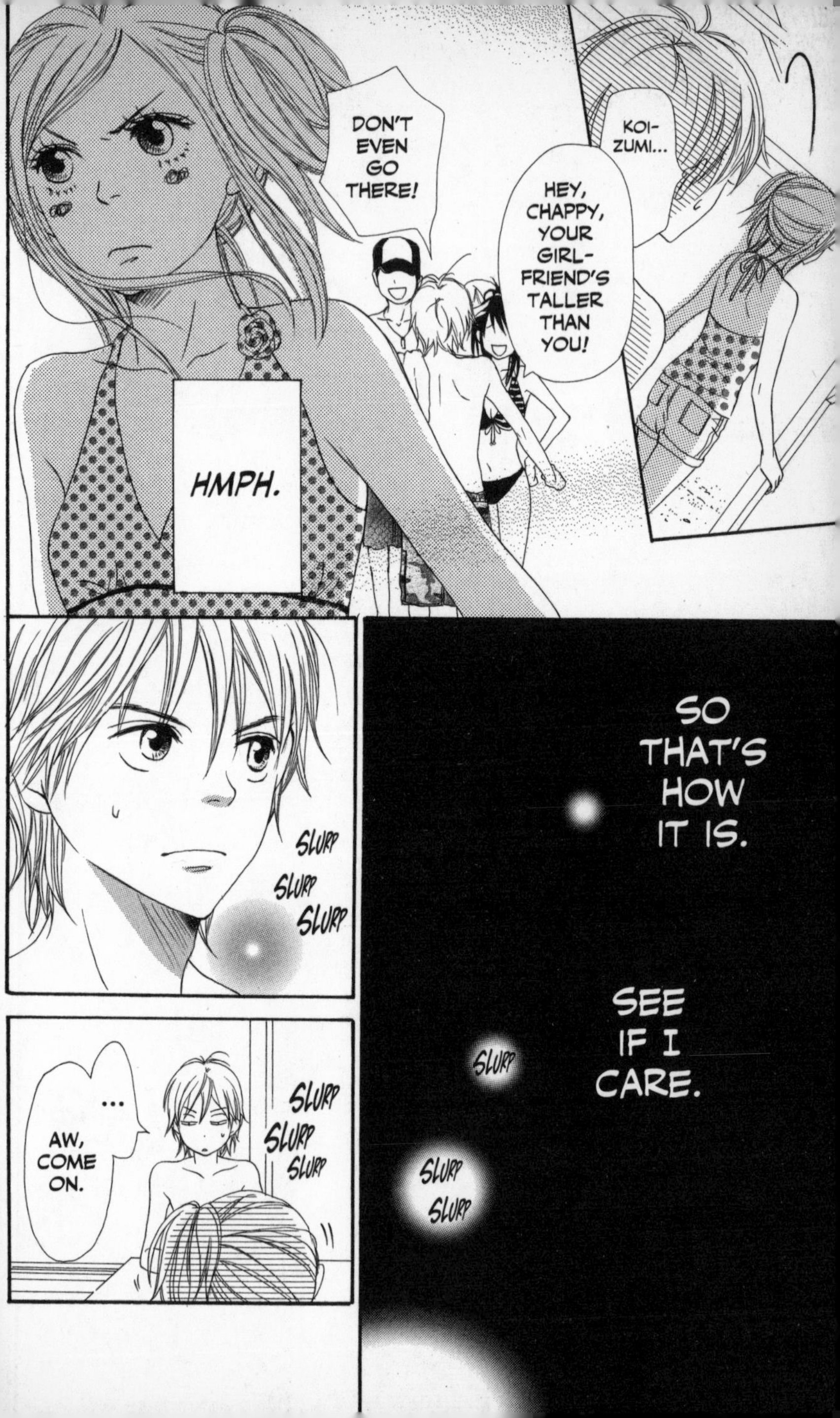
KOI-ZUMI...
HEY, CHAPPY, YOUR GIRL-FRIEND'S TALLER THAN YOU!
DON'T EVEN GO THERE!
HMPH.
SO THAT'S HOW IT IS.
SEE IF I CARE.
SLURP
SLURP
SLURP
SLURP
SLURP
SLURP
SLURP
...
AW, COME ON.
SLURP
SLURP
SLURP

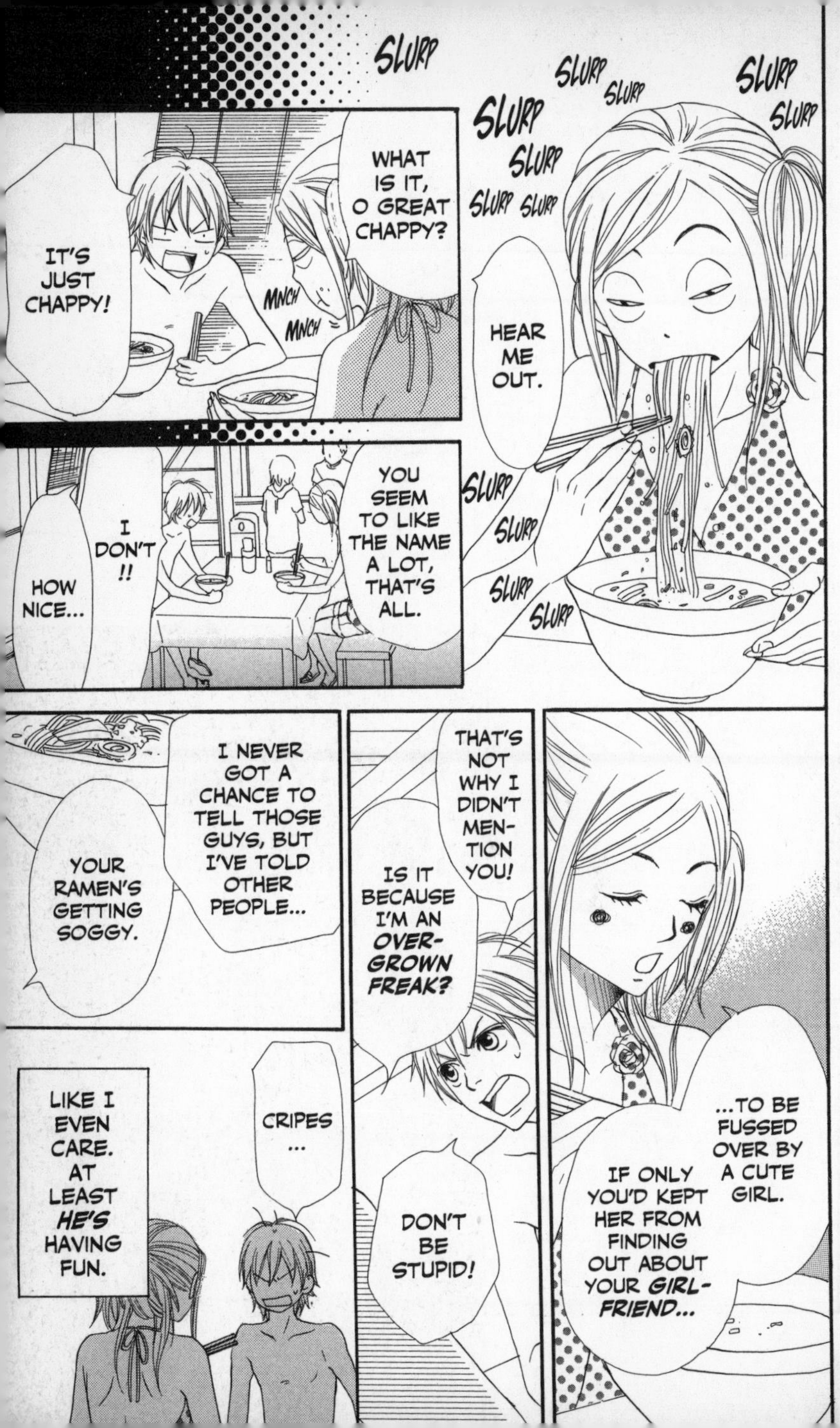
SLURP
SLURP
SLURP
SLURP
SLURP
SLURP
SLURP
SLURP
SLURP
HEAR ME OUT.
SLURP
SLURP
SLURP
SLURP
WHAT IS IT, O GREAT CHAPPY?
MNCH
MNCH
IT'S JUST CHAPPY!
YOU SEEM TO LIKE THE NAME A LOT, THAT'S ALL.
I DON'T !!
HOW NICE...
...TO BE FUSSED OVER BY A CUTE GIRL.
IF ONLY YOU'D KEPT HER FROM FINDING OUT ABOUT YOUR *GIRLFRIEND*...
THAT'S NOT WHY I DIDN'T MEN-TION YOU!
IS IT BECAUSE I'M AN *OVERGROWN FREAK?*
DON'T BE STUPID!
I NEVER GOT A CHANCE TO TELL THOSE GUYS, BUT I'VE TOLD OTHER PEOPLE...
YOUR RAMEN'S GETTING SOGGY.
CRIPES ...
LIKE I EVEN CARE. AT LEAST *HE'S* HAVING FUN.

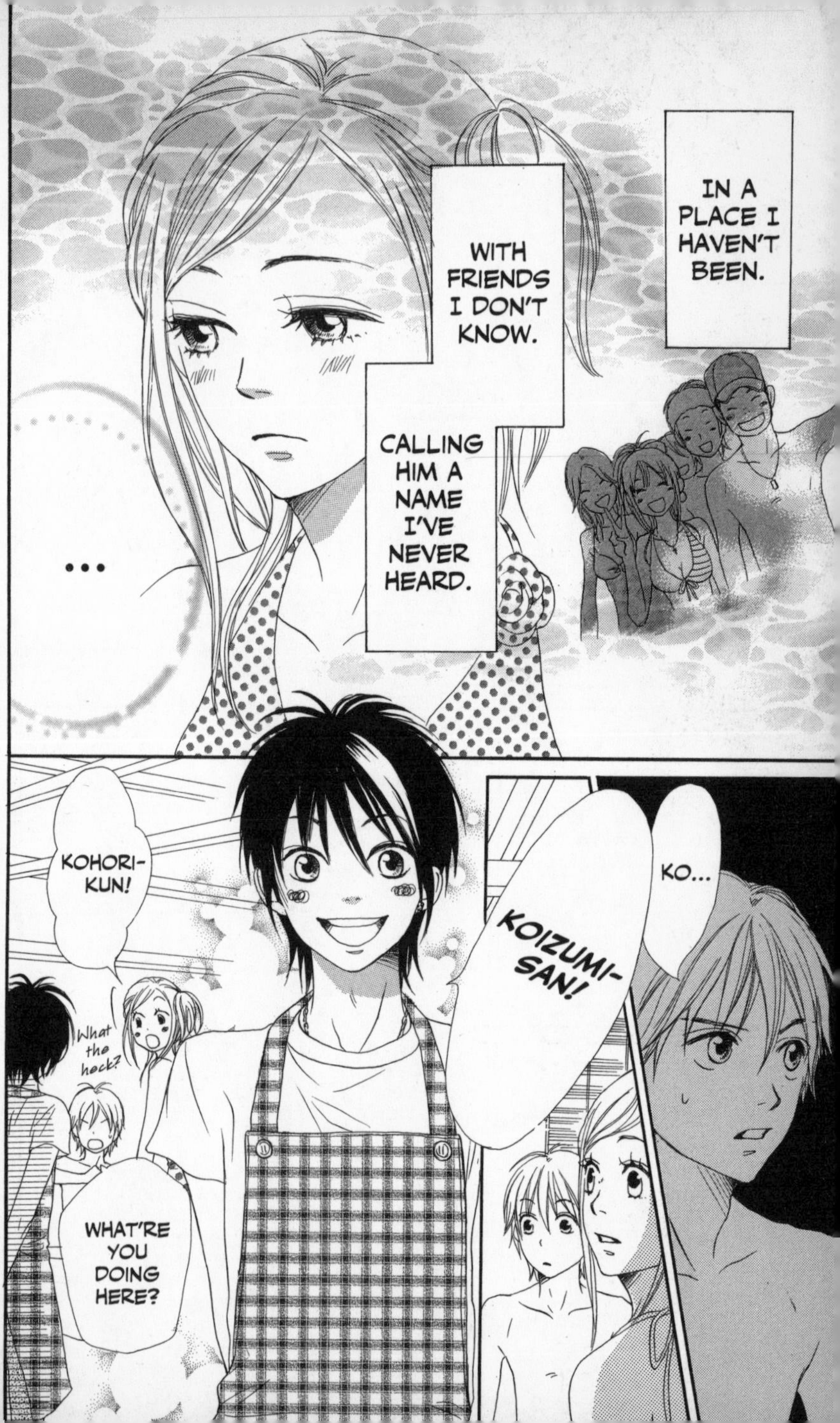
IN A PLACE I HAVEN'T BEEN.
WITH FRIENDS I DON'T KNOW.
CALLING HIM A NAME I'VE NEVER HEARD.
...
KO...
KOIZUMI-SAN!
KOHORI-KUN!
What the heck?
WHAT'RE YOU DOING HERE?

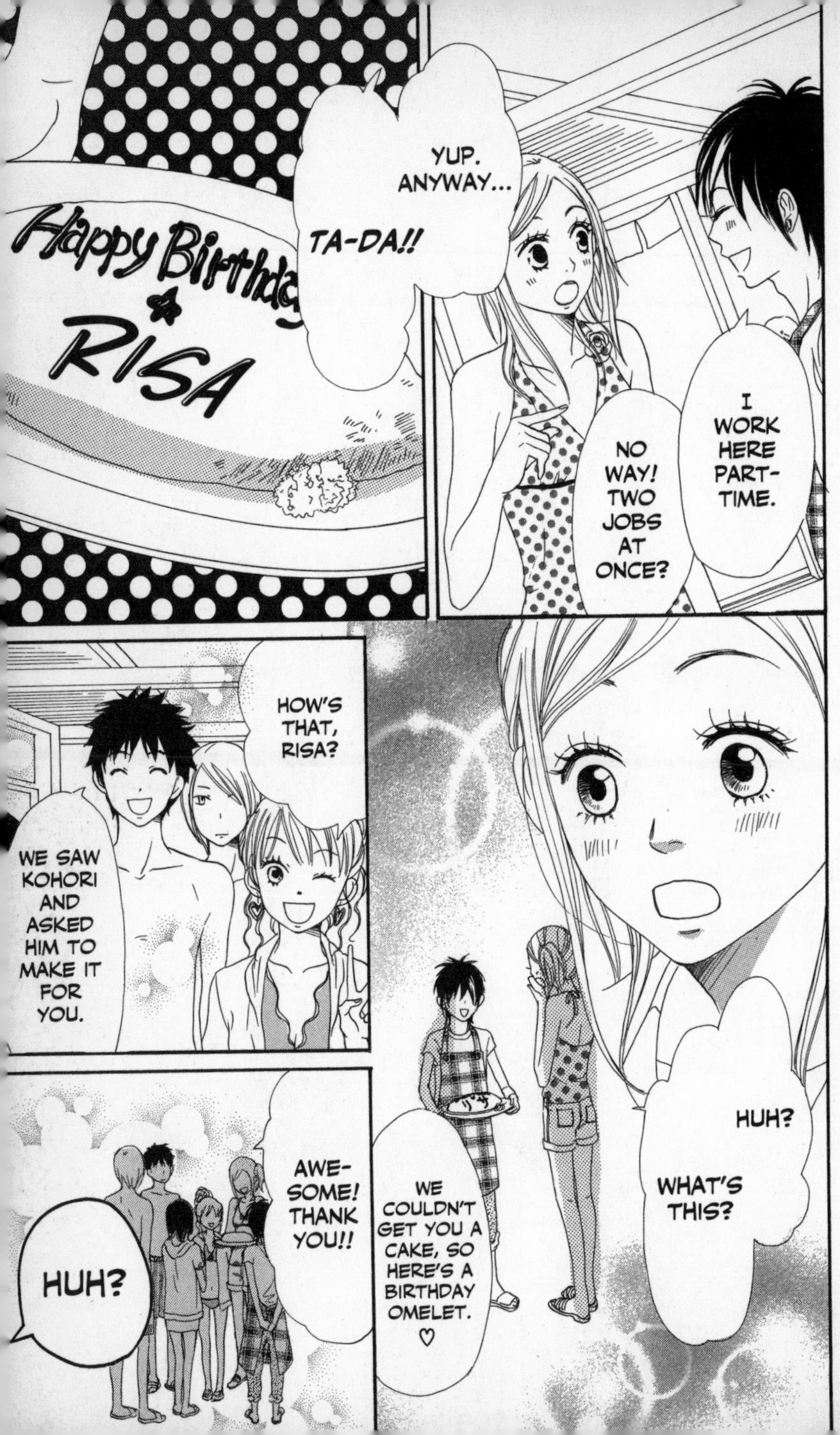
I WORK HERE PART-TIME.
NO WAY! TWO JOBS AT ONCE?
YUP. ANYWAY... TA-DA!!
Happy Birthday ✿ RISA
HUH? WHAT'S THIS?
WE COULDN'T GET YOU A CAKE, SO HERE'S A BIRTHDAY OMELET. ♡
HOW'S THAT, RISA?
WE SAW KOHORI AND ASKED HIM TO MAKE IT FOR YOU.
AWE-SOME! THANK YOU!!
HUH?

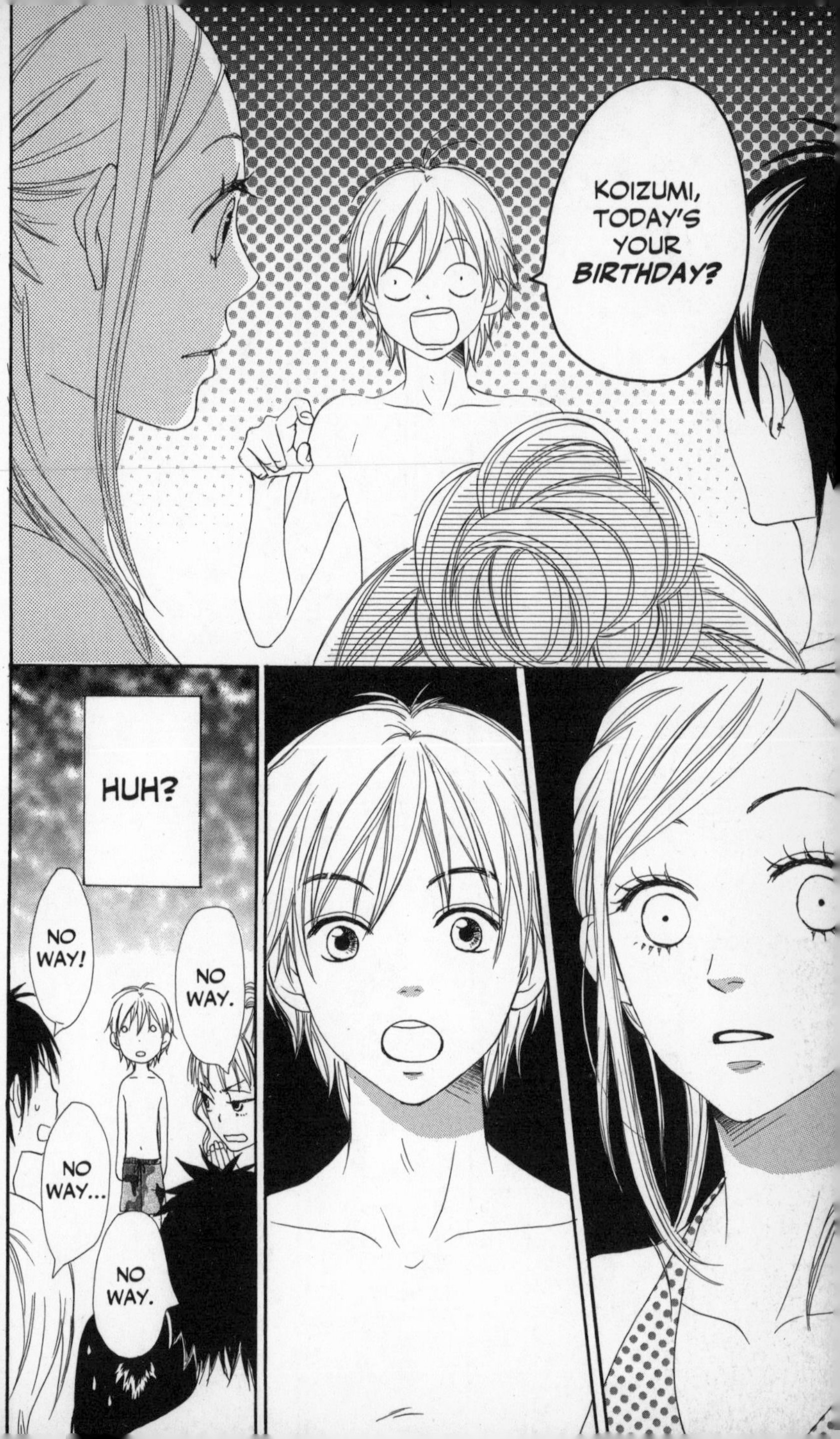
KOIZUMI, TODAY'S YOUR BIRTHDAY?
HUH?
NO WAY.
NO WAY!
NO WAY...
NO WAY.

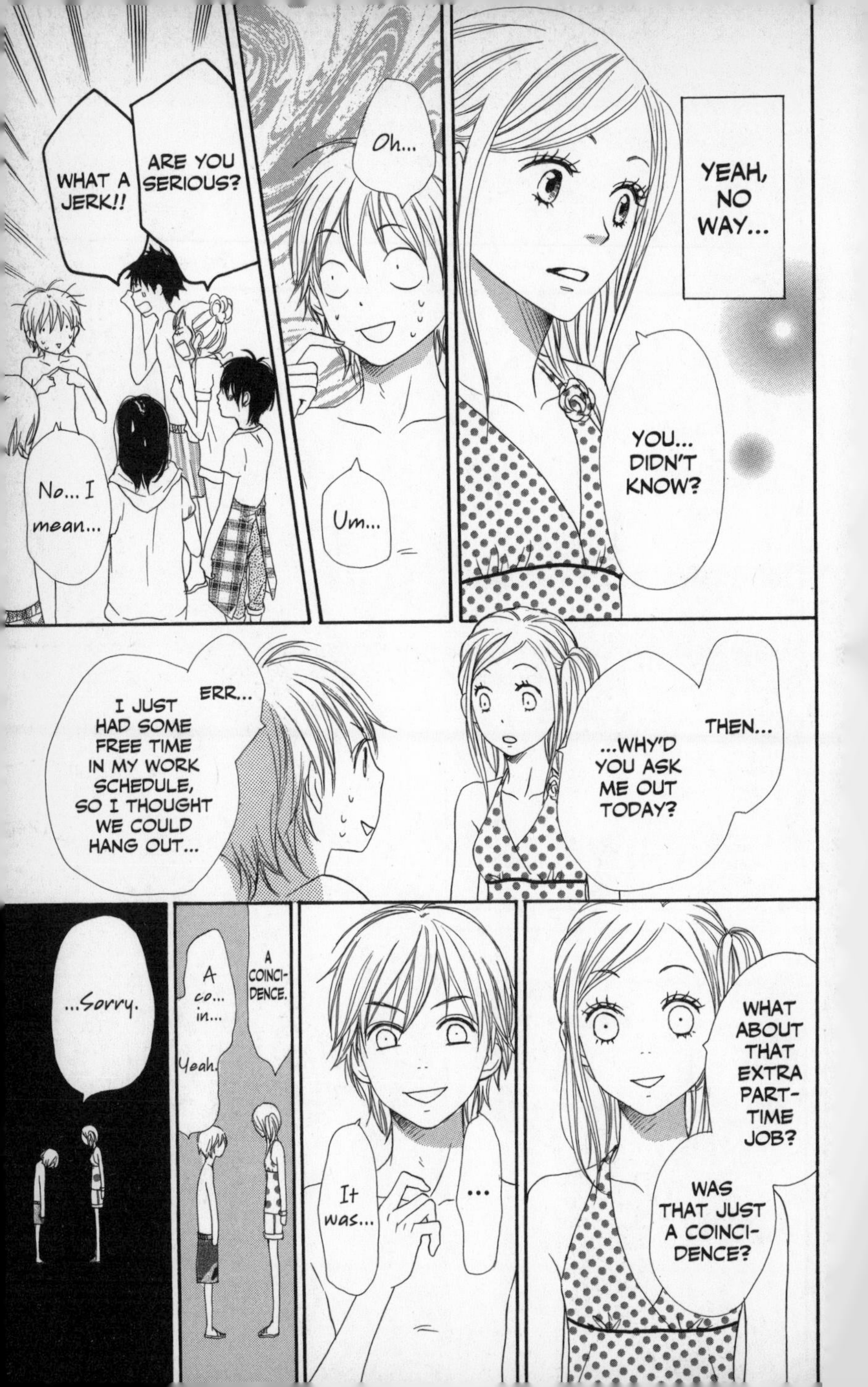
YEAH, NO WAY...
YOU... DIDN'T KNOW?
Oh...
Um...
ARE YOU SERIOUS?
WHAT A JERK!!
No... I mean...
THEN...
...WHY'D YOU ASK ME OUT TODAY?
ERR...
I JUST HAD SOME FREE TIME IN MY WORK SCHEDULE, SO I THOUGHT WE COULD HANG OUT...
WHAT ABOUT THAT EXTRA PART-TIME JOB?
WAS THAT JUST A COINCIDENCE?
...
It was...
A COINCIDENCE.
A co... in...
Yeah.
...Sorry.

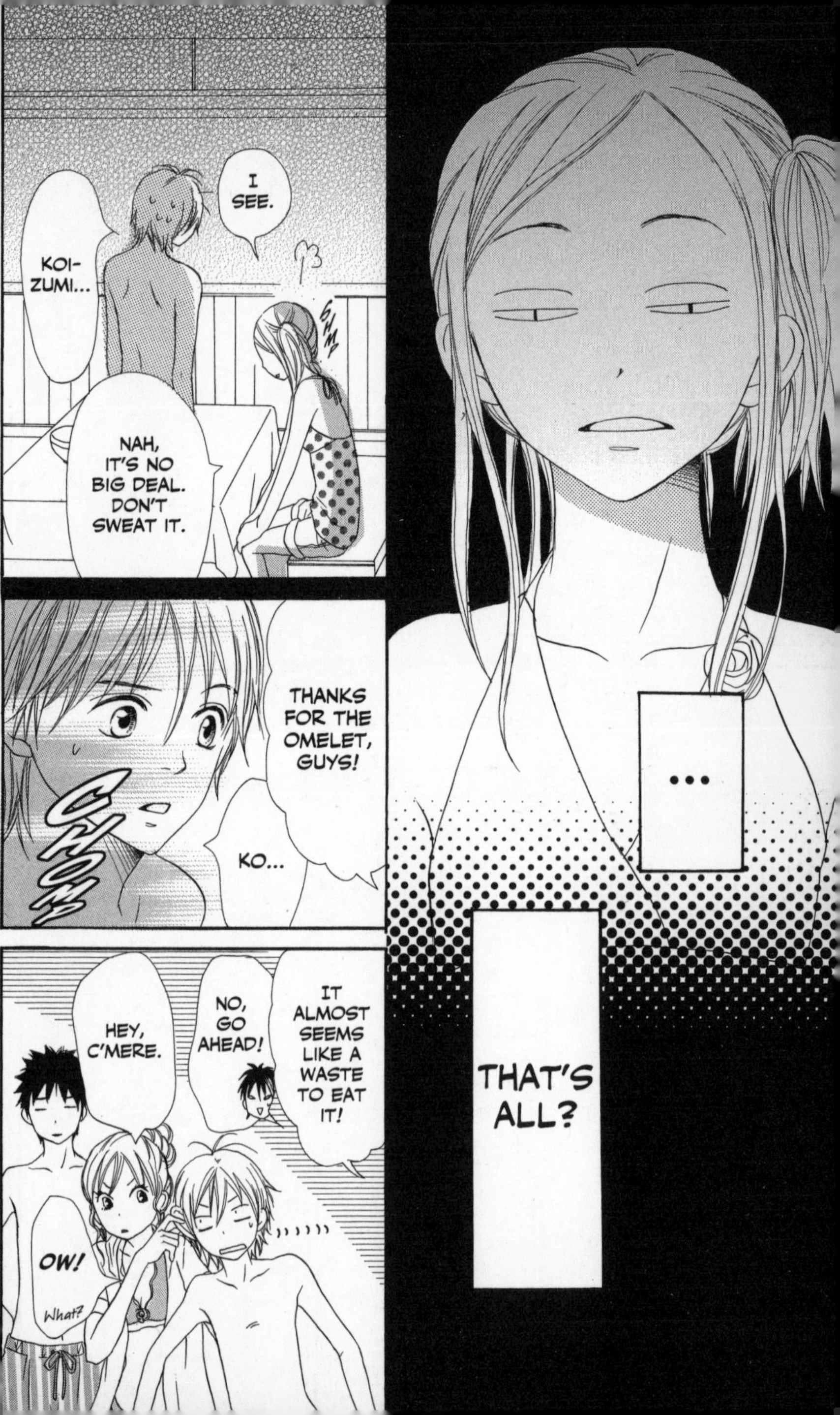
...
THAT'S ALL?
I SEE.
KOI-ZUMI...
NAH, IT'S NO BIG DEAL. DON'T SWEAT IT.
THANKS FOR THE OMELET, GUYS!
KO...
CHOMP
IT ALMOST SEEMS LIKE A WASTE TO EAT IT!
NO, GO AHEAD!
HEY, C'MERE.
OW!
What?

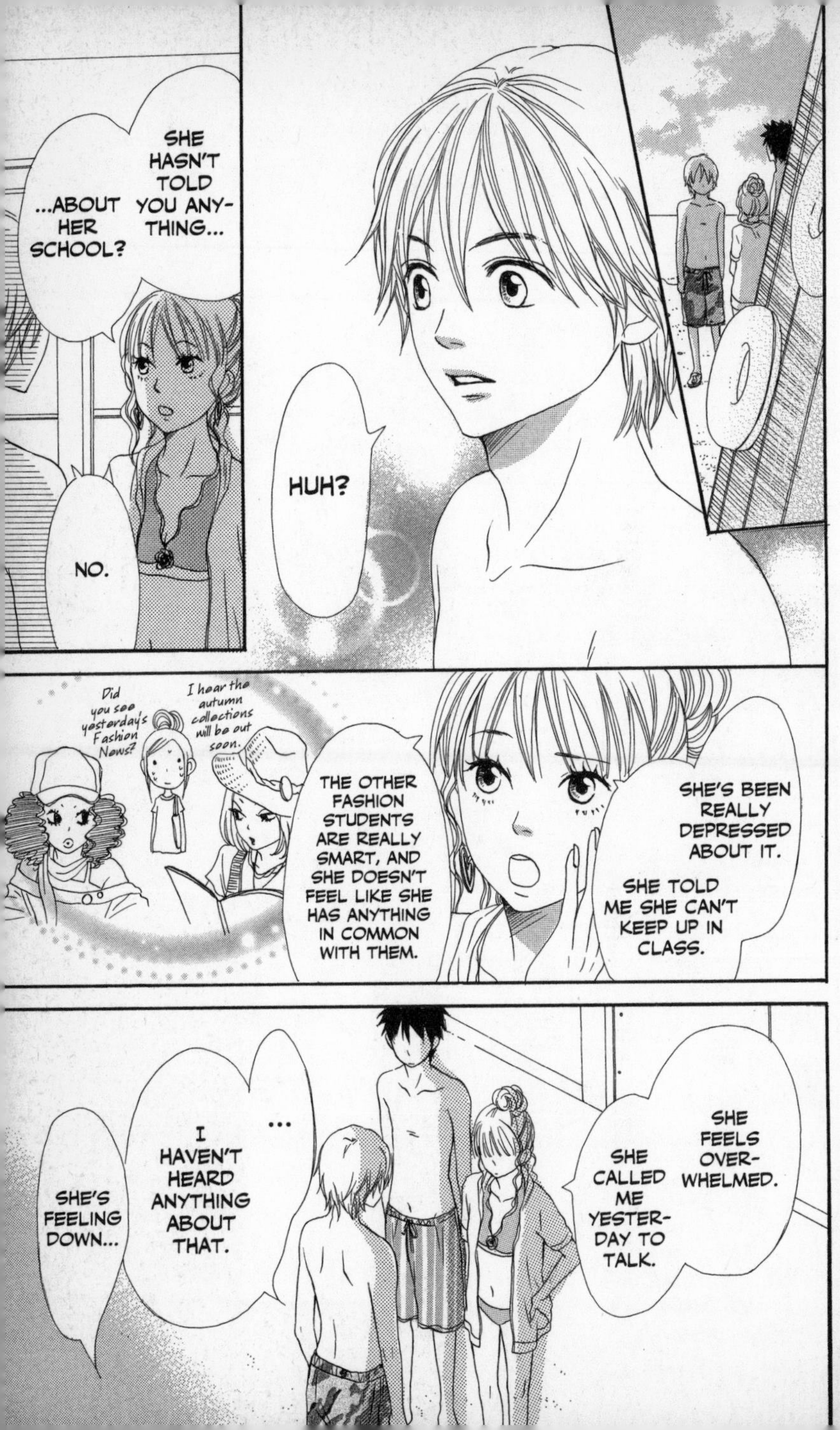
HUH?
SHE HASN'T TOLD YOU ANYTHING...
...ABOUT HER SCHOOL?
NO.
SHE'S BEEN REALLY DEPRESSED ABOUT IT.
SHE TOLD ME SHE CAN'T KEEP UP IN CLASS.
THE OTHER FASHION STUDENTS ARE REALLY SMART, AND SHE DOESN'T FEEL LIKE SHE HAS ANYTHING IN COMMON WITH THEM.
I hear the autumn collections will be out soon.
Did you see yesterday's Fashion News?
SHE FEELS OVER-WHELMED.
SHE CALLED ME YESTER-DAY TO TALK.
...
I HAVEN'T HEARD ANYTHING ABOUT THAT.
SHE'S FEELING DOWN...

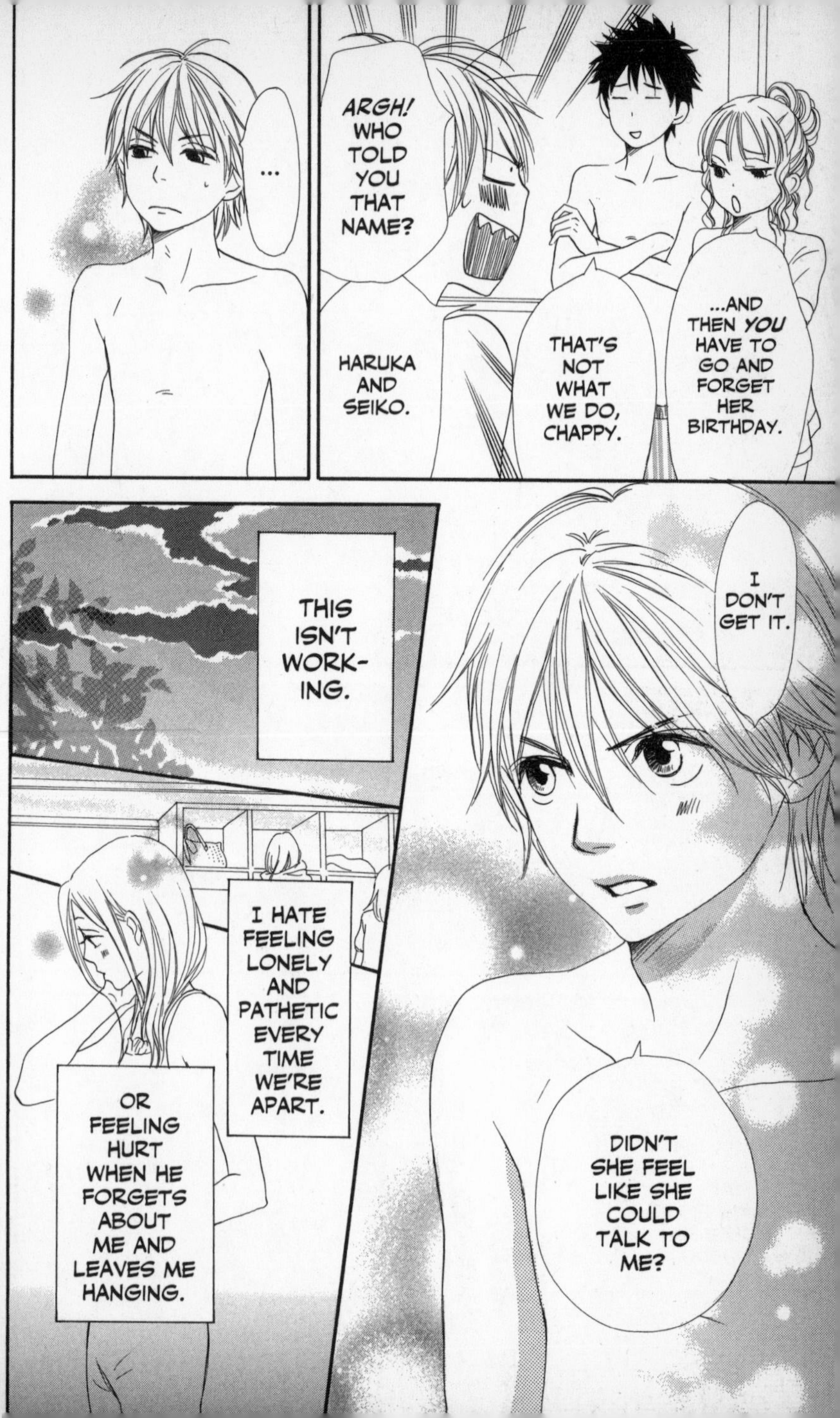
...AND THEN *YOU* HAVE TO GO AND FORGET HER BIRTHDAY.
THAT'S NOT WHAT WE DO, CHAPPY.
ARGH! WHO TOLD YOU THAT NAME?
HARUKA AND SEIKO.
...
I DON'T GET IT.
DIDN'T SHE FEEL LIKE SHE COULD TALK TO ME?
THIS ISN'T WORK-ING.
I HATE FEELING LONELY AND PATHETIC EVERY TIME WE'RE APART.
OR FEELING HURT WHEN HE FORGETS ABOUT ME AND LEAVES ME HANGING.

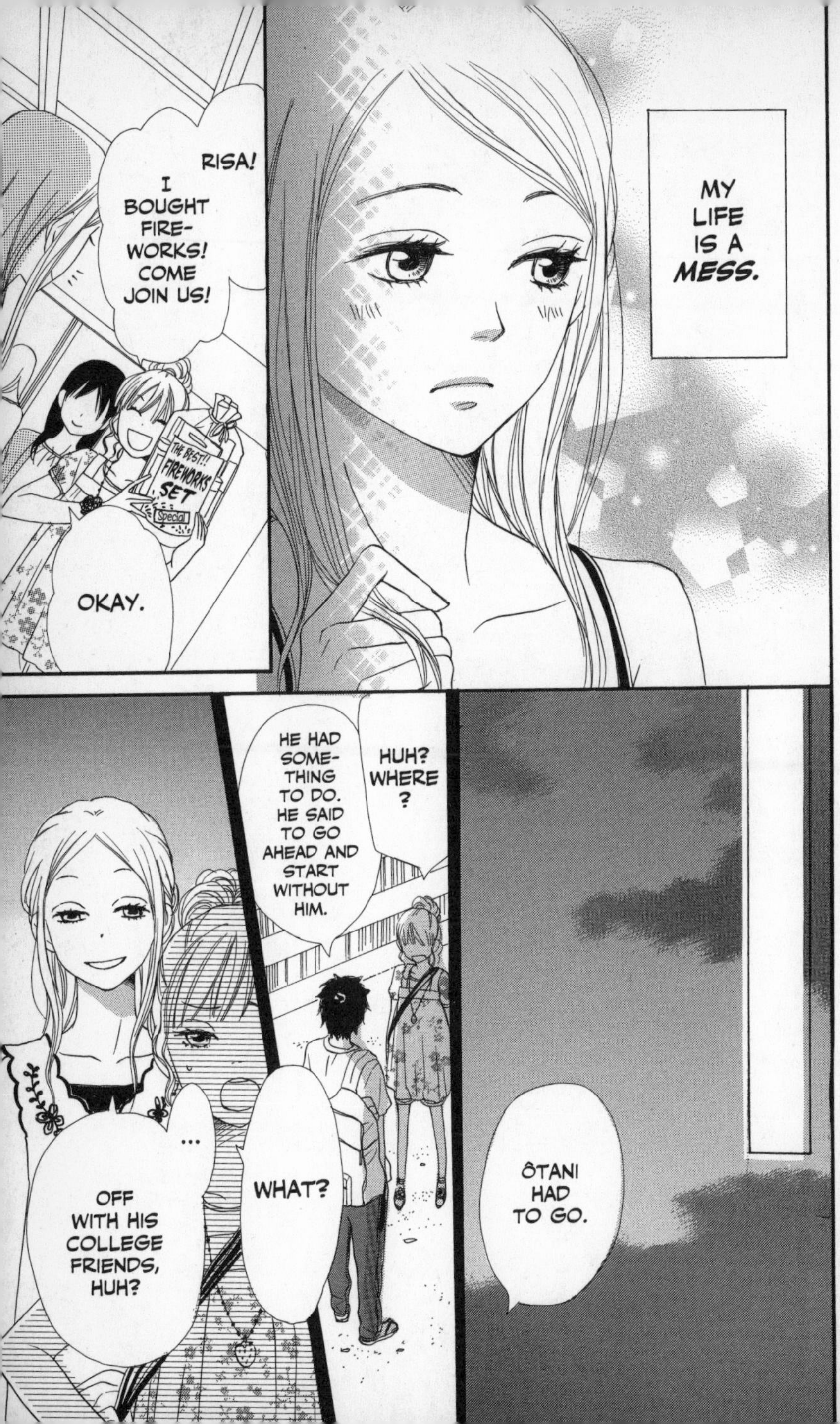
MY LIFE IS A MESS.
RISA! I BOUGHT FIRE-WORKS! COME JOIN US!
THE BEST!! FIREWORKS SET
Special
OKAY.
ÔTANI HAD TO GO.
HUH? WHERE?
HE HAD SOME-THING TO DO. HE SAID TO GO AHEAD AND START WITHOUT HIM.
WHAT?
... OFF WITH HIS COLLEGE FRIENDS, HUH?

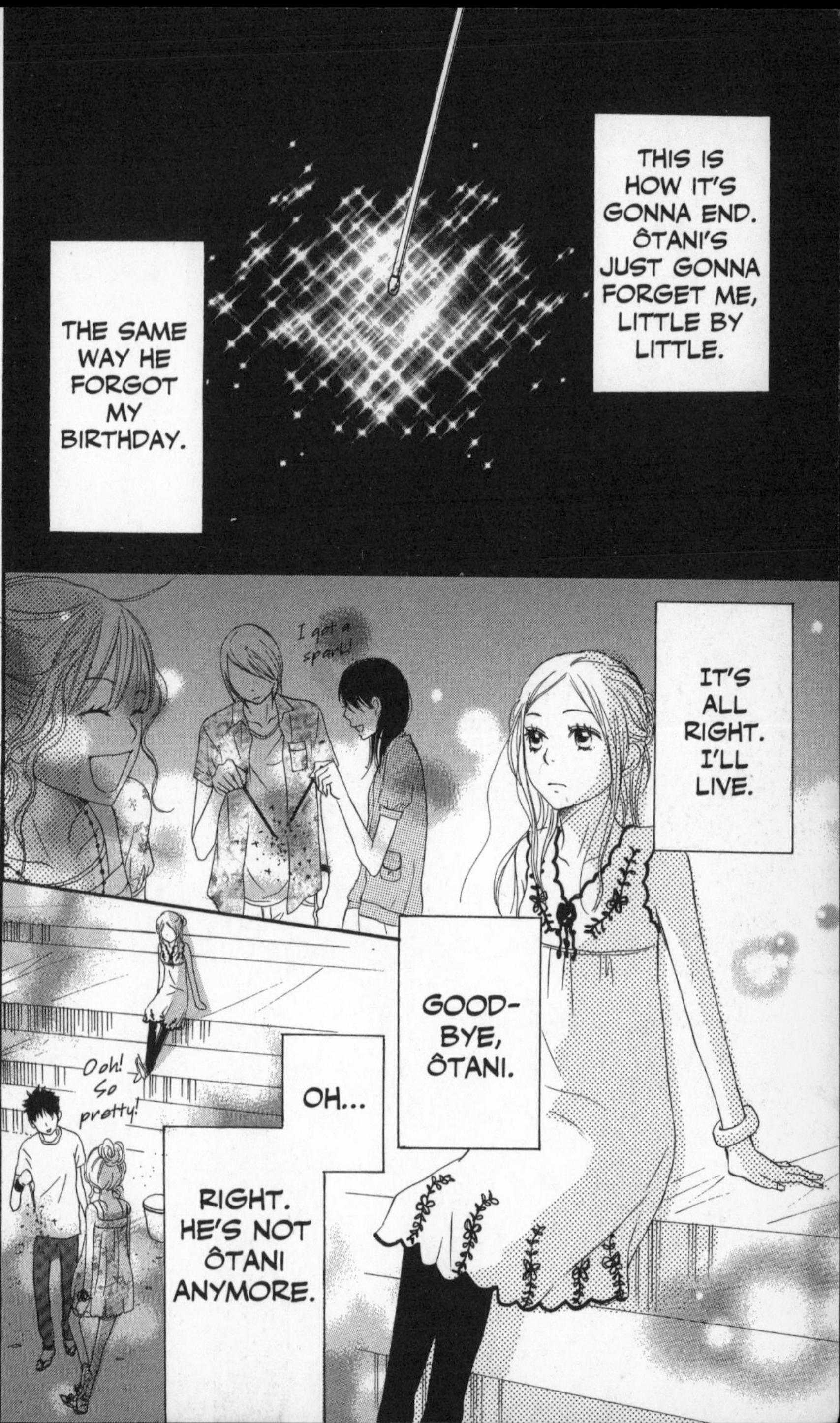
THIS IS HOW IT'S GONNA END. ÔTANI'S JUST GONNA FORGET ME, LITTLE BY LITTLE.
THE SAME WAY HE FORGOT MY BIRTHDAY.
IT'S ALL RIGHT. I'LL LIVE.
I got a spark!
GOOD-BYE, ÔTANI.
OH...
RIGHT. HE'S NOT ÔTANI ANYMORE.
Ooh! So pretty!

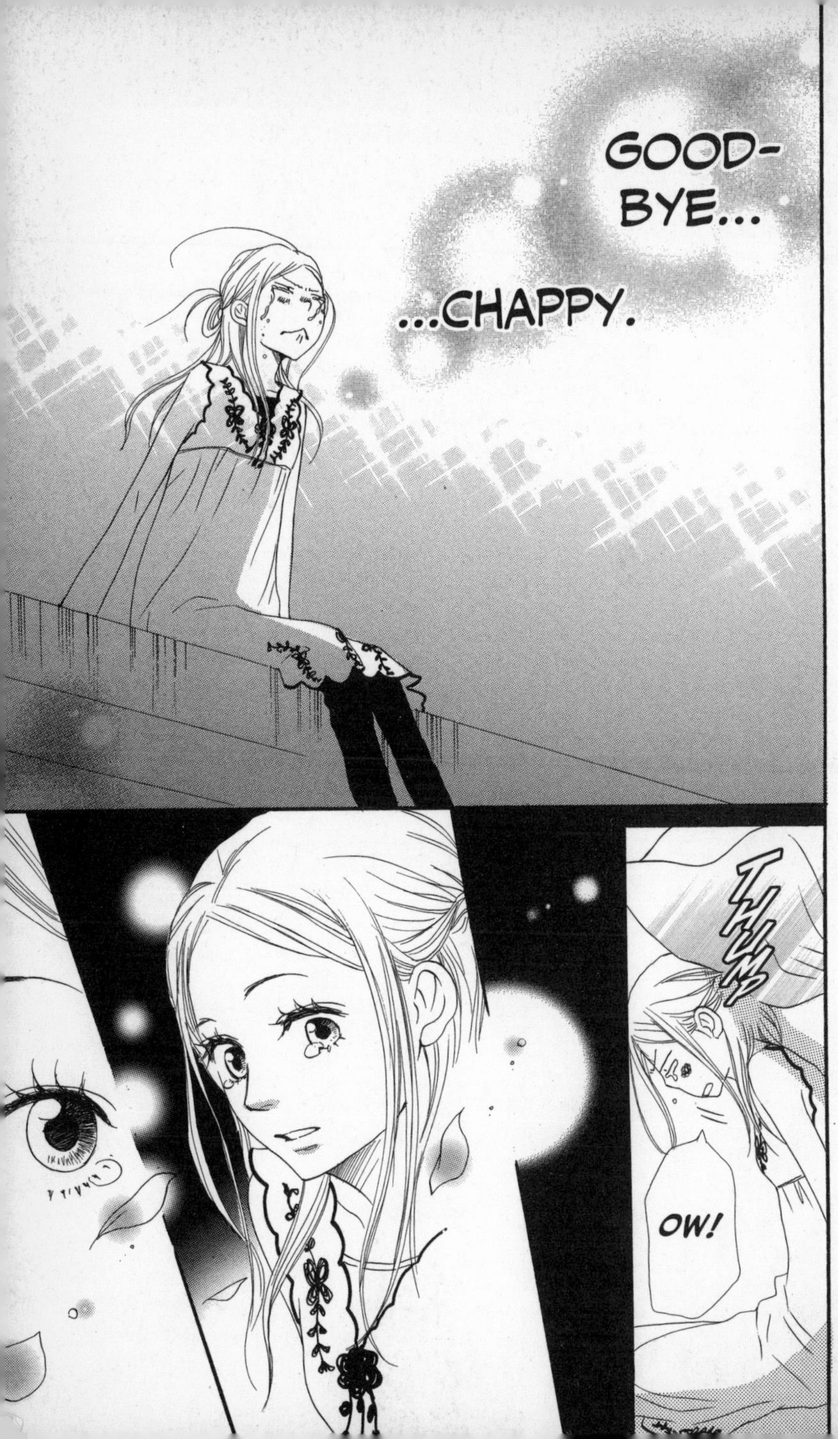
GOOD-
BYE...
...CHAPPY.
THUMP
OW!

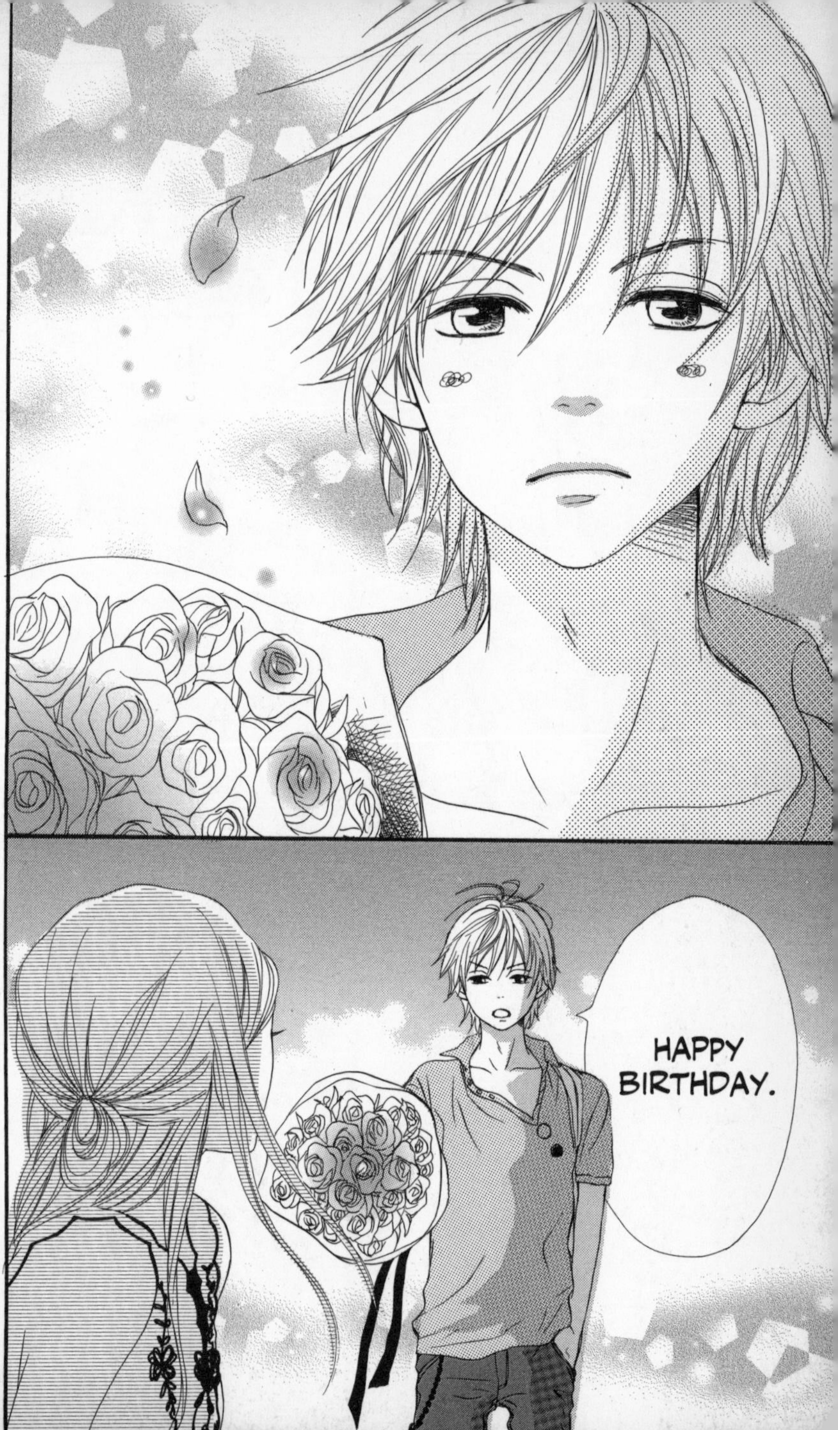
HAPPY BIRTHDAY.

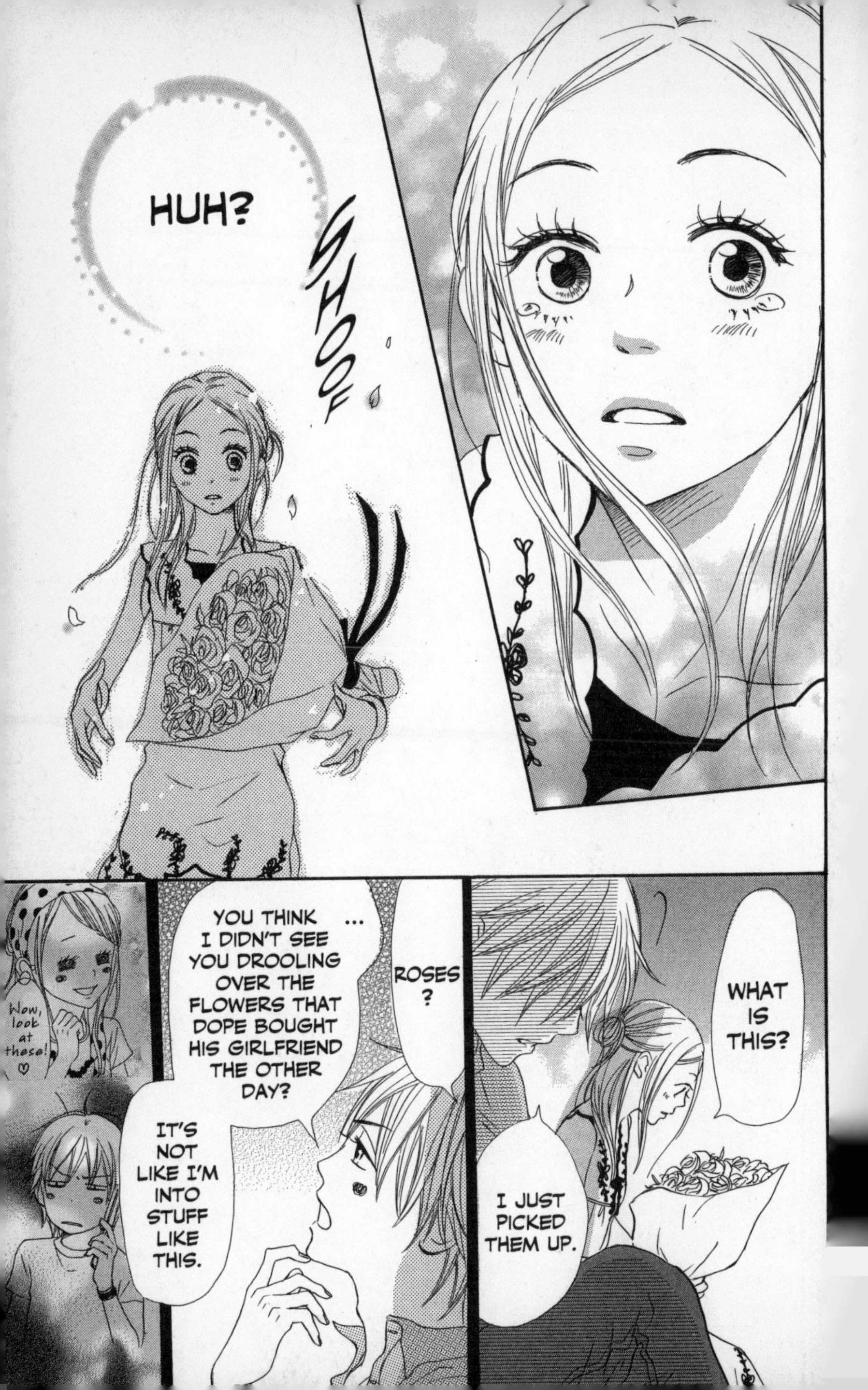
HUH?
SHOOF
WHAT IS THIS?
I JUST PICKED THEM UP.
ROSES?
...
YOU THINK I DIDN'T SEE YOU DROOLING OVER THE FLOWERS THAT DOPE BOUGHT HIS GIRLFRIEND THE OTHER DAY?
Wow, look at these! ♡
IT'S NOT LIKE I'M INTO STUFF LIKE THIS.

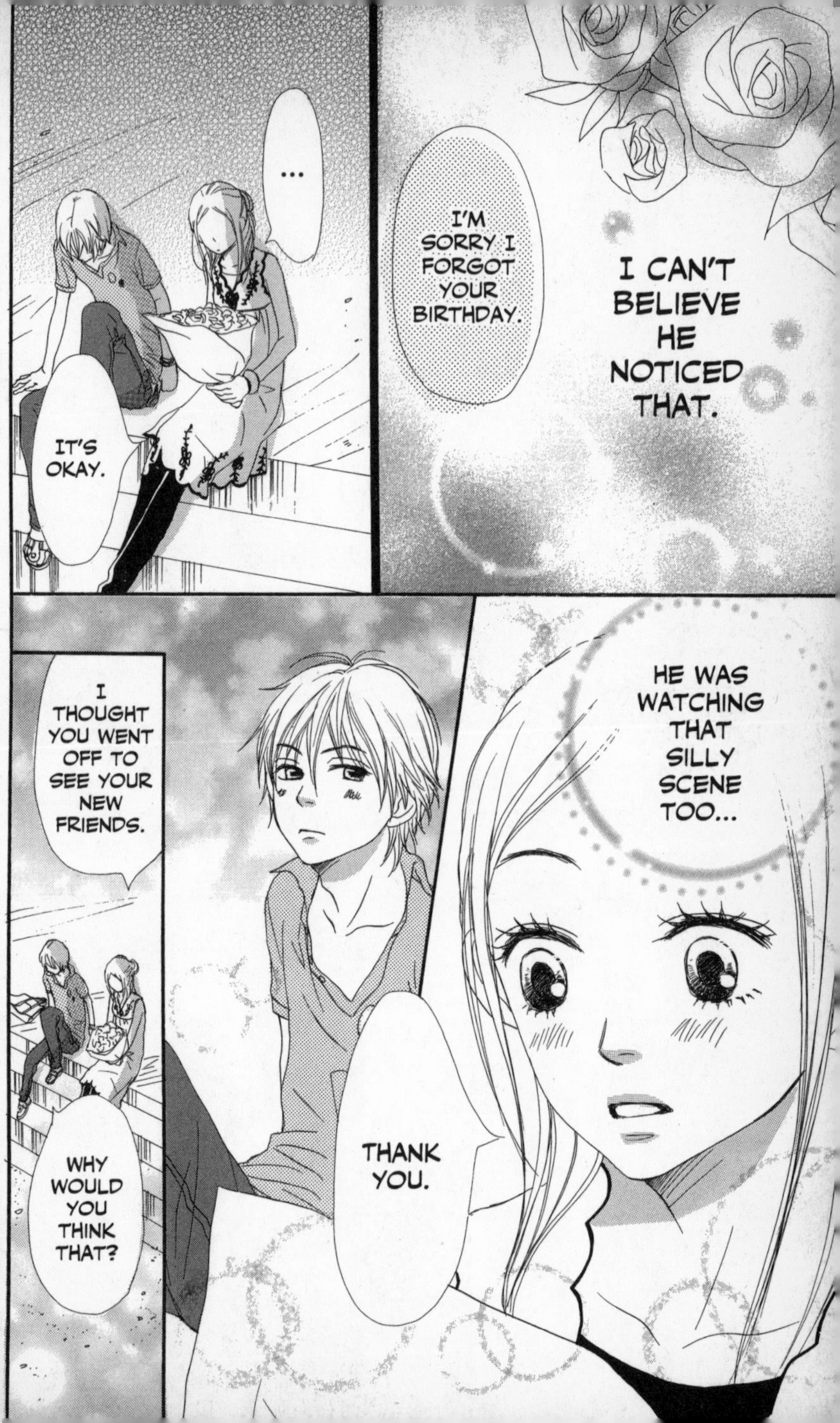
I'M SORRY I FORGOT YOUR BIRTHDAY.
I CAN'T BELIEVE HE NOTICED THAT.
...
IT'S OKAY.
HE WAS WATCHING THAT SILLY SCENE TOO...
THANK YOU.
I THOUGHT YOU WENT OFF TO SEE YOUR NEW FRIENDS.
WHY WOULD YOU THINK THAT?

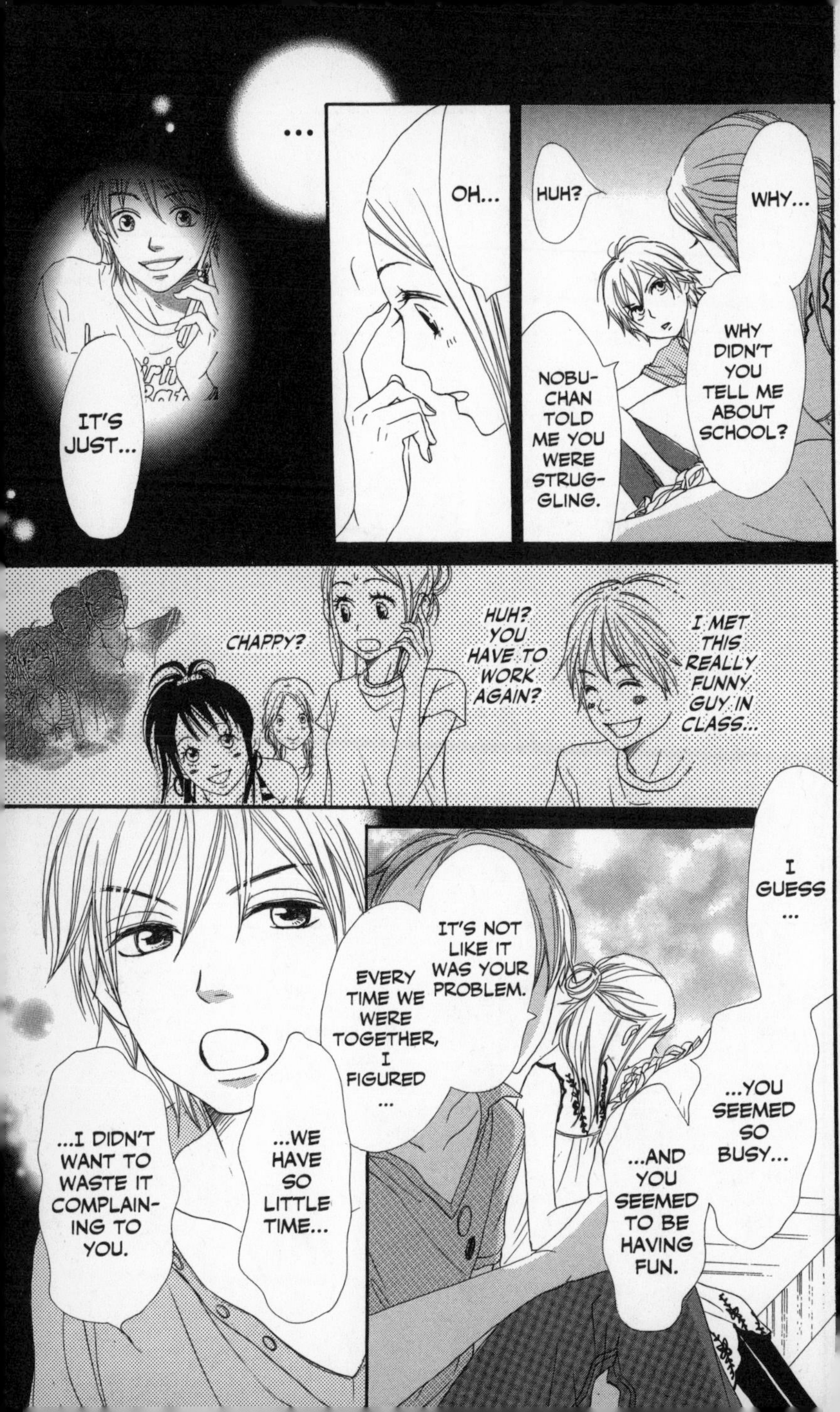
WHY...
HUH?
WHY DIDN'T YOU TELL ME ABOUT SCHOOL?
NOBU-CHAN TOLD ME YOU WERE STRUGGLING.
OH...
...
IT'S JUST...
I MET THIS REALLY FUNNY GUY IN CLASS...
HUH? YOU HAVE TO WORK AGAIN?
CHAPPY?
I GUESS...
...YOU SEEMED SO BUSY...
...AND YOU SEEMED TO BE HAVING FUN.
IT'S NOT LIKE IT WAS YOUR PROBLEM.
EVERY TIME WE WERE TOGETHER, I FIGURED...
...WE HAVE SO LITTLE TIME...
...I DIDN'T WANT TO WASTE IT COMPLAINING TO YOU.

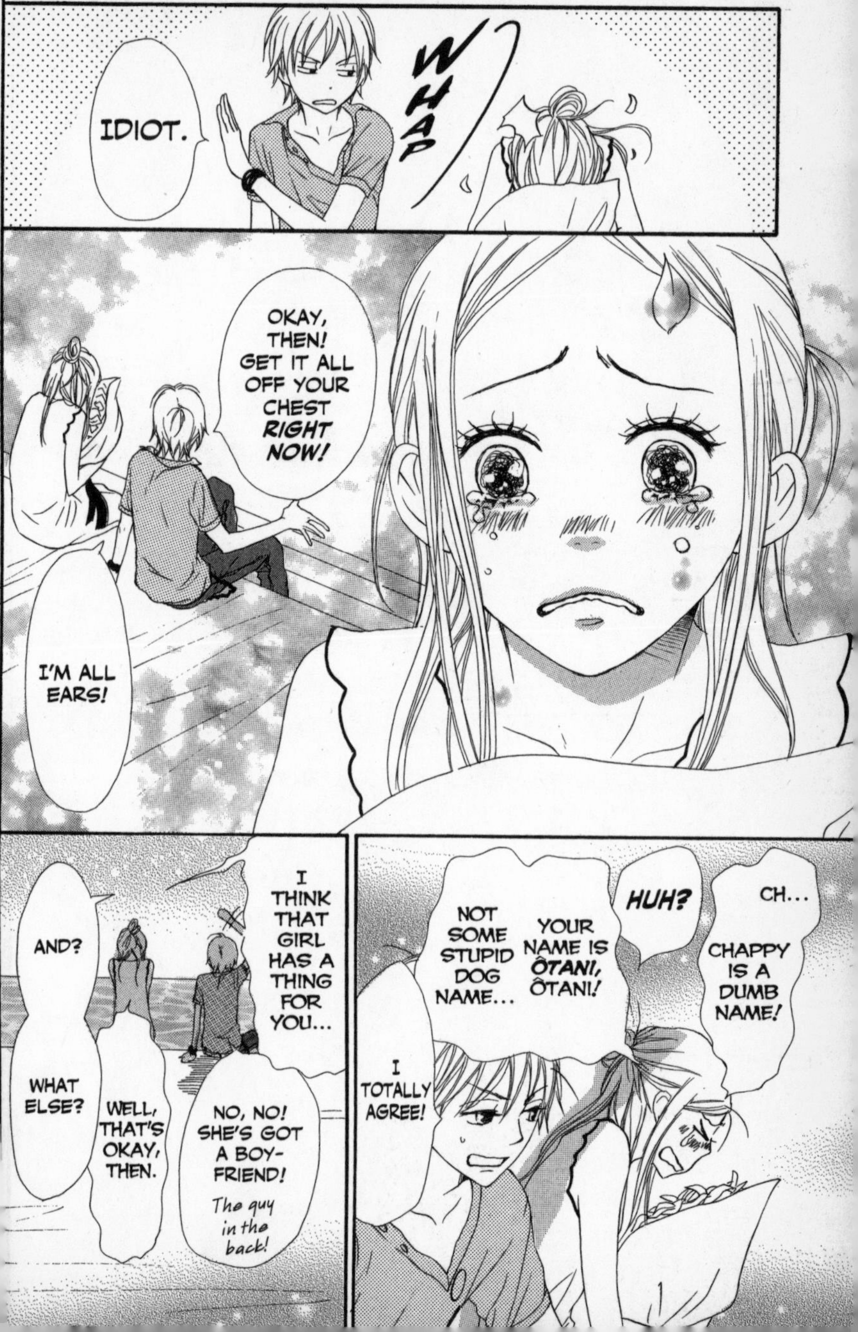
WHAP
IDIOT.
OKAY, THEN! GET IT ALL OFF YOUR CHEST RIGHT NOW!
I'M ALL EARS!
CH...
CHAPPY IS A DUMB NAME!
HUH?
YOUR NAME IS ÔTANI, ÔTANI!
NOT SOME STUPID DOG NAME...
I TOTALLY AGREE!
I THINK THAT GIRL HAS A THING FOR YOU...
AND?
NO, NO! SHE'S GOT A BOY-FRIEND!
The guy in the back!
WELL, THAT'S OKAY, THEN.
WHAT ELSE?

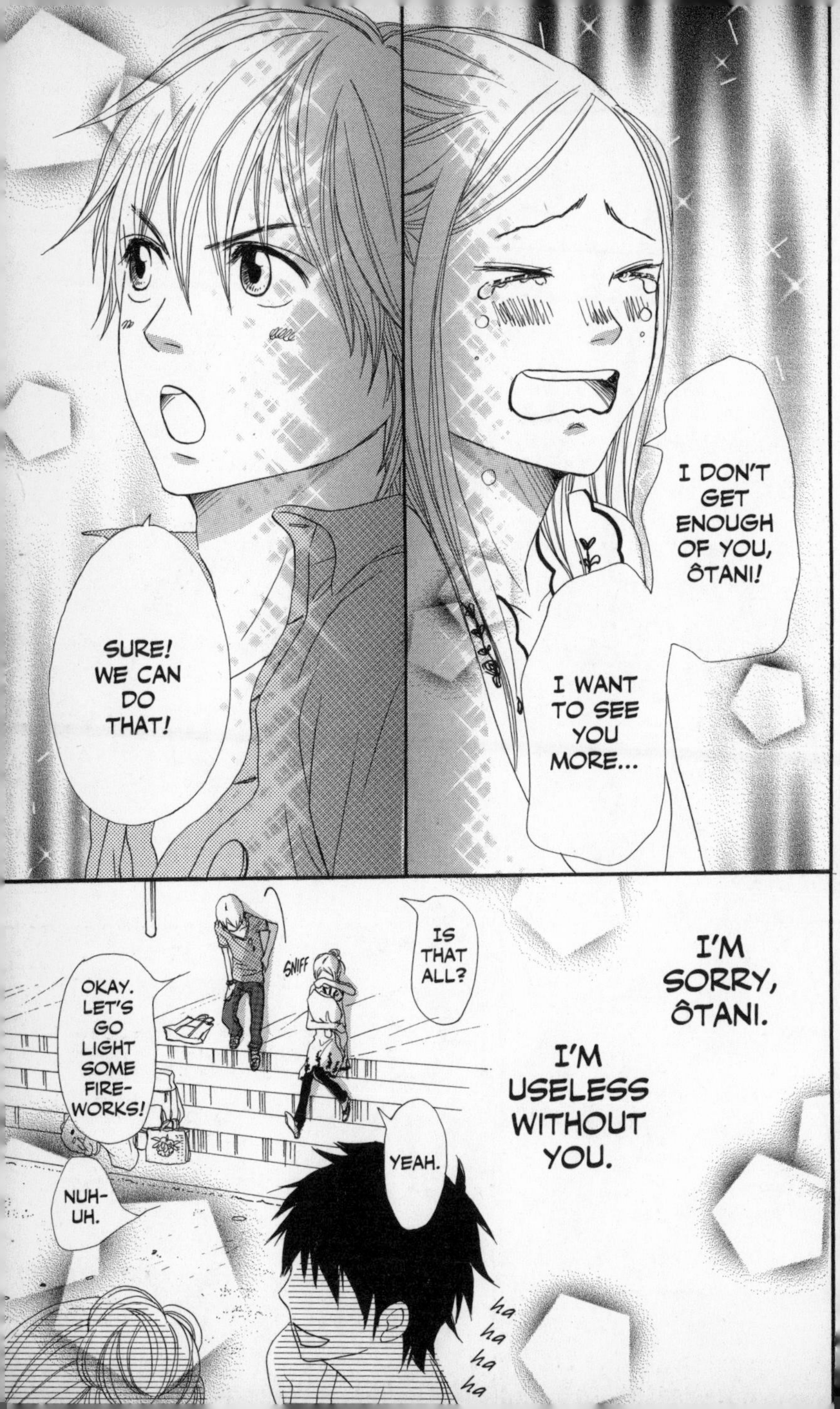
I DON'T GET ENOUGH OF YOU, ÔTANI!
I WANT TO SEE YOU MORE...
SURE! WE CAN DO THAT!
I'M SORRY, ÔTANI.
I'M USELESS WITHOUT YOU.
IS THAT ALL?
SNIFF
OKAY. LET'S GO LIGHT SOME FIRE-WORKS!
YEAH.
NUH-UH.
ha ha ha ha

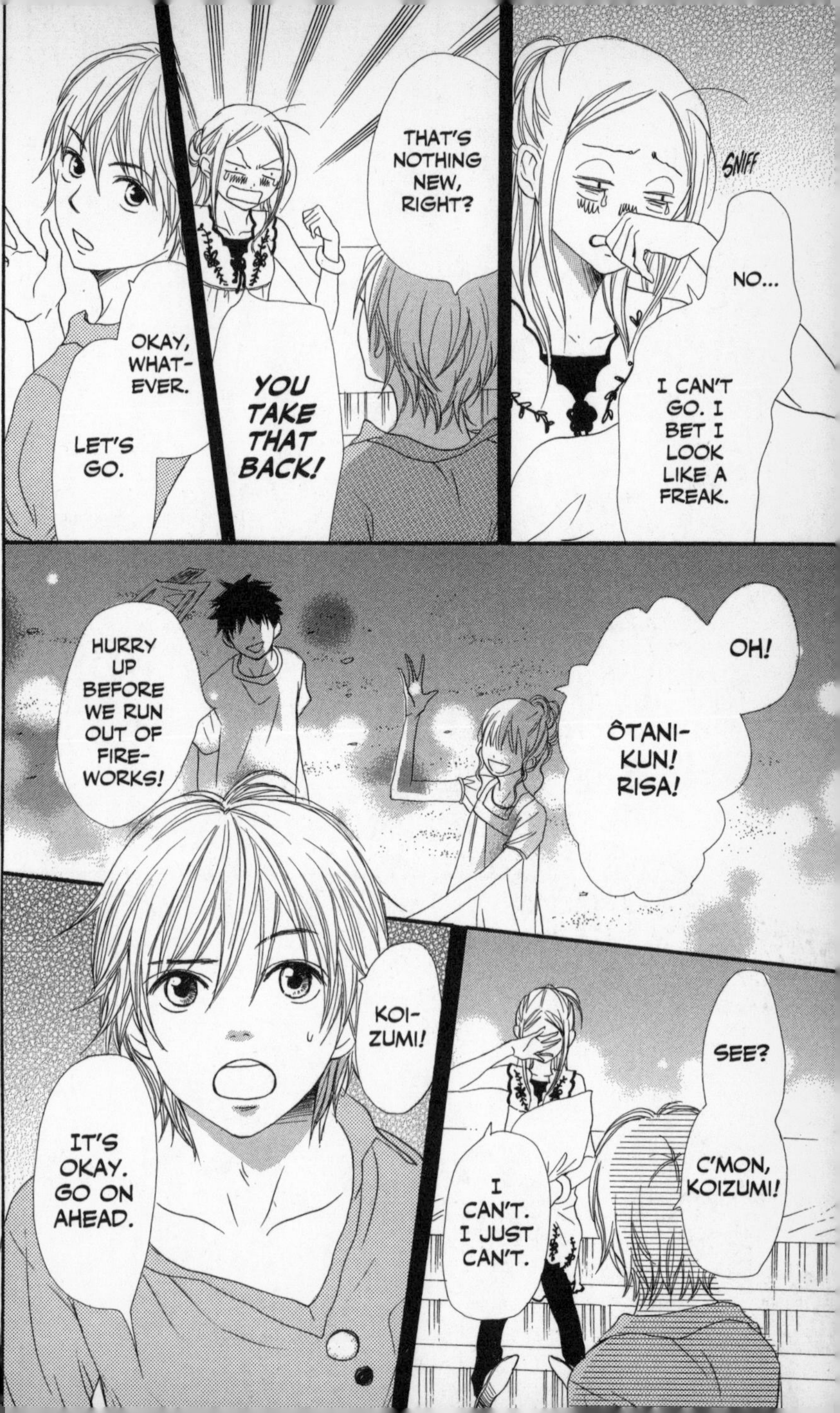
SNIFF
NO...
I CAN'T GO. I BET I LOOK LIKE A FREAK.
THAT'S NOTHING NEW, RIGHT?
YOU TAKE THAT BACK!
OKAY, WHATEVER.
LET'S GO.
OH!
ÔTANI-KUN! RISA!
HURRY UP BEFORE WE RUN OUT OF FIREWORKS!
SEE?
C'MON, KOIZUMI!
I CAN'T. I JUST CAN'T.
KOIZUMI!
IT'S OKAY. GO ON AHEAD.

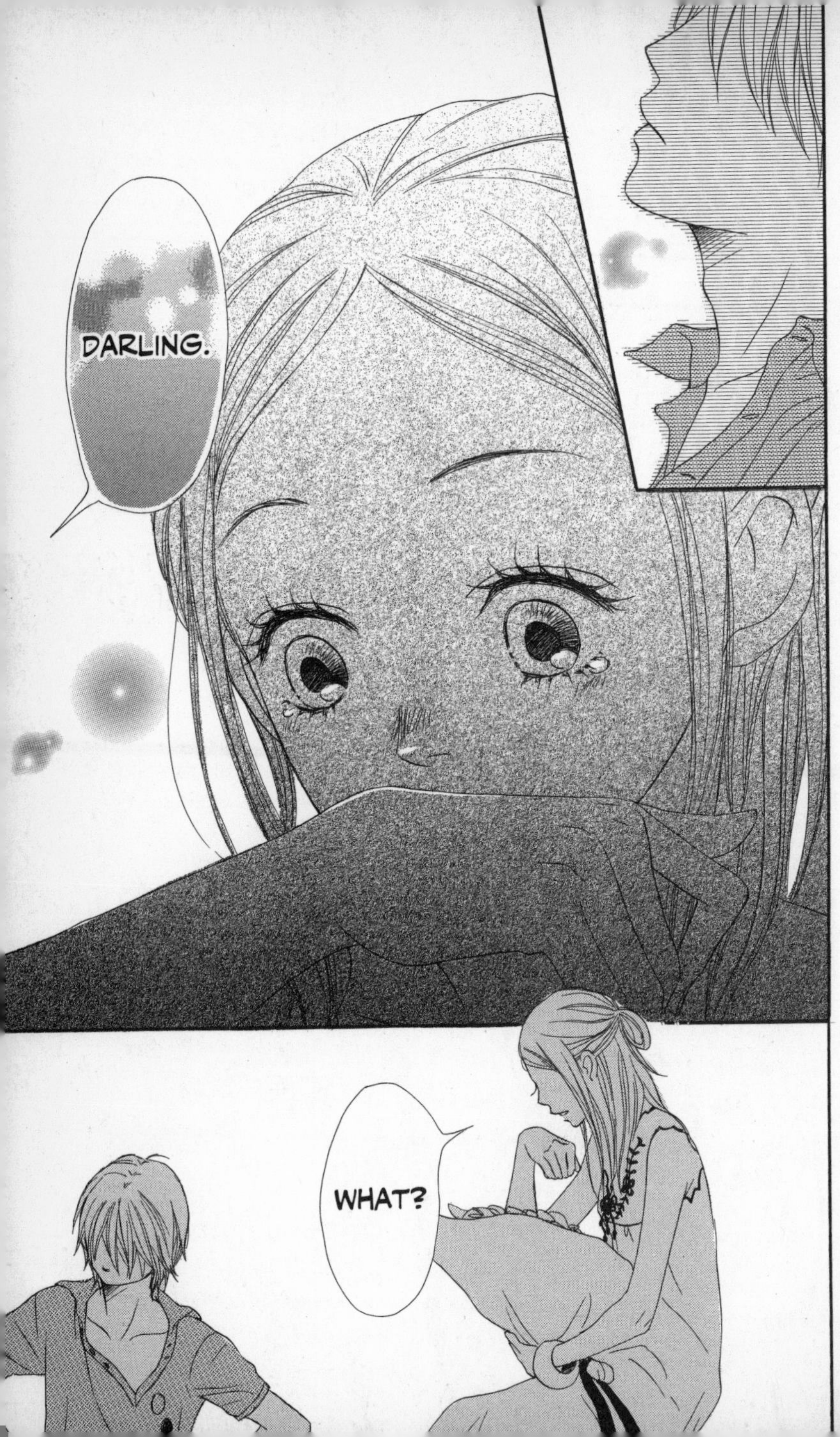
DARLING.
WHAT?

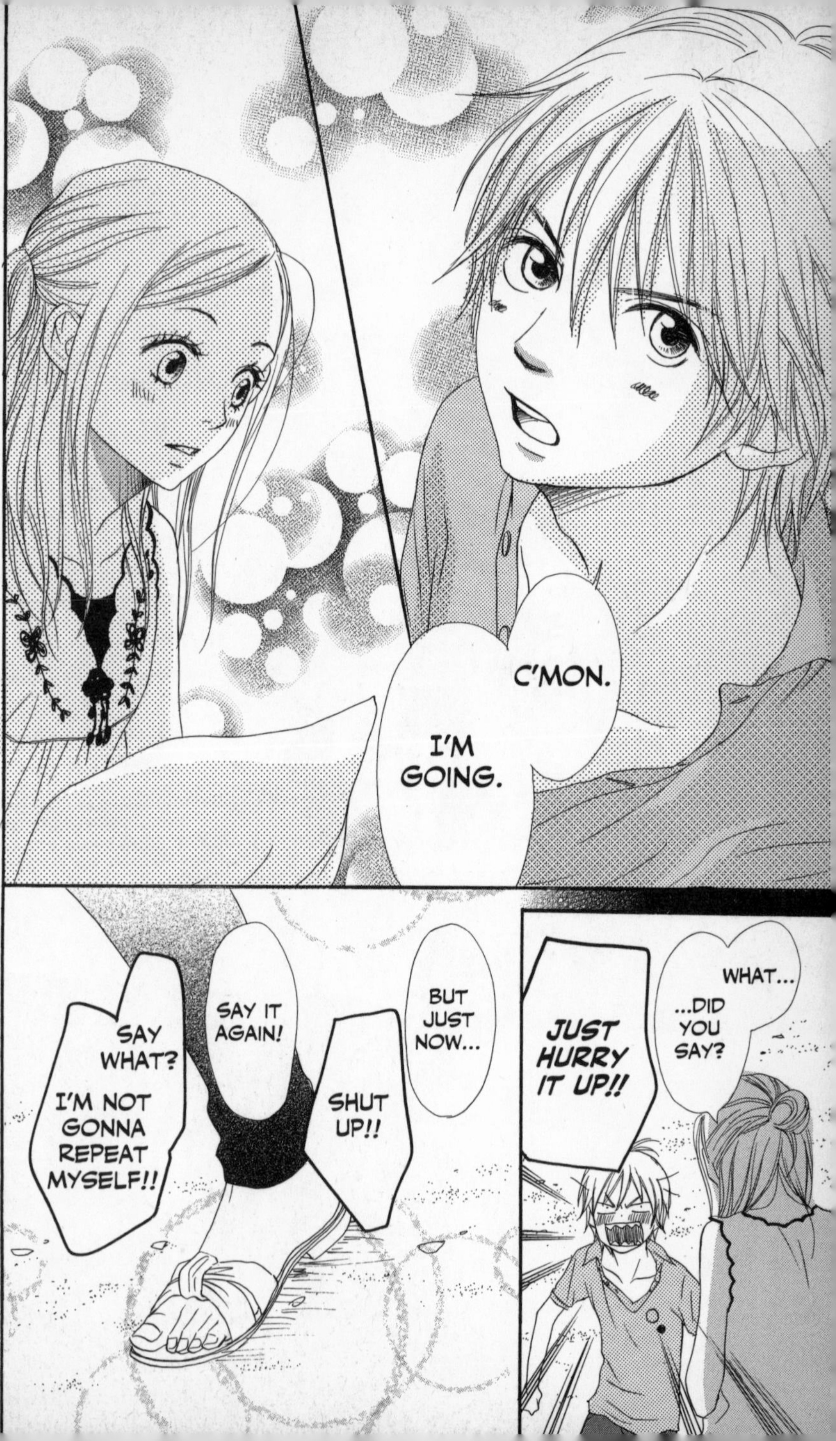
C'MON.
I'M GOING.
WHAT...
...DID YOU SAY?
JUST HURRY IT UP!!
BUT JUST NOW...
SAY IT AGAIN!
SHUT UP!!
SAY WHAT?
I'M NOT GONNA REPEAT MYSELF!!

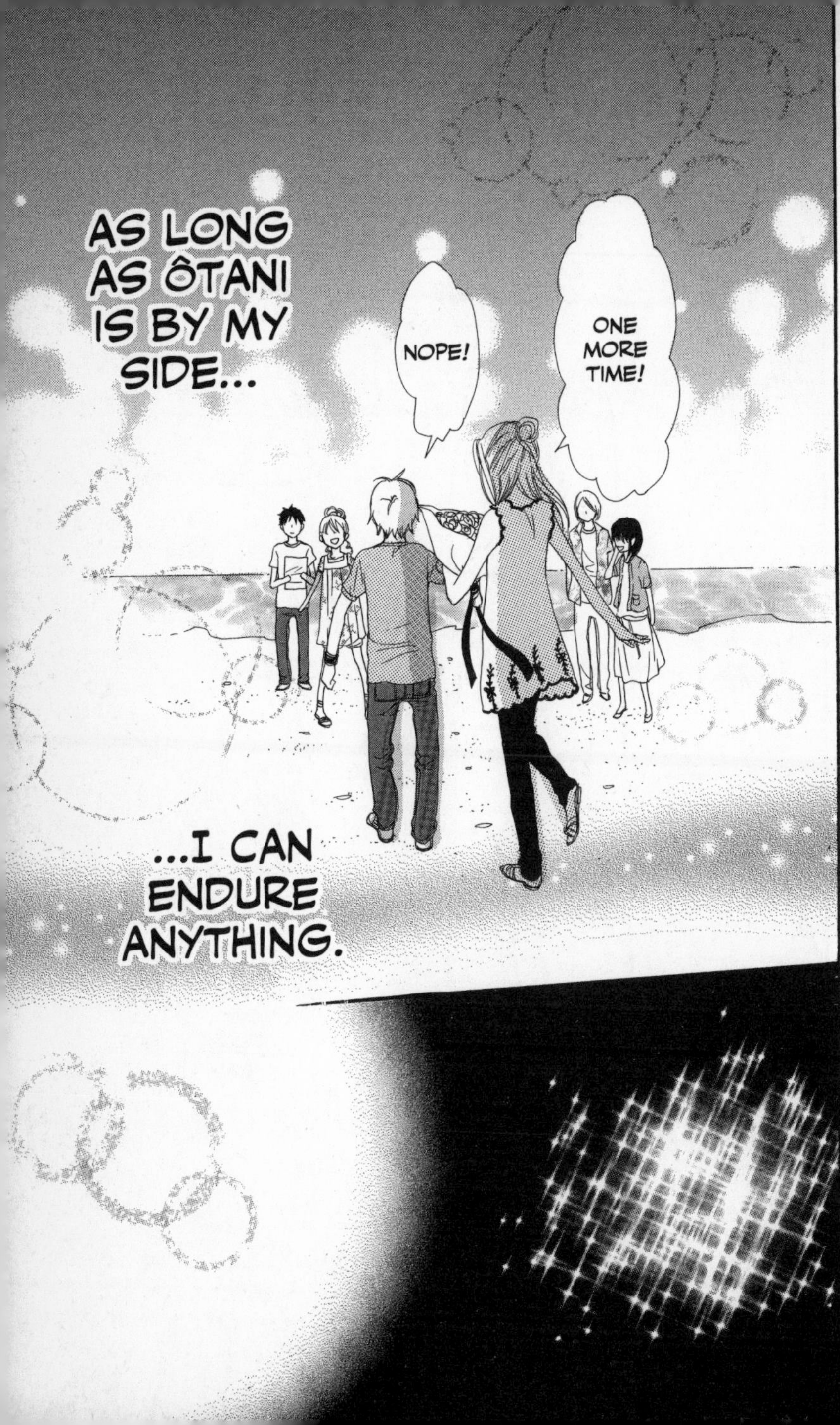
ONE MORE TIME!
NOPE!
AS LONG AS ÔTANI IS BY MY SIDE...
...I CAN ENDURE ANYTHING.

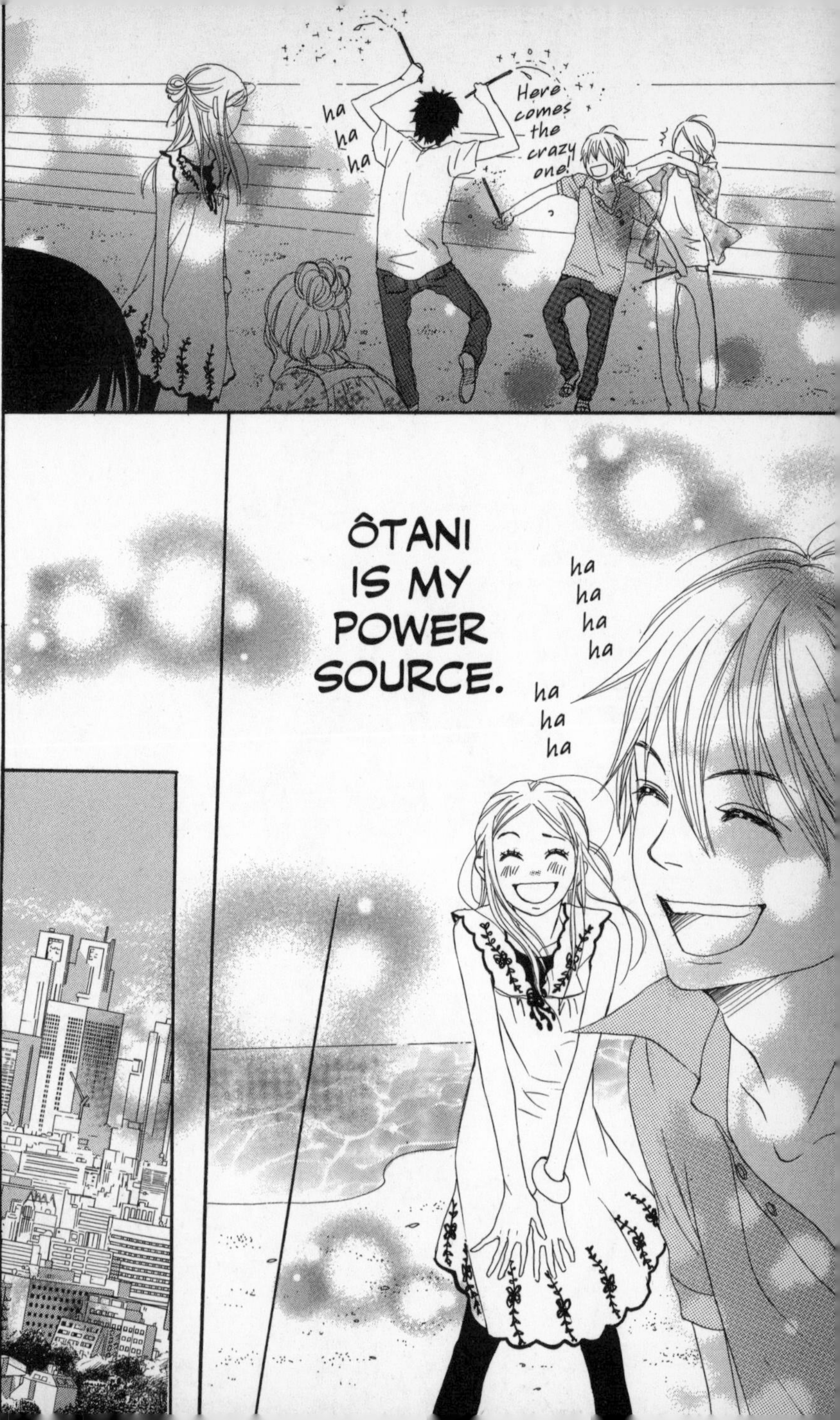
ha ha ha
Here comes the crazy one!
ÔTANI IS MY POWER SOURCE.
ha ha ha ha
ha ha ha

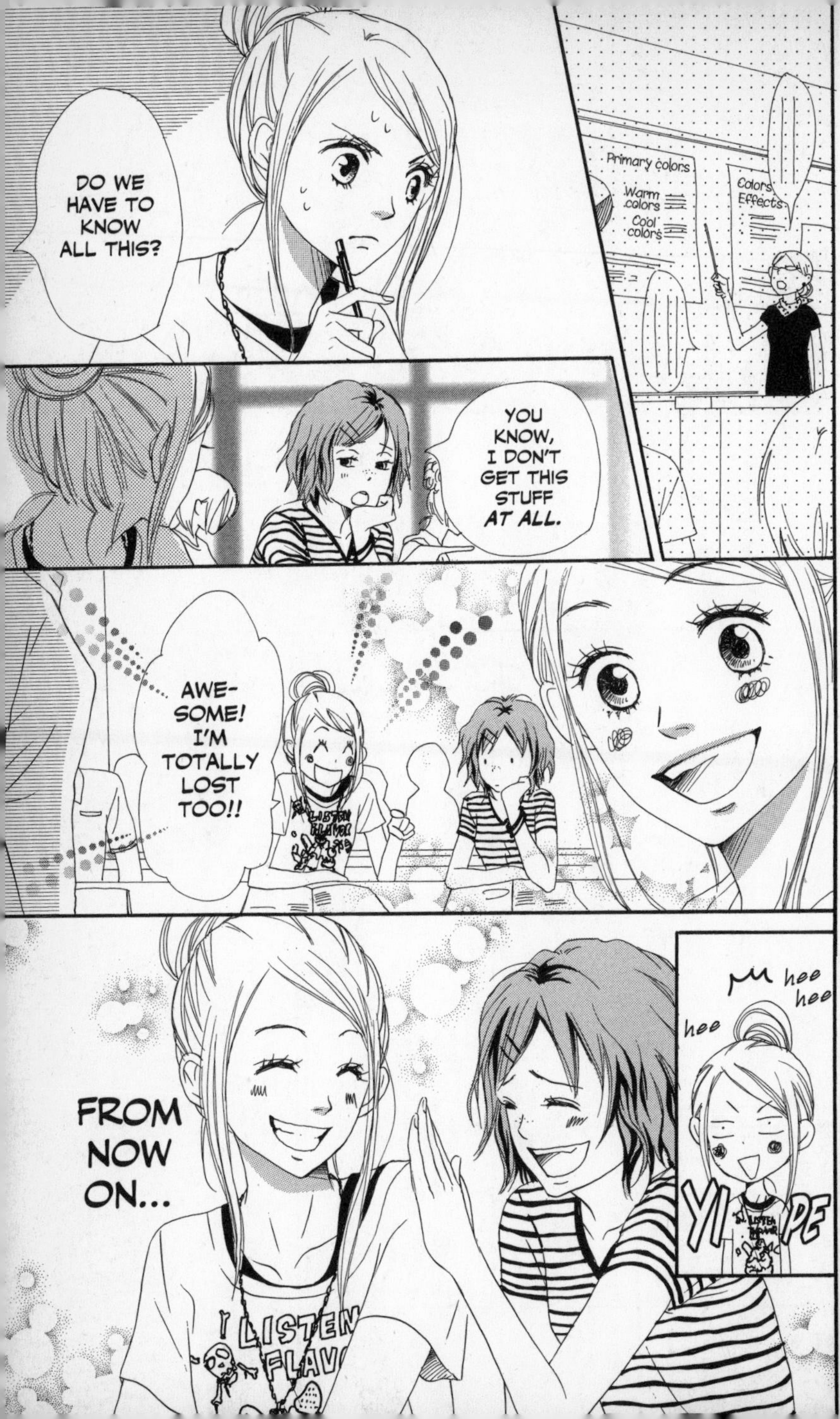
Primary colors
Warm colors
Cool colors
Colors Effects
DO WE HAVE TO KNOW ALL THIS?
YOU KNOW, I DON'T GET THIS STUFF AT ALL.
AWE-SOME! I'M TOTALLY LOST TOO!!
hee hee hee
YI
PE
FROM NOW ON...

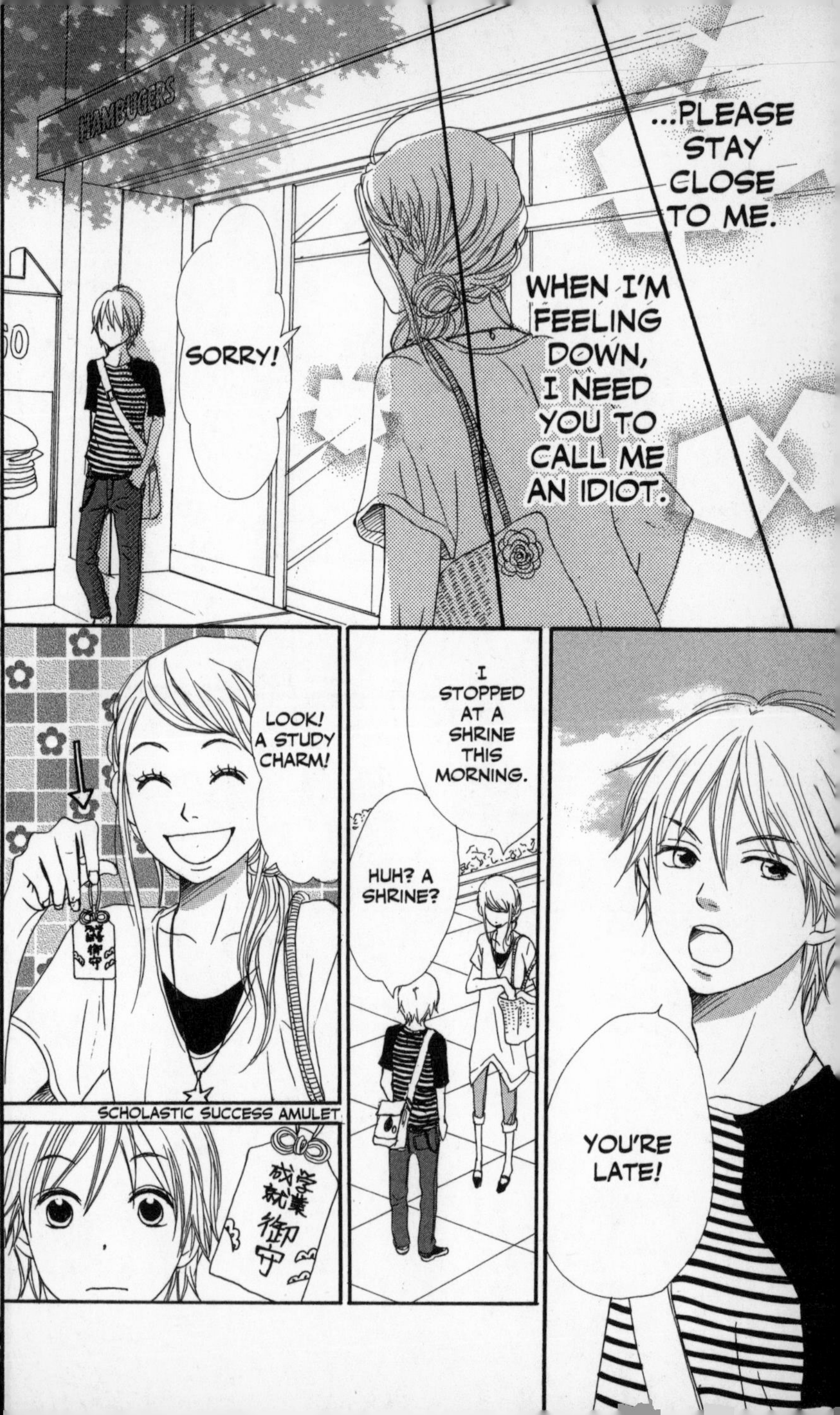
...PLEASE STAY CLOSE TO ME.
WHEN I'M FEELING DOWN, I NEED YOU TO CALL ME AN IDIOT.
HAMBUGERS
SORRY!
YOU'RE LATE!
I STOPPED AT A SHRINE THIS MORNING.
HUH? A SHRINE?
LOOK! A STUDY CHARM!
SCHOLASTIC SUCCESS AMULET
学業成就御守

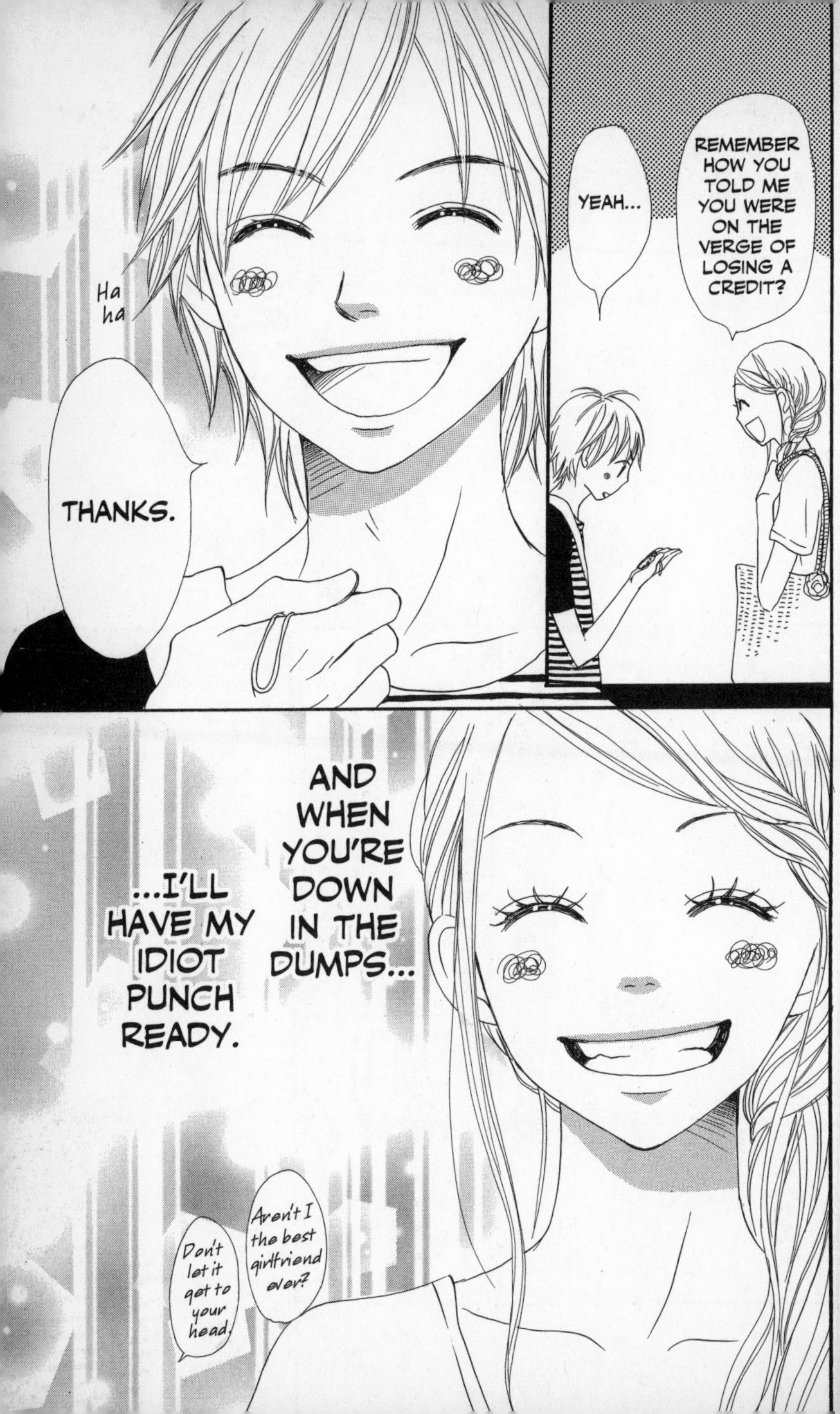
REMEMBER HOW YOU TOLD ME YOU WERE ON THE VERGE OF LOSING A CREDIT?
YEAH...
Ha ha
THANKS.
AND WHEN YOU'RE DOWN IN THE DUMPS...
...I'LL HAVE MY IDIOT PUNCH READY.
Aren't I the best girlfriend ever?
Don't let it get to your head.

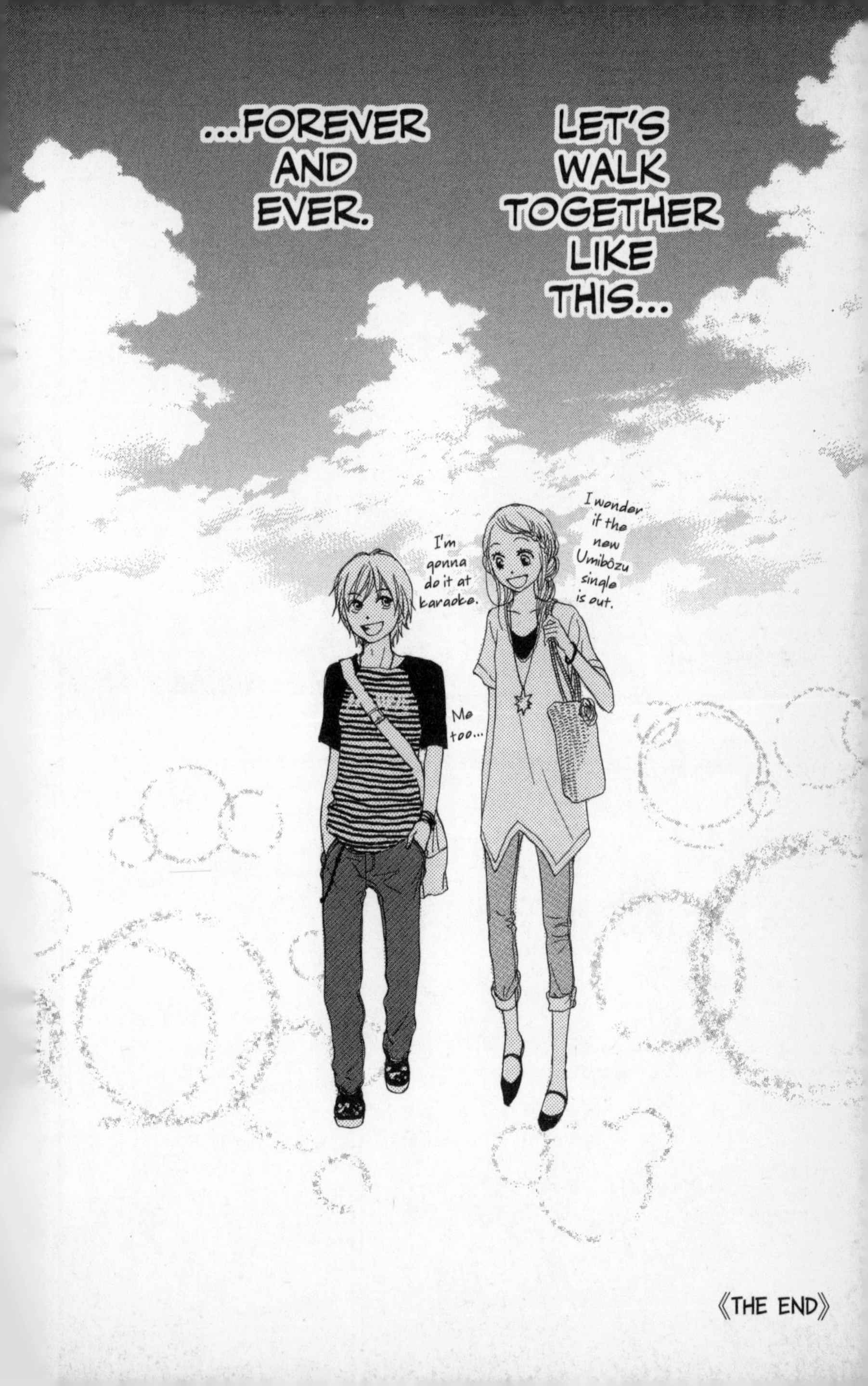
LET'S WALK TOGETHER LIKE THIS...
...FOREVER AND EVER.
I wonder if the new Umibôzu single is out.
I'm gonna do it at karaoke.
Me too...
《THE END》

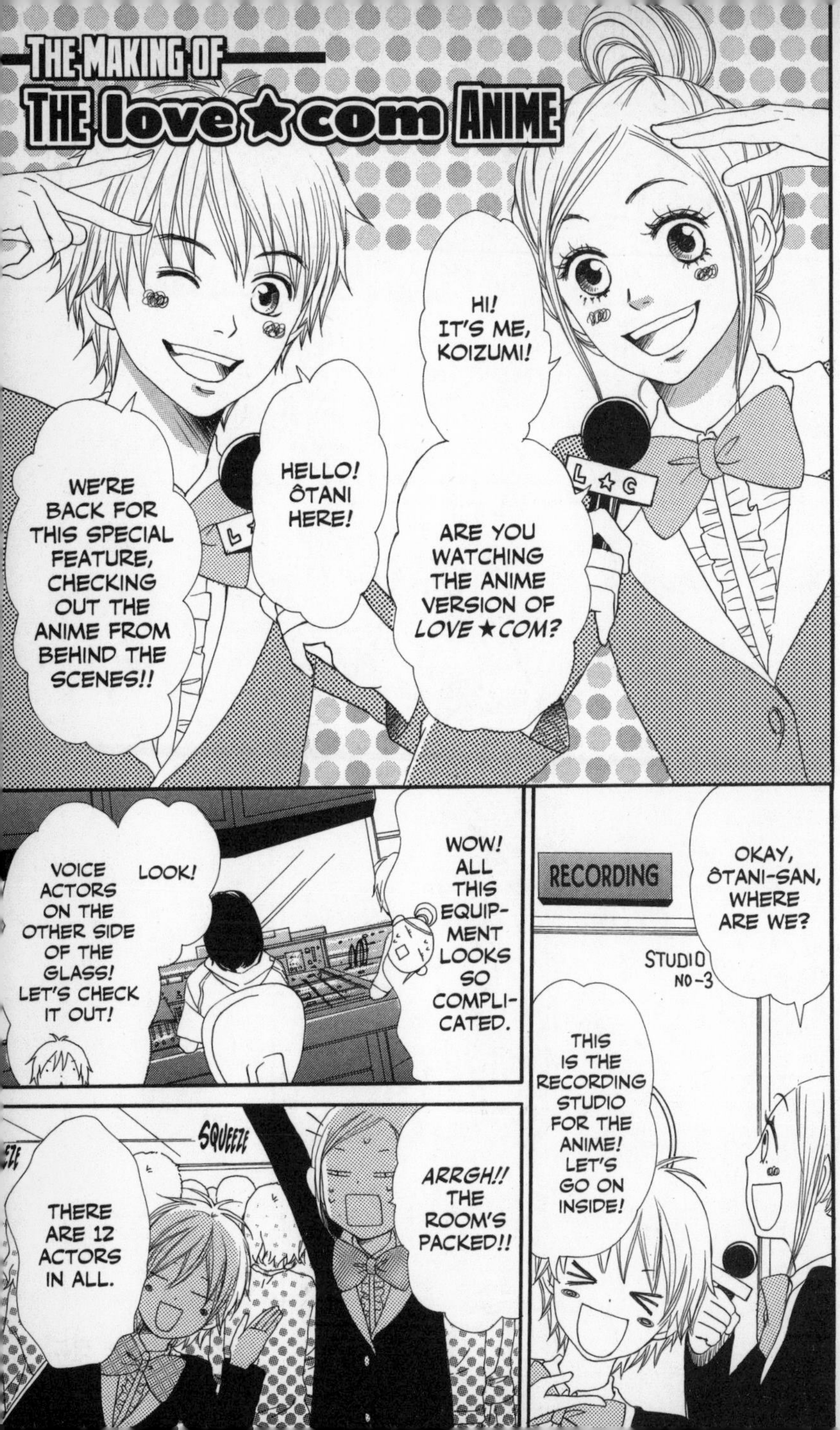
THE MAKING OF
THE love★com ANIME
HI! IT'S ME, KOIZUMI!
ARE YOU WATCHING THE ANIME VERSION OF *LOVE★COM*?
HELLO! ÔTANI HERE!
WE'RE BACK FOR THIS SPECIAL FEATURE, CHECKING OUT THE ANIME FROM BEHIND THE SCENES!!
RECORDING
OKAY, ÔTANI-SAN, WHERE ARE WE?
STUDIO NO-3
THIS IS THE RECORDING STUDIO FOR THE ANIME! LET'S GO ON INSIDE!
WOW! ALL THIS EQUIPMENT LOOKS SO COMPLICATED.
LOOK!
VOICE ACTORS ON THE OTHER SIDE OF THE GLASS! LET'S CHECK IT OUT!
SQUEEZE
ARRGH!! THE ROOM'S PACKED!!
THERE ARE 12 ACTORS IN ALL.

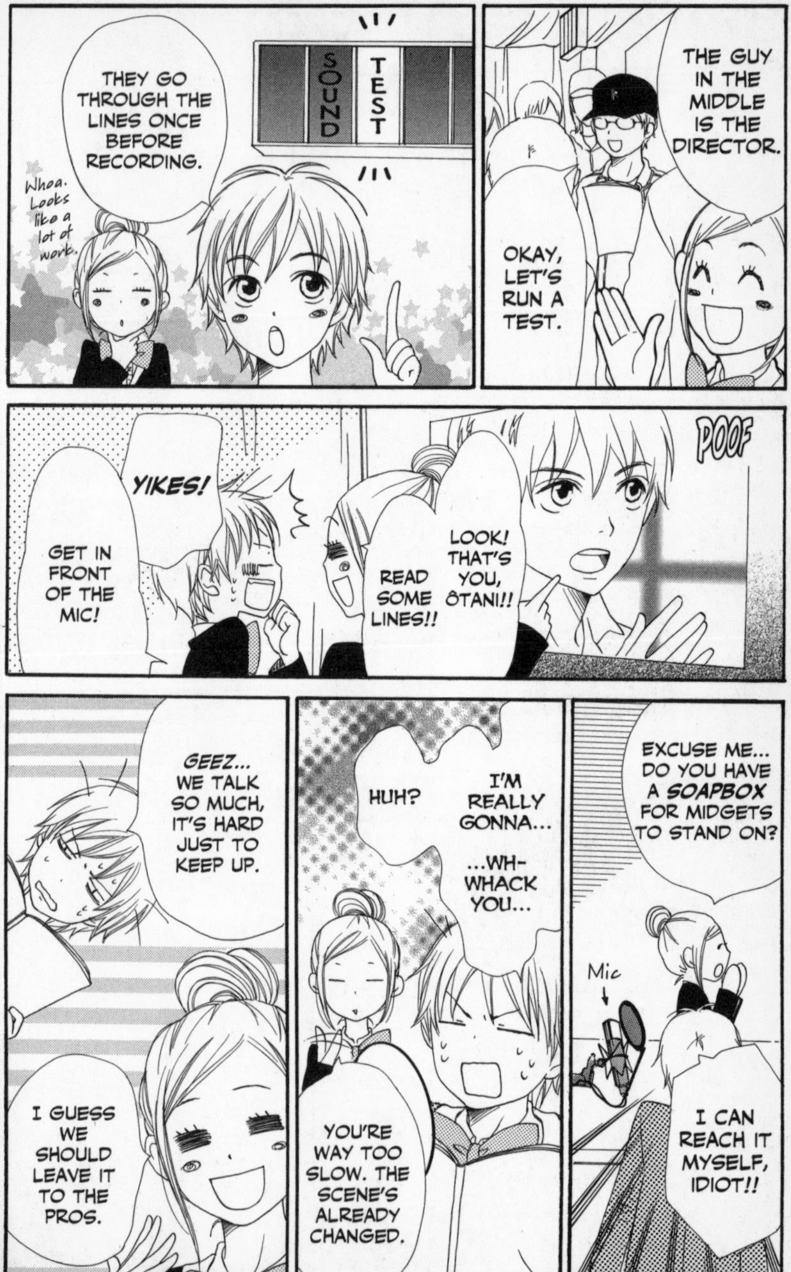
THE GUY IN THE MIDDLE IS THE DIRECTOR.
OKAY, LET'S RUN A TEST.
SOUND TEST
THEY GO THROUGH THE LINES ONCE BEFORE RECORDING.
Whoa. Looks like a lot of work.
POOF
LOOK! THAT'S YOU, ŌTANI!!
READ SOME LINES!!
YIKES!
GET IN FRONT OF THE MIC!
EXCUSE ME... DO YOU HAVE A *SOAPBOX* FOR MIDGETS TO STAND ON?
Mic
I CAN REACH IT MYSELF, IDIOT!!
I'M REALLY GONNA...
...WH-WHACK YOU...
HUH?
YOU'RE WAY TOO SLOW. THE SCENE'S ALREADY CHANGED.
GEEZ... WE TALK SO MUCH, IT'S HARD JUST TO KEEP UP.
I GUESS WE SHOULD LEAVE IT TO THE PROS.

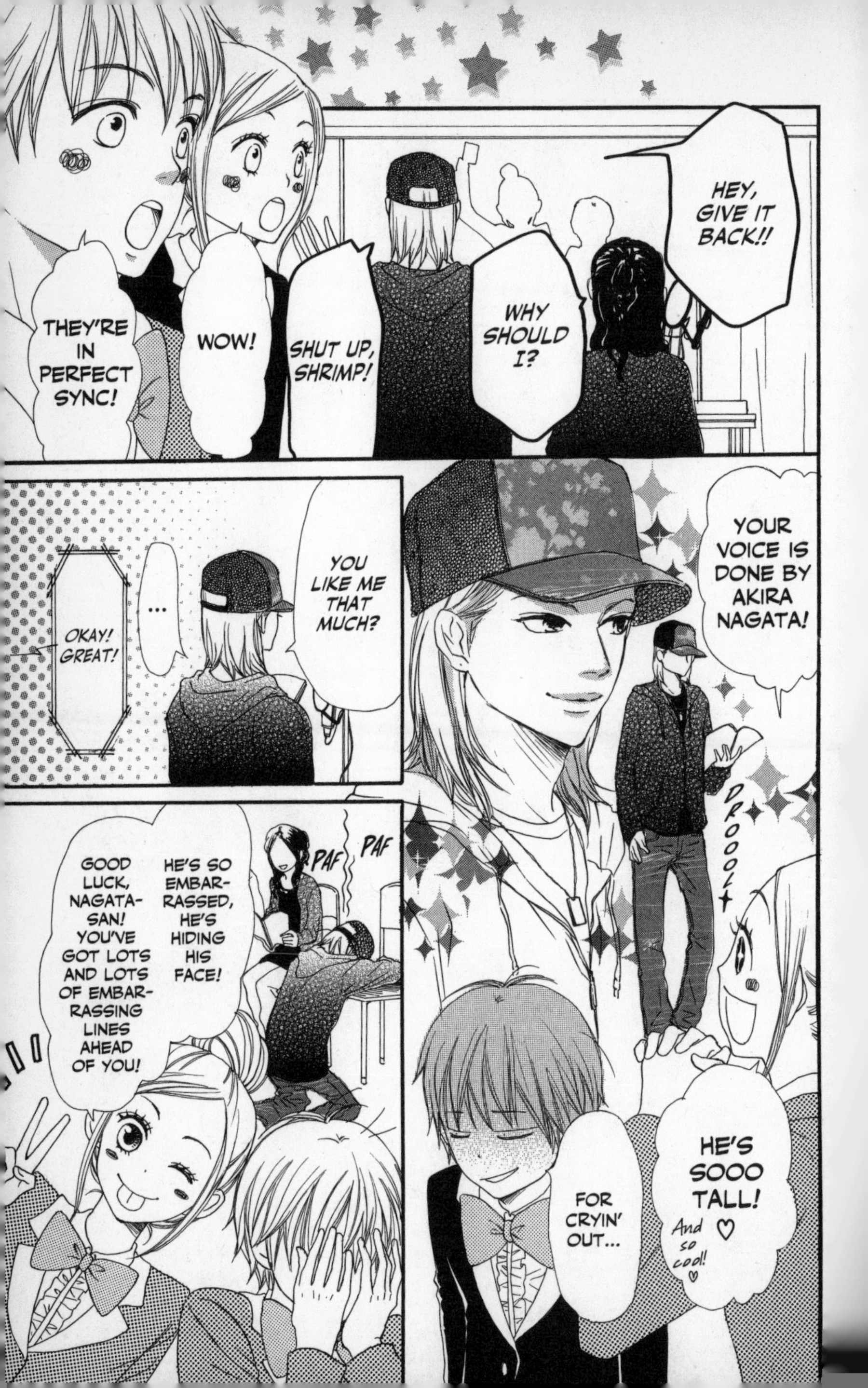
HEY, GIVE IT BACK!!
WHY SHOULD I?
SHUT UP, SHRIMP!
WOW!
THEY'RE IN PERFECT SYNC!
YOUR VOICE IS DONE BY AKIRA NAGATA!
DROOOL
HE'S SOOO TALL!
And so cool!
FOR CRYIN' OUT...
YOU LIKE ME THAT MUCH?
...
OKAY! GREAT!
PAF PAF
HE'S SO EMBARRASSED, HE'S HIDING HIS FACE!
GOOD LUCK, NAGATA-SAN! YOU'VE GOT LOTS AND LOTS OF EMBARRASSING LINES AHEAD OF YOU!

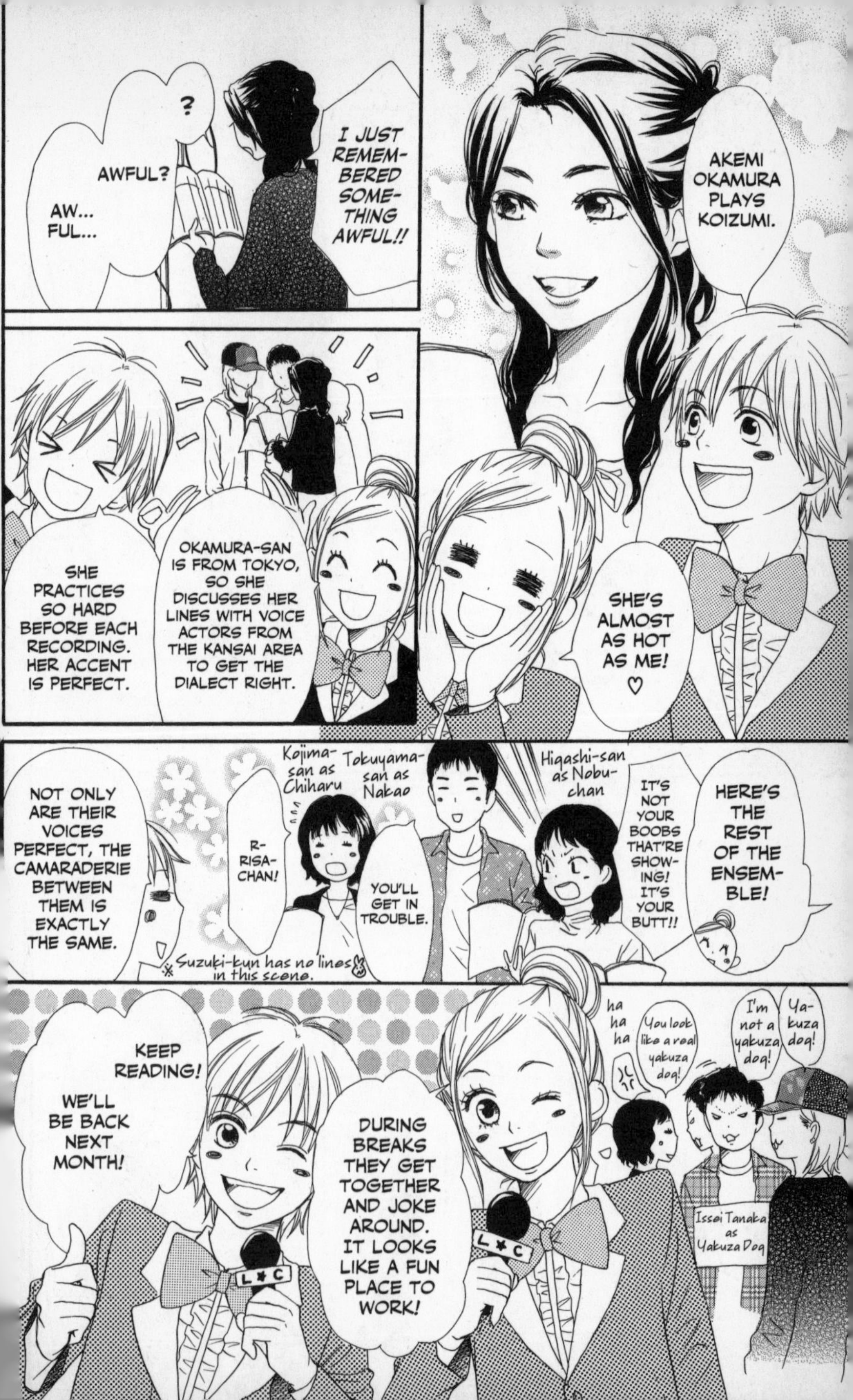
AKEMI OKAMURA PLAYS KOIZUMI.
SHE'S ALMOST AS HOT AS ME! ♡
I JUST REMEMBERED SOMETHING AWFUL!!
?
AWFUL?
AW... FUL...
OKAMURA-SAN IS FROM TOKYO, SO SHE DISCUSSES HER LINES WITH VOICE ACTORS FROM THE KANSAI AREA TO GET THE DIALECT RIGHT.
SHE PRACTICES SO HARD BEFORE EACH RECORDING. HER ACCENT IS PERFECT.
HERE'S THE REST OF THE ENSEMBLE!
IT'S NOT YOUR BOOBS THAT'RE SHOWING! IT'S YOUR BUTT!!
Higashi-san as Nobu-chan
Tokuyama-san as Nakao
Kojima-san as Chiharu
YOU'LL GET IN TROUBLE.
R-RISA-CHAN!
NOT ONLY ARE THEIR VOICES PERFECT, THE CAMARADERIE BETWEEN THEM IS EXACTLY THE SAME.
※Suzuki-kun has no lines in this scene.
Ya-kuza dog!
I'm not a yakuza dog!
You look like a real yakuza dog!
ha ha ha
Issei Tanaka as Yakuza Dog
DURING BREAKS THEY GET TOGETHER AND JOKE AROUND. IT LOOKS LIKE A FUN PLACE TO WORK!
KEEP READING!
WE'LL BE BACK NEXT MONTH!

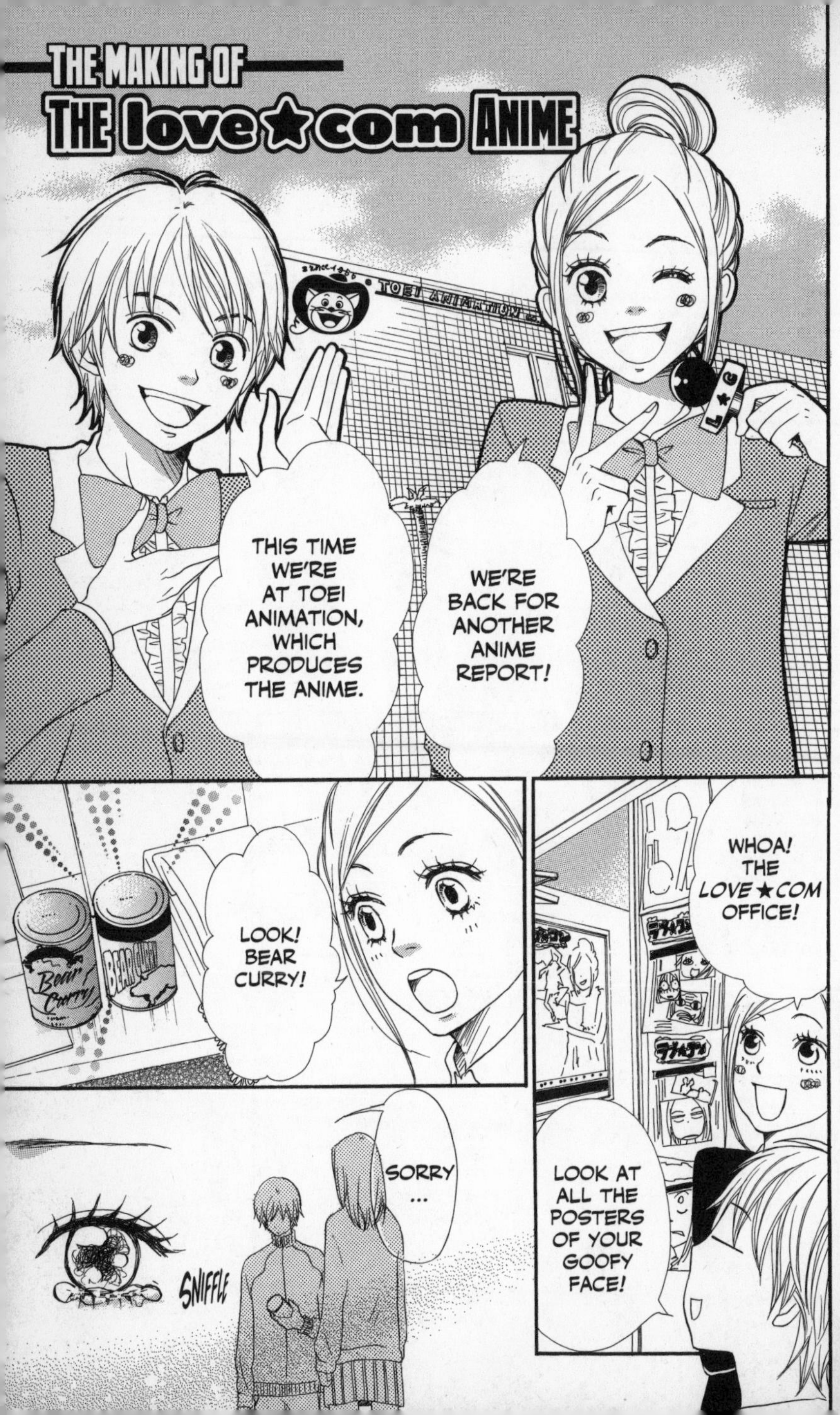
THE MAKING OF
THE love★com ANIME
TOEI ANIMATION
WE'RE BACK FOR ANOTHER ANIME REPORT!
THIS TIME WE'RE AT TOEI ANIMATION, WHICH PRODUCES THE ANIME.
WHOA! THE *LOVE★COM* OFFICE!
LOOK AT ALL THE POSTERS OF YOUR GOOFY FACE!
LOOK! BEAR CURRY!
Bear Curry
SORRY ...
SNIFFLE

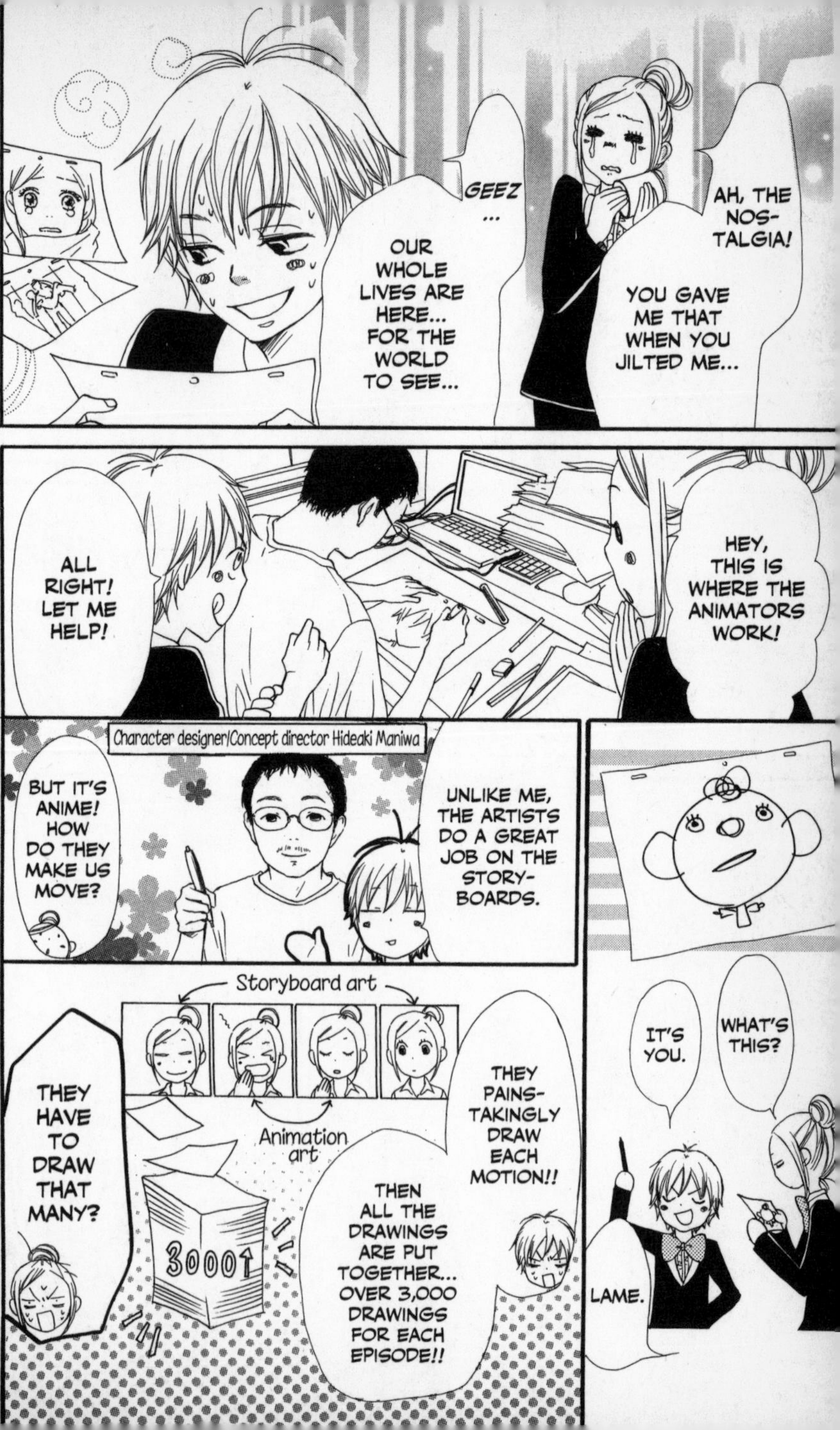
AH, THE NOS-TALGIA!
YOU GAVE ME THAT WHEN YOU JILTED ME...
GEEZ ...
OUR WHOLE LIVES ARE HERE... FOR THE WORLD TO SEE...
HEY, THIS IS WHERE THE ANIMATORS WORK!
ALL RIGHT! LET ME HELP!
WHAT'S THIS?
IT'S YOU.
LAME.
Character designer/Concept director Hideaki Maniwa
UNLIKE ME, THE ARTISTS DO A GREAT JOB ON THE STORY-BOARDS.
BUT IT'S ANIME! HOW DO THEY MAKE US MOVE?
Storyboard art
THEY PAINS-TAKINGLY DRAW EACH MOTION!!
Animation art
THEN ALL THE DRAWINGS ARE PUT TOGETHER... OVER 3,000 DRAWINGS FOR EACH EPISODE!!
3000↑
THEY HAVE TO DRAW THAT MANY?

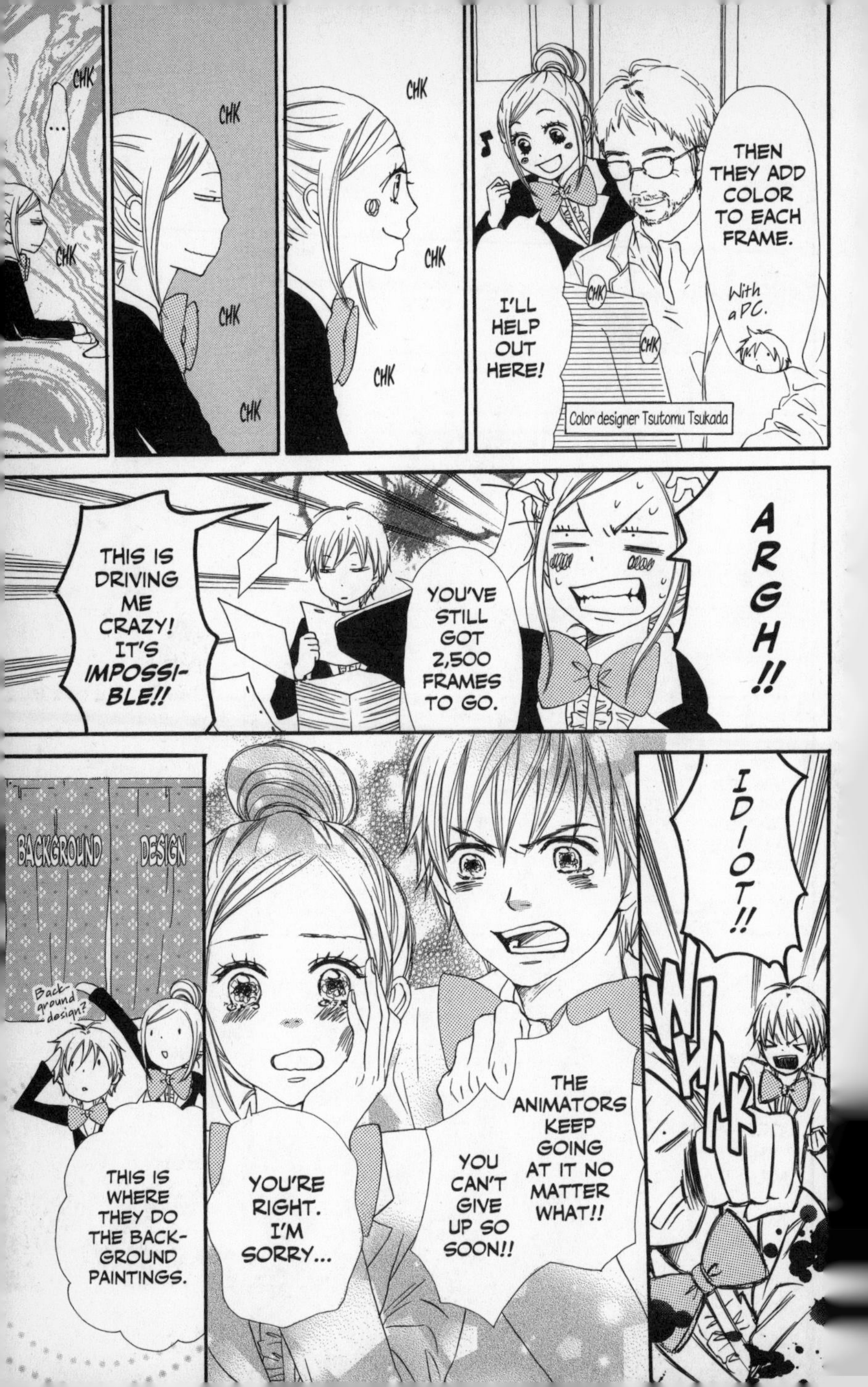
THEN THEY ADD COLOR TO EACH FRAME.
With a PC.
I'LL HELP OUT HERE!
CHK
CHK
Color designer Tsutomu Tsukada
CHK
CHK
CHK
CHK
CHK
CHK
CHK
...
CHK
ARGH!!
YOU'VE STILL GOT 2,500 FRAMES TO GO.
THIS IS DRIVING ME CRAZY! IT'S IMPOSSIBLE!!
IDIOT!!
WHAK
THE ANIMATORS KEEP GOING AT IT NO MATTER WHAT!!
YOU CAN'T GIVE UP SO SOON!!
YOU'RE RIGHT. I'M SORRY...
BACKGROUND DESIGN
Background design?
THIS IS WHERE THEY DO THE BACKGROUND PAINTINGS.

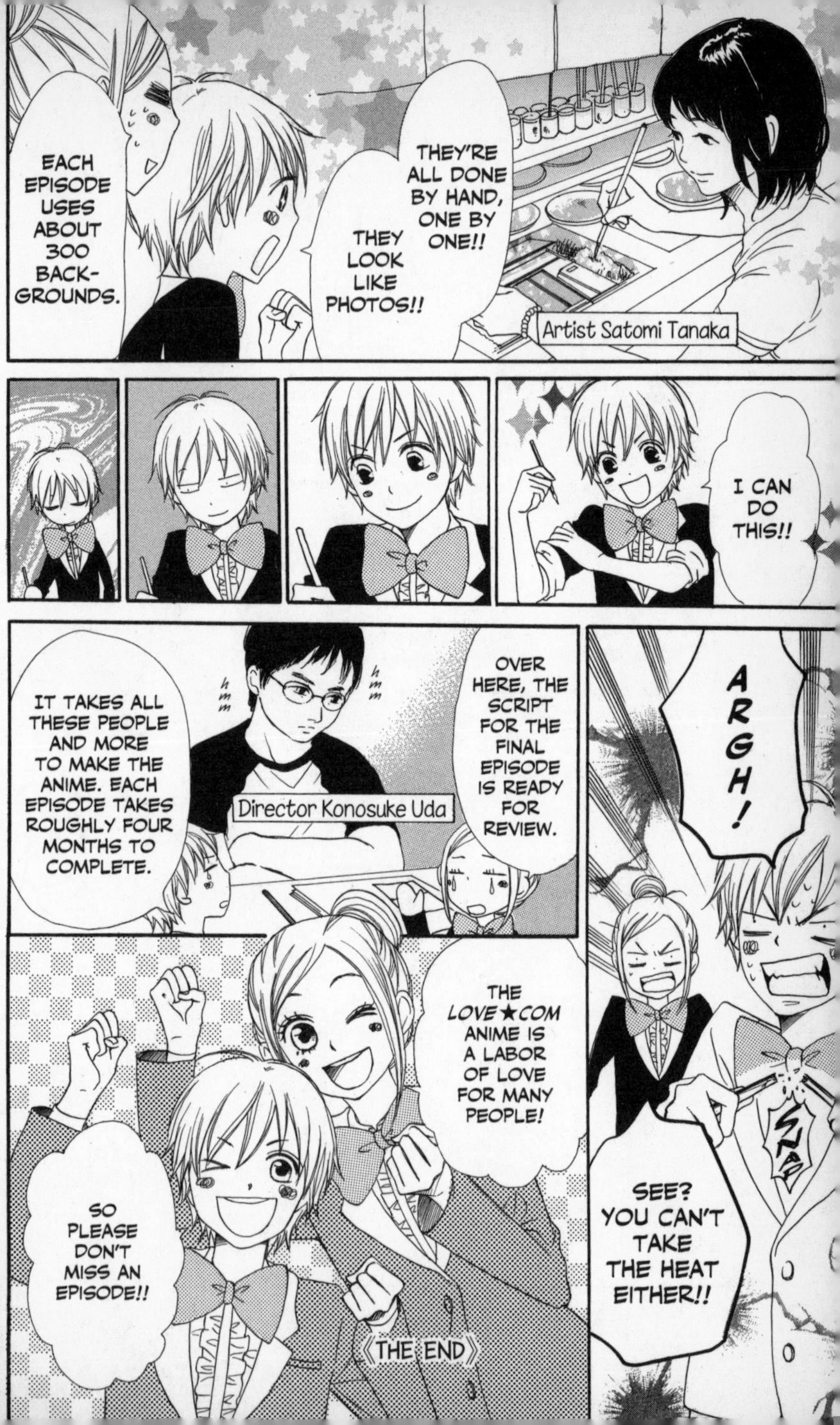
THEY'RE ALL DONE BY HAND, ONE BY ONE!!
THEY LOOK LIKE PHOTOS!!
Artist Satomi Tanaka
EACH EPISODE USES ABOUT 300 BACKGROUNDS.
I CAN DO THIS!!
ARGH!
SNAP
SEE? YOU CAN'T TAKE THE HEAT EITHER!!
OVER HERE, THE SCRIPT FOR THE FINAL EPISODE IS READY FOR REVIEW.
hmm
hmm
Director Konosuke Uda
IT TAKES ALL THESE PEOPLE AND MORE TO MAKE THE ANIME. EACH EPISODE TAKES ROUGHLY FOUR MONTHS TO COMPLETE.
THE *LOVE★COM* ANIME IS A LABOR OF LOVE FOR MANY PEOPLE!
SO PLEASE DON'T MISS AN EPISODE!!
《THE END》

This is the final volume of this long series. I was able to reach this point thanks to the help and support of many people. Thank you all so much. Manga is truly a wonderful thing!

Aya Nakahara won the 2003 Shogakukan Manga Award for her breakthrough hit *Love★Com*, which was made into a major motion picture and a PS2 game in 2006. She debuted with *Haru to Kuuki Nichiyou-bi* in 1995, and her other works include *HANADA* and *Himitsu Kichi*.

LOVE★COM VOL 17
Shojo Beat Edition

STORY AND ART BY
AYA NAKAHARA

Translation/JN Productions
English Adaptation/Shaenon K. Garrity
Touch-up Art & Lettering/Gia Cam Luc
Design/Yuki Ameda
Editor/Carrie Shepherd

VP, Production/Alvin Lu
VP, Sales & Product Marketing/Gonzalo Ferreyra
VP, Creative/Linda Espinosa
Publisher/Hyoe Narita

Printed in Canada

Published by VIZ Media, LLC
P.O. Box 77010
San Francisco, CA 94107

10 9 8 7 6 5 4 3 2 1
First printing, March 2010

RATED T FOR TEEN
PARENTAL ADVISORY
LOVE★COM is rated T for Teen and is recommended for ages 13 and up.
ratings.viz.com

www.viz.com

www.shojobeat.com

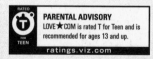

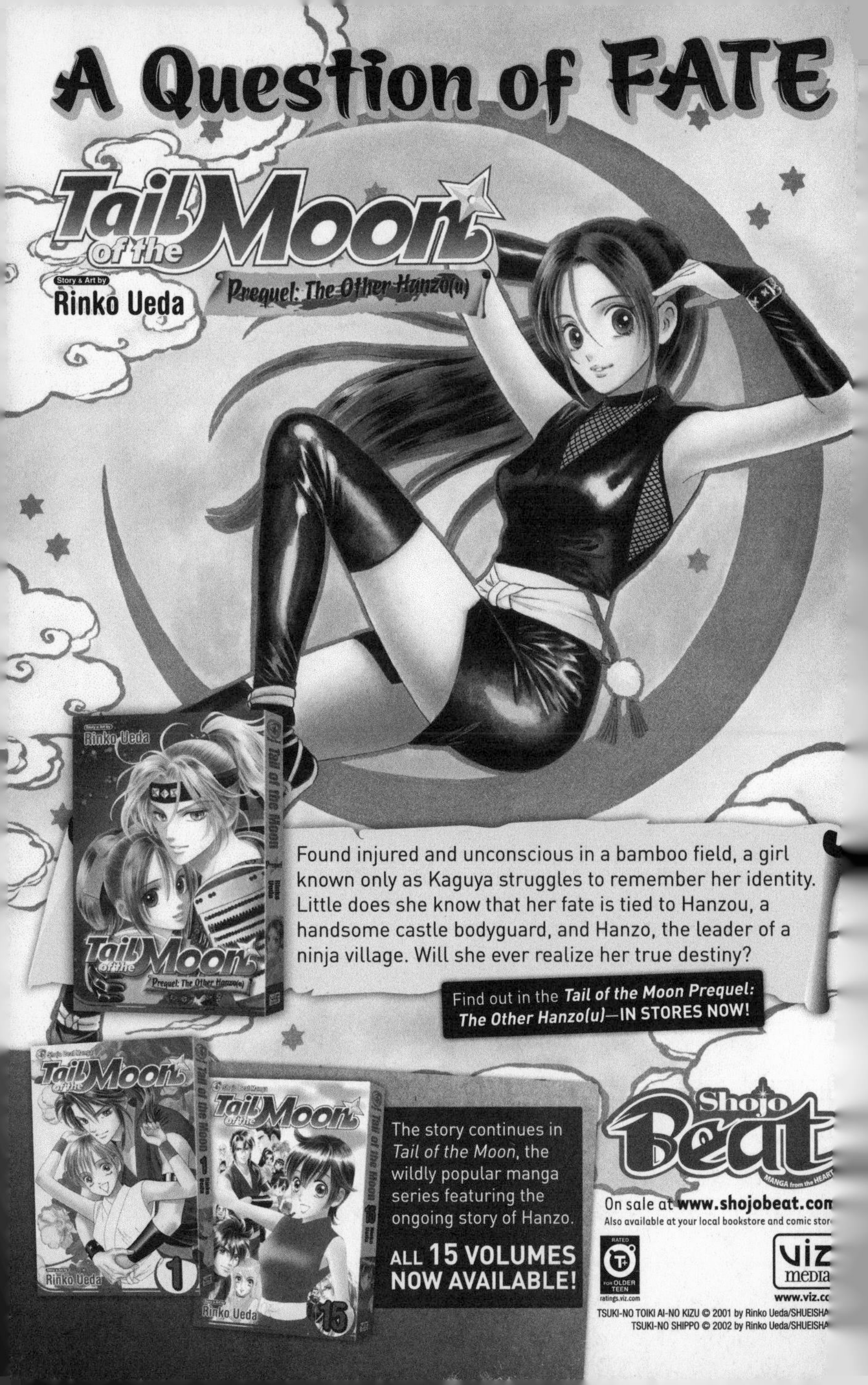

A Question of FATE
Tail of the Moon
Story & Art by
Rinko Ueda
Prequel: The Other Hanzo(u)
Found injured and unconscious in a bamboo field, a girl known only as Kaguya struggles to remember her identity. Little does she know that her fate is tied to Hanzou, a handsome castle bodyguard, and Hanzo, the leader of a ninja village. Will she ever realize her true destiny?
Find out in the Tail of the Moon Prequel: The Other Hanzo(u)—IN STORES NOW!
The story continues in Tail of the Moon, the wildly popular manga series featuring the ongoing story of Hanzo.
ALL 15 VOLUMES NOW AVAILABLE!
Shojo Beat
MANGA from the HEART
On sale at www.shojobeat.com
Also available at your local bookstore and comic store.
RATED T+ FOR OLDER TEEN
ratings.viz.com
VIZ media
www.viz.com
TSUKI-NO TOIKI AI-NO KIZU © 2001 by Rinko Ueda/SHUEISHA
TSUKI-NO SHIPPO © 2002 by Rinko Ueda/SHUEISHA